KYLIE KINLEY

~ BETWIX ~

PublishAmerica
Baltimore

© 2008 by Kylie Kinley.
All rights reserved. No part of this book may be reproduced, stored in a retrieval system or transmitted in any form or by any means without the prior written permission of the publishers, except by a reviewer who may quote brief passages in a review to be printed in a newspaper, magazine or journal.

First printing

PublishAmerica has allowed this work to remain exactly as the author intended, verbatim, without editorial input.

All characters in this book are fictitious, and any resemblance to real persons, living or dead, is coincidental.

ISBN: 1-60474-071-X
PUBLISHED BY PUBLISHAMERICA, LLLP
www.publishamerica.com
Baltimore

Printed in the United States of America

To Kris, my mentor, and to Mom, my everything

Chapter 1

The Sneeze That Never Happened

"ALLEE!" a voice screamed. Allee sighed and shut her book.

"WHAT?" she yelled back, wondering for the hundredth time why little sisters had to be so loud.

"Where are you?" Arian called, rounding the corner of the house. She saw Allee and her face lit up. Allee shifted in her hammock to discourage Arian from sitting with her.

"Whatcha doing?" Arian asked, ignoring Allee's feet by sitting on them.

"Well, I was," Allee said, pulling out her feet from under Arian, "reading my book." She stood up quickly and smiled as the hammock dipped and swung.

"HEY!" Arian yelled, trying not to get tipped over. Allee grinned mischievously.

"But now I think I'll go play fetch with Maisy," she said.

"Okay, I'll watch," Arian replied. Allee sighed again, pushing her auburn hair out of her face. She had hoped Arian wouldn't want to watch, and she could go back to reading her book. Instead, Allee stuck it in a pocket attached to the hammock and started off towards the house, tying her hair up as she went. It swung to her waist and when she put it in a knot, it was too large to lie on comfortably.

Suddenly, Allee heard something rip behind her. She whipped around, expecting Arian to have broken her hammock, but her little sister was just sitting there, puzzled at Allee's close scrutiny.

"What?" she asked, tilting her head. Allee peered at her, surprised. The noise she had heard had been unmistakably a ripping noise, and a loud one, too.

"Didn't you hear that?" she asked. For some reason, her eyes were drawn to the air above the hammock. *But that's silly*, she thought, *air can't rip.*

"Hear what?" Arian answered. Allee was beginning to get frustrated.

"That...that...tearing noise," she replied. Arian frowned for a moment and shook her head. Then she grinned.

"Ooh, you're starting to hear things. It's okay, Allee, I already knew you were crazy." Allee glared at her, and Arian collapsed in giggles.

"If I am, it's all your fault," Allee muttered darkly. Arian was too busy laughing to hear her. Allee rolled her eyes and continued on to the house.

Her dog, Maisy, saw Allee coming and got out from underneath the picnic table. She padded over to her, and tried to lick Allee's face, stepping on the girl's bare toes in her eagerness. Allee tried to push her away, but Maisy was too enthusiastic.

"Ow, Maisy, you big fur ball, get OFF!" Allee exclaimed, running across the patio. Maisy followed, tail waving. Allee laughed and opened the screen door. The rush of cool air that greeted her almost made her stay inside, but she quickly decided against it. Summer was too short to waste by staying indoors.

Allee was almost to the door with the fetch ball before she remembered her crunched toes, and she quickly grabbed her socks and tennis shoes. Her hand on the latch, she heard the clatter of silverware being set on the table. Allee felt guilty she was not helping her mom start supper, but assured herself that she would make up for it by cleaning up afterwards and went outside.

She waved the fetch ball and Maisy started bouncing up and down, her black and white tail a blur. Allee laughed again and led the dog around to the backyard. Maisy tried to bite the ball out of her hand, so Allee threw it with a hearty,

"GO FETCH!" Maisy chased after it, narrowly missing Arian's legs.

"HEY!" she yelled, getting up off the hammock to come stand by Allee. Maisy was right behind her. Allee shook her head in amazement at how fast she was. She hadn't even had to teach Maisy how to play fetch; the dog had learned all by herself. Those instincts could be a blessing with the one hundred head of cattle Allee's dad raised, or they could get Allee into big trouble if Maisy chased cows when she wasn't supposed to.

Allee picked up the fetch ball and threw it in an arc; meaning for it to go high and far, but instead the ball flew through the air into the branches of a cedar tree. Allee waited for it to fall, but, strangely, the ball seemed to have disappeared. Maisy searched all around the base, but soon returned, looking as puzzled as a dog can manage. Allee shared her sentiments.

"That's weird," she mused, walking toward the tree. It was a little smaller than the rest in the windbreak, and its branches looked too far apart to be able to catch anything. "How could it have gotten stuck?" she asked Arian.

"Maybe it landed in a bird nest or something!" Arian suggested. "That would be cool."

"Yeah, well, Maisy thinks it would be cool if she could play fetch. And that's my only fetch ball," Allee replied. She gazed up into the branches. There wasn't a bird nest in the whole tree, but up towards the top were some close-clustered branches that could conceal a slobbery tennis ball. The trunk supported one end of her hammock. She looked at the rope thoughtfully. It could hold her. She grabbed it and announced,

"I'm going to climb it." Arian stared at her with wide eyes.

"Ooh, Allee, be careful," she said. Allee hated climbing cedar trees, but Arian's worry strengthened her resolve. Maybe she'd pretend to fall, just to scare her. Hiding a grin behind her hand, she pulled herself into the tree.

Although its limbs were sparse, they were sturdy, and Allee didn't have any trouble climbing to the top except when she got her hair tangled in the sharp needles. She took a quick survey of the branches, but the fetch ball was nowhere in sight. After putting her foot in the middle of a V shaped branch to see the other side, she suddenly felt a sneeze coming on. *Maybe I won't have to pretend to fall out of this stupid tree,* Allee thought with a surge of panic and closed her eyes.

The next moment, the tickling feeling passed. Allee opened her eyes and screamed. In front of her was a bare expanse of rock, as if she was looking at a stone wall. She spun around and screamed again. Hundreds of feet below her was the largest expanse of trees she had ever seen in her life. She realized she was on some sort of cliff. All of a sudden her legs gave away, and she sat heavily on the ground, her back to the forest.

"What's happening to me?" she whispered to the rocks, her voice quivering. "Have I gone crazy?" She knew talking to inanimate objects was pretty high on the list of things you do if you are nuts, but the sound of her own voice soothed her. She took a shaky breath and her heart stopped beating at warp speed.

Suddenly, there was a noise like glass tinkling and shiny gold letters appeared on the rock face in front of her. She yelped and scooted back. Her hand hit something wet, and her trembling fingers closed around the fetch ball.

"What do you want?" she yelled, her fright turning into anger as she pulled her arm back to throw the fetch ball at whatever was there. She heard the tinkling sound again, this time sounding almost like a laugh, and words formed from the letters:

> *You are not insane or asleep,*
> *But through time and space you did leap,*
> *Don't worry, it's easy to fix.*
> *But for now, you're in Betwix.*

The words shimmered and then disappeared.

"Don't worry?" Alee cried. "But what about my house? My parents? My dog? MY LITTLE SISTER!" The air remained empty. In frustration, Allee threw the fetch ball at the rock. It bounced back harmlessly. The tinkling sound came again, but this time it was more of a rattle, and Allee felt an undercurrent of anger. She was afraid again, but swallowed hard and did not let it show on her face in case whatever was making the letters could see her. The letters blazed brighter than before:

BETWIX

Time in your home world will stay,
While you perform the part you're meant to play.
Now leave, be gone, go away!

With another rattle, the words vanished. Allee tried to swallow against the lump that was rising in her throat.

"But where am I supposed to go away to?" she whispered, her last word ending in a squeak. Tears sprang to her eyes as she thought of never seeing her home again, but she blinked them away angrily. No stupid rock that made lame attempts at writing poetry was going to make *her* cry.

She stood up brusquely, shaking her head to clear it. She would get her bearings and then decide what to do so she could "perform the part she was meant to play." The sooner that was done, the sooner she could go home.

Allee put the fetch ball in her pocket, took a deep breath, and turned around to face the forest. Scanning it, she realized she had missed something in her earlier panic. About three miles away was a huge castle, its many windows reflecting the late afternoon light. Behind it spread a city, and on all sides water sparkled. Since she could vaguely see the other shore, Allee guessed the city was on an island in the middle of a huge lake. She had an idea and spun around.

"Am I supposed to go there?" she asked the rock. Nothing happened. Allee gave an exasperated sigh. It could at least give her a little hint. "Hello-oo?" she continued, taking a step forward. Something crunched. She jumped back, looking at her feet. Beside her big toe was the biggest ruby she'd ever seen. The *only* ruby she'd ever seen.

Forgetting her conversation with the rock for a moment, she bent down to pick it up. It fit snuggly in the palm of her hand. Allee was about to pocket it when she heard a voice roar,

"MINE YOU THEIF!" Something large and heavy dropped on her from behind. Allee fell to the ground and lay there, temporarily dazed. She felt a fist come in contact with her ribs and finally realized the thing wanted the ruby.

"I didn't steal it!" she cried, kicking with all her might. Her feet came in contact with air. Her attacker was only a child! Allee forgot her shock and gritted her teeth. She relaxed for a moment, letting the thing think she was giving up. As soon as it paused its assault to wonder what had happened, Allee bucked with all her strength. In retaliation, the thing stopped trying to pry open her hand and began pulling her hair. She cried out in pain and bit its hand. It gave a yelp and pulled her hair harder.

"Hold still, you," it growled. Suddenly, she heard another voice.

"GNARRISH! GET OFF OF HER!" it cried. A hand seized Gnarrish and sent him tumbling into the dirt. Roughly, Allee was pulled to her feet. As soon as she was sure she was all in one piece, she quickly yanked away to see her rescuer better.

He was a boy about her age and height, with blond hair and pale skin. But that was all that was familiar about him. His strangeness began with his maroon shirt with belled sleeves, and continued down to his brown trousers and funny shoes. The boy hadn't noticed her inspection; he was goggling at her the same way she was at him. Allee flushed in embarrassment. The boy noticed and broke off his gaze, but he was unable to take the astonished look off his face.

"Are you all right?" he finally asked her. She noticed he spoke with a subtle British accent.

"I might be," she replied as calmly as she could, checking herself over and brushing off the dirt to hide the way she was trembling. The boy looked relieved and whirled on Gnarrish, who was sulking against the cliff face. Examining him from a safe distance, Allee realized he was not a child, but a dwarf-like creature.

"Apologize!" the boy snapped. Gnarrish shook his head and mumbled,

"Saw it first, I did!" The boy sighed and turned back to Allee.

"Please excuse this shameful *dung scraper*." He twisted his head to glare at Gnarrish, who looked quite shocked. The boy seemed pleased. "That I have in my service. He has a passion for shiny objects. I guess he couldn't resist. You know gnarfs." He rolled his eyes in his servant's direction. Allee had no idea what he was talking about, but tried to play along.

"Yeah," she agreed, "You know, he can have it if he wants it so bad." She held the ruby out to the boy. Suddenly, the jewel burned like fire in her hand. Allee felt like dropping it, but instinctively held it tighter. The burning stopped, and she looked at the ruby in confusion. It was like it wanted to go to the boy. Allee berated herself for being so stupid. Rubies did not think. She turned her attention back to her rescuer.

"No, you keep it," he was saying. "After all, not many people can hold their own against Gnarrish." Allee wanted to ask if that was a compliment or not, but she knew right now was not a time to be rude.

"If you're sure," she replied, stuffing the ruby into her pocket. When she looked up, Allee saw the boy looking at her jeans like he had never seen anything like them before. She blushed and tried to distract him.

"My name is Alethea Laurena Quintin," she said, and although she did not know why, she bowed. The boy looked like he was trying not to smile. "But I would prefer to be called Allee," she added.

"I am Ferdinand Nickolas Denerite," he announced, performing an elaborate bow of his own. Allee thought he was being a show-off, but couldn't help being impressed. "But you can call me Ferdy," he offered.

"Nice to meet you," Allee said, wondering if she was supposed to shake his hand or something, but he started talking again.

"Where can we take you?" he asked. Allee struggled to keep her face and voice casual.

"Take me?" she repeated. She was still trying to adjust to everything that was happening to her and didn't think she was safe to be around people without having them think she was crazy. And she was not quite sure if Ferdy and Gnarrish were to be trusted.

"That's what I said," Ferdy replied, a hint of impatience entering his tone. "We owe you something for the way you were treated." He turned to glare at Gnarrish again, who was pointedly not looking at his master. Allee was still a little hesitant of going anywhere with a complete stranger, but she did not want to seem ungrateful.

"I want to go there," she said, pointing at the city on the island. Ferdy's face relaxed into a grin.

"Excellent," he replied. "That's where we live. It would be our *pleasure*," he enunciated the word while shooting a glance at Gnarrish, who continued to ignore him. "to take you wherever in Goldham you want to go." Allee thought fast, not wanting to lie to Ferdy.

"Umm...the castle...to umm...be a maid," she said making it up on the spot. Even though it sounded incredibly lame, she was desperate and a castle always needed extra help, didn't it? She swallowed hard as she thought of all the things that could go wrong. This new world did not look very civilized and Allee knew she would attract a lot of attention with her strange clothes and mannerisms. She didn't even know why she wanted to go to the city; there were endless other possibilities. But something told her that the city was the place she should go. And Allee knew that when everything else seemed to be going against you, the last thing you needed to do is go against yourself. She came out of her reverie to see Ferdy looking horrified.

"A maid at the pastle?" he repeated, aghast. Allee could have sworn she heard him add a "p" to castle, but focused on what he was saying. "After Gnarrish almost *killed* you? Oh, no, you will stay as my guest!" Now it was Allee's turn to be horrified. She just knew that if she didn't do whatever she was supposed to do all by herself the thing in the rock wouldn't send her home. Fear strengthened her resolve.

"I couldn't..." she began to protest, but Ferdy went right over top of her.

"We'll be there in time for supper," he announced, smiling at her cheerfully. "Gnarrish and I will even have enough time to get the umm...flowers we were supposed to get." His ears turned red, and Allee suspected him of making up a story to explain his presence in the mountains. Gnarrish confirmed her suspicion.

"The only flower you've even *looked* at today is her," he said sullenly. His earlier madness was gone, and Allee was surprised to hear he spoke with an accent not unlike a Scottish brogue. She was absolutely bewildered with this strange place. Ferdy looked embarrassed.

"I wouldn't have even done that if it weren't for you," he growled. He strode over to Gnarrish, pulled him off the ground, and gave him a push down the path. Gnarrish grinned at his master's discomfort and set off whistling. Ferdy frowned at him and turned to Allee. "Are you coming?" he asked. Allee decided not to question the little episode that had just happened.

"Lead the way," she replied. He nodded curtly at her, and followed after Gnarrish.

They walked single file down a dirt track that must have been designed by mountain goats. Allee had to cling to roots and pieces of dirt to keep from hurtling off the side. After a while, though, the path leveled out enough that they were able to talk.

"So," Ferdy began, and Allee braced herself for an onslaught of questions, hoping she wouldn't have to lie. "Why are you going to Goldham? You really want to be a maid?" Allee was relieved that was all he wanted to know about.

"That's my plan," she responded, trying to act nonchalant. But she was sure Ferdy would hear her heart beating if it didn't calm down.

"But why travel through the Amalgams?" he pressed, his face quizzical. "There are much easier ways."

"Maybe I felt like finding some flowers, too," Allee replied, her voice bland. As she had predicted, he colored in embarrassment. She wasn't sure, but she thought she heard a chuckle from the gnarf. She had hoped her retort would shut him up, but he plowed diligently on.

"Has your family fallen on hard times or something?" Allee was tired of being interrogated, and was worried about forgetting part of her story later if she made it up.

"I just needed a change, okay?" she said, irritably. She glared at him, and he threw up his hands in defeat.

"All right, all right, keep your secrets," he said, grinning at her in amusement. *The nerve*, Allee thought, and copied Gnarrish by turning her head away from him. She heard Ferdy laugh at her, and haughtily began to examine the forest around her. She saw him shrug out of the corner of her eye, and breathed a sigh of relief. With any more questions, she just might come out with her real story, and then Ferdy really *would* think she was crazy.

Allee pushed aside her worries and tried to enjoy the strange scenery around her. Everything about the forest fascinated her. Growing up on the plains, she had never seen more than a hundred trees at the same time. This forest stretched on for miles. But its size was not what was unusual to her. What was strange was that when she tried to name the type of tree she was seeing, she came up with two different options. It was almost like there were two kinds of tree in one.

When Allee wasn't looking at the scenery, she would glance in front of them to make sure Gnarrish was still where she could see him. Even though he was acting normal, he still made her nervous. With growing apprehension, Allee had watched him get farther and farther away from Ferdy and her. Soon, Allee could not see him anywhere. Forgetting her earlier annoyance, she sidled up to Ferdy, who turned to grin at her. She didn't let him start teasing her again before asking her question.

"So, what else do gnarfs like?" she inquired, trying to sound casual. "I want to be prepared." Ferdy stopped so he could stare at her. Allee winced. *I've blown it now* she thought.

"You don't have gnarfs where you come from?" he asked, incredulous.

"No," Allee replied, her heart sinking farther as the truth came out unwillingly. Ferdy frowned.

"Where *do* you come from?" he asked, narrowing his eyes suspiciously. Allee panicked.

"Earth," she blurted, thinking fast. "It's umm...a small farming community. We're very isolated, ignorant of the rest of the world." She prayed Ferdy didn't notice the panic in her voice. He must not of, for his face relaxed, and he shrugged.

"That's probably why I haven't heard of it," he replied. Allee let out the breath she'd been holding. He shook his head. "But of course, many of our villages are unaccounted for," he added. Disgust laced his last words, though Allee couldn't imagine why. She kept her eyes on the path and didn't say anything else. After a few steps, Ferdy answered her query.

"Gnarfs are a dedicated, down-to-earth people," he began, his eyebrows drawn together in concentration as he tried to explain it so she would understand. "who work hard and enjoy doing it. They like to dig for stuff, like jewels or precious metals. That's why he attacked you." Ferdy looked around quickly, and lowered his voice to a whisper. "He's quite ashamed of himself now," he confided. "He messed up his reputation of being very cool headed. He's been trying for years to make me think he is." Ferdy gave Allee a mischievous smile and continued in his normal voice. "They also enjoy gardening and growing things. You really should have at least a couple of gnarfs in a farming community."

He frowned in puzzlement again, and Allee gave him a weak smile, her heart beating wildly. Ferdy gave another of his shrugs. "But then again, there aren't that many that live around humans; they have their own colonies. Anything else you need to know?" Allee knew he was making fun of her and was about to reply when she saw the centaur behind him. She bit back a scream.

"Yes," she said faintly, trying to slow her rapidly beating heart for what seemed the twentieth time that day. "Why is there a centaur behind you?" Ferdy looked startled and whirled around, but relaxed as he seemed to recognize the creature.

"Good evening, Neiy," he said, bowing. Alee followed suit, still gawking. "How go the heavens?" Neiy surveyed the humans gravely.

"The heavens, Young Lord, are in discord with your wanderings," he said in his serious, gravelly voice. Then a twinkle came into his eyes. "As is your aunt." His deep voice made Allee shiver, but the last part almost sounded like a joke. And Ferdy was a Lord, Neiy had said. Somehow this didn't surprise her.

"Yeah, I know," Ferdy said, shrugging. Allee wished he would quit doing that. It was driving her crazy. "I need to get back, fast. I don't suppose…you could…maybe?" his voice took on a wheedling tone, and his eyes begged Neiy, who was looking bemused. Ferdy put his face into a pitiful mask, and Neiy shook his head in defeat.

"All right, Young Lord," he sighed, and the pout turned into a grin. "But if my father finds out, it will never happen again." Ferdy was already climbing up on his back. After making sure Ferdy didn't pull all of his hair out, Neiy turned to Allee. Although from his size and the smoothness of his face he appeared to be a very young centaur, his penetrating hazel eyes seemed to hold centuries of information. Allee felt lightheaded; an hour ago centaurs didn't exist and now she was expected to *sit* on one.

"Well, youngling, can you ride a centaur?" he asked, his eyes boring into her. Suddenly, they went unfocused and his mouth dropped open. He looked as if he had just realized something important. Allee was extremely unnerved and tried not to gape at him more than she already was. After what seemed an eternity to her, he shook himself, and the look passed. "Of course you can," he murmured, kneeling and offering her his arm. Blushing furiously, she clambered onto his back. Ferdy was goggling at her as she slipped into the place where human met horse. Neiy turned back to give her another piercing look, and then jerked forward. As Neiy began to gallop, Ferdy leaned over and whispered,

"What secrets do you have to awe a centaur?" Allee was too distracted by Neiy's behavior to think about her answer.

"Oh, they're out of this world," she replied. She saw Ferdy open his mouth to talk again, but Neiy was going so fast they had to focus all of their attention on hanging on. Allee fervently hoped she wouldn't be sick, (at least not all over herself or Neiy, she really wouldn't care what happened to Ferdy) but the feeling only lasted for a minute or two. Then Allee began to thoroughly enjoy her ride, for as long as it lasted. Neiy brought them to the edge of the trees in a little less than fifteen minutes.

As they neared the break in the forest, Allee realized that she had been right; the castle was on an island in the middle of a lake. The only way to get to it was a causeway of stone that led to a gate in the city's surrounding wall. The castle rose majestically out of the sparkling water, obscuring all view of the city behind it. The building and its massive walls reminded Allee of a huge gray dragon guarding the riches of its hoard. The causeway was made of a different type of stone that reflected the sun and the sparkle on the water to give the whole scene a dazzling, unreal quality. As they got closer, Allee realized the causeway was made of pure white marble. She gave a low whistle under her breath as she estimated what something like that would have cost. However, the people and animals scurrying over the gorgeous bridge seemed to care little for its value.

Allee watched with particular interest as a family of gnarfs tried to get a stubborn sheep onto the walkway. Then she frowned. There was something peculiar about the sheep. Allee looked closer, and did a double take. The sheep looked like it had the face of a pig! Before she almost fell off of Neiy to get a better look, the animal bolted and the gnarf clinging onto the lead rope was hanging on for dear life. Something in the expression on his face reminded her of their third companion.

"What happened to Gnarrish?" she whispered to Ferdy.

"He must not have wanted a ride, but I'm sure he's right behind us," he said, totally unconcerned. "He'll show up later." Allee felt a twinge of guilt for leaving him, but quickly banished it as Neiy smoothly came to a stop in the shadow of the forest. Ferdy and Allee slid off, and Neiy looked them over each in turn, carefully avoiding Allee's eyes and making her blush.

"I leave you now," he said, bowing. Allee followed Ferdy's example and bowed in return, her head whirling with all she had just seen. "Good luck with your aunt, Young Lord," Neiy added, a hint of a smile playing on his lips. "Though I'm sure you have some story invented." Ferdy's brow creased.

"Yeah, I'm working on it," he said. Distractedly, he moved off towards the causeway, rubbing the back of his neck. Neiy appeared amused. Allee moved to follow Ferdy, but Neiy grabbed her arm.

"Do not trust Betwix's beauty," he said, his voice deep and resonating. Allee looked at him in bewilderment. "For beauty is always deceiving. Remember this, Alethea. Fare thee well." And without any explanation, he galloped off. Alee stood staring after him, speechless. *What is that supposed to mean*, she cried silently, frustration overwhelming her. And then, suddenly, she remembered something. She had not told him her name.

"Are you coming?" Ferdy's voice demanded, cutting though her perplexed fog. Allee shook herself and tried to smile.

"Of course," she said, forcing her hands to stop shaking and wiping her palms on her jeans. She didn't know if it was from nerves of the unknown or the shock of what she had already been put through, but it was extremely annoying.

"Great," Ferdy said shortly, "And um…kind of keep behind me, okay? I um…don't want you to get lost." His ears turned red again and Alee knew he wasn't telling the entire truth. As they got closer to the people, Allee understood why. All of the women wore dark colored dresses and had their hair pinned up in neat braids or under headscarves. Allee brushed the loose strands of hair off her face and looked down at her bright purple t-shirt and blue jeans, her heart sinking down past her shaking knees to her tennis shoes. So much for pretending she was a native.

"I'll be right behind you," she promised. Still looking doubtful, Ferdy turned and began making his way down the causeway. Allee followed, gaping at all of the strange animals. There were more of the sheep things, and a goat that wasn't quite a goat. But the most astonishing creature, in Allee's opinion, was the braying llama. She was so preoccupied with it that she almost ran into the city wall.

Craning her neck, she goggled at the enormous gate they were now passing through. Doors made of the same white marble were folded back against the inside of the wall. Allee noted with puzzlement that the hinges were rusty and there were no guards posted anywhere. Were there no wars or enemies in this strange new world?

"Do I have to hold your hand, redkin?" Ferdy hissed in her ear, making her jump. Allee didn't know how to retort to an insult that she didn't know the meaning of, so she just followed him into a broad, cobblestone lane between the outer wall and the one that surrounded the castle. They followed the flow of people moving along this avenue until an archway in the inner wall appeared. Ferdy made a sharp turn into it and Allee gasped in surprise as the courtyard and workshops of the castle spread out before her.

"Wow," she breathed, too much in awe to say anything else. Ferdy turned to look back at her, grinning.

"Welcome," he said, bowing and sweeping with his arm, "to the pastle of Goldham, pride of Taween." Allee was again puzzled over the strange word "pastle", but was too enthralled with the people streaming in and out of the different archways in the building to think about it.

The courtyard they were standing in seemed to be dedicated to metal work; the entire left side was covered with men and boys working in forges, their bodies and clothes darkened with sweat and soot. To the right was a single wall of the giant pastle. The stone wall was almost obscured by the multitudes of servants entering and exiting the doors. Red-cheeked laundry women, parcel-laden pages, and stockmen leading protesting animals made up the blur of activity that was the lifeblood of the pastle. Then, one person in particular caught Allee's eye. A tall woman with light brown hair streaked with gray in glittering green skirts was storming towards them, her eyebrows and mouth pinched in an expression of intense annoyance. Allee immediately knew who she was.

"Umm…Ferdy…" she said, gesturing nervously, "I think someone wants you." Ferdy's eyes went wide, and he spun around. Allee saw his face contort as he tried to decide whether to run for it or stand his ground, but before he could decide the woman put on a burst of speed and latched onto his ear. Ferdy grimaced but didn't struggle.

"Hi, Aunt Cardolyn," he said. His cheerful greeting seemed to make the woman even angrier.

"Prince Ferdinand," she began quietly, breathing heavily. Everyone in the courtyard stopped whatever they were doing to watch. Allee saw many jab their neighbors with their elbows, snickering, and decided that this must be a regular event. Cardolyn must have noticed, too, for her face reddened before she continued, "Did you enjoy your outing?" Ferdy winced as she twisted his ear harder and nodded. "Do you know what I did?" Ferdy responded by closing his eyes, waiting for the blow. Cardolyn delivered it.

"I TOOK YOUR PLACE AT THE COUNCIL!" she bellowed, making Allee (and she was sure Ferdy) want to cover her ears. Oblivious to how loud she was, the woman's voice took on a higher pitch. "I arranged this for you to actually *learn* something, but, no, *Prince* Ferdinand is too *busy* to be able to sit in on the discussion of the affairs of his own country! Did you think *I* needed to sit in on the conference?" She paused for his answer. Ferdy shook his head vigorously. "Do you know *why* I don't need to sit in on the conferences?" she asked calmly, and Alee breathed a sigh of relief, but it was too soon. "BECAUSE I ATTENDED THEM WHEN I WAS YOUNG!" Cardolyn roared. Ferdy finally seemed to get his tongue back.

"But I'm not *going* to be king," he protested. "Esendore is! And," but Cardolyn cut him off.

"I DO NOT CARE! Your father is on his deathbed and YOU, Prince Ferdinand, are second in line to the throne, heaven forbid you ever make it there. Nevertheless, I will *not* let you be ignorant of your station or your responsibilities." She paused for breath, her face scarlet.

"Esendore looks pretty healthy to me," Ferdy replied sullenly. Cardolyn just twisted his ear even harder.

"IMPUDENCE!" she shrieked. "I will not tolerate it, Ferdinand. We are going to go through the minutes of the conference until you have no breath left for cheek," she finished, dragging him toward a large wooden door in the side of pastle. Allee wished he would hurry up and remember her. Most of the people in the courtyard were hiding grins behind their hands, while some smiled encouragingly at Ferdy, but a few were starting to stare at her quizzically. Ferdy plodded desolately along behind Cardolyn, but then he seemed to think of something.

"Your Grace, what about Allee?" he asked in a final plea. Cardolyn turned and blinked at Allee, letting go of Ferdy in her surprise. He started rubbing his ear with one hand and raised the other in a victory pump. Some blacksmith youths whistled and stomped their feet in support. Cardolyn didn't notice them in her preoccupation with Allee, who gulped and fought to stay calm under her scrutiny.

"Well, hello, dear," Cardolyn said, kindly. Allee wondered how someone who was so loud one moment could sound so nice the next. "How did you fall into such bad company?" Allee opened her mouth to tell her story, but Ferdy jumped in, eager to redeem himself. Allee glared at him, annoyed, but he was busy trying to distract his aunt from his misbehavior.

"Gnarrish attacked her, Aunt Cardolyn," he explained quickly. Cardolyn looked surprised, but didn't interrupt. Ferdy continued, talking very fast, "Allee was coming to be a maid here and he attacked her on the mountain, so I brought her here, to make up for it. You know, since he is *my* servant," he paused for breath, smiling winningly at his aunt. "And I thought it would be the *responsible* thing to do," he added, hopefully. Cardolyn looked suspicious. Allee knew that she was wondering what a peasant girl could possibly have that would interest a gnarf. Thinking fast, she dug the ruby out of her pocket.

"He wanted this, Your Grace," Allee said, and hoping she was acting the right way to the second in line to the throne's aunt, she knelt. Cardolyn held out her hand and Allee offered the ruby to her. As she did, a jolt passed down her arm and she was filled with a feeling of giddiness that wasn't her own. Instinctively, she held tighter to the ruby. Cardolyn saw her fingers twitch and drew back.

"Very pretty, dear," she said, smiling kindly. Allee, drenched in cold sweat from whatever had just happened, gave a watery smile back. Cardolyn's face finally softened to match her voice. "I'm sure it's very important to you," she said. "And Ferdinand was right to bring you here. You need to be repaid for any inconvenience Gnarrish caused you." Ferdy caught Allee's eye and grinned. Allee wanted to hit him, but couldn't with Cardolyn watching.

BETWIX

"Now, come along and we'll get you situated," Her Grace continued, flicking her skirts out of her way and walking towards the pastle door. She seemed to have entirely forgotten Ferdy. Allee scrambled to her feet, pushing the ruby into her pocket, and half-trotted to keep up.

"I will be situated as a maid, won't I, Your Grace?" Allee asked, determined to stick to her plan. She wanted to be inconspicuous until she had Betwix a little more figured out. Cardolyn stopped to stare at Allee.

"You don't want to be a guest of His Royal Highness?" she asked, her voice both surprised and a little insulted.

"No!" Allee objected, horrified. "I didn't mean that! I would take the Prince up on his noble offer, it's just...I...I don't want to be a burden," she finished, her voice small. Cardolyn's features relaxed into a soft smile.

"Well said, um—," Cardolyn stopped, looking startled. "I don't even know your name!" Again, Alee opened her mouth to tell her, but Her Grace was shouting for Ferdy. "Ferdinand! Introduce...drat it! He's inside already." Cardolyn sighed, and strode over to the door. She yanked it open and disappeared.

Allee followed closely, but her heels got smashed in the heavy wooden door. It did not bother her much; rubbing them gave an excellent cover so she could stare at her surroundings. The stone corridor they were in was long and dark, lit only by thin torches in heavily wrought sconces. At the end, the hall made a sharp L with a huge wooden door with black hinges guarding the corner. Right in front of them was a large wooden staircase. Ferdy was halfway up, but before he could make it the rest of the way Cardolyn spotted him.

"Ferdinand! Introduce me to your friend. NOW." Ferdy stopped and gave a broad, forced looking smile while going into one of his elaborate bows.

"This," he said, gesturing to Allee, "is Alethea Laurena Quintin, from a place called Earth, who prefers to be called Allee. Allee, meet Her Grace Cardolyn Reaneece Denerite, the Duchess-Princess of Taween. And I," he said pointing to himself, "am out of here." And he turned and ran up the stairs. Cardolyn was utterly speechless, at least for a millisecond.

"FERDINAND!" she bellowed loud enough to make the candles flicker. "Get back here!" But Ferdy was gone. "That boy!" she fumed. Allee was thinking along the same lines.

"Don't worry, Your Grace," she said, trying to comfort her. "That's just human nature." There was a silence, and Allee realized that criticizing, borderline insulting, the Prince was probably treason. She clapped her hand over her mouth and slowly lifted her eyes to the Duchess's face. Their eyes met, and for a second, Cardolyn's hazel eyes went unfocussed like Neiy's, but then she began to laugh. Allee was a little frightened at first, but was reassured when Her Grace laid a hand on her shoulder.

"I needed that," she said, smiling. Allee smiled weakly back, relief flooding her. "So you want to be a maid," Cardolyn continued, her eyebrows twitching, like it was some kind of a joke. Allee nodded, and Her Grace turned brisk. "You shall need garments, of course. There are storerooms off the kitchen. Come along, dear." She swept down the hallway towards the black-hinged door.

Allee looked at it apprehensively, wondering if she was to spend all her time in Betwix behind it. But, suddenly, movement on the floor averted her attention. Cardolyn saw it, too, and stopped with a squeak. It seemed to sense her and scuttled closer to them. Allee realized it was a huge spider. She *hated* spiders. Instinctively, she lifted her foot and brought it down with a satisfying crunch.

"There," Allee said triumphantly, "one less bug in the world." Her elation evaporated when she saw the shocked expression on the Duchess's face, which had gone deathly pale. Cardolyn took a shaky breath.

"Do you know what you just did?" she asked, her eyes each the size of the ruby. Allee slowly shook her head, totally bewildered at the Duchess's reaction. "That was a taranion!" Allee gave Cardolyn another blank look. The Duchess looked even more astounded. "A taranion, child!" she repeated, looking at Allee like she was stupid. "The most dangerous insect in the world! A single sting and you're...you're dead! Don't you have them where you come from?" For the third time in five minutes Allee opened her mouth to explain herself, and much to her chagrin, was again interrupted.

"But, dear!" Cardolyn cried, seeming to suddenly realize something. "You killed it with your *foot*. You could be hurt! Let me see, let me see!" And without a by-your-leave Cardolyn picked up Allee's shoe to examine it, leaving Allee balancing on one foot.

"I feel just fine!" she protested, hopping to avoid falling over. This was not her idea of meeting royalty. Cardolyn paused in her probing, and stared at Allee's shoe quizzically.

"What workmanship is this?" she asked, fingering the plastic sole. Allee blushed. Her footwear contrasted sharply with Cardolyn's, which looked to be made out of felt.

"My um...traveling shoes," she replied. Cardolyn nodded, somewhat skeptically, and set Allee's foot back down. Allee breathed a sigh of relief.

"Quite interesting," Cardolyn said absently. "Now move a bit, there's a dear, I want to look at the remains." Sweeping her skirts into her hand, she bent to peer intently at the taranion guts. Feeling foolish, Allee knelt beside her. As she did, she took the opportunity to really study the Duchess. Allee guessed that her hair had once been a mahogany brown, but it was now faded to a light honey color. Her Grace was not long over forty, but Allee knew that the combined stress of raising a nephew like Ferdy and helping oversee the country had made her age before her time. She probably hadn't been ravishingly gorgeous in her youth; her nose and cheekbones were too prominent, but now age and experience had given the Duchess a very subtle beauty that would attract any male who could look past her age. Allee knew Her Grace was still unwed because her name was the same as Ferdy's, and was just wondering why she had stayed single so long when Cardolyn made a noise in her throat.

"Oh, see here, Alethea. It has a stinger *and* fangs, that means it's a male!" Allee blinked at her stupidly. Cardolyn sighed.

"You really don't have taranions at Earth, do you?"

"Nope," Allee replied, entirely truthful. Cardolyn sighed again.

"Female taranions only have fangs," she explained patiently, as if Allee was a small child, "And their poison isn't lethal—if you have the antidote. They are fairly common, but there's never been one in *this* pastle." The Duchess sounded outraged at the very thought. "But the males have both fangs and stingers. I've never seen one of those *anywhere*, but I do know they sting anything that moves. And there is no antidote to their poison. It kills within minutes." Allee digested this information. It sounded sort of like a scorpion, but the remnants were that of a tarantula.

"Good thing it's dead, then," Allee replied, peering at it. She looked up to see Cardolyn gazing at her with saucer-like eyes. Allee felt a little unnerved. "Kind of hairy, isn't it?" she said to break the silence.

"Don't you know what this means?" Cardolyn asked. Allee looked at her uncomprehendingly.

"Uh...we need to find a trash can?" she guessed, wishing she did not sound so stupid. Cardolyn grabbed a hold of her hand.

"You saved my life," she breathed, squeezing it. "I am in you debt." Allee felt her mouth drop open.

"WHAT?" she said, wanting to laugh but knowing she shouldn't. "You can't possibly think...that I—" Cardolyn continued to stare at her with admiration. "Oh, come on! I just stepped on it!" Cardolyn just kept gazing up at her with soppy eyes. Allee started to babble in desperation. "It was there, so I stepped on it! It's dead now, it doesn't matter who killed it. Anyway, it was closer to me, or otherwise I couldn't have done it! Would you quit looking at me like that?" Cardolyn just squeezed her hand harder.

All Allee wanted was for people to leave her alone so she could figure out what she needed to do here and go home. She did not want to draw attention to herself, she did not want people gushing over her like Cardolyn was doing, and she wanted to get home *all by herself*. Frustrated beyond keeping herself in control, Allee totally lost it. "I JUST STEPPED ON IT!" she shouted, not caring about the shocked look on Cardolyn's face as Allee tugged her hand out of her grip. "I DON'T GO AROUND SAVING DUCHESS'S LIVES!" she yelled. Suddenly, the door in front of them opened and a dark head appeared.

"Who's making that racket?" the woman barked. "Ferdinand, I'll make you clean out the—," she finally realized who it was, and her face instantly changed to puzzlement at what they were doing. Allee realized how ridiculous they must look, bent over on the floor looking at bug guts. Cardolyn didn't seem to notice.

"Yes, I understand this ordeal has upset you," she replied, one eye watching Allee suspiciously, obviously wondering if she was going to blow up again and gesturing to the remains. "Look at this taranion,

Caysa, and tell me what you see." Obediently, Caysa knelt beside them. There was moment of silence as she examined it, and then a gasp.

"It's a male!" she shrieked. "How horrible! Who killed it?"

"Alethea did," Cardolyn replied proudly. Caysa turned to Allee with wide eyes.

"You saved her life," she said. Allee wanted to scream.

"I did NOTHING!" she yelled, breathing hard as she tried to control her emotions. Cardolyn shook her head and gracefully got to her feet.

"Whatever you say, dear," she replied soothingly. She exchanged a glance with Caysa. Allee bit her tongue to keep from bursting out again. "But, so I can show my thanks, you will dine with me tonight." Allee didn't dare try to argue a royal order.

"If it pleases Your Grace," she said humbly. Cardolyn gave her another smile.

"Wonderful," she replied, and turned to the other woman. "Caysa, would you show Allee to a room? And find her something suitable to wear, please. I will send someone else to oversee the kitchens." And with single flick of her skirts, Cardolyn disappeared behind the door.

Allee stared at the door with some degree of desperation. The one person who had been truly nice to her in this strange new world was gone, leaving her with a stranger who radiated no-nonsense strictness. She gave the servant woman a tiny smile, trying to be friendly but just a little too overwhelmed by what was happening to her to give much of an effort.

Casya got to her feet briskly, straightening her skirts with brown, work worn hands while running her eyes up and down Allee's profile. Allee stood up so quickly that her feet got tangled under her and she almost fell over again. She could feel Caysa staring at her disapprovingly, but Allee bravely lifted her head to meet the servant woman's gaze, all the while flushing bright red.

"Let's go then," Caysa said, walking back the way they had come. Allee followed meekly.

Caysa led her up the wooden staircase and through the door at the top, explaining that the staircase was strictly for servant use. Indeed, when Allee looked behind them, the door almost blended into the wall, leaving the pattern in the tile uninterrupted. Ferdy was waiting for them at the end of the little hall.

"Is she gone?" he whispered. Allee had been appalled at his behavior towards Cardolyn and figured that while she was yelling at people she should make sure Ferdy got his share.

"Yes, as a matter of fact she is," she snapped, her eyes flashing. Ferdy drew back in surprise. Allee ignored him and continued, "But let me ask you something, Your Rudeness, have you ever considered that someday the Duchess might decide not to bail you out and let you take whatever you deserve?" She paused to let him think about it. "What then?" she pressed. "Have you ever thought to *thank* her for being there for you?" Ferdy started to sputter, but Allee cut him off. "Apparently not."

For lack of a better thing to do, she turned the corner and walked a few paces to cool herself off. She desperately hoped she hadn't just committed high treason and leaned her head against the cool tile wall in despair. She just wanted to go home!

Caysa appeared a minute later and put her hands on her hips, again giving Allee a piercing examination. However, this time she was looking at Allee with interest instead of contempt. Allee cringed, waiting for her sentence. But instead, Caysa's face broke into a grin.

"I like you," she declared. Allee started, wondering if she had heard Caysa right. "*Nobody* ever gives His Highness what he deserves," Caysa continued, her grin widening. "Though heaven knows Her Grace has tried. He needed that in the worst way." Allee couldn't believe what she was hearing.

"I don't need to apologize?" she asked, looking at Caysa in disbelief.

"APOLOGIZE?" Caysa was astounded. "Girl, you just do that more often and you can stay her forever. As for His Highness, he just went down to *apologize* to Her Grace."

"Then I'm not in trouble?" Allee couldn't help asking. Caysa chuckled.

"Of course not! But *I* will be if you're not ready for dinner on time. Come on." Marveling at how well everything had worked out, Allee followed Caysa down the tiled hallway.

This level was very different from the one below. Whereas the first had seemed like a fortress, Allee now felt like she was in a palace like the ones described in fairy tales. Colorful tapestries and glass vases in niches adorned the walls between the doors, and the sparkling arched windows boasted flowers on every sill. To top it off, Allee could have sworn she heard music playing softly as they passed an alcove with a tinkling fountain. Each block of the beautiful white marble floor was masterly crafted so that the ground seemed to be made from a single block.

Caysa finally stopped at a door and pulled a ring of keys from her belt. The door opened with a click.

Allee gasped in surprise. The room looked to have come right out of a very expensive home décor magazine. A magazine that was obsessed with the color purple, that is. *Everything* in the room was purple (the rich rugs on the stone floor, the candles in the elaborate gold sconces, the bed with its velvet comforter and many pillows, and even the flowers on the windowsill.) The bed seemed big enough to sleep Allee's entire family, including the dog, though Allee thought Maisy would go berserk if the heavy velvet curtains were closed around her. Looking around at the room's richness, Allee realized that she was not being taken seriously.

"This isn't a maid's room," she said, accusingly.

"It matches your…uh…garment," Caysa said, smiling sweetly. Allee looked down at her purple, only slightly ratty t-shirt and wondered if that remark was a thinly veiled insult. "I'll go start your bath," Caysa continued, disappearing into an adjoining chamber.

Allee was a little cross for not being taken seriously, but she quickly got over it after another sweep around the room and a quick bounce on the four-poster. Part of her still wanted to stubbornly cling to her first plan, but staying in a room like this and eating as a guest of a Duchess sounded like a much better idea.

Allee's stomach growled at the thought of food. She was very hungry. She figured she had left Earth around six, and she guessed it to be around eight now, if they had the same clocks in this world. As Allee looked around for a clock to check what time it was, Caysa came back from the bathroom, the funny smile still on her face.

"It's all yours,'" she said, nodding her head in the direction of the bathroom as she walked over to the wardrobe. "I'll find you something to wear while you bathe." Allee was almost scared of what would be waiting for her when she returned, but she decided not to worry about it and walked into the bathroom, closing the door softly behind her. She quickly undressed and stuck a leg into the lilac-tiled tub. The vessel was so deep the water came up to her hip. The water came out of a tap and was so hot it was steaming, but Allee hadn't seen any signs of electricity anywhere else in the pastle. She figured that the water must have been piped out of underground springs.

Allee lowered herself into the water and let herself relax in the warmth for a minute, but she was too hungry to sit doing nothing for long. She grabbed a promising looking bottle from a shelf at her shoulder and set to washing her hair. She had barely lathered up before she stopped with a gasp. Her hair was bright red! Suddenly, Allee was aware of all the different shades of purple in the bathroom. The colors jumped out at her, and she closed her eyes to escape, but light whirled inside her eyelids, making her eyeballs burn. Fighting nausea, she stuck her head under the water, desperate for the glare to go away. Then something occurred to her, and she breathed in water in surprise, the sickness gone. Choking and coughing, she quickly lifted her head back up.

"It's because I'm in a different world," she whispered. "It's catching up to me." The colors were not so bright now, but they still made her eyes hurt. Allee hurriedly put some white syrupy stuff that she hoped was conditioner in her hair, rinsed, and got out of the tub. The amethyst towel she found to wrap herself in was as thick as her bedspread at home. Doing her best to ignore the brightness, she grabbed a brush off a golden tray and tackled her hair, starting almost every time she saw it. As soon as she had finished, she began looking around the room for something less revealing than a towel. She found a violet bathrobe and after putting it on, walked into the other room. Caysa was sitting in a chair in front of the fireplace.

"Done already?" she asked, her tone startled.

"I don't take long baths," Allee replied. "I hate getting wrinkly." Casya smiled again and walked towards the wardrobe.

"I have found a dress for you," she announced, pulling out a navy blue piece of fabric with more flounces than a wedding dress.

"You want me to wear *that*?" Allee half-shrieked.

"No, just the petticoats," Caysa said, sarcastically, pulling out a cream-colored under-gown. "Of course. And you should be wearing more, but I don't think we have a corset that wouldn't kill you, untrained as you are. Now come here so I can help you put it on."

"I can dress myself," Allee said stiffly, not wanting a stranger to help her, especially a stranger as prickly as Caysa. Caysa arched her right eyebrow again, but handed the dress over without a word. Allee took it and started back towards the bathroom.

"*Now* where are you going?"

"To get dressed."

"What is your *problem*, child?" Allee ignored her, closed the bathroom door, and looked at the dress helplessly. She had absolutely no idea how to put it on; it was even a guess to which hole her head went through. She chose the biggest and hoped for the best.

Allee did manage to get her head and arms in what felt to be the right places in the dress, but, somehow, she got her leg caught in part of the petticoat thing. Admitting defeat, Allee went back to Caysa. She stood in the doorway, not knowing how to ask the woman to help her get dressed. Fortunately, Caysa seemed to pity her.

"Come here, child," she said. Allee obeyed and Casya deftly pulled and fastened until everything was in its proper place. "Hold still another minute," Caysa murmured and Allee froze as Caysa fastened something cold across her neck. It was a silver chain with a silver ivy leaf on it. Then metal bit her ears, and Allee realized Caysa had fastened ivy leaf earrings onto them.

"There we are," Caysa said, her face triumphant. "You clean up nice." She frowned. "But your hair," she continued, fingering it. "It's still wet. We'll just have to do something simple with it." Allee knew a ponytail was very simple, but dared not suggest it. Caysa pulled out a drawer in the open wardrobe and produced a comb. She wrapped it in Allee's hair and turned her to look at herself in the mirror above the vanity.

Allee looked at her reflection and scowled. Somehow, the dress managed to highlight her least favorite body parts. Apparently, Betwix women were differently shaped than she was. She hadn't expected a total transformation, but she had hoped not to look silly. As if in agreement, one of the little bows fluttered to the ground. Caysa was busy putting away the jewelry box and didn't notice.

Her scowl deepening, Allee forced herself to resist the temptation to stick her tongue out at her image. Then she noticed her bare feet sticking underneath the dress.

"What about shoes?" Casya reached into the wardrobe again and brought out blue slippers. Allee eyed them.

"Those are going to be too small," she said. Caysa pulled at the toe and the heel, and the slipper was suddenly bigger. Allee wanted to ask how, but Caysa seemed to be in hurry.

"Here," she said, handing Allee the slippers. "You have very big feet," she added. Allee blushed, wondering if every single part of her looked ridiculous to Betwix eyes.

Caysa gave Allee a last long look, and nodded.

"You're ready now." Allee slipped the shoes on and followed Caysa out into the hall. She led Allee up and down several corridors until the shoes began to pinch her feet and she had tripped over her long skirt so often that all she wanted to do was run back to her room and hide behind the heavy velvet curtains of the four-poster. But she was so hopelessly lost that she knew it was pointless to even try. Finally, they reached their destination: a heavy, gold-wrought door surrounded by a large group of people. Allee was painfully aware of the light reflecting off of the jewels and silks they all wore. She blinked furiously, and they toned down.

"Any questions about your order?" Caysa called to the crowd. They all shook their heads. She turned back to Allee as a trumpet blasted on the other side of the wall and the first man went through the door.

"This door opens onto a stairway that leads into the Hall of Affair," Caysa explained, eyeing Allee sternly. "You are to walk down the staircase, *without* tripping," Allee blushed. She had never worn a skirt this long in her life. "And sit with Her Grace. Remember to smile." Caysa straightened Allee's hair.

"They aren't going to say what I did, are they?" Allee asked, nervously.

"No. You are simply a guest of Her Grace. Smile and don't trip." And with that, Caysa turned and walked briskly back the way they had come. Allee watched her go with a sinking heart. She felt like a fool in this dress and would look even more so if she tripped. Trying not to think about it or draw attention to herself, she stood by the wall and fiddled with her necklace.

The line grew shorter and shorter until Allee was next. As she grasped the doorknob, the trumpet echoed again, and a voice called, "Guest of Her Grace the Duchess-Princess of Taween. I present to you, Alethea Quintin."

Allee found herself at the top of a white marble staircase. At the bottom were long wooden tables full of people on a canvas-covered floor. The walls were also white marble, but the ceiling seemed to be made of brightly colored stained glass. Allee gasped in awe. Every creature imaginable was elaborately etched in the glass, from jewel-scaled fish and bright-eyed woodland animals to proud, stern centaurs and breathtakingly beautiful mermaids. Allee decided it was the most gorgeous piece of artwork she had ever seen.

Although she wanted keep looking at the ceiling, Allee jerked herself back to the task at hand and slowly began to descend. She concentrated on her feet, gripping the banister tightly. There was some polite applause, and Allee lifted her head and gave the onlookers a weak smile. Another two steps, and the descent was over. Allee breathed a shaky sigh of relief and fervently prayed she would *never* have to do that again.

Once she was on the floor, Allee quickly became nervous again. She couldn't see Cardolyn anywhere. Frantically, she searched the tables, finally noticing one that was raised higher than the others. And, to Allee's great relief, the Duchess was waving at her.

As she walked to the table, Allee took notice of its occupants. On the end closest to her was Cardolyn. To the Duchess's right was Ferdy, looking bored and uncomfortable in a fancy suit of russet silk with heavy silver braid. Seated next to him was a tall, stately young man dressed in a golden, heavily embroidered tunic with a velvet robe of midnight blue that perfectly enhanced his gorgeous blue eyes. Almost all of the young women in the Hall were gazing at him in adoration. Allee wasn't sure she was too impressed with him; his smile seemed fake to her.

Allee was fairly certain that the man was Prince Esendore, and her suspicion was confirmed when she saw the glint of a crown underneath his dark blonde hair. He didn't need it to assert his station; every inch of him screamed royalty. Allee couldn't help compare him to Ferdy, but there was little similar between the two. Their completely different personalities were evident just by the way the held themselves. While Esendore was surveying his subjects with haughty indifference, Ferdy was making faces at a boy at the trestle tables. The two brothers didn't even look alike. Esendore had a finer bone structure, and was more slender than Ferdy. Esendore was also darker haired, and while his tresses were pulled into a neat ponytail; Ferdy's golden tresses hung raggedly around his collar. The Princes had the same nose, but Ferdy's wasn't exactly centered in his face like Esendore's was.

Allee shook her head in puzzlement and began climbing the steps to the dais. In her haste to be seated, she tripped on the top step and had to bite her tongue to keep from crying out in pain and frustration. Cardolyn pretended not to notice and smiled at her, patting the empty chair on her left. Allee flopped into it and folded her hands in her lap. Although she had only walked a hundred feet or so, she felt exhausted. Taking a deep breath, she forced herself to focus on Cardolyn's chatter.

"Do you like your room, Alethea? We have others, if it doesn't suit you. Green, yellow, pink, blue, even puce, if you like." Allee wanted to see what color puce was (she had always wondered), but she shook her head.

"I like purple. And I never imagined I would be so comfortable here. I—" Cardolyn interrupted.

"No comfort can express my thanks, dear," she gushed, giving Allee that same adoring look that had frustrated her earlier. "I just don't know what would have happened if you had not been there. We are bringing in a specialist to investigate. I just can't imagine how it got here! We barely have fliquitos, this is just so strange, oh, good, here comes the food!"

Allee looked to her left. Servants with platters of food were filing out of a door, invisible when closed, to the right of the staircase. Suddenly, there was a voice at her elbow.

"Hello, Flower." It was Gnarrish.

"Hello," Allee said, coldly. He smiled, served her food, and then moved on to Her Grace. When he had finished, Cardolyn turned back to Allee.

"See, he does like you. He couldn't help it, the incident with the jewel and all. Oh, what's wrong, dear?" Allee had been staring at her plate of food, trying to decide if it was safe to eat it. With all that Betwix had thrown at her, she was just a little suspicious. Cardolyn took her hesitancy to be of politeness.

"Oh, don't wait for the everyone else to be served, dear! You can start in anytime you want." Allee gulped, but had no choice except to start eating. To her surprise, the pasta tasted a lot like spaghetti, though the meat had a rather gamy taste to it, not quite venison, but not quite beef.

She began to eat with gusto, but slowed down after she almost spilled on the dress. Normally she was a fast eater, and consequently very sloppy, but she did not want to ruin her gown. Still, she finished before Cardolyn, who was filling Ferdy in on the missed conference between bites.

Seeking entertainment, Allee scanned the crowd before her. She guessed the people sitting at the tables to be nobles and merchants by the way their elaborate garb contrasted with servants who were offering trays of food. Strangely, but mercifully to Allee's eyes, there wasn't a single bright color in the entire lot. All of them were wearing dark colors, as if in mourning.

Allee remembered Cardolyn mentioning that the King was on his deathbed, but that meant he was still alive. She had not heard anybody talk about a Queen, but there was not exactly an air of gloom over the dining hall, more of subdued apprehension. Women in glittering skirts were laughing at whatever their dinner partners were telling them while old matrons surveyed them disapprovingly, sharing gossip behind hands. The older men seemed to be keeping an eye on the high table. Allee wondered if they were sizing up their future King, plotting how they could win his favor. All the people looked to be enjoying themselves, except for the servants. Allee thought they looked overworked and in want of a solid meal.

"We have quite a full house tonight, on account of Esendore and Dariel's wedding." Cardolyn voice said, cutting through her thoughts, and Allee jumped in surprise. She hadn't realized her inspection of the people had been so obvious.

"Wedding?" Allee asked, feeling ignorant. Cardolyn blinked at her, startled.

"Why, of course, dear. Prince Esendore is to wed Countess Dariel of the Western Strand. The ceremony is to be held next week. Her parents, Count Daneald and Countess Fariel are here already," Cardolyn nodded at a couple seated by Esendore. "But Dariel doesn't arrive until tomorrow. She wanted to see a little bit of the country, so she'll come with the wagon train carrying her belongings. There will be a Grand Ball tomorrow night to celebrate her arrival, and then dances every night until the ceremony. That will be fun, won't it, dear?" Allee could think of several things more fun than wearing a dress every night for a week and dancing with total strangers, but Cardolyn seemed so excited she murmured an agreement. Suddenly, Cardolyn changed the subject. "Why did your parents send you at this time, then, if you did not know about the wedding?" Allee thought fast.

"We hoped that the pastle could always use one more servant," Allee said, hoping she didn't sound stupid.

"Oh, I see." Cardolyn sounded disappointed in not being able to find anything interesting about Allee. To discourage her from asking anything else, Allee stared up at the ceiling.

"This is a beautiful room," she said, knowing that Cardolyn would realize she was changing the subject, but the Duchess seemed quite eager to talk about the chamber.

"Oh, yes," she gushed, "It is the most splendid in the pastle. As you know, Taween is famous for the craftsmanship of its marble. It lasts three thousand years when we've treated it," she boasted, gazing fondly at the walls. "That's why there's a block on our banner." She gestured to the far wall, where a bright blue banner hung. In the middle was a sword with a silver blade and black handle embedded in a block of white marble, with silver diamonds in an arc over the entire picture. When she thought Allee had looked enough, Cardolyn continued,

"The ceiling is what interests you though, of course. Every single creature that has ever been and lives now is etched into the glass. And do you see the writing on the edges?" Allee nodded, staring at the silvery script. She didn't recognize any of the words, though the letters were familiar.

"What does it say?" she asked, curious. Cardolyn sighed.

"We really do not know. We did once, or at least some scholars did, but it has faded away from memory. There are some old songs, so we know the pronunciation, but most of the meanings are lost to us." Allee was even more intrigued, and craned her neck to get a better look. She still could make nothing of the jumble of letters. With an effort, she turned her attention back to Cardolyn. "Quite a lot of things happen in here," she was saying, "Balls, coronations, wedding receptions. It's not called the Hall of Affair for nothing."

"Though you must realize that not only affairs of state have begun here, right Aunt Cardolyn?" Ferdy had joined in their conversation. Allee was confused, but Cardolyn seemed shocked.

"Ferdinand! What a thing to say!" she exclaimed, blushing. Allee thought she understood. Some time or another Cardolyn had met someone here, and the encounter had led to a relationship. But there had been no mention about Her Grace being married. Allee guessed that Ferdy was trying to imply that Cardolyn was some type of a flirt. Allee snorted at the very thought. Ferdy just grinned at her. Cardolyn made a sound of disapproval, but then her expression abruptly changed to one of delight.

"Alethea, so you don't learn about the wrong type of things that happen in this pastle," she paused to glare at Ferdy, "you can come to my embroidery group tomorrow. Won't that be fun?" Allee knew how to embroider, but not without poking her finger along with some choice words aimed at the needle. She shot a look of panic at Ferdy. His eyes flashed mischievously and for a second Allee thought he wasn't going to help her, but then his face folded into a simpering mask.

"Oh, but Her Grace, didn't Allee tell you? She misses her farm horribly and wants to find something more engaging than embroidery. Why don't I take her with me tomorrow?" Ferdy made her sound like she was a huge cry baby and Allee wished very much to hit him or boldly declare that she would be happy to go with Cardolyn, but she was too desperate not to. She just gritted her teeth and gave Ferdy a terse smile. Cardolyn looked astounded.

"Oh, you poor dear, why didn't you say something?" she cried. Allee cringed while Ferdy tried to stifle an evil-sounding laugh. "I had no idea! Of course you can go with Ferdinand! Now, since you are to have a busy day tomorrow, I think it's best you go to bed. Goodnight,

Ferdinand." Cardolyn abruptly stood up and swept down the stairs, assuming Allee was following her. Allee was too stunned to do anything. Ferdy laughed.

"Don't worry, you don't owe me for that. The look on you face is enough."

"So glad I could amuse you," Allee snapped, standing up.

"Sweet dreams, Allee," he replied, still laughing. Not caring how childish it was, she stuck her tongue out at him and carried his look of shock all the way to the door, where Cardolyn was waiting for her. They passed through it into a dim corridor. After several twists and turns, Allee realized that they were in the corridor where the taranion incident had happened. Allee sighed. The pastle's floor plan was going to take some getting used to. She had no idea how they had gotten here.

Allee was worried Cardolyn would start making a big deal about the taranion thing again, but they climbed the stairs without a word between them. Two minutes later they were at her room. Cardolyn opened the door and immediately started to bustle around, leaving Allee standing on the threshold.

"Would you like a fire, dear? It can get chilly, even though it's summer. It's the lake, you know." Looking at the thickness of the comforter on the bed, Allee doubted she would get cold.

"No thanks," she said, feeling out of place. Allee couldn't understand why Cardolyn was doing this. Weren't there servants to take care of the guests? Allee decided it must have something to do with Cardolyn's obsession with the taranion. The Duchess finally seemed to notice her still standing in the doorway and paused in her efforts to turn down the bed.

"There's a nightgown in the wardrobe, if you want to get changed. Let me unbutton you." Allee complied, feeling extremely foolish having her buttons undone by a Duchess. Cardolyn respected Allee's desire for privacy, though, and as soon as she finished untying the sash she turned her back. Walking stiffly so her gown wouldn't fall off, Allee went over to the wardrobe and opened the door. Neatly folded on a shelf was a lavender nightgown. Allee disliked nightgowns; she usually slept in a t-shirt and shorts.

"Do you have any pants to go with it?" she asked Cardolyn. The Duchess looked up from fluffing the pillows, her surprise plain on her face.

"Pants? Whatever would you want them for, dear?"

"Never mind," Allee sighed. She made a face at the nightgown and went into the bathroom.

She slipped into the nightgown and then brushed her hair again. She was not quite sure if she liked it being so red. It felt strange not brushing her teeth, but Allee doubted Betwix had anything to improve dental hygiene. Then again, none of the people she had seen had had rotten teeth. On impulse, she opened the top drawer. Resting on a little tray was a crude purple toothbrush.

Allee wet it and stuck it in her mouth. Mint flavor exploded on her tongue and the toothbrush started to foam. Allee was delighted, and disappointed when the flavor went away after a couple of minutes. She put the toothbrush back on the tray, and re-entered the big room. Hearing her footsteps, Cardolyn turned from watering the flowers on the windowsill.

"Are you ready for bed, dear? Or do you need some help getting ready? I used to help Ferdinand when he was little, but he won't let me anymore." She sounded so sad that Allee pretended that she needed her hair braided. Cardolyn was elated.

"I've always wanted to do this," she sighed, tying the end with a bow. Allee smiled, glad that she had made her happy. She crawled up into the four-poster and Cardolyn tucked the covers around her, though Allee could have easily done it herself. She decided then that Cardolyn was tucking her in out of loneliness, not gratitude. Allee finally relaxed and gave Cardolyn a sleepy smile.

"Sleep well, dear," Her Grace murmured. She hovered another moment, as if wanting to do something yet not sure if she should. Whatever it was she decided against it and left the room, though the smell of her perfume still lingered. A minute later the candles went out.

The warmth Cardolyn had brought with her disappeared and Allee was left alone in a canopy bed five times too big for her in a pastle in a different world where not a soul knew who she really was. To fight her homesickness, Allee tried to think of something else, anything else. Her mind landed on the word "pastle." The language of this world was exactly like English, except for those few strange words. It sounded like a combination of palace and castle.

Suddenly, the truth hit her like a brick. Betwix sounded like a combination of the words "between" and "mixed". So, naturally, each of the creatures and places in Betwix would be a combination of two species or two places on Earth. A gnarf was both a gnome and a dwarf and that's why they liked both flowers and jewels, a pastle was a palace and a castle, which was why the first story was like a fortress and the second a palace. So she *had* seen a braying llama that afternoon! Allee's thoughts spun wildly, imagining all the possibilities of a world that was combined with her own. As a result, her head began to ache and she got up to get a drink.

She raced across the deep purple carpet and drank deeply from a lilac tumbler on the sink. She drank two cupfuls, but wasn't ready to go back to bed just yet. With relief, she realized that the bathroom was cluttered with her stuff and set about tidying it. She hung up the robe and folded the towel on the edge of the bathtub. When she shook out her jeans to lay them on the chair, something heavy fell out of the pocket and landed on her toe. Biting back a yelp of pain, Allee picked it up. The jewel fit snugly into the palm of her hand.

"I'm glad I found you," Allee told it. She smiled wryly at her foolishness, and, for no particular reason, decided to take it to bed with her.

While crossing the floor again, Allee wished for some slippers. She went over to the wardrobe to see if there were any. She could not find any, but she did solve the mystery of her shoes. There was a sliding panel that made the sole get bigger or smaller when you pulled on the ends. She could not see the need for shoes that fit different wearers; after all, didn't most people bring their own clothes? She guessed that the pastle must entertain a lot of people and it went to any expense to make sure they were taken care of. She wondered, briefly, if any of the guests had been like her. Rolling her eyes at the very thought, she crawled back into bed, pressing the ruby against her cheek.

Suddenly, she had a vision of herself giving the ruby to Cardolyn, as a token of her appreciation to Her Grace for being so kind to her. *Cardolyn will be so happy with me*, Allee thought dreamily, swinging her legs over the side of the bed to go give Cardolyn her gift right away. Then she stopped. Something was nagging at the back of her mind. In response, the urge to find Cardolyn grew stronger. Allee was annoyed.

Stop that, she commanded the urge, slowly grasping that Cardolyn probably had all the rubies she could want, and she hadn't even seemed interested in the jewel earlier that day. With that realization, the urge disappeared as fast as it had come, and Allee could think clearly again. *That was weird* she thought, shaking herself to rid herself of the vision. She rolled over and homesickness took hold of her again. She didn't have the slightest guarantee as to when she would see her family again. She had no idea what was going to happen to her. A painful lump rose in her throat at the thought of never seeing her home again and her eyes began to burn uncomfortably.

"I *hate* crying," she whispered to the ruby. In response, a subtle warmth seemed to come from the jewel, and suddenly a voice started singing from its depths. Allee was so happy to hear a friendly noise that she did not even question how bizarre and unreal it was. Even the language was strange, but the singing was as soothing as a lullaby. She began to feel sleepy, but this time the feeling was not a trance. As her eyes closed, the singing stopped.

"There now," a female voice said. "Go to sleep." And Allee did.

Chapter 2

Winning Over His Highness

Allee woke up the next morning to a clattering noise by the fireplace. She sat up and was about to open the curtains when she remembered the ruby. Suddenly wide awake, she tore through her sheets, eventually finding it underneath her pillow. Her shoulders sagged in disappointment. It was just a plain, ordinary ruby. She knew she was being foolish, but deep down, she had hoped it would have taken her home.

"Are you awake, Alethea?" a voice called. Allee put the ruby back under her pillow and opened the curtains. Caysa was dishing up food onto two plates that lay on a little table by the fireplace.

"I'm awake," Allee replied. Caysa looked up and smiled.

"Wonderful. There's a dress laid out for you on the end of the bed. You should hurry or your eggs will get cold." Allee scrambled out of bed, briefly wondering what the bird that laid the eggs was named, and inspected the garment she was to wear today. She supposed it was nice, but brown velvet was really not her thing. She had been hoping that dresses were only worn for formal occasions. This one was not as fancy as the gown from the night before, and it didn't have a petticoat shift to wear underneath it, but it still had a lot of skirt. Sighing, Allee went to put it on.

Once inside the bathroom, Allee held the dress at arm's length. Again, there was no obvious way to get into it. She decided to just stick her head through and hope for the best. She shucked off her nightgown and pulled the dress on. The garment went on a lot easier than she had expected, but it still looked silly on her. To make herself feel better, she put on her tennis shoes and hoped Caysa wouldn't notice them underneath the long skirt. Much encouraged, she brushed her hair, stuck it in a ponytail, and went back into the bedroom.

Caysa was unfolding a napkin on her lap, but jumped up when Allee entered.

"You can't go on a tour with His Highness looking like that," she scolded. Allee couldn't keep from rolling her eyes.

"Like Ferdinand cares what hair looks like," she said scornfully. Caysa smiled wryly, as if she knew something Allee did not.

"Oh, he cares alright," she said, giggling. Allee realized that Caysa was implying that Ferdy was a girl-chaser.

She could believe that very easily. Caysa continued.

"But it wasn't *him* who requested your hair to be done up properly; it was Her Grace. Now come here." Allee blushed. She did not want to be an embarrassment to Her Grace. Wincing at the thought, she slowly pulled out her ponytail and stuck the band on her wrist.

Caysa took a box out of the wardrobe and positioned Allee so she couldn't see herself in the mirror. The servant woman then began to grab fistfuls of Allee's hair, twisting them into braids as she did so. Next, she slid bronze rings up to hold the hair in place and stuck some pins in to link the braids all together. Allee's hair felt like it was being pulled out of her scalp, and she almost cried out when Caysa took out two bronze disks with clips on the back.

"Didn't you say the eggs would get cold?" she asked, trying to defer her tormenter.

"They'll wait for now," Caysa replied firmly, sliding the disks over the two places where the braids met. Allee's head nodded with their weight. Caysa stood back and turned Allee so she could see herself. "What do you think?" Allee thought of several, nasty things; like no one's head is supposed to resemble the tires on a car, but she couldn't say *that*. She tried to look on the bright side. Caysa wore her hair this way (minus the hubcaps), and she looked all right. It would just take some getting used to. Allee gulped, trying to think of something nice to say.

"It's much better than what I had done," she said, her voice very small. Caysa smiled at her and moved towards the table. Her head wobbling, Allee followed her and sat down, punching at her skirts in frustration. Caysa was too busy dishing up to notice.

"Do you want some aplrange juice?" she asked. Allee looked up, breathless and frustrated at the stubborn skirts. She had almost fallen off her chair.

"What? Oh, sure," she replied, finally getting the skirts to sit right. She took a sip, her mouth puckering at the unfamiliar combination of apples and oranges. She decided she liked it and turned her attention back to Caysa, who was asking her a question.

"Do you ride? Ferdinand would be more than happy to go for a ride with you. He loves that beast of his." Allee had ridden the camel at the State Fair, and had sat on a horse at a friend's house, but she couldn't tell Caysa that.

"A little," she said, hoping riding wouldn't be required of her. "But I'm not sure if I would be up to an entire morning." She knew she could ride if she had to, but wanted to see what she would be riding first. Caysa nodded.

"I know how that is. The last time I rode an entire morning..." Allee contentedly listened to Caysa'a story while marveling at her food. The toast did not taste like Earth bread, yet Allee knew it had to be made of some kind of grain. From its dark color, she guessed the plant was a combination of wheat and rye. Whatever it was, the end result was quite pleasant. The sausage that she had dared to try was also okay, but it had the same gamy taste as the meat in the spaghetti. The juice was fantastic. Just as Allee was draining her second cupful, there was a knock on the door.

"Come in," Caysa called. Ferdy stuck his head in.

"Ready yet, Allee?" he asked. "It's going to get hot out there if you don't hurry." Allee stood up, glad to be going outside, no matter how hot it was.

"Ferdinand, don't you even say good morning?" Caysa chided.

"Nope," Ferdy grinned. "But I will if you insist. Good morning, Caysa. Allee, are we going yet?" Allee turned back to thank the servant woman.

"Thanks for breakfast, it was delicious," she said, bowing. Caysa gasped.

"Wait!" she cried, her face horror-stricken. "You must learn how to curtsey!" Allee practically pushed Ferdy out the door and shut it firmly behind them. Bowing was just fine with her. She turned to see Ferdy silently laughing at her, but he quickly composed himself.

"So, what do you want to be bored with first?" he asked.

"I won't be bored," Allee said, sure that boredom would be the last thing she would encounter in this strange place. She was eager to see the different kinds of animals. "Let's just go outside."

"Whatever," he said, and started off down the hall. Allee tried to follow, but she was finding walking difficult while her hair was being pulled out by the roots.

"Wait," she called to Ferdy. While Ferdy stared at her in disbelief, she slid off the bronze disks and nimbly undid the braids. Once her hair was free of its bonds, she grabbed the ponytail holder off her wrist and put it in her hair.

"Do you know where I could put these?" she asked. Ferdy continued to goggle at her. She sighed and tried to put things as simply as possible. "Look, they hurt my head. I don't like stuff to hurt my head unless I absolutely *have* to look proper." Can you please show me somewhere to put these so they won't get lost?"

"It can't hurt that bad," Ferdy scoffed.

"Come a little closer and you can find out first hand," Allee said, reaching for his hair. He looked startled.

"Are you threatening me?" he asked.

"I will be in a minute if you don't show me somewhere to put these," Allee retorted. Ferdy rolled his eyes.

"Okay, okay, give them here." He took the pieces and hid them behind a flowerpot on a shelf. "Are you happy now?"

"Absolutely," Allee said. "Are we going yet?" Ferdy rolled his eyes again and guided her down the stairs and to the door that opened into the courtyard. He flung it open and Allee was almost deafened by the noise. The sounds of hammers pounding and men shouting were almost intolerable. It was much louder than yesterday. Allee guessed that the smiths did most of their work in the morning.

"This courtyard is the smige's!" Ferdy yelled in her ear. *Smith/forge* Allee thought instinctively and looked around in awe. She counted at least ten buildings with fires in them, each of them big enough to hold fifteen men and half a dozen horses. Even though she was standing some fifty feet away, the heat was almost unbearable.

"Can we go somewhere quieter?" she yelled.

"WHAT?" he yelled back.

"CAN WE GO SOMEPLACE QUIETER?" she bellowed.

"WHAT?"

"CAN WE GO—" Then, she realized he could hear her perfectly fine and was just making her scream. "I'm going to hit you," she said right in his ear. First, he looked surprised at the threat, but then he laughed and led her around the corner of a room attached to the pastle. The noise was muffled considerably and Allee forgot her anger to pump Ferdy for information. "What are they doing out there?" she asked.

"They serve about four hundred people every week," he replied, eager to boast. "All of the nobles in Taween come to the pastle to get their ironwork done. Or gold. There are goldsmiths and silversmiths over there." He pointed to the right to a group of wooden buildings with large glass windows in front. Inside the little shops, Allee could see the smiths bent over pieces that caught the light and dazzled her eyes. Ferdy mistook her gasp of surprise as one of delight. "We can go look if you like." He didn't sound very enthused and neither was Allee. She wanted to see the creatures of Betwix.

"Don't you have any animals?" she asked.

"Yeah, sure," Ferdy said, relief in his voice. "We can go see Lunar and Majesty. Lunar is mine, and Majesty is Esendore's."

"The Prince's horse's name is Majesty? Don't you get them mixed up?" Allee asked, puzzled. Ferdy stared at her for a second, and then burst out laughing. Allee glared at him.

"What's so funny?" she demanded. Ferdy caught his breath.

"Esendore getting confused with a zeorse! That's HILARIOUS!" He went off into peals of laughter again. Allee was a little annoyed, but she could see why he thought it humorous. The tall, poised man at supper last night had not seemed someone to take lightly.

"What's going on out here?" a voice suddenly yelled. A door in the side of the extension opened and a woman was framed in the doorway. Her hair was pulled in to a tight bun and her face was contorted in anger, but that's not what made Allee shiver. The apron she wore was covered in blood. Allee felt Ferdy stiffen beside her.

"I'm entertaining a guest of Her Grace, Nerin," he said. Nerin smirked at him.

"You couldn't entertain the backside of a llonkey," she sneered. Ferdy drew himself up to his full height.

"However, unlike you, I have never acted like the backside of a llonkey," he growled, his voice cold. Allee wondered why Ferdy didn't have Nerin arrested on the spot for insulting him, but guessed it was because he did not care for acting like a Prince—ever. She realized that that was why Nerin had dared to insult him in the first place.

However, Ferdy was not going to let the serving woman get to him, and met her eyes defiantly. "I'm not doing anything wrong," he declared. Watching him stare Nerin down, the lines of his body radiating command, Allee noted with a shock that Ferdy *could* look as imposing and royal as his older brother. "Go scold someone who cares about your pointless harping." The moment he finished, there was a loud squawking and a thunk from inside the doorway.

"Aaahhh!" a girl's voice screamed. "I missed the head! It's gonna get me! I'm sorry, ducken, I'm sorry!"

"Not again, Orla!" Nerin cried, half-turning. She sent a glare in Ferdy's direction and then slammed the door. There was another scream, a ba-quack, and then all went silent. Ferdy and Allee looked at each other and started to laugh. Allee could not believe such perfect timing. Then she pictured Nerin chasing a chicken-duck all over the room and laughed even harder.

"What was that place?" Allee asked after they had recovered themselves.

"It's an extension to the kitchens," Ferdy replied. He looked around and lowered his voice. "The place where they butcher the animals. It's on this side to be close to the starns. You know...for easy access." Allee grimaced.

"I didn't need to know that," she protested.

"You asked." Seeing her face, he tried to smooth things over. "I suppose you want to go see the looms now?" Allee wrinkled up her nose.

"I told you, I want to see the starns." She tried not to stumble over the unfamiliar word. Ferdy's eyebrows went up.

"Okay, if you're serious." He began to walk towards a wall at the end of the courtyard. Allee ran to keep up.

"What?" she demanded. "Why do you think it's strange I don't want to see a bunch of people making cloth?" Ferdy stopped and turned to her.

"I just know that if Cardolyn finds out I took you to the starns first instead of the looms, she'll yell at me for not looking out for your best interests." Allee frowned at him.

"Number one, you do not now, nor will you ever, care for my best interests, and number two, it's *my* idea," she said. Ferdy rolled his eyes.

"But I'll still get in trouble," he replied. Allee sighed in exasperation.

"If that happens, I will tell her that I *wanted* to go see the starns and make her believe me. And, by the way, what exactly do you do that makes you the number one suspect if anything goes wrong or someone's unhappy?" Ferdy tried to look innocent, but failed miserably by grinning.

"It's just that nobody's forgotten the manure fight me and the blacksmith's boy had with the Earl's niece and her maid, or the time I put bugs in that horrible brat, the Duke of Betwa's daughter's soup, or when—"

"You did *what*?" Allee interrupted. Ferdy shrugged.

"She called Lunar an ugly brute."

"Don't forget the time when that stuff blew up in your bathtub," a voice said. Allee and Ferdy looked up. Sitting on the wall, grinning broadly, was Gnarrish.

"You helped!" Ferdy exclaimed. "And you never told me that baking powder and vinegar *exploded* when they were combined."

"What were you trying to do?" Allee asked, very interested. Ferdy gave an evil laugh.

"Dying Cardolyn's hair piece green." Allee gaped at him.

"It was ugly," he said, defending himself. "We were doing her a favor."

"It was still your idea," Gnarrish reminded Ferdy. Allee laughed.

"Okay, okay, I've heard enough. Can we please go see Lunar before you get *me* into trouble?"

"We're going!" Ferdy declared, throwing up his arms. "Bye, Gnarrish!" The gnarf waved at them lazily as they passed through a gate under an arch in the wall.

Allee gasped in surprise. The smige courtyard had been made entirely of gray stone so nothing would burn, and the sun had been blocked by the heights of the pastle. Now, they were fully exposed to the dazzling sunshine and the smell of growing things. Green pastures spread out endlessly before them, almost swallowing a group of buildings further north from where they were standing. To the east, Allee saw neat, well-kept fields that went all the way to the wall that ran between the island and the lake. She turned her head to the left and saw the road that led to the city, which lay to the north. Allee could just barely see masses of people moving about in the city at the bottom of the hill they were on.

"Beautiful view, isn't it?" Ferdy's voice said in her ear.

"The city seems so alive," she agreed.

"I wouldn't know," Allee cringed at the bitterness in his voice. "The King does not like to see nobles mingling with the common folk. I've only been there three times in my entire life." Allee almost shivered. When Ferdy was angry, he seemed to radiate a powerful, intimidating aura. Allee pretended to push her hair out her eyes and peeked a look his face. Although the sun was shining brightly, a shadow seemed to have crossed his features. He obviously hated his father. As soon as it had come, the shadow passed, and he smiled at her.

"Are we going to see Lunar or not?" he asked.

"Lead the way," Allee replied cheerfully. She was dying of curiosity to find out who exactly the King of Taween was and why Ferdy hated him so much, but she swallowed her questions and silently followed Ferdy down the gray brick path.

"The starns with the zeorses are farther down. These are the kennels for the dokats," he explained as they approached pens made of thin slats of wood.

Allee didn't even have time to wonder. On either side of the path were thigh-high fuzzy creatures with pointy ears, long snouts and bushy tails. Some were rubbing themselves against the boards and emitting a throbbing noise that sounded sort of like purring while a few others simply sat at the back of their pens and stared at her coldly. Allee looked at each one with delight, exclaiming when one stood on its hind legs and meow-barked in her face. Then she saw the black one and a wave of homesickness washed over her. It was a combination of Maisy and Nightlight, her favorite cat.

"Oh," she said longingly and grasped the front of the cage. The dokat rubbed its silky head against the fence.

"Her name is Lullaby," Ferdy said, his eyes soft with affection. "You know, since she's black like night and that's when mothers, you know, sing to their…their children." His voice trailed off. Allee forgot her homesickness at the sad tone of his voice and looked up at him. The shadow had come back over his face. Allee's curiosity finally got the better of her.

"You never had a mother to sing lullabies, did you?" she asked. His pain was so deep that he did not question her ignorance. He closed his eyes, remembering, but trying to not to.

"You don't have to tell me," Allee said quickly. She certainly would not want to talk about her mother's death to an almost stranger. But Ferdy didn't seem to hear her.

"I was nine," he said heavily, his breathing shaky. "And there was an outbreak of Blossom Fever. The King was not taking strong enough action to prevent an epidemic. The Queen told him how she would handle things, and suggested that he take more action." Ferdy took a deep breath, but his voice shook with anger, "And he locked her in the Tower Room for her outburst, saying that he knew what he was doing, and she should know better than to meddle in affairs she didn't understand. He was kind enough to allow her one servant," Ferdy gave a short laugh and Allee shivered, wishing he would stop.

"But then the servant got sick. My mother nursed her, until she caught it herself. Her own children were forbidden to see her, and no one knew until the servant crawled out and said the Queen was dying." His voice lowered to a pain-filled whisper. "There was nothing anyone could do," he choked out, his hands balled up in fists. "She was too far gone and passed away that same night. Locked up in a tower because she stood up for the people." He wiped a tear from his cheek, and Allee turned her head so she could pretend she hadn't seen it.

Out of the corner of her eye she saw Ferdy shake his head and recover his composure.

"Now His Majesty has locked himself in that Tower, because he realized she was right. But he still hasn't accepted that a King can be wrong. And that *he* was wrong." Allee was silent, biting her lip to keep her emotions in check. She understood Ferdy's anger, and his behavior. Why should he want to be King if the only one he had ever known had killed his mother? To distract herself, she reached her hand farther through the fence to stroke Lullaby. Ferdy saw her gesture.

"Oh, you want to pet her? Here." With a flick of his finger, he opened the gate and Allee was hit by twenty pounds of very excited dokat. The tension in the air evaporated as Allee laughed and tried to prevent Lullaby from licking off her nose.

"Well, she certainly isn't as calm as a lullaby," Allee said, glad for a diversion. Lullaby got off of her to go over and rub against Ferdy's pant leg. He reached down to pet her and some of the sadness left his face. Allee was very relieved.

"Hey, can she come with us?" she asked, as Lullaby flopped down in her lap. Ferdy shook his head.

"No, she's going to have kips soon. I can't risk something happening to her."

"Oh, I understand," Allee said, though she was disappointed. Maisy followed her everywhere at home.

Ferdy held out his arms and Allee deposited a squirming Lullaby in them. He walked to the back of the run and set her in the dokat house. Allee could still hear her throbbing even as Ferdy came out and latched the gate. He smiled absently, and they started off towards the starns again.

Allee noticed then that many of the cages were empty and in disrepair. The kennels clearly did not hold as many dokats as they could. She did not say anything to Ferdy, who seemed to be concentrating intently on the path. Allee looked down at her feet, too, and found that she had to be careful where she stepped; most of the cobblestones were missing and pieces of trash frequently littered the edges. The grounds of the pastle were obviously less well kept than the inside was.

Allee looked up from the path and stopped dead in her tracks. Before her were two rectangular buildings, one on the left and one straight ahead of her, forming an L shape. And, sticking their heads up from their feed troughs to the left were the biggest buffaloes she had ever seen in her life. Or at least that is what they looked like at first.

As Allee peered closer she realized that some were cream-colored, others brown, and quite a few were spotted like Holsteins. In a separate pen, a little behind the building, grazed Angus and Hereford-looking buffaloes. However, they were four times as big as normal cattle and at least three times as big as Earth buffalo. If they hadn't been colored like cows, Allee would have thought they were a buffalo and elephant combination. Before she could ask the hundreds of questions that were buzzing around her brain, Ferdy began explaining.

"The ones in the shed are the milk coffaloes and the others grazing are for beef," he said. Coffaloes, Allee said to herself, wishing her father could see this.

"In a few days," Ferdy continued, "the beef coffaloes will be taken into the summer pastures, off the island. In the fall, the old ones will be slaughtered and the younger ones will stay here for the winter. There's a pasture further down where they're kept." Allee knew the island was at least eight miles in diameter, but she was still finding this hard to absorb.

"*All* of the old ones?" she asked, unbelieving. There must be two hundred head here, not counting the calves and each animal probably weighed three tons. She wasn't even going to guess how they controlled those monsters.

"Well, all the ones that aren't good mothers. And the steers." Allee reeled. That was still a lot of beef.

"Where does all of it go?" Ferdy shrugged.

"Some is sold to the butchers in the city or nobles whose land isn't suitable for raising coffaloes buy it. The rest is used by the pastle. The servants get free meals, you know. Though that hardly makes up for the little the King pays them." His face hardened again. Allee was glad that there was no time for him to brood on it, for a horse whickered at them.

She turned her head to look at the other side of the yard and shrieked in surprise. Now there were zebras sticking their heads over their stalls. But like the coffaloes, they weren't exactly what they seemed. Instead of the usual black and white stripes, these creatures came in a variety of combinations. Some were brown with white stripes, others roan with black, or white with buckskin; basically, any color a horse could be. The one that was whickering at them was a blue roan with black stripes. Ferdy grinned and strode over to pet him.

"This is Lunar," he said, proudly. Lunar nuzzled his master affectionately. Allee stood a little back in awe of this strange creature.

"Can I pet him?" she asked. Ferdy looked surprised.

"You really want to?" Allee was getting annoyed at Ferdy's stereotype that all girls did not like animals that were bigger than they were and smelled a little. She rolled her eyes at him.

"Oh, come *on*, Ferdy, I am NOT scared," she said, striding over. Involuntarily, she gasped. The stalls were in a sad state of disrepair. Nails and pieces of garbage seemed to be all they were made of. Now Allee *was* hesitant to go near; the stall looked close to collapsing. She'd never seen such unsafe conditions for an animal in her life, and these were *royal* buildings. Allee realized Ferdy had turned a bright shade of red in embarrassment. Her heart sank. She had not meant to be so obviously shocked. He seemed to think he needed to explain.

"The King doesn't like to "waste" money on the animals when he can use it to pamper the royal treasury," he mumbled. Suddenly, Allee had to ask something.

"He *is* your father, isn't he?" Ferdy frowned.

"Who?"

"The King."

"Yes."

"Then why don't you call him that?"

"Because he doesn't act like one!" Ferdy exploded. Allee bowed her head and didn't look at him. She had known better than to ask. She held out her hand for Lunar to sniff and decided to apologize.

"I'm sorry." She realized Ferdy had apologized at the same time. They both blushed.

"I didn't mean to pry," Allee said, softly.

"No, you have every right to," Ferdy replied, scuffing his shoe in the dirt. "I asked stuff about you. It's only fair. And, my behavior needs an explanation. I just don't know how to explain it." Allee almost felt sorry for him.

"You don't need to," she said, "I understand." He gave her a wobbly smile and changed the subject.

"Do you want to go get some carrishes to feed Lunar?" Allee smiled back.

"I'd love to," she said, glad that there were no hard feelings.

They started walking towards the big building that connected the coffaloe and zeorse stalls. As they did, Allee peered into the stalls. Most were empty, so she figured the zeorses were either out grazing or the stall wasn't occupied. She was getting used to the empty ones when a black head suddenly appeared in front of her and neighed. She stumbled back and grabbed a hold of a door, trying to catch her breath. Ferdy laughed.

"This is Majesty. He doesn't like to be ignored." Allee reached up to stroke the zeorse's nose. Majesty leaned down his head with its narrow white stripes and blew in her face.

"I guess," she said, laughing. Another zeorse next to Majesty stuck its head out and nickered. It was a palomino with black stripes.

"Wow," Allee said in admiration. The palomino was the most beautiful zeorse she had seen yet.

"That's Dazzle," Ferdy said. "She's Esendore's wedding gift to Dariel. Allee rubbed Dazzle's nose, too, and they continued on their way.

The courtyard was crawling with people, all of them carrying buckets of feed for some cages with birds in them or hauling milk pails down the path that led to the kitchens. When they saw Ferdy, they would bow and mumble, "Your Highness." He would nod his head, but otherwise seemed nonplussed. Allee was a little embarrassed and was kept quite busy bowing in return, which seemed to surprise the servants.

Allee turned her gaze from them and noticed a man who wasn't carrying anything, but seemed to be looking for someone. Ferdy saw him, too, and his face lit up with glee. Allee wondered why, but then she realized the man was completely bald. And she knew that if Ferdy had the sense of humor other adolescent boys had, he would love bald jokes. The man seemed to be searching for them, and strode over. Ferdy looked overjoyed to see him.

"Hello, Roeland!" Ferdy said brightly. "How goes the recession?"

"Just fine, Your Highness," Roeland said dryly. Some of the air went out of Ferdy's sails at his failed attempt to needle him. Roeland continued on.

"Highness, do you know where my favorite pitchfork is? The one that you also seem to have taken a fancy to?" Ferdy looked thoughtful. Roeland sighed. "While you think about it, I have another question. Do have any idea, even an inkling, why I keep getting boxes of tonic to get rid of flice?" Ferdy tried to look innocent. Allee figured that flice was a flea and louse combination. She also figured that Ferdy had sent the boxes to tease Roeland. Her suspicion was confirmed when Ferdy grinned wickedly.

"Just some friendly concern from someone who cares about the well-being of your hair, I bet," he said. Roeland snorted.

"Whatever, but that someone better knock it off. I am running out of places to put it. My pitchfork, Your Highness."

"Yeah, yeah, I'm going," Ferdy said, and disappeared up the cement ramp into the starn. Allee watched him go, amazed. Although she was a little amused, she also found him annoying. Not to mention rude. But to her surprise, Roeland was not staring after Ferdy with a look of contempt, but bemusement.

"Doesn't that bother you, sir?" she asked. He smiled at her.

"He thinks it does, but it really doesn't," he replied. Just then Ferdy came back.

"Here you go." Roeland accepted the pitchfork with a nod and continued down the row of stalls, whistling. Allee was puzzling over the response he had given her. Ferdy took her expression to be one of disproval.

"I know it's probably not very nice..." he started.

"But it is still funny." Allee finished for him. "Where in the world did you get the idea to send him flice remover?" Ferdy grinned and they began walking up the ramp.

"I really don't know. I was just helping one of the kitchen woman make it and I thought it would be a good joke."

"Wait a minute," Allee interrupted. "*You* were in the kitchen actually doing something productive?" He flushed.

"Well, I thought it was interesting. Keep going straight." They had come to the top of the walkway to enter the starn. The enormity took Allee's breath away. She had to crane her neck to see the roof. Two stories above was a wooden walkway with bins and hay bales to one side. People were swarming all over with wheelbarrows, loading them full of feed and then winding their way down the ramps to ground level. Sometimes the stable hands were obscured by the thick dust motes floating in the air, made visible by the sunshine coming in from five huge skylights. Again, there was nothing clean or new about this place, to the point of looking uncared for. It did not really surprise Allee, but it still disturbed her. Ferdy seemed to pick up her distaste.

"Again, the King cares for his own wants before the animals'," he explained bitterly. Allee knew Ferdy had a point, but she was tired of him complaining.

"I wish you would quit doing that," she said.

"Doing what?"

"Blaming your father for everything. Maybe it's some your fault, too."

"My fault?" Ferdy repeated, sounding outraged. Allee wished she hadn't said anything, but continued.

"If you want to get repairs done or something, spend less on your own needs. How many pairs of clothes do you have?" She winced, knowing she was sounding more stupid by the second.

"What does *that* have to do with anything?" he asked.

"Just tell me," Allee said, exasperated. "More or less than twenty." He thought a minute.

"More."

"You only need ten, you know. Seven for everyday and three pairs for dress." Ferdy stared at her with a look of pure unbelief.

"Where exactly are you going with this?"

"I'm trying to show you that if you spend less on clothes and other luxuries you'll have more to spend on things you need. It's simple, really." Allee paused to see his reaction, vaguely aware of a rumbling noise off in the distance. Ferdy stared at her with more disbelief than she thought was possible to show on a person's face. But, to her surprise, he seemed to go along with her idea.

"I'll think about it," he shrugged, "even as crazy as it sounds. You think of the weirdest things." Allee was relieved he was not angry with her.

"Thanks, I think," she said. Suddenly, she was very much aware of the rumbling noise. She looked around for its source.

"Where does that ramp lead?" she asked, nervously, pointing to the one to their right.

"The zeorse pasture," he said, clearly not noticing anything. "But they drive the dairy coffaloes through that pasture because the milking room opens up into it. Then they go through here to get back to their own pasture...uh-oh." The doorway was suddenly filled with giant shaggy heads charging towards them. Allee looked for a way to get out of their path and her mind registered the space to the side of the ramp. She grabbed Ferdy's arm.

"Jump!" she yelled, and pulled him over the railing into the air beyond. Allee closed her eyes as the bottom dropped out of her stomach, but seconds later she landed in something soft. She heard the soft plop that was Ferdy landing next to her and opened her eyes. To her great relief, they had landed in a pile of straw in what appeared to be the milking room. Directly across from the straw pile they were sitting on were rows of stalls where Allee guessed the coffaloes were milked. They were empty, as was the rest of the room, but she could still feel someone staring at her.

Finally, she noticed that Ferdy was looking at her. He was almost indistinguishable from the straw underneath him, since he was almost buried in it. All Allee could see were his eyes. The only thing that kept her from laughing was his extremely unnerving gaze.

"What?" she asked, her voice echoing in the big room. "What's wrong?" Ferdy's eyes got bigger.

"You, that's what," he retorted. "You must be wrong in the *head*. Do you have any idea how long that drop was?" Allee craned her neck towards the ceiling, which was made of the ramps of the ground floor.

"Oh, I'd say about twenty feet or so. Not horribly far," she said. Ferdy made a choking noise. Allee rolled her eyes. "Oh, come on," she said, "don't tell me your devious little mind has never thought of jumping off the ramp into the straw before. It's fun." His face told her he hadn't. "You're pitiful," she laughed, and threw a handful of straw at him, which he promptly threw back.

"I usually have better things to do than to play in the hay," he retorted. Just then, a war cry split the air, followed by a resounding crash. Allee jumped up and peered down the hall where it sounded to have come from, curious. Ferdy groaned.

"Like lessons, for instance, which you completely made me forget." He scrambled out of the straw and started down the hall. Allee ran to keep up.

"What lessons?" she asked. Ferdy ignored her and disappeared through a doorway. "Hey!" she protested, and skidded to a halt. She was on the top tier of a set of stone bleachers that surrounded a sand-filled pit. In the middle were two boys fencing with each other.

"Oh," Allee said to herself. "Sword fighting lessons." She had always wanted to learn how to fence, but now that she was seeing a real match in progress, she was not so sure. Again and again the boys would lock swords and again and again they would spring back. It made her tired just watching them. The boys wore simple leather pads and were so intent on each other that they did not seen to notice the blows, but Allee knew they had to hurt. Suddenly, a voice cut through the clashing.

"Watch your side, Louzre!" the deep, booming voice echoed. Allee looked for its source. In the front row of the bleachers was a large, heavily muscled man with his arms crossed over his chest, scowling at the boys. Then she noticed Ferdy trying to sneak past him and ran to follow. She caught up right when he was directly behind the instructor. Ferdy put his finger to his lips to show she had to be quiet. Allee didn't even have time to nod before the voice growled,

"You're late." Ferdy froze and winced.

"I was entertaining for Her Grace," he said, his voice almost shaky. Even though the man still wasn't facing them, Allee could see one of his heavy eyebrows raise. Ferdy cringed.

"Okay, Your Highness," the man said slowly, as if speaking to a little child, "When you meet an enemy who wants to slice you to pieces, do you entertain him?" Ferdy didn't say anything. Now both eyebrows were up. "I think not. What do you do, Your Highness?" Ferdy still didn't say anything. This seemed to make the big man even angrier, and he finally turned to look at them. "YOU FIGHT HIM,

FERDINAND!" he screamed. "And you can't fight him if you don't blooming know how, can you?"

"No," Ferdy squeaked.

"THEN GO GET INTO YOUR GEAR SO I CAN TEACH YOU!" the man roared. Ferdy *scampered* to the opposite end of the arena where some other boys were awaiting their turn in the ring. Either Ferdy got chewed out a lot, or the man yelled constantly, for none of them even glanced up from their conversations. Allee stood awkwardly on the bleachers, wondering what to do next. She had decided to follow Ferdy when the voice erupted again.

"You the one he was entertaining?" Allee jumped and swallowed hard, her mind racing wildly.

"He was just showing me around, sir. I'm sorry he was late," she said, proud that her voice didn't squeak like Ferdy's. He chuckled and Allee realized he was not mad at all.

"Come sit and watch the boys make fools of themselves," he offered. Warily, she went to sit beside him, careful to place herself far enough away she would not be deafened the next time he spoke. She had just got her dumb skirts arranged when a huge, callused hand appeared under her nose.

"I'm Mort. The combat instructor." Allee realized his hand was in a fist. Surprised, she looked up in to his face. His eyes smiled at her for a second, but then they went unfocused. Allee felt like she was sinking, and if she sunk much further, she would never come back. She jerked herself away and banged her own fist against his, hoping it was the right response.

"My name is Allee," she mumbled. Fortunately, Mort hadn't seemed to notice anything and had turned back to the boys in the ring.

Allee stared at her hands angrily. What was it in her eyes that made people do that? And why did it bother her so much? It was not exactly the people's reaction; it was the way she felt during it. When she looked into people's eyes she had a sense of rightness...of belonging in this world. But she did not want to belong; she wanted to go home! Then panic struck her. Did her eyes tell people she was from a different world? She did not mind Neiy knowing her secret, because he was a centaur and centaurs just knew stuff. Humans were different. They would not trust her. And with all the royal family had done for her, Allee desperately wanted them to trust her. Her thoughts were broken by a bellow from Mort.

"COME ON, RAF! DON'T LET LOUZRE GET YOU!" The boys in the corner started to laugh, but Allee didn't get the joke. Mort saw her puzzled expression.

"His real name is Louisander, but when you call him Louzre he fights harder," he explained. Allee nodded and looked back to the ring as a cheer exploded. Lou, flushing triumphantly, had his sword point at Raf's neck. Mort jumped to his feet.

"BRAVO, gentlemen! Now I believe it is His Highness's turn, and gentlemen, it would undoubtedly make my day if one of you could beat the spit out of him." Ferdy glared darkly at his teacher as he got into his gear, but Mort just chuckled. "So," he continued, "Do we have a challenger?" Lou stepped forward.

"I would be happy to deflate His Highness," he said, bowing.

"You go ahead and try," Ferdy said, stuffing on his helmet and walking into the ring. Mort crawled over the railing to oversee the match, looking excited. Allee was left in full view of the boys. As soon as they saw her, they began whispering and several phrases floated across the still air.

"She saved the Duchess's life!" one said.

"That's nothing," another scoffed. "I heard her yelling at His Highness last night!" There were several noises of disbelief, and Allee looked at her feet, embarrassed someone had heard her outburst. The boys' comments were cut short by Mort's roar.

"On your mark!" he bellowed. Ferdy and Lou took fighting stances on opposite sides of a white circle painted on the sand. "Get set." They raised their dull practice swords, their bodies taut. "GO!" Instead of the clash Allee was expecting, Lou and Ferdy stayed as far apart from each other as possible, each circling his opponent.

After a minute of tense waiting, Ferdy gave a war cry and sprang to the center of the ring. Lou eagerly jumped to meet him, but Ferdy sidestepped right before they made contact. Lou, expecting the impact of Ferdy's body, almost lost his balance. Ferdy was on him in a second. He jammed his sword under the hilt of Lou's, and with a little twist, Lou's sword went flying. Mort and Lou groaned in unison. Ferdy gave a cry of victory and sent a triumphant look at Mort, who pointedly ignored him. Ferdy kept grinning.

"Oh, come *on*, Louzre, " he said, picking up Lou's sword, "Do you have to let me disarm you *every* time?"

"Oh, eat coffalo crap," Lou said, smiling good-naturedly. He held out his hand for his sword. Ferdy gave it back to him.

"Doesn't the loser usually do that?" he replied. Lou grimaced at him and walked out of the arena.

"Next victim," Ferdy called. Another boy walked into the ring. He and Ferdy faced each other and on Mort's "Go!" they began.

It took a little longer for Ferdy to beat this one, but in the end he used the exact same trick, and the fight was over. Three more boys tried, and Ferdy disarmed them all. It made Allee feel sick. She did not think the boys were letting him win; they looked sincere enough, yet she could not see how he beat them so easily. She watched each match closely and could have disarmed Ferdy with his own trick. She just didn't get it. Neither did Mort.

"Could *somebody* please, please, please, beat the snot out of him?" he pleaded. Allee felt even sicker when she saw the gloating triumph on Ferdy's face.

"I'll do it," she heard herself saying. Wondering what she was getting herself into, she gathered her skirts and jumped over the railing. Ferdy's jaw dropped. All of the boys turned to stare at her. Allee was surprised at her brashness herself. Mort looked a little startled, but took her challenge without question.

"Find her some gear, boys," he called. The boy named Raf walked over with shin pads, armguards, helmet, and a leather vest. Allee stuck them on determinately. They were a little big, but not unbearably. They fit her a lot better than the dress she had worn last night.

Then Mort handed her a sword. It was not as heavy as she had thought it would be, but she knew she would definitely be sore tomorrow. She also knew that she would have to beat Ferdy quick or her arm would give out. Mort surveyed her, looking a little doubtful.

"Go get him, kid," he said, slapping her on the back. She stumbled a little from the impact and walked to the circle. The other boys were watching her silently from the rail, but none of their stares were hostile. Allee was a little surer of herself when a female voice suddenly rang out,

"Yay, Ferdinand!" Allee whipped her head around to see a dark-headed girl dressed in calico with a white apron hanging over the railing by the door. Ferdy saw her, too, and waved, grinning. She giggled and blew him a kiss. Allee smiled wickedly. So Ferdy had a girlfriend.

Ferdy and Allee took their places on opposite ends of the circle amidst catcalls from the boys and cheers from the girl.

"On your mark," Mort said. Allee put her toe on the line, sweating nervously. "Get set—"

"To be pummeled by a girl, Ferdinand!" Lou's voice rang out. There were appreciative snickers from his friends. Allee smiled weakly, silently thanking the boy named Lou. Ferdy's jaw hardened into a resolute line, and Allee realized that she could take advantage of Ferdy's temper before he could take advantage of her inexperience. Mort waited for the boys to settle down again, and then—

"GO!" he yelled. Allee heard the girl yell, "Yay, Ferdinand!" again, but she kept her eyes fixed on her opponent. Ferdy also remained standing at the edge of the circle, leering at her. She knew he was expecting her to rush in and decided to surprise him.

"That your girlfriend?" she asked shrugging her shoulder in the girl's direction. He looked taken back by her question.

"Yes," he said, narrowing his eyes. Allee raised her eyebrows and started to circle him. Startled, he began moving, too.

"Well, I see two options, then," she said, her eyes flicking from Ferdy's face to his arm muscles to see if he was about to spring. "Either she's not really your girlfriend," she paused for effect. "Or you paid everyone off so that Cardolyn won't find out." Just as Allee had expected, Ferdy lost his temper. He sprang forward, and she dodged. He did not expect her to be so fast and almost lost his balance. Allee moved back in front of him and quickly performed the disarming move. With a flick of her wrist, Ferdy's sword went flying. Allee smiled, and put her sword point on Ferdy's chest. He looked at her for a second in disbelief. Their eyes met, but instead of the sinking feeling, Allee felt like a shock of electricity had passed between them. Suddenly, a cheer erupted from the stands and the moment was over.

"You are my new favorite person, kid!" Mort cried. Blushing furiously, Allee went to retrieve Ferdy's sword to hide her face and her confusion. The girl was gone from the railing. Allee was not really surprised. She turned back and handed Ferdy his sword. He was still standing where she had left him, his arms at his sides, dumbstruck.

"You didn't tell me you knew how to sword fight," he said reproachfully.

"I don't," Allee replied, relishing in the look on his face while carefully avoiding his eyes. "I've never touched a sword until today." Mort came up behind her.

"That was the most spectacular sword fighting for a first-timer I've ever seen," he boomed. Allee blushed again.

"I just watched the other boys and kind of picked it up," she said. Mort laughed.

"Just kind of," he repeated, slapping her on the back once more. Allee felt like she had been hit with a brick. Mort, chuckling to himself, went to bark a couple of words to the rest of the class. They began taking off their gear and throwing it in the corner. Without looking at each other, Allee and Ferdy walked over to throw their stuff in the pile with the others. Suddenly, bells tolled overhead, and the boys rushed out of the door. Bewildered, Allee began to follow, but Mort stuck his head out of a room that appeared to be his office.

"And, kid," he said, "skip the tour tomorrow and come straight here, okay? Can't let your talent go to waste." Allee nodded, pleased, and he disappeared again.

"You're lucky," Ferdy said, jealous, "All he ever tells me to do is leave." Mort stuck his head back out.

"Ferdinand, are you still here? What are you, crazy? You're going to miss all the food! LEAVE!" Ferdy sent Allee an I-told-you-so look and jumped over the rail. Allee tried to follow as smoothly as he had, but her skirts got caught, and she fell on the bleachers. Thankfully, Ferdy did not say anything, but Allee thought he might as well have. Tapping his foot was just as bad. As soon as she was on her feet he set off at a jog, and Allee, rubbing a bruised shin and thoroughly annoyed, hurried to catch up.

Ferdy raced back through the hallway and up a ramp to the ground level floor of the starn. Allee had to follow closely so she would not lose him. She was so close, that when he stopped at the doors, she ran into him. The stupid dress kept trying to trip her, and it did not need Ferdy's help.

"Now what?" she asked irritably. Ferdy turned to look at her.

"What would people think if they saw me running like that?"

"Oh, puh-lease," Allee said, but she did try harder to walk like she wore a dress everyday.

The courtyard was deserted now; it seemed everyone had went on lunch break. Ferdy decided no one would see them and quickened his pace again. Allee also abandoned trying to look dignified and just tried to keep up.

"Where are we eating?" she asked as they passed the courtyard wall.

"With Her Grace. I don't want to be late." Allee stopped dead in her tracks, her heart sinking.

"But I can't," she protested. Ferdy turned to give her a look of disbelief.

"What do you mean, "you can't"?"

"You know when we hid my hair stuff behind the vase? Cardolyn wanted my hair to be that way." Ferdy looked outraged.

"What do you mean 'we'? *You* told me to hide it. And it's just a hair thing." Allee had known he wouldn't understand, but she wasn't going to give in just because he was being a stubborn male.

"I just can't go eat with her. What if she gets upset?" Ferdy sighed, but Allee knew she had finally won him over. He knew his aunt's moods firsthand.

"So where do you propose we eat, then?" he asked. Allee could hear voices and smell food behind a door in the pastle.

"What's in there?" she inquired.

"That's where the servants eat."

"Excellent. They'll have plenty of food. Let's go." She moved to open the door, but Ferdy grabbed her arm.

"We can't go eat with the servants," he hissed. Allee tossed her head.

"Why not? Shouldn't Princes eat with their subjects once in a while?"

"Well, Esendore never—" he stopped abruptly. Allee could practically see the wheels turning in his head. If Esendore never ate with the servants, then by eating with them Ferdy would be better than Esendore. And Cardolyn would not mind him not eating with her because he had been acting like a Prince. "Of course they should," he said, rolling his eyes at her like her question had been a stupid one. He opened the door. "After you."

Allee entered the room and blinked, letting her eyes adjust to the dimmer light. When they had, she found herself in a whitewashed cafeteria-like room with a beamed ceiling. The eighty-plus people had been chattering a moment before, but a hush fell on the room as soon as she had entered. Ferdy was busy shutting the door, but when he turned many of them gasped. The entire assembly dropped to both knees and bowed their heads, some knocking over plates to do so. Allee expected Ferdy to just shrug and sit down, but to her surprise he spoke.

"I am not here to be worshipped," he said, "I'm here to eat! Just like the rest of you! On your feet!" He emphasized his command with his hands. The people slowly rose from the ground, looking bewildered. The chatter slowly started up again as Ferdy and Allee slipped into two empty places on the nearest bench. Allee looked at Ferdy with new respect as he ladled some soup stuff into their bowls.

"You handled that well," she complimented, feeling generous after beating him. He rolled his eyes again, threw a sandwich on her plate, and started eating. Allee followed suit, consuming one half of her sandwich in record time. She ate her other half more slowly, and was drawn into listening to a group of three women sitting across the table from her.

"Well, I heard the dowry was over five-hundred gold pieces. And that they're bringing fifty of their finest coffaloes," a woman with a red headscarf said.

"No, no, I tell you it's fifty zeorses, their lineage hundreds of years old," argued another, this one with a green scarf.

"And where did you get this information? I got mine from the butcher's apprentice's sister, a very reliable source, you know."

"She is not," the first retorted. "She said she saw me kissing Tenner behind the woodshed last night and I did no such thing, and I should know." The last woman, her head bare, snorted and rolled her eyes.

"It's not only Brit that knows you're sweet on Tenner, Shantal, the entire pastle does." Shantal blushed.

"I didn't say that I did not kiss him altogether, I just meant that I didn't kiss him behind the woodshed. It was behind the wash house." Both Shantal and the red-topped women collapsed in giggles, but the bare headed woman shook her head in disgust.

"What does it matter how much the dowry is, anyway?" she said. "We won't see any of it. The King will take it for himself." That shut the other two up. All three of them sighed, and Shantal rubbed at a patch on her worn dress. Then the first perked up.

"What does the King have planned for the young Prince, do you think? The Duke's daughter form Betwa sure left in a hurry." They all snickered. Allee had a feeling that the Duke's daughter was the girl whose soup Ferdy had put bugs in. Shantal leaned in closer.

"Who is the one he is hanging around with now? Has he done anything to her yet?" With a jolt, Allee realized they were talking about her, and listened harder. The bare headed woman shrugged.

"She's a guest of Her Grace, that's what they said at dinner last night. They didn't announce a title. But she must have some upbringing."

"How do you know, Marlyn?" the first woman breathed. Marlyn tossed her head.

"She disarmed Ferdinand in sword fighting!" The other two gasped. Allee's head spun at how fast the news had traveled.

"No!" they squealed.

"Yes!" she said, "Jermenain, he's friends with my Bo, you know, and he told Bo, and Jermenain saw it himself." There was a stunned silence.

"But His Highness is the best swordsman in the class, Mort said so when I was sweeping the courtyard the other day. How did she do it?" Shantal wondered aloud.

"Who cares?" Marlyn said. "I just want to know her name so I can congratulate her. Didn't let him beat her, and she being a girl and all." Allee felt it was time she spoke up.

"Thank-you," she said. The women jumped, looking for the speaker. They saw that she was sitting right next to them and their eyes grew round. "My name is Alethea Quintin," Allee continued, and she held out her hand in a fist to Marlyn. Ever so slowly, Marlyn raised her fear-filled eyes to Allee's face.

"I'm not angry with you," Allee reassured her. "I might be if what you said wasn't true, but it is. I did beat Ferdinand. I think this morning was mostly luck, but you never know." Hesitantly, Marlyn laughed. Allee jiggled her hand. Marlyn bumped it and introduced herself and her companions.

"I am Marlyn and this is Saren," she said, gesturing to the woman with the red headscarf. "And Shantal," she finished, pointing at the woman in green. "May I ask how you managed it?" Allee was quite surprised at the question and a little shy, but she was never one to deny an audience. She gave them a blow-by-blow account of her duel. Suddenly, Ferdy spoke beside her.

"You forgot the part when you held the sword point to my chest," he said. Allee stiffened, not sure if he was angry or teasing. The three women were definitely afraid. Terror showed in every inch of them. Ferdy tried to smooth over their discomfort.

"Not that it matters much," he said, smiling broadly at them. "Marlyn, I've been meaning to ask you, what is it that you put into this stew that makes it so delicious? It's driving me crazy." Marlyn blushed, and spoke softly.

"It might be garlion, Your Highness."

"Ah, that would be it. Make sure you put in the cakes, too, if it makes them this flavorful." Allee didn't know if he was joking or not, he probably did not even know what garlion was. She could only guess that it was a cross between garlic and an onion and knew she was going to have bad breath. The women thought it was funny and seemed more at ease. Ferdy smiled at them.

"Now, I'm very sorry," he said, "but I have to take your entertainment away from you." Allee took this as her cue to stand up, and the women waved good-bye. Ferdy steered her out of the room through an inner door. As the door shut, she heard Saren say,

"Well, whoever she is, she sure is a good influence on him."

Ferdy closed the door quickly and leaned against it, running his fingers through his hair.

"I, Ferdinand, just ate with the servants," he said, almost to himself. His look of pure disbelief made Allee want to laugh, but he suddenly turned brisk.

"Sorry, Allee," he said, "but you're going to have to go join Cardolyn's embroidery group or go somewhere to hide from her, because I have to go to indoor lessons." Allee was desperate not to go waste the entire afternoon with a bunch of old women. She would even put up with Ferdy to avoid them.

"Can't I come with you?" she almost pleaded.

"And do what? We're studying algebra and philosophy today. You'd be bored out of your skull. I know I will be." Allee knew he was right, but she didn't want to give up that easily.

"Can't I read a book or something?" she asked. Ferdy looked startled.

"Since when do peasant girls read?" Allee was almost as surprised as he looked, but did not let him see it.

"Since they can swordfight," she retorted. His mouth tightened for a second, but then he sighed.

"Fine. Just don't complain how bored you are," he said, and began walking down the hall. Allee followed, afraid she had offended him in some way, but not eager to bring it up. After walking a few minutes in silence, she couldn't hold herself back.

"You aren't mad…that I told them how I beat you…are you?" she asked hesitantly. When he didn't say anything, she rushed on. "I mean, I didn't mean to brag about it, and it was probably just a fluke on my part, they did say that Mort had said you were the best swordsman in the class, and—"

"Don't worry about it," he interrupted. "It's better they know the truth than rumors anyway."

"Oh," Allee said, relieved. A few moments later he looked sideways at her.

"He really did say that then? About me being a good swordsman?" Allee felt like laughing again, but didn't.

"That's what Shantal said," she replied. Ferdy seemed to mull this over and was silent. Allee turned her head to hide her grin and noticed the peculiar shape of the lamp sconces. They were worked into figures of books and scrolls. Around them were hung dark-hued tapestries depicting scholars surrounded by rolls of papers and huge tomes labeled history, philosophy, and mathematics. Ferdy saw her looking and explained.

"This floor on the East Wing is kind of an education center of sorts. Though only the smallest rudiments of learning go on here; the funding all lies in the King's treasure chamber." The familiar bitterness entered his voice. Allee stole a quick glance at him. He was just not himself when he talked about his father. She decided to see how far she could shove her foot in her mouth this time.

"You could start a university," she suggested. She cringed, waiting for his reply, but instead he gave a short laugh.

"Like His Majesty is going to give his least favorite son any gold, especially to start a university."

"Then go make your own gold," she said, wincing as she dug her hole deeper.

"And how do I do that, short of selling all of my possessions?" Allee thought fast, wishing she would stop opening her mouth.

"Get a job?"

"What?" he yelped. "Are you—"

"Oh, don't get upset," Allee said, "I know a job won't buy a university, but at least it was a suggestion."

"You're crazy," Ferdy replied. For a second, he looked like he was going to say something more, but then he lapsed into silence, looking thoughtful. Allee let him be.

Suddenly, they rounded a corner and faced a small flight of stairs, which turned sharply into another corner, around which Allee could not see.

"My room's up there," Ferdy explained. "I have to go get my books and stuff." Allee was curious to see what his rooms were like, but she did not know if Ferdy would want her tagging along there, too.

"Do you mind if I come?" she asked.

"Why would I care?" he replied, and bounded up the stairs. Allee followed, trying to think of a retort. She rounded the corner and instantly forgot what she had been thinking about. The pastle had changed from castle to palace once again. The Hall of the Royals was made of white marble with glass mosaics from floor to ceiling portraying centaurs, dragons, mermaids and a wolf-like creature Allee couldn't name intermingling with people wearing elaborate dresses and handsome suits. Sunshine streamed in from skylights, making the mosaics sparkle as if they were alive. At the end of the hall were two glass windows that looked out over a flower garden.

"Wow," Allee breathed, barely able to take it all in. Ferdy looked over at her, pride in his eyes, as if he had made it all himself. "Wow," she said again, getting her breath back, but then she frowned. "I thought you told me the looms were on the east side of the pastle, not a garden."

"They are," he replied. "It's just that the east side is split in two. Half is the looms, and half is the flower and kitchen gardens. This looks out over one of the flower gardens. Then if you walk a little farther north, you get to the fields and pastures." Allee was almost as confused as before.

"Uh, okay," she said. Ferdy rolled his eyes.

"I'll just have to show it to you sometime. This is my room." He walked over to the wall. Allee watched him in puzzlement; there seemed to be no door. But then he reached out a finger and pushed in a tile in the mosaic. Immediately, part of the wall slid back, revealing a room decorated in deep red. Ferdy disappeared into it and reappeared moments later with several books in his arms. Allee quickly shut her gaping mouth before he could tease her.

"An extra precaution, in case some one wants to murder me or something," he said, watching her reaction. Allee couldn't hide her look of disbelief fast enough. "What?" he said, clearly enjoying himself. "You think that no one would want to do away with the second in line to the throne?" Allee snorted.

"No, I was wondering how you've lived this long. Who *wouldn't* want to kill you?" He gave a strained grin.

"Ha, ha, ha, very funny," he said. "Let's go before you get any ideas." Smiling, Allee turned back to the stairwell. They had just made it to the edge when a shout echoed behind them. Ferdy and Allee both looked back to see a very angry Cardolyn bearing down upon them. They both braced themselves.

"Where have you been, Ferdinand?" she asked shrilly, "I gave you *explicit* instructions to come dine with me, and then you go and not show up! And, you had to go drag poor Alethea along to wherever you just *had* to go! Absolutely shameful, Ferdinand. You had better have a good excuse this time!" She paused for breath, her hands on her hips and her eyes blazing. Ferdy looked bored, but Allee could see the spark in his eye as he waited for Cardolyn's response to his bombshell.

"We were eating with the servants, Your Grace," he replied. Cardolyn took a deep breath.

"A likely story! That's just like you—," she stopped in mid-sentence and blinked. "Wha-what did you say, dear?" she said, her voice shaking, all of her hot air gone.

"We were eating with the servants," Ferdy said again, smirking. Allee tried not to crack her ribs from withheld laughter. Cardolyn's jaw went slack.

"You ate with-with the servants?" she repeated, looking at Allee for reassurance. Allee swallowed her laughter.

"We did, Your Grace," she said. For a second, Cardolyn stood dumbfounded. Suddenly, with a sweep of her arm she crushed Ferdy to her bosom and began stroking his head.

"Oh, I am so *proud* of you, Ferdinand! Finally, finally you have realized your station, and even accepted it! I knew you would! I just knew it! Oh, Ferdinand!" She gave him one final squeeze and let go. He gasped for air, his face red with embarrassment and lack of oxygen.

"Gotta go...lessons," he wheezed, and sprinted for the stairway. Allee followed, but took one look back at Cardolyn. She was still standing in the middle of the Hall, her hand to her face, as if to wipe away a tear.

As soon as they reached the bottom of the stairs, Allee collapsed in laughter. Ferdy gave her a disgruntled look as she laid crumpled on the bottom step.

"Don't know what's so funny," he muttered, trying to fix his hair from the reflection on a shiny silver doorknob. "It's not like it's *abnormal* to be petted like a dokat, she does that all the time." That made Allee laugh harder.

"Yes, it is very abnormal," she gasped, clutching the stitch in her side. Her voice squeaked, and Ferdy started to laugh, too. They both ran out of breath at the same time. Ferdy shook his head.

"Come on," he said, and once again they started down the corridor. Only a couple of hundred feet down was a set of wooden double doors. Ferdy opened them, and Allee realized they were in a library. Books covered the walls from top to bottom; there weren't even any windows. To her left were three rows of wooden desks facing a chalkboard. Sitting in them were boys that Allee recognized from her sword fighting experience, but some of them she had never seen before. They took one glance at her and bent their heads to whisper to each other. Lou even whistled, but she ignored him and walked towards the shelves, very impressed by the number of books. She touched the spine of one entitled *Customs of Centaurs*.

"Go ahead and pick one out and then sit over there to read it," Ferdy instructed, pointing to a maroon armchair. "I'll be right over here, but try not to interrupt unless you've got a gargantuan paper cut and you're bleeding to death." Allee rolled her eyes.

"I wouldn't bother you even if I cut my whole finger off," she retorted.

"Good," he said, and walked over to his desk.

Seething, Allee pulled the book about centaurs out and flopped into the armchair, her head on one armrest and her feet hanging over the other. She relaxed, pleased she would get an entire afternoon to read and be away from Ferdy. Smiling, she wiggled farther down into the chair and opened the book.

Chapter 3

Playing Dress-Up and Boys' Games

Allee awoke with a start, her neck stiff from sleeping with it at a sharp angle. She raised her head slowly, ashamedly rubbing at a spot of drool on the lace doily. After turning the doily over, she sat up. The boys in the corner seemed to be gathering up their things to leave. Allee was relieved Ferdy had not caught her sleeping. She was not quite sure that he wouldn't do something evil to get back at her for beating him in sword fighting. She got up and put the book away and then went to join Ferdy by the door.

"How far did you get?" he asked, obviously trying to be polite only because the teacher was still sitting at his desk.

"I finished it," she replied. The book had been an interesting read and had only taken her an hour and a half. Now she was ready to meet Neiy again.

"Finished it?" Ferdy repeated. Allee was annoyed.

"Centaurs live in tribes, ranging from ten to one-hundred of their kin," she recited. "The biggest is called the Weald and the leader is the King or Wealder. His duties include—"

"Okay, okay, I'm sorry," Ferdy interrupted. "It's just that it's not very often that a peasant can read, especially a girl. Not that they're stupid or anything," he added, seeing her face. "It's just the way things are."

"Yeah, I know," she said. An awkward silence descended, and Ferdy gave a small cough.

"Let's be going then," he said. "Good-bye, Master Ritter." The old white-haired man lifted a hand in farewell and then returned to his books. Ferdy and Allee tiptoed out and Ferdy started back the way they had come.

"Where are we going now?" Allee asked.

"To get ready for dinner," he replied.

"What?" she exclaimed, glancing at a clock on the wall. "It's only five o'clock. Dinner isn't for another three hours." Ferdy shook his head.

"Nuh-uh. It's at six-thirty tonight because Dariel's arriving and there's going to be a banquet and a ball and all that good junk in her honor."

"That's still an hour and a half away," Allee protested. Ferdy grinned wickedly.

"It'll take that long for Caysa to get you ready, trust me," he replied, his eyes lighting up. "She'll be waiting for you. Just go straight down this hallway, go behind the tapestry next to the first lamp sconce with pictures of food on it. Climb the stairs and four corners down is your room. Have fun." Allee realized that they had come back to the steps that led to Ferdy's room. She watched him disappear up the stairs, wanting to follow him and ask him to give her the directions again, but he was already out of sight. She sighed and continued down the hall.

She watched the lamp sconces carefully and as soon as hams and bags of flour appeared, she ducked under the nearest tapestry. She recognized the hallway immediately. It was the corridor where she had killed the taranion. It seemed like she always ended up here. Shaking her head, she climbed the stairs with a light step. She realized she was actually looking forward to being at a banquet and seeing all the people, except for the dressing up part.

Ten minutes later Allee was at the door to her room. She had gotten lost twice and bumped her head on a wall sconce when she had bent to retrieve the metal hairpieces from behind the flowerpot and then stood up too fast. Relieved at reaching her destination, she composed herself and opened the door, fearing the worst. She was quite surprised by a soft voice.

"Good evening, milady. Should I start you bath?" Allee peered into the shadows to see a slender brunette about her age standing by the wardrobe.

"Oh, hello," Allee said, shutting the door. She was not only relieved it was not Caysa, but also eager for companionship that wasn't Ferdy's. "My name is Allee. What's yours?" The girl looked surprised.

"Melior—, I mean, Meli, milady, but you need not remember it." Allee frowned, wondering why the girl had stumbled over her own name.

"Why shouldn't I? It's your name, isn't it?'

"Ladies do not need to address their servants by name, milady," the girl said, her voice fluttering a little. Allee frowned.

"Well, they should. And I am certainly not a Lady. Just call me Allee. Go ahead and try. Al-lee." Meli looked uncertain, but complied.

"Al-lee would you like me to start your bath?" she said, the words coming out in rush. Allee felt uncomfortable having someone do things for her that she could easily do herself.

"I can do it myself," she said. Meli seemed a little confused at Allee's strange behavior. Allee hated seeing her ill at ease. "But could you help me unbutton my dress?" she added. She was awarded with a soft smile and Meli nimbly undid the buttons.

Allee hurried into the bathroom, started the bath, and hopped in before it was even a quarter of the way full. She soaped her hair and impatiently waited for it to fill the rest of the way, wishing she could take a shower instead. Ten minutes later she was ready for whatever Meli had to do to her, and she entered the bedchamber.

Meli was fiddling with a dress in the wardrobe, and jumped when she saw Allee. *Why is this girl so nervous* Allee wondered.

"Would you like this one, mi—Allee?" she said, and coughed to hide her embarrassment. Allee feigned that she hadn't noticed by looking very intently at the gown. It was pale lavender with tons of ruffles and little pearls sewn everywhere. Allee liked purple, but this shade almost looked gray. Bright colors did not seem to bother her anymore, and she was ready to wear some. She sent a quick glance at the wardrobe, but all of the garments in there were pastel or dark colors.

"Why are the colors so pale?" Allee asked, wondering if it was some kind of fashion. Meli gave her a quizzical look, but quickly hid it.

"We are still mourning for Her Majesty," she said, very softly. Allee was shocked.

"But it's been...what, at least five years since she died, hasn't it?" Allee said, quickly calculating Ferdy's age now if he was the same age as she, fourteen, and how old he had been when his mother died.

"Six," Meli said, so softly that Allee had to strain to hear her. "The king sees it as fit." The sadness in her eyes was astounding, like she had known the Queen personally. Allee swallowed hard, wishing she hadn't brought it up.

"This dress will work fine," she said, pretending nothing had happened. She picked it up, and Meli moved to help her. Allee backed away.

"I'll be right back," she said, leaving Meli standing with a very puzzled expression on her face. Allee hoped she would just need help with the buttons, but the dress decided to be stubborn, and she could only get the very top of her head through. More embarrassed than if Meli had just helped her in the first place, she went back into the other room. Meli rushed to help her, and began pulling on the skirt. She tugged for five minutes before the dress would slide down to the right spot. They both collapsed into chairs, breathing hard.

"I do not understand," Meli panted, "It should not be this difficult. You are thin enough and just the right height." Allee stood up to look at herself in the mirror and scowled. None of the folds fell in the right places, and all of the curves curved where there weren't supposed to be any. She looked like a little girl playing dress-up with her mother's old prom dress. She sat back down again and buried her face in her hands. If she had to wear a dress she did not want to look stupid in it. Meli patted her on the shoulder.

"Don't worry, milady. I will do something so spectacular to your hair that no one will notice your dress." Allee peeked out from between her fingers.

"I'm sure you will," she said, and lifted her head, aware that she was being rude. "I'm sorry." Meli shrugged and picked up a brush.

"Every Lady wants to look her best." And, for some reason, Meli's brown eyes softened with sadness. Allee made a mental note to ask Meli about her past as soon as she felt she had gained her trust.

"But I'm NOT a Lady," Allee said. Meli gave Allee another quizzical look, but continued.

"Don't worry. I would be depressed if I had to go eat in front of a whole bunch of people and was unsure of myself, too." Allee gave a little smile and tried to keep the conversation going.

"Your name is very pretty. Does it mean something?" she asked. Strangely, Meli seemed to stiffen.

"No, its just a name," she said, very slowly, almost as if she was frightened. "There's nothing unusual about it; it's just like any other servant's name."

"What do you mean?" Allee asked, wondering why Meli was so defensive.

"You don't know?" Meli asked, bewildered. "Servants and the lower class always have one or two syllable names. Only nobles have three or four." Allee laughed.

"I'm not from around here, so I've never heard of that before, but I'm not a noble and I have four syllables in my name. Does it really matter that much?"

"To some people it does," Meli said, and before Allee could pursue the matter, she picked up a hand mirror. "Do you like it?" she asked, holding it in front of Allee. Allee gasped. All of her hair was piled on top of her head, with her curls ringed around the tips of her ears. She had only seen hair as fancy as this in the movies. And Meli had done it with only a brush and a few clips. Meli seemed to take her gasp as one of horror.

"Milady, I can change it, we have plenty of time. I'm very sorry—" she reached to pull out the clips. Allee grabbed her hand and squeezed it.

"It's beautiful," she said, and let go. Meli, blushing furiously, bent swiftly to the bottom of the wardrobe.

"Here are your shoes," she said, handing Allee a pair of lavender slippers that had pearls sewn onto them to match the dress. Allee adjusted them to her feet and slipped them on. As soon as she looked up, Meli handed her some dangly pearl earrings and a five-rope pearl necklace. Allee balked.

"Nu-uh," she said, handing the necklace back. "My head will fall into my soup." Meli giggled, shaking her own head, but took back the necklace. Allee put on the earrings and stood up.

"Am I ready?" she asked, throwing out her arms.

"Well, I am supposed to teach you how to curtsey," Meli said. Allee froze.

"What?" she squeaked. Meli giggled again.

"I'm joking. Caysa was complaining that you didn't know how, but she didn't tell me to teach you. She did say that you should wear a necklace, though. Will two ropes work?" Allee, eager to keep Caysa from getting angry, nodded. She also realized that Meli had very subtle persuasion skills.

"Alright." Meli fastened the necklace and stood back.

"Now you're ready," she said, crossing to the door and opening it. "Caysa said you are to use the door you left by last night to get into the Hall."

"Thanks, Meli," Allee said, sorry to be leaving. Meli gave another one of her soft smiles.

"You are just glad that I wasn't Caysa."

"Of course not," Allee said, smiling in return. "I'm glad I got to meet someone as nice as you." Meli ducked her head, blushing, and Allee left the room.

She was a little worried about getting lost again, but the noise of the people in the kitchens (some of it not very nice) led her to the wooden staircase easily. From there it was just guesswork, but once she started using the lamp sconces as guides, she quickly found the hallway they had come through the night before. She knew which door was the right one because its handle was engraved with pictures of men and women dancing. She silently thanked whoever had thought of such a thing and opened it.

The steady roar of people's voices and the clatter of dishes greeted her. At least a hundred extra people sat at the tables than the night before, forcing a few of the less wealthy-looking to stand against the wall. Allee looked around nervously, searching for Cardolyn at the high table. When she finally spotted her, the Duchess was engaged in conversation with the Countess Fariel and did not notice that Allee had no idea where to sit.

Allee was almost panicking when she suddenly saw Ferdy wave at her. Tonight, he was crowned with a circlet and wearing a robe and tunic in the royal colors. She exhaled and hurriedly walked to the high table, looking neither right nor left. Much to her disgust, she tripped on the stairs again. Ferdy grinned wickedly as he pulled out her chair. Allee rubbed her bruised shin, her temper rising.

"Let's see *you* in a dress and see how well you do," she hissed, and sat down. Ferdy's grin went wider.

"You should be nice to me, you know, I'm your dinner partner," he whispered. Allee rolled her eyes.

"Ooh, lucky me, I get to sit with the weaset," she said sarcastically, using one of the words she had learned in the book she had read that afternoon.

"Actually, you are," he replied. "It was either the weaset or Duke Marsel." He pointed to a man half way down the table who was so old he looked ready to die any second. Allee shivered.

"Weasets are actually quite nice," she said, picking up her napkin.

"If you like little buggy eyes," he replied.

"Don't forget the pointy teeth," she reminded him.

"And the sharp claws."

"Nah, that doesn't bother me. It's the *smell*." They sent a quick glance at each other and smothered their laughter in their hands as the trumpet blew and the announcements began.

Allee tried to watch and listen to each introduction, but after the fifteenth they all began to look and sound the same and her attention wandered to those already seated. After a minute, she noticed one who was moving around the room. A short man in a dark green tunic with a mud stained red cloak was weaving his way through the tables. His eyes never left the high table. Allee followed his progress intently until he disappeared into the crowd against the walls.

She searched in vain for a minute, but then found him at Esendore's elbow, whispering furiously. Esendore's brow furrowed and when the man finished, his face fell as if the man's news was disappointing. Esendore nodded and gave a forced sort of smile, slipping something into the man's hand as he did so. The man bowed low and began his way back to the floor, where he was soon lost in the crowd again. Allee suddenly realized that the announcements had stopped, but everyone was still staring at the staircase, as if waiting for someone important. Esendore, looking a little more like Ferdy tonight since their clothes almost matched, stood up, and everyone turned to him for an explanation.

"Let the feast begin," he said, and sat back down. Every face in the Hall registered some sort of bewilderment. When they realized he was not going to say anything else, a confused buzzing started.

"Wonder what happened to Dariel," Ferdy mused, looking at Esendore, who was holding a glass to be filled by a servant and acting if nothing was out of the ordinary. "She was supposed to arrive tonight." His face darkened. "He knows, but he thinks he's the only one *special* enough to know." He banged his fist on the table. "Now we're going to have to have *another* feast and *another* ball, and I just wish they'd hurry up and get this wedding over with."

"No, you don't," Gnarrish said at their shoulders, bearing a platter full of food. "The sooner the wedding is finished, the sooner you will have *two* women to carp at you." Ferdy gave him a small smile.

"You're right."

"When have I not been?" Gnarrish asked, setting a plate in front of Allee. Ferdy gave him a friendly punch on the shoulder and helped him unload some baskets full of breadsticks. Allee still felt uncomfortable in Gnarrish's presence so she looked at her plate instead of him. And, much to her surprise, she was looking at a calzone, one of her favorite foods. She blinked, thinking it was just a trick of the light on her glass crystal plate. To test it, she poked it with her fork, and, sure enough, it was real. She thought it strange that this was the second night in a row that they had been served an Italian dish when the people here spoke with British accents.

She surveyed the crowd for a second time, looking more closely at the people's appearances. Most of them had dark hair and dark complexions, but there were a few with dark blond hair like Ferdy and Esendore's. Then a thought struck her. If the animals, plants and buildings of Betwix were combined, why couldn't the people be? True, Italy was a long ways from Great Britain, but there had been no indication that the geography was the same in Betwix as Earth.

With a jolt, Allee realized everyone else was eating and quickly looked back down at her plate. She blinked, unable to believe what she was seeing. Ferdy was cutting her food for her.

"Hey!" she said angrily, taking a stab at him with her dessert fork. "That's mine!" Ferdy yelped and drew his hand back.

"Have you gone crazy?" he demanded, bringing his hand up to his mouth.

"You're pawing at my food!"

"I told you I'm you're dinner partner!" he replied. "And I am not pawing at your food, I am cutting it, which is part of section two of dinner partner proper protocol."

"What's section three say, that women are too helpless to take a drink out of their water goblet? I can cut my own food, thank you," Allee replied. Ferdy glared at her, dropped her fork and knife, and viscously began attacking his own food. Allee, feeling a mixture of triumph for proving a point and guilt for upsetting him, quietly began to eat her food. She finished eating at the same time as Ferdy, but was still hungry, so she followed his example of grabbing a breadstick. Ferdy looked at her sideways.

"Are you mimicking me?" he asked, holding his breadstick half way to his mouth. He seemed to have forgotten their earlier spat.

"Are you mimicking me?" Allee repeated in a high, squeaky voice. Ferdy narrowed his eyes and took a huge bite out of his breadstick. Allee laid hers on her plate and began cutting it into tiny bites, surprised to see that they were filled with cheese.

"Honestly, Ferdinand," she said, putting a piece in her mouth. "Whaf beaswy table manners." Ferdy tore off a piece of his breadstick and flung it at her. She took a bigger piece and threw it at him. He pitched it right back. On impulse, she opened her mouth and caught it in her teeth. Ferdy goggled at her.

"Do that again for me," he commanded. They were tied at two pieces each and enjoying themselves immensely when Esendore stood up again. Ferdy choked on his piece, and Allee had to pound him on the back. Esendore sent them a searching look, but they were both taking small sips out of their water glasses by then. The Prince cleared his throat and the Hall went quiet.

"I am very sorry to inform you that the Countess Dariel has been detained," he said. His light tenor was just loud enough to drown out the sighs of disappointment from the crowd. "One of the wagons in her caravan broke a wheel. Rather than leave it, the entire caravan halted. She will arrive tomorrow morning and we will welcome her with another feast tomorrow night."

"Oh, bother," Ferdy said under his breath as Esendore paused. Allee suppressed a giggle.

"But since you are all here, and we have entertainment, I see no reason not to continue with the ball, which was also meant to welcome the Count and Countess Farholt. I wish you all a pleasurable evening." Several cheers erupted from the crowd, and servants began clearing the rugs off to the sides to reveal a floor of the purest white marble, but Allee didn't even notice. She had just realized what a ball meant. A ball meant dancing and dancing meant she was going to be miserable. She was not against learning the dances of Betwix or meeting new people, but she hated dancing and she certainly was not going to learn to like dancing while dressed in a circus tent in a place where they probably hadn't heard of the chicken dance, especially since they did not have chickens. Ferdy heaved a sigh and stood up.

"Well, let's get this over with." Allee looked around for an escape. She decided just to tell him.

"Ferdy, I can't dance," she said bluntly. He rolled his eyes.

"Come on, don't you peasants have starn dances and stuff?" Allee forgot her panic in irritation.

"Like we have the same dances as nobles do. Have you even heard of the hokey pokey?"

"Huh? What's that all about?"

"Never mind," Allee said, shaking with suppressed laughter. "But I don't think you are the one to give me noble dancing lessons."

"You got that right," he said, shuddering at the very thought. "And I pity anyone who does." Allee grimaced at him. He threw up his arms. "Look, I would be more than happy not to dance. It makes me dizzy and all the people I have to dance with smell funny."

"You dance with other boys?" Allee asked innocently.

"Ha, ha. You haven't got a whiff of some of the Countesses and Baronesses and Duke's daughters, and—"

"I get the point," Allee interrupted. "But we shouldn't have to be here if we are not enjoying ourselves. That's what this thing is for, right?"

"Yeah, but if I don't dance Cardolyn will be on my back so fast..." He let his sentence trail off. Allee thought quickly.

"Then let's distract her." Ferdy's mouth dropped open.

"Do what?" Allee ignored him.

"Don't you know of any eligible bachelors that would give their right arms to be commanded by the Prince to dance with the Duchess?" Ferdy opened his mouth to argue, but then fell silent. An evil grin spread over his face.

"I believe that is the best Cardolyn ditching plan that has ever been planned," he said, awe in his voice. That was the first compliment Ferdy had ever given her.

"Thank-you," Allee said. He rolled his eyes.

"Yeah, yeah, come on." He grabbed her arm and pulled her along the back of the high table. For a second, she was afraid he was going to choose the ancient man, but he stopped in front of a good-featured gentleman who looked to be in his early fifties like Cardolyn. He was surveying the dance floor, his head resting on his fist. He saw Ferdy and smiled.

"Ferdinand!" he cried. "You look like you're up to something." Ferdy grinned.

"Good evening, Archibald. Right as always." Archibald leaned close, his face serious.

"Let me just say one thing," he said, and for a moment Allee was afraid he was going to forbid them to do whatever they were going to do. "How can I help?" Allee let out her withheld breath, and Ferdy's grin widened. Allee silently complimented Ferdy on his choice of friends.

"Well, you see," Ferdy said, putting his face into a sad mask, "I'm worried about Her Grace." All the faith Allee had just gained in Ferdy evaporated. Even Archibald looked taken back.

"*You* are worried about the Duchess?" he repeated, blinking in surprise. Ferdy nodded.

"Yes, I'm afraid so," he sighed, his voice dripping with woe. Allee forced herself to stop looking bewildered. "Every time we get done with a ball, she seems hassled and depressed. I think it's because she has to dance with people that nobody else would dance with because she feels sorry for them." Allee goggled at Ferdy. He sounded so sincere it amazed her. Archibald looked thoughtful.

"And so what do you suggest?" he asked, a smile playing on his lips.

"For you to monopolize her, of course," Ferdy said, his voice incredulous, as if Archibald should have known from the beginning. "Then she won't have to dance with anyone she doesn't want to, and she'll be happy."

"And you'll be happy, too, because she won't be on your back to dance with people you don't want to," Archibald guessed, his eyes twinkling. Allee held her breath, wondering if he would still agree. Ferdy just shrugged.

"That, too," he said, as if he did not really care. "So will you do it?" Archibald chuckled.

"Aye, I'll do it. Not only because Her Grace is a good dancer, but," he looked around to see if anyone was listening and leaned his head in closer to theirs. "But that is one of your better stories." He winked at them and stood up. "Have fun, you two," he said, scanning the crowd for Her Grace. "I know I will." He winked again and walked off the dais. Allee felt that she should return the compliment Ferdy had given her earlier.

"That was a very good story," she said. She did not know if he heard her, at first, for he was watching Archibald with a faraway look in his eye.

"Yeah, and surprisingly enough, it was your idea." Allee's temper flared.

"Does that mean that most of my ideas aren't good?" she demanded, her hands on her hips. He turned back to her.

"Jumping off that ramp certainly wasn't. I got straw stuck in places I didn't even know I had," he said.

"Well, fine then," Allee snapped. "Next time, I'll just let you be pounded into the ground and SWEPT off the ramp in little bitty pieces instead of in one piece, okay?"

"That would be better than having pieces of straw in my—" He coughed and turned pink. Allee held back her laughter as he composed himself. "It doesn't matter. What are you going to do now?" His question caught her unprepared. She had not thought about what she would do if she did not have to stay. She really did not want to tag after Ferdy, but she really did not want to go back to her room, either.

"I guess I'll just hang around here…watch the dancing," she said, trying to convince herself that she would have fun.

"What happens if someone asks you to dance?" he asked.

"I'll growl at them," she replied, feigning seriousness to see what he would say. He didn't say anything, just gave her his you-are-crazy-beyond-all-reason look.

"All right, then," he said, turning to leave. He walked a few steps and stopped, as if considering something. He sighed and turned back around. "You got me out of dancing so you shouldn't have to be all by yourself. Come on." Allee was surprised at this, but did not hesitate to gather her skirts and follow him off the dais to a row of tables covered with finger foods. In front of them lounged people who were not getting ready to dance. Ferdy ignored the food and went up to a group of boys looking bored and apprehensive. Allee recognized the boys named Lou and Raf from that morning.

"You guys want to do something other than get your toes stepped on?" Ferdy inquired.

"What kind of question is that?" Lou replied. "You think we like having to endure hours of twirling, and spinning, and twirling, and more spinning—"

"Yeah, we get the point," Ferdy cut in. "Anyway, then meet me in the storeroom in five minutes." The boys looked pleased, nodded their heads, and disappeared into the crowd. Ferdy turned back to Allee.

"Okay, just follow me, and be discreet. I don't know if we're exactly allowed to do this."

"Oh, great," Allee replied, but she followed him as quietly as she could.

As they wove their way through the crowd, Allee noticed Archibald talking to Cardolyn. Just as she had thought, Cardolyn seemed to notice no one else as he led her out onto the dance floor.

"Who is he?" she asked as soon as she and Ferdy were out of all the people. He turned and saw whom she was talking about.

"Archibald?" Ferdy shrugged. "He's my godfather and my mother's fist cousin. Only one of her family that still comes to these things. The rest are still mad at the King." *Like you*, Allee thought, but she remained silent as he opened the door that led to the cavernous kitchens. No one seemed to notice them; all the servants were occupied with washing dishes or putting away food. Ferdy and Allee quietly threaded through the people until they moved between two shelves. At the end was a wall with a little door in it. Ferdy opened it and ushered Allee in. Except for wavering candlelight at the far end, the room was pitch black. As her eyes adjusted, Allee realized they were in a storeroom full to the ceiling with crates and bags. Light flooded the room as the door opened again, but someone quickly shut it. There was complete silence then—

"Yee-ow! That's my foot!" Ferdy cried.

"That's the squishiest foot I've ever stepped on."

"Well, I never knew you were some kind of expert, but I really wish you'd get off." Allee tried to move out of the way, but something was holding her down. She realized what, and snorted.

"Ferdinand, you are a big baby. He must have just bumped your foot because he's standing on *my* skirt." She could feel Ferdy glaring at her in the dark, but ignored him as she concentrated on getting all her skirts back. She heard someone snicker.

"That's the first time I've ever heard *anyone* called a weakling by a *girl*," a voice said. Ferdy made a noise of disgust.

"Yeah, yeah, are we going to play or not?" he asked.

"We're going," another voice replied.

"How did you manage this anyways?" Raf asked as they started toward the candlelight. Always eager for an audience, Ferdy launched into the explanation. From what Allee heard as she picked her way through the boxes, none of his brilliant escape had included her. She really did not mind; she could not care less how she got out of dancing as long as she got out of it. Suddenly, she heard that she *was* in the conversation.

"She just going to hang all over you like Brit did or sit in a corner and watch?" Raf asked. For a moment, Allee wondered what the butcher's apprentice's sister had to do with this, but then realized that Brit must also be the dairymaid and shuddered at being compared to her.

"Actually," she interrupted, annoyed when both Ferdy and Raf turned and looked at her as if she had popped out of the ground. "If you don't mind, I would like to play." Their jaws dropped, Ferdy's the farthest.

"You want to play?" Raf repeated.

"If you don't mind," Allee replied.

BETWIX

"Mind?" Raf repeated. "Uh, no, that' fine, I guess. We'll have a full game then." He went on ahead, and Allee began to follow, but Ferdy held her back.

"*You* know how to play Deceit?" he hissed.

"No, but I'm sure you're a great teacher," Allee replied sweetly. Before he could answer, they walked into the ring of candlelight. It illuminated a group of crates gathered around a low table. Lou was stretched out on three of the crates.

"You took the longest five minutes to get here," he said.

"Whatever, you came in behind us," Ferdy said, pushing Lou's long legs off so he could sit down. Allee slipped in on the crate between him and Lou before Lou could use it as a footrest again.

"You got the bones, Jermenain?" Ferdy asked. A tall boy dressed in forest green nodded and pulled a long black box out from under his crate. With names like bones and deceit, Allee was almost worried that they were doing something illegal. But, then again, if the Prince was doing it, was it still illegal? Allee quit thinking about politics and forced herself to pay attention.

Jermenain opened the black box, and Allee saw that it was divided into six parts with each section holding a different color of dominos. Each boy quickly grabbed a set, and Allee picked green. Soon only Lou and the pink set were left. He looked crestfallen as the other boys teased him.

"Don't you want the pink, Allee?" he queried. Allee really did not care one way or the other, but decided to lead him on.

"I just thought *you* would want them more," she replied. The look on his face made everyone laugh, and she pushed the green set over to him and took the pink for herself. Ferdy cleared his throat.

"All right gentlemen," Allee kicked him under the table. He glared at her. "And Allee," he added, rolling his eyes. Lou chuckled. Ferdy glared at him, too. "Anyway, are we going by points and number of bones, or just number of bones?"

"Ah, let's go with both," Raf said. "It's more fun that way. I'll keep score, if no one else wants to." Everyone seemed to accept his decision, and Allee passionately hoped she could catch on to what they were talking about. Ferdy turned to Jermenain, who was on his left.

"Since you brought the bones, you can go first." Jermenain nodded and laid a domino face down in the middle of the big crate.

"One," he said, tapping the side that was darker ivory, "and two," he continued, tapping on the lighter side. There was a pause of silence, but then Lou leaned forward.

"Deceit," Lou said, looking triumphant. There was a chorus of groans from the other boys.

"Oh, come on, Lou, it's the first one!" Jermenain said. "Like I need to lie on that one. Take it!" Lou peeked under the domino, sighed, and took it.

"Five points from Louzre," Raf said, marking it down on a piece of paper. Lou grimaced at him. Raf ignored him, and picked out a domino for his turn. "Seven, three," he said. Nobody questioned it. The next boy, who Allee didn't know, laid his domino and called out, "Nine, three," with the three touching Raf's. Nobody said anything.

As Allee watched, she realized that this game was a combination of dominos and the card game, when nicely called, was titled "B.S.". When Lou called out "Five, six," she almost challenged him, but she didn't want to make a fool out of herself if he was actually telling the truth. She picked up a four, five domino and placed it next to Lou's. Then it was Ferdy's turn.

"Three, five," he said. Allee glanced down at her dominos and smiled.

"Deceit," she said, reveling in the look on Ferdy's face. The other boys looked at her strangely. "Deceit," she said again, flipping over the domino to reveal a three and nine. "I have that one." The other boys laughed as Ferdy gathered all of the dominos into his pile.

"Five points to Allee," Raf said, jotting it down. "Next." And so the game went on. Her next turn, Allee lied since she did not have an eight or a two, and didn't get caught, but on her fourth round she did. Just to keep the game interesting, she challenged the boy across from her in the eighth round and won another five points. Ferdy and Lou tested the most people, so they were constantly winning or losing points, but in the eleventh round, no one was challenged. Allee only had one domino left, as did the boy across from her, who was named Nikolas. Ferdy with two dominos, called out, "Six, eight." Allee looked down at her domino and felt an evil grin spread over her face.

"Deceit," she said, almost laughing with glee. "I have that one, too." Everyone roared as Ferdy had to take his domino back and five others, bringing his total to seven.

In the next round, the game ended as Nikolas went out. Since Allee only had one domino left and fifteen points, she came in second. Raf, with two dominoes and ten points was third, Ferdy with seven and fifteen was fourth, and Jermenain and Lou tied for last with eight and ten both. As soon as Raf had declared the standings, everyone stood up and put their crates against the wall. Jermenain scooped up the dominos, Lou grabbed the candle, and they wove their way back to the kitchens, chattering cheerfully about the game.

The kitchens were still filled with people washing dishes, and Allee heard music and voices of people on the side of the door that led to the Hall of Affair. The four boys said good night to Allee and asked Ferdy to come with them, but Ferdy said he did not feel like going back to the Hall and that he was going to bed.

"What—afraid you'll sleep through sword lessons again?" Lou joked.

"I wasn't *sleeping* this morning," Ferdy protested.

"Yeah, that's right, you did that in Philosophy," Raf said. Ferdy rolled his eyes at them, and laughing, they left.

Ferdy did not say anything to Allee as he led her through the kitchens and to the corridor that held the wooden staircase and would eventually lead to Ferdy's wing. He did not even say goodnight, just nodded curtly and started down the hall. Allee watched him go, too tired and pleased with her win to care that he was angry with her for beating him.

Allee was even more pleased with herself when she reached the door to her room; she had not gotten lost once on the way there. Congratulating herself, she opened it. Surprised, she saw Meli was sitting on a chair waiting for her.

"Have you been waiting all this time?" Allee asked, shutting the door.

"Oh, no," Meli said, rising from her chair. "I've been straightening the other guests rooms. I just got here five minutes ago." Allee breathed a sigh of relief.

"Do you always have to wait for your people to get back?" she queried. Meli shrugged.

"I'm supposed to, but if they do not return in three hours I usually assume they found another place to sleep, and I retire myself."

"That's horrible, making you wait for three hours and then not showing up," Allee said. Meli smiled her soft smile.

"I think it is better for them to fall asleep under a table somewhere than to come back and expect me to help them when they are too intoxicated to stand." Allee sputtered in indignation, but Meli interrupted her. "But I like working in the pastle. I meet lots of interesting people. Let me help you with your dress." Allee offered her back obediently.

"Exactly what do you mean by "interesting people"?" she asked. "I hope I'm not one of them." For the first time, Meli laughed, and deftly undid the buttons.

"You're a nice kind of interesting, Allee, don't worry," she replied. Pondering this comment, Allee took off her shoes, and when Meli moved to put them in the wardrobe, she escaped to the bathroom where she changed and brushed her hair, grabbing her day dress and ball gown as she exited. Meli took them from her as soon as she entered the bedchamber.

"I'll take them to the wash for you," she offered.

"Good," Allee replied, glad to be rid of them, "I would probably stick them down the garbage chute instead of the laundry." Meli laughed again, and Allee realized how tired she looked.

"You can go to bed, Meli," she told the other girl, "I can tuck myself in."

"Not many nobles can," Meli said, moving towards the door. Allee made a face.

"Don't ever forget that I am *not* a noble," she commanded.

"I don't think you'll let me," Meli answered, going out into the hall. She stuck her head back around the door. "Good night, Allee."

"Sweet dreams, Meli," Allee responded. Meli closed the door softly, and a second later, all the candles except the small one on the nightstand went out. Allee made a mental note to ask someone how they did that.

Although she was sleepy, she was still too restless to go to bed. With relief, she realized she had forgotten to brush her teeth. The mint taste was not as strong as the night before, but it still did the job. Allee finished and re-entered the big room. She was still reluctant to get into bed, but the booming of a clock scared her so badly she jumped under the covers.

After fighting with the heavy bed covers for a minute, she realized she was not restless; she was just trying to keep herself from being homesick. As soon as she comprehended this, thoughts of her parents and sisters overwhelmed her.

Trying to escape her emotions, she rolled over and pressed her head to her pillow. Her cheek came in touch with something hard. She removed her hand and brought out the ruby, eager to see if it would sing to her again. She peered at it intently. Nothing happened. She tapped it with her forefinger and brought it up to her ear. Still nothing. Feeling foolish, she put the ruby to her mouth and asked,

"Could you sing for me again, please?" As soon as the words were out of her mouth, pure, sweet music erupted from the jewel. The voice wrapped Allee in an invisible security blanket. She could still not understand the words, but she understood their meaning all the same. Happily, she felt her eyelids droop and she crawled deeper into her covers. The singing stopped.

"Thank-you," Allee whispered.

"You're welcome," the voice replied, but Allee was already asleep.

Chapter 4

Foggily Clear Bubbles

Someone was shaking her. Expecting to find Meli trying to awaken her for breakfast, Allee opened her eyes. The room was still dark, but enough light was coming from somewhere that she could see that the profile outlined against her room was definitely not Meli's. With a start, Allee realized it was Ferdy. She groaned. He leaned in closer to peer at her.

"Allee, you awake?" he whispered. Allee groaned louder.

"No. What do you want?" He didn't answer right away, and even in her sleep-clouded mind, she knew he was up to something. "Is this pay back for beating you?" she asked, extremely annoyed. "'Cause if it is you are one lame revenge-taker. Waking me up in the middle of the night? Come on Ferdinand! Put garlion in my breakfast, challenge me to another duel, anything, just do it TOMORROW!" Allee couldn't see the look on his face because it was too dark, but his voice was horribly cheerful.

"Actually," he said, "It's four o'clock, so it's not the middle of the night. And, no, this isn't payback. I just…um…wanted to talk to you." Allee shot him a glare that she hoped he would feel in the dark and rolled over.

"Allee!" he said.

"Go away!" she replied, her voice muffled by her pillow.

"Please, Allee, I need you." Allee was so startled that she sat up. Ferdy usually acted as if he needed nobody, and she certainly hadn't heard him say please before.

"I'm listening," she said. She heard him take a deep breath.

"Dariel has been kidnapped," he said, speaking very fast. "It seems that she's been missing since the day before yesterday when the caravan stopped to fix the broken wheel. There's been three messengers sent after the one who was a dinner last night, but a fourth just got here. Esendore has decided to secretly leave to rescue her, and he's taking me to help. And I decided that um…you might, um…like to come, too." Allee almost laughed out loud. That was one of the most ridiculous things she'd ever heard.

"Why do you think that?" she asked.

"Oh, just because."

"Just because?" Allee repeated. "Just how stupid do you think I am?" She saw him open his mouth, but interrupted. "Don't answer that." Suddenly, she realized what he was after. "You want me to cook and clean for you, don't you?" she accused. She saw his head shake furiously, and he sputtered in indignation.

"Nu-uh," he started, but then stopped. She saw the outline of his head drop. "Yeah, pretty much." Allee still could not see why he wanted *her* to come along.

"Why me? Why not your dairymaid? What's her name—Brit?" Five hours earlier Ferdy hadn't been speaking to her and now he wanted her to come on the mission to save the future queen. She heard him sigh.

"'Cause Esendore said I had to find someone who was smart enough to keep her mouth shut and make sure we got fed. And I thought that since you were smart enough to beat me in sword fighting, and Deceit, and outwit Cardolyn twice, that you could do the job." Allee was extremely taken back. Ferdy had never been this nice to her before; he must be desperate.

"Aww, Ferdy, I'm touched," she said.

"I was kind of hoping you might be," he replied, his eagerness plain in his voice.

"Touched in the head, that is," she said, sliding off the bed. She headed towards the bathroom.

"Where are you going?" Ferdy demanded.

"To get dressed," she said over her shoulder.

"Does that mean you're coming?" He sounded as if it were too good to be true.

"Yes. I really don't want to be around when Cardolyn realizes that you two went off on a rescue mission without her permission."

"Why do you think I'm going?" he answered. Allee shut the bathroom door, shaking her head. Lovingly, she donned her jeans and purple t-shirt. When she sat down, she realized that the fetch ball was still in her back pocket. Since it was one of the few things she had from home, she decided to bring it. After folding the nightgown on the chair, she went to join Ferdy. He looked surprised to see her.

"That's the fastest any female I know has changed," he said. Allee tossed her head.

"That's because the rest of the females you know like wearing things that take a long time to put on. Do you have a problem with what I'm wearing?" He looked startled.

"Nope. Because now I don't have to worry about you tripping on me all the time." Allee wished she had something heavy to throw at him. He grinned at her frustration and walked to the door.

"Shall we go?" he asked, opening it. Allee walked stiffly over to him. At the last second, she noticed her crumpled bed.

"Oh, wait," she said, running over to it. She arranged the pillows down the middle of it and smoothed the creases in the velvet comforter.

"What are you doing?" Ferdy asked again.

"Making it look like I'm still in it," she replied, without looking up. She'd always wanted to try this trick and see if it actually worked. "That way they won't notice I'm gone if they come to check on me."

"Oh, puh-lease," he said, leaning against the doorframe. She ignored him and pressed the last wrinkle down. As she did so, she found the ruby. She turned it over once in her hand and then pocketed it, figuring that it was what had brought her here in the first place, it might as well come along. She rejoined Ferdy by the door, and he gave her one of his looks.

"Whatever time you save getting dressed you lose trying to be sneaky," he grumbled.

"Oh, yeah," Allee said, shutting the door. "Well, at least I'm good at it, unlike—" Ferdy put a finger to his lips, but he needn't have bothered. Allee was stunned into silence when he pulled on the candle sconce opposite her door and a secret passage way opened up.

"Wow," she breathed, "a real honest to goodness secret passage. How does it—," but she couldn't finish her question for Ferdy's persistent pulling on her arm. He tugged her into the passage, and the panel soundlessly closed.

"How much do you use this?" Allee asked, noting the cleanliness of the floor. Ferdy shrugged and grabbed a small burning candle from a shelf above their heads.

"A little. Now be quiet, people can still hear you through the walls." Allee snorted.

"How many people are crazy enough to be awake at four o'clock in the morning?" she said, scornfully.

"You for one," he replied. Allee scowled at him.

"Look who's talking." He sighed and shook his head. Allee decided to be quiet.

There were many other tunnels leading off of the one they were in, which seemed to be leading down, so Allee had to keep right behind Ferdy in order not to get lost. Some of the smaller ones looked like they had light at the end, and cold air wafted out of others, making Allee shiver. She was going to ask where all of them led to, but Ferdy abruptly stopped. Allee peered around him to see that their tunnel made a sharp right turn.

"This passage ends in the kitchen," he said, pointing to the wall in front of them. "I just need to find the latch." He set his candle in a niche and started to run his hands over the stones. Allee took a step forward to see if she could help, but her shoe caught in a crack. She fell, landing on Ferdy. Suddenly, they were spilling out into the darkened kitchen. Allee cracked her head on the door and bumped her elbow on Ferdy's knee. As soon as the pain abated, she sat up. She realized that they had come out of a false cupboard. Ferdy, who had been groaning in a little heap a few feet away from her, lifted his head.

"That is a ridiculous place to put a secret passageway opening," Allee said, examining the cupboard. Ferdy moaned and stood up.

"I hurt in places that have no business hurting," he complained, "and you want to move the secret passage. Ug." He limped over and shut the cupboard door.

"I want you at least three feet behind me at all times, okay?" he said, touching a spot on his head and wincing. Allee didn't know whether to laugh or be angry, so she just nodded and fell into step three feet behind him. He opened the door, peered out, and when he deemed it safe, stepped out into the courtyard.

An early morning mist hung low over the ground, but Allee could see stars in one bare patch of sky. They were the only light in a night black as pitch, so Allee stayed as close to Ferdy as she dared.

As they passed under the archway she looked for some kind of guard, but there was no one. Allee thought it was odd that the pastle had such loose security measures, but then she was too busy keeping up with Ferdy to think about it more. He didn't stop his fast clip until they reached the starns.

The figures of two people and three horses emerged from the mist. Allee recognized Roeland at once and realized the other man was Esendore, for she doubted anyone except him would wear such elaborate clothes for riding. His black shirt and green pants had fancy embroidery up and down the sides, and his shoes didn't look fit for bedroom slippers, let alone riding.

Roeland's garb depicted the early hour: his shirt was untucked and his bootlaces were shoved in the top of his shoes. Allee sent a quick look at Ferdy, and realized he was dressed almost as nicely as Esendore, except all in maroon. She doubted that they could be secretive about their identities when the Princes were so plainly dressed like royalty. Esendore's voice cut through her deliberations like a knife.

"Have you found a suitable one then, Ferdinand?" he asked, his voice clear and commanding. Ferdy threw a glance at Allee, plainly still mad at her for falling on him and thinking her anything but suitable.

"I guess," he said. Allee thought of all the things she would love to say to him, and moved to introduce herself.

"I am Alethea Quintin, at your service, Your Majesty," she said, bowing. She looked up, and she tried to stop herself, but she could not help but look into his steel gray eyes. They went unfocused, like everyone else's, but to her horror, Esendore's body began to tremble. She quickly looked away, appalled. *Don't do that*, she berated herself, *your otherworldliness does something to them.* Then she realized that

Ferdy had never been affected. She could give him her coldest glare, and he wouldn't flinch. With an effort, she turned back to Esendore, who didn't seem to have noticed anything.

"Yes, I know you, Alethea," he was saying, "You saved Her Grace's life. I am very grateful." Allee wished everyone would just forget about that. She hadn't even meant to. It was embarrassing. She bowed to him again.

"Begging your pardon, Majesty, but I no more saved her life than saved her the inconvenience of killing an insect." Carefully avoiding his eyes, she looked up to see a smile playing on his lips.

"I still thank you," he said. The sound of hooves came out of the mist, and Gnarrish, along with a pony loaded with saddlebags, materialized.

"I have the supplies, Sire," he said, bowing.

"Excellent," Esendore replied, "And the cloaks?" Gnarrish held out three dark bolts of fabric. Esendore took one and passed one each to Ferdy and Allee, who felt much better about the secrecy issue. Once she had clasped the bronze fastener and drawn the hood close to her head, the cloak covered all of her quite well. Allee saw that Gnarrish had donned one, too, and realized he was coming the same instant he realized she was.

"She's coming?" he said, his face aghast.

"He's coming?" Allee said at the same moment, horror in her voice. She had bruises the size of her fist from their first meeting. Esendore didn't seem to notice their dislike of each other.

"Why, yes," he said, his voice cheerful. "Gnarrish will be our manservant, and Alethea our maid. Let's mount up." Roeland hurried to help Esendore into Majesty's saddle. Ferdy must have detected the undercurrents, for he peered at Gnarrish and Allee with narrowed eyes. He opened his mouth to say something, but then changed his mind and moved to take Lunar's reins from Roeland. Gnarrish glanced sidelong at Allee and left to get on his pony. Roeland finished with Ferdy and offered the other horse's reins to Allee. She realized who it was.

"I get to ride Dazzle?" she gasped. Roeland started to reply, but Esendore's voice interrupted him.

"You are to take care of Dazzle until the Countess is found," he explained, "and then we will find you a different mount and she will ride Dazzle. Take good care of her until then." Allee swallowed hard and hoped she would be able to do just that. She looked up at the stirrup, which seemed a long, long ways up. Roeland noticed her distress and cupped his hands for her to use as a foothold. Gently, he lifted her into the saddle. Once in it, Allee felt very tall and very foolish riding a noble woman's zeorse. She drew her cloak tighter for reassurance.

"Is everyone ready, then?" Esendore asked, his eyes sweeping over their group. He gave no time for an answer. "Roeland?" he questioned.

"Both gates are open, Your Majesty," Roeland replied. "And I will shut them behind you. You should make good time." Allee could not believe the subdued change in him from the morning before. She guessed it was because of Esendore's presence, for he had never been this formal with Ferdy.

"All right then," Esendore said. "Be as quiet as you can until we leave the causeway." He nodded to Roeland, who bowed low to the ground, and kicked Majesty into a fast walk. Ferdy was after him, and Gnarrish followed. Allee shook Dazzle's reins, but then felt a nudge by her foot. Roeland had grabbed hold of it.

"Don't let them get to you," he said, his voice serious. "They haven't been around peasants much." Allee lifted her head.

"Then I'll teach them how to act around a peasant and to like it," she promised. Roeland threw back his head and laughed, slapping Dazzle on the rump as he did so. The zeorse was startled into a trot.

"Good luck," he called after them, but Allee was too busy clinging to the saddle to reply.

They did not meet anything or anyone as they rode through the pasture, but Allee got worried that they would be heard as soon as they started on the stone road. Even though it was pot-holed and overgrown, the zeorses' hooves made a lot of noise. But they had absolutely no trouble leaving the city; there wasn't even a guard on the city wall. Allee looked back at the wall with distaste; anyone who wished to could just walk right in and do whatever they pleased. She reasoned that either the King didn't care or Taween had no enemies. Or both. But then why would anyone kidnap Dariel? Allee just didn't understand.

The causeway seemed to worry Esendore, for the mist was rapidly disappearing and they were out in the open. When they reached the end, Allee could see beads of sweat on his usually composed face. He looked apprehensively toward the dark forest and cleared his throat.

"Well, then," he said, his voice uncertain, "I guess this is where we begin." The tremor in his voice made Allee look carefully at his face. Gone was the assurance and arrogance of a few minutes before. Instead, he seemed nervous and hesitant, and with a jolt, Allee recognized fear. She remembered Ferdy mentioning that he had only been to the city three times in his entire life. If that was the same for his brother, Esendore had no idea what he was doing. There was a silence—no one knew what to say. Ferdy broke it.

"Are we going yet?" he asked, sounding bored. Esendore squared his shoulders and spurred Majesty into a canter. Allee urged Dazzle to follow, hoping desperately that she wouldn't fall off, that she could learn to cook over a campfire really fast, that Esendore found Dariel quickly, and, for some strange reason, that she wouldn't get hurt in the process.

Allee didn't think she would be able to stay awake, but she did. She credited most of her awareness to all of the different sights, sounds, and smells she was busy with. As soon as the sun was up, so were the flowers and animals. Allee got a crick in her neck from looking at everything. The hardest thing to keep track of was the smells. Her favorite was one purple flower on the side of the road that she guessed to be a cross between a violet and a daisy, which gave off a very pleasant odor. Even the dirt smelled different. She never did see a weaset, but the other creatures kept her occupied. The best was a bushy-tailed rabbit that would pop out of a hole, shoot up a tree, and then wiggle its nose and chatter at them.

The creatures kept her awake, but it was Esendore's detours that kept her aware of what they were doing. Even when it was still half-dark and no one was using the road, Esendore would take them into the forest on paths hardly fit for deer (or whatever they were) at the smallest rustle that sounded suspicious to him. As the sun got higher and there actually were people using the road, Esendore often had them in the forest holding their breaths for a half an hour at a time.

The day was already warm, but when they were forced into the close underbrush Allee was afraid she would pass out from the stuffy heat.

"He said that he doesn't want Cardolyn or whoever has taken Dariel to know our whereabouts," Ferdy told Allee. "But the real reason is that he just isn't a people person. Little children especially. They scare him," he whispered to her after the fifth time they had gone off the road. Allee snorted, but she almost believed him. Most of the time the offender was a coffalo drawn wagon full of goods for market or, if the driver was a little richer, a zeorse-drawn trap. Twice it was just a group of people with their wares on their backs, and once there was a man on a zeorse who was dressed in royal colors, but he came from the wrong way and sang a bawdy drinking song the entire time they could hear him. Esendore turned beet red, but Allee could hear Ferdy singing along under his breath.

"Wanna teach me?" she asked. He grinned.

"Sure, it starts like—"

"FERDINAND NICKOLAS DENERITE!" Esendore roared. "You are NOT teaching the young lady vulgar drinking songs. I should take you home right now if this is how you are going to behave. The very idea!" Ferdy made a face at Esendore's back as he turned Majesty back onto the road.

"I swear, he's going to put on skirts and go with Cardolyn to her sewing circle any day now." Allee nodded her head in agreement, trying hard not to laugh at the image of Esendore in a dress, and they continued on their way.

After five hours of riding and hiding, they had only covered eight miles. When they were forced to hide in the brush from a would-be pursuer who turned out to be a skunkish-badger creature, Allee was about ready to strangle the Crown Prince. Ferdy had already tried.

"So, what message from Her Grace did *that* messenger have, Esendore?" he wisecracked, out of breath from their tussle. Esendore reddened and didn't reply, but after that they stuck to the road.

Soon afterwards a stream appeared, and Esendore consented to a break. The zeorses drank greedily, and the humans received one trail biscuit apiece. Allee wolfed hers down, but was still starving. She had been swept out of the pastle so fast she hadn't had time for breakfast.

"How much longer?" she asked Ferdy. He squinted at their surroundings.

"I don't know," he sighed irritably, "I'm completely lost because of all the detours and sniffing the flowers we were obligated to do by that...that..." He seemed to be at a loss for words on what to call Esendore.

"Dunderhead?" Allee said without thinking, and immediately realized what she had just said. Ferdy just stared at her.

"You just made that up," he accused.

"No, it means someone who messes up," Allee replied. She could tell that Ferdy was getting ready to argue with her, but at that moment, Esendore called for them to get ready to leave again.

A half an hour later Allee was tired of not knowing where they were going and rode up to ask Ferdy. He was scanning the trees along side of the road as if looking for something. He ignored her, but she knew he knew she was there. After ten minutes, Allee interrupted him.

"What are you doing?" she whispered, though she didn't know why she lowered her voice.

"Looking for centaurs," he said, his eyes still glued to the forest. Allee was not sure she wanted to meet another centaur; their air of knowing everything about her made her nervous. But she was still curious.

"Why?" she asked. Ferdy sighed, as if it should be obvious, and finally turned to look at her.

"Because if I find Neiy, he will give us a straighter answer than Espy will about where Dariel is, and that's saying something." Allee's brow furrowed.

"Aren't we looking for Dariel *now*?" she queried. He sighed again.

"No, stupid, we have to know where she is first."

"I'm only stupid because no one around here tells me anything," Allee snapped. She didn't want to give Ferdy any more cause to call her stupid, but she couldn't help asking, "Who's Espy?" Ferdy rolled his eyes.

"Espy the Effervescent. She is Taween's Seer, and the only one on Betwix that I know of, Record Keeper, Healer, Map Holder," he was ticking them off on his fingers as he spoke. His eyes went blank as he struggled to remember the last one. "Oh, and the Princess." He sighed with his last words. Allee's eyes widened.

"She's your *sister*?" Ferdy shrugged.

"Yeah, and she tries to be my mother. Except she really doesn't know how, and she can't stay with it...she's kind of...kind of..." He gestured to his temple.

"An airhead?" Allee said before she could stop herself. Ferdy gave her his look, and she winced in anticipation. He just laughed.

"An airhead, yep, that's Espy." Allee relaxed, but still felt puzzled.

"If she "sees" stuff, whatever you mean by "sees" than how can she be an airhead?" Ferdy shrugged.

"She just is. Centaurs may just predict things, and they may give foggy answers to what they've predicted, but it's never as bad as Espy. She *knows*, but gives you hazy answers. Just a bunch of hints and stuff. She thinks it's fun to make you guess." He paused to shake his head in disgust. Then he brightened. "But if I ask Neiy, I know I'll get an answer as straight as he can give me. And if I find him *now*, we can find out where Dariel is and I won't have to put up with Espy and her airs." Even though Allee didn't know Espy, she still didn't think Ferdy should be so judgmental. Ferdy saw her frown and exhaled noisily.

"I know she's my sister, but I just don't like her breathing down my neck all the time and playing with us because she likes to be paid attention to. I can't help it." He sighed again. Allee was about to sympathize with him, but realized that he had just sighed for the fifth time in the last two minutes.

"Would you stop doing that? You're depressing me," she said.

"Doing what?" he asked, looking bewildered. At loss for a word, Allee made one up.

"Heahing."

"Alright, I *know* you made that up. I'm not stupid you know."

"Sure seems like it to me," Allee snapped.

"Oh, really?" He seemed about to get fired up, so Allee changed the subject.

"Why isn't His Highness going to see Neiy instead of Espy?" she asked.

"What?" he said, trying to figure out where the conversation had went to. He realized what she'd said, and scowled. "Long story," he said.

"Looks like I have time," Allee replied. "And if you sigh one more time I'll throw something at you." He gave a pitiful cough instead and then started explaining.

"One day when Esendore was practicing his trail riding skills by himself in the forest his zeorse threw him, and Neiy happened to come across him. Esendore was all hot and bothered because the zeorse had ran away and he wanted to ride Neiy back to the pastle because Esendore is a lazy idi—" Esendore chose that moment to turn back to straighten something on his saddle, and Ferdy choked in mid-sentence. Allee snickered while Ferdy took a deep breath and continued,

"Anyway, Neiy didn't want to give him a ride because Esendore didn't ask very nice, and Neiy would get in trouble with his father for letting a human ride him." Ferdy saw Allee's startled look and quickly reassured her. "But his father won't get mad at *us* because Neiy offered and he's not going to find out. Well, then Esendore started acting all Esendoreish, pulling the I'm-the-future-king-so-obey-all-my-wishes sort of thing. And Neiy pulled it right back since his father is the Wealder, and then Esendore called him a half-breed or some nonsense and now all the centaurs hate him for insulting their Prince. They wouldn't even accept his gift of twenty rare trees he imported from Betwa as an apology." From the tone of his voice, Allee guessed that the trees had been a very generous offering.

"Harsh," she agreed.

"Huh?" Ferdy asked, but she was saved from explaining when Ferdy had to rein Lunar in to avoid running into Gnarrish. Allee craned her neck around to see why they had halted. The forest of broadleaf tress they had been traveling in all morning suddenly changed, as well as the land. They were standing on top of a hill, looking down into a forest of evergreens. Beyond the forest was a lake, only a mile or so in diameter, but Allee guessed from the color of the water that it was at least a hundred feet deep. She realized that they were standing on the edge of a very old crater from a blown-out volcano.

On the side of the lake closest to them was a small village, with a fishing fleet tied up to the dock. Between the village and where they were standing was a curious landform; at first Allee thought it was just a bunch of boulders, but as she looked closer she saw that it was a solid sheet of rock, but with doors embedded at different intervals. She realized that it was a system of caves. Esendore gave a relieved sigh.

"Wonderful," he said, his eyes surveying the caves. "We'll be there in time for lunch. Come on then." He kicked Majesty into a trot. Ferdy and Gnarrish followed and Allee brought up the rear, hoping that Espy was not so much of an airhead she didn't make decent food.

They made a fairly good pace down to the base of the crater, but slowed down again as the trees thickened. Allee was having a such a terrible time staying on Dazzle and keeping the tree branches out of her face (she suspected Ferdy was making no effort to hold them for her) that when the bubble appeared she didn't even notice until she ran into Gnarrish. It was very hard to miss, though, being the size of a basketball and giving off a blue-green light. Allee stared at it in awe. There seemed to be something flickering in its depths.

"Ah," Esendore said, eyeing the bubble nervously as it circled around his head. "She knows we're coming." The bubble stopped circling and started drifting away in the direction of the caves. Esendore watched it for a moment and then urged Majesty to follow. Allee moved up to ride beside Ferdy to avoid getting left behind.

"Well, I certainly hope she knows we're coming, that is her job," Ferdy muttered. Allee was still too transfixed by the bubble to rebuke him. She was feeling very funny, like her head was plugged up or something.

"Espy's job is to make bubbles?" she asked, trying to shake off whatever was holding on to her. Ferdy rolled his eyes.

"No, stupid, don't you know anything? That is how she sees stuff." Allee snapped out of her trance as soon as she heard that, but had no time to pursue the matter further, for they had broken out of the trees and the caves were right in front of them.

Standing in the doorway was a woman garbed in a brilliantly white shift. Allee grasped that it wasn't only the woman's gown that was white, but her skin and hair, too, and realized that Espy was an albino. However, her eyes were not colorless. Instead, they were a bright, piercing blue.

"Welcome," Espy said, her voice as piercing as her eyes, but with a strange lilting quality. "I hope you find what you are looking for." Allee's first impression of the woman was that she was stern and cold and wise, but then Espy laughed and the feeling vanished. Esendore dismounted to give her a hug. He kissed her forehead in greeting and she giggled.

"I've missed you," she said, her voice high and childish, completely different from a moment before. "Please say you'll stay a long time." Esendore smiled, but then his face grew serious.

"We are on a matter of some urgency," he told her. "Espy, do you know where she—" Espy interrupted by putting a long white finger to his lips.

"Shhh," she said, her voice changing from playful to powerful. "There will be time for that later, Esendore." Esendore looked disappointed, but did not protest. Espy smiled at him and turned her stare to Ferdy, who hurriedly dismounted.

"I have neither seen nor heard from you for six months," she said. Ferdy raised an eyebrow.

"You haven't?" Espy frowned at him.

"Not in person, I mean. We will have to change that. I miss you." Ferdy's cold demeanor vanished, and he let himself be embraced by his sister. Allee felt like saying, "Aww!" but restrained herself.

"Gnarrish," Espy continued, still keeping an arm around Ferdy. The gnarf, already out of the saddle, bowed to her.

"Lady, I give you my humblest greetings," he said, not looking up. Espy raised his head with her finger to look into his face.

"Courteous as always," she smiled, and Allee tried hard not to snort. "I have a lunch laid out for you in the stable, if you would be so kind as to see to the mounts. And, if you please, when you've finished, I have some bushes that sorely need your attention. Take whatever you need from the storeroom." Gnarrish's eyes lit up in anticipation.

"It would be an honor, Lady," he said, taking the reins of Majesty and Lunar. Allee knew what was coming next and braced herself.

"And Alethea," Espy breathed. Allee had tried to be prepared, but she was so surprised Espy knew her name that she fell off her zeorse. Ferdy started laughing, but Espy rushed to help her. Allee hopped up from the dirt and brushed herself off, trying to hide her blushing face by bowing.

"Your Highness," she mumbled. Espy looked surprised.

"I renounced that title when I became the Effervescent," she said, and Allee blushed again. "You may call me Espy." Allee bowed deeper.

"My apologies," she said, and when she raised her head a smile similar to the one that had been on Esendore's face that morning was playing on Espy's lips.

"I have *so* looked forward to meeting you," she said, and before Allee could look away, Espy's eyes were locked on her own. Espy's eyes did not go unfocused, but Allee felt very strange. It was almost as if her outer eye had gone foggy, but her inner eye was growing, growing so large that she saw all of Betwix playing out before her. Rivers, mountains, villages, and forests all sped by, and Allee's heart yearned for them to stop so she could look at them closer. Something was tugging on her heartstrings, and Allee let out a gasp of pain and longing.

"*Come*," it said, "*Come and see the wonder of this world.*"

"But I can't," Allee's new inner voice cried, "I don't belong here. This is not my world."

"*But it can be,*" the little voice told her, its tone wheedling. "*Renounce the world of your birth and then all that you see will be yours.*"

"NO!" Allee yelled. The voice laughed, and Allee felt her frustration come to a boiling point. "Stop that," she commanded, but the voice laughed harder.

"*I will wait*", it said, "*I will not give you up so easily. I will wait.*" Before Allee could think anything else Espy looked away and Allee was left feeling lost and more than a little bit breathless. All the pictures of green fields and blue waters with all sorts of amazing new things in them kept playing through her head, and she struggled to find that voice again and tell it off for thinking it could claim her so easily. Then Espy started talking again.

"We should eat before the food gets cold or you will have to wait for me to heat it up again," she reminded them, apparently oblivious to what her gaze had done to Allee. With a flounce, she turned back to the caves. Gnarrish took Dazzle's reins and Allee followed her hostess, trying to get the memory of the unearthly voice out of her head.

Espy led them down a hallway of stone and then turned to the left. The room they entered was clearly a kitchen, though a strange one.

Everything was made of stone, from the cupboards to the sink to the table. Even the benches were stone, carved out of the mother rock along the long sides of the table. Espy gestured for them to sit down and dished the stew that was simmering in the fireplace into bowls, humming as she went. The humming grew louder as she sliced some bread and cheese to go with the stew. She set the plates on the table and sat down, her waist-length hair swirling around her.

"Enjoy," she sang out, taking a bite out of her bread. She laughed out loud in delight when Ferdy began slurping his stew. Even though she was starving after not having any breakfast, Allee raised her spoon slowly to her mouth. She was in awe of this strange woman who made her have visions and saw things in bubbles and could watch her better if she ate slowly. However, Espy didn't do anything else unusual, so Allee gave up and enjoyed her meal.

When the last bit of cheese had disappeared from the plate, Espy spoke again.

"As soon as everyone is finished, I would like to give you a tour of my home." Her words seemed to be directed at Allee, who swallowed nervously.

"Sounds great," she said, smiling weakly. Esendore looked upset.

"But Espy—" he started.

"Hush, little brother," she said, turning her stare onto him. "I am not ready yet." Esendore fell silent, but his eyes still protested. Espy stood up and with a sweep of her arms she deposited the dishes in the sink. "We'll do them later," she said. "Come on," she giggled, looking like an anxious little girl. "I have many rooms I want you to look at," she added, and walked out. Allee looked around the table at the Princes. Esendore was moping and didn't return her gaze, but Ferdy shrugged at her and stood up. Allee followed him, and a moment later, she heard the scrape of boot on stone as Esendore came after.

Espy was waiting very impatiently outside the door with a lighted candle. As soon as she was sure they were all there, she led them down the hallway at a brisk pace.

"This room is the infirmary," she said, throwing open a set of double doors to a room full of cots. There was not a single person in any of the beds, and they looked as if they had been vacant for a very long time. Allee remembered Ferdy calling Espy a Healer, but what was the point of being the Healer if you had no one to heal?

It wasn't like Espy wasn't prepared. She showed them a medicine room that had enough bandages and healing herbs for an epidemic. The whole place was immaculate; the gleaming stone counters and sinks looked like they had never been used. Allee did notice that they were very smooth, as if at one time they had been used frequently. When she saw the next room full of medical journals and card-cataloged remedies that had a very unused air, Allee could not hide her bewilderment any longer.

"But what is all this for?" she queried, her voice echoing against the stone. "There's no one using it." Espy turned to her, her eyes pulsing with incredulity.

"You don't know?" Before Allee could answer, Espy's face contorted, as if she had just remembered something. "Ah, yes," she said, almost to herself. She shook her head, and continued,

"This system of caves was designed to be a sort of hospice, for anyone who needed it. All are accepted for treatment, even if they cannot pay. The job of the Effervescents is to seek out those who need the services here and send them aid. There was a school for the Seers here, also, since they needed to be trained in the arts of seeing and healing. But it wasn't just the Effervescents-in-training who studied here. Others did, too. Kings, princes, dukes, sultans…" Espy's voice drew on a dreamlike quality and she looked off into the distance, twirling a piece of hair around her finger. Ferdy and Esendore didn't notice her lapse of silence, they were examining a crate of bottles marked RUMSKY, but Allee was almost concerned. Espy was so zoned out Allee felt that she had fallen away from them. Suddenly, she smiled at Allee.

"But I am the only one left now," she said, her voice sad. "No others have presented themselves for tutoring."

"Why don't they come?" Allee asked, feeling sorry for Espy in her solitude. Espy's brow furrowed.

"There seems to be a…a…mistrust of me and the Effervescent craft in general," she said softly. "My last two predecessors were not very capable women, and people have drawn the wrong conclusions. The people seem to think me a…a…witch, among other things."

"They said WHAT?" Esendore's voice cut in. Allee jumped. He *had* been listening. Espy looked frightened.

"Nothing important," she said quickly, giving a forced laugh. Esendore frowned at her, and she crumpled.

"They told me they didn't want to be healed by sorcery and didn't want their children to be taught by a witch and to stay away from them," she babbled, her eyes wide. Suddenly, they filled with tears, and she bit her lip to keep in a sob. "But five in the village have died from the Wasting Sickness, and they blame me, but I could have saved them. I know I could have." Her blue eyes shone even brighter with the withheld tears as she looked up at Esendore. "I could have," she half-sobbed, as if begging Esendore to forgive her. He ignored her plea, and Allee could actually *feel* the anger he was holding in check. The vibe was not as strong as Ferdy's was when he was angry, but very close.

"What were the other things? Other than calling you a witch?" he demanded. Espy was really frightened now. She swallowed hard, looking as though she was regretting saying what she had.

"That was the largest reason," she said, avoiding his eyes.

"What were the others? Tell me Espy," he commanded, putting his hands on her shoulders. She flinched and shut her eyes.

"They mistrust the King because all he does is sit in his treasure chamber that is growing larger by the day from the taxes he imposes and makes the working people starve to death. They also say that all who associate with him are as evil as he is," she said in a rush. Her tears spilled over. "I've been here for five years and only three people have come to me for help! The records show that a hundred a day came in the old days! There has not been that many for almost fifty years because of some stupid fear these people have. What can I do?" Allee laid her hand on Espy's arm in sympathy, and they both winced as Esendore exploded.

"How dare they say such things!" he shouted, his body trembling in rage. "Who are they, Espy? These...these...TRAITORS! If they would work harder they would not worry about starving. Lazy." He spit the last word out. Allee felt her temper rising, and fought to control it. She doubted Esendore could know more about the peasants' working conditions than they themselves did. "Are you sure you're seeing right, Espy?" he continued, trying to find someone to blame. "Surely they cannot be so ignorant." Now it was Espy's turn to get annoyed. She brushed away her tears angrily.

"Of course," she snapped. "I have seen the same complaints many times." Esendore ran his fingers through his hair.

"Stupid peasants," he spat. "Making judgments on things that have nothing to do with them." Allee opened her mouth angrily, but she saw Ferdy shaking his head at her, so she bit her tongue, but her eyes were still shooting sparks.

Espy seemed to have gotten control of herself again and burst into cheerful chatter to ease the awkwardness.

"Shall we go see the Record Room?" she asked, brightly. Allee was just a little annoyed at the way Espy was handling the situation, especially when the Effervescent bounced back into the hallway without waiting for an answer. Ferdy seemed to feel the same way, but followed her without question, rolling his eyes. Allee took a step after him, but Esendore put a hand on her arm. A tremor of disgust went down her spine, but she forced herself not to move.

"Alethea," he said, his voice low, his eyes searching her face. Allee quickly lowered her head to hide her eyes. He thought she was ashamed of herself. "No, no, Alethea," he said hurriedly, "Don't be ashamed. It is I who should be sorry. I should not have said the things I did. I forgot myself. You have every right to be angry when your people are being insulted. Maybe what they are saying does have some basis in fact. Please forgive me." Allee was so surprised at his apology she almost looked up into his face.

"Of...of course, Your Highness," she said, looking at his chin instead of his eyes. He looked about to say something else, but Espy suddenly called for them.

"Esendore, Alethea, hurry up!" Esendore sent a quick glance at Allee and squeezed her arm.

"Coming!" he called back, hastening to join her. Allee followed slowly, unnerved with Esendore's apology. Ferdy never apologized for anything. *But Ferdy would never say anything like Esendore just did*, a little voice said. Allee ignored it and ran to find the others.

Allee had known that the Record Room would have all of the maps and books needed for a center of learning, but she had expected it to be like the pastle's library, which had been dark, dusty and mostly unused. But the Record Room was like everything else in Espy's domain—immaculate and well cared for. *For being an airhead, she sure takes good care of her stuff,* Allee thought, looking around at the colossal room, its thousands of bindings gleaming in the sunlight. Espy giggled at Allee's look of awe.

"You...you keep this up all by yourself?" Allee asked, her voice almost lost in the vastness of the room.

"Yes, all by myself. Don't I do a good job?"

"Amazing," Allee told her. Espy beamed.

"And I cataloged everything, too," she gushed. "It's over here. Come see." She led Allee over to the cabinet, chattering gaily.

They spent an hour looking at maps and records that Espy said Allee just *had* to see. Allee really didn't mind too much. Espy was a very entertaining lecturer, but Allee did see what Ferdy meant when he had said his sister was a little dramatic. Espy waved her hands a lot and had a tendency to gush on and on about trivial things. Ferdy and Esendore followed them around listlessly; it was clear they had experienced the tour before.

When they reached the end of the section devoted to the different colors of toenail fungus (which caused Esendore to turn green and Ferdy to punch him for being a sissy), Espy stopped and clapped her hands.

"That's certainly not all the books I have, but these are just what I think are the most interesting," she said, letting her shining eyes sweep back over the room. "I just love it here, don't you? It's so peaceful." She sighed, the expression on her face as if she were looking on her dearest friend. Allee had a distinct impression that Espy needed to get out more.

"But I do like the Dining Hall, also," Espy continued, her fingers stroking the binding on a book. "It has the most beautiful murals. I just finished restoring them. Come see!" She grabbed Allee's arm, and Allee would have followed willingly, but Esendore interrupted them.

"Espy," he said, his voice wheedling but firm. "I need to know where Dariel is." All of the elation left Espy as if she had been punctured. She even stuck her bottom lip out in a pout. Allee was strongly reminded of her little sister after she had been told to eat her broccoli.

"Very well," Espy sighed, her head drooping. "I will do it." Dejectedly, she led them out of the room and down the hall, back towards the kitchen. She turned left, and the doors lining the new hallway were much smaller and closer together than those of the previous one. Seeing the heavy wooden doors, Allee assumed that they were private bedrooms. They were all exactly the same, so she was surprised to see one doorway covered with strings of glass beads. Her surprise evaporated as soon as she saw Espy turn into it. Espy would have to be different.

Allee followed right behind the Effervescent, shivering when the icy beads touched her skin. She felt like she had just walked through a cold shower. She was a little unnerved at first, but the simple room they entered put her at ease. The walls were bare except for a blue brick fireplace against one side and a blue silk curtain on the opposite one. Allee realized it hid a bed that was built into the wall. The other furniture consisted of a wooden table and chairs and an indigo clay pot next to the fireplace.

Espy sat down, her back to the fire, and gestured for them to take a seat around the table. Esendore and Ferdy sat on either side of her and Allee took the other chair. Once they were comfortable, Espy took a deep breath and began to speak.

"Two days ago, about mid-morning, one of the wagon wheels in the Countess Dariel's caravan snapped in two." Allee was more than a little unsettled at the way Espy was telling them this information. She spoke in a monotone and her eyes weren't focused on anything. The Princes didn't seem to notice; they were too busy hanging on Espy's every word, but Allee wished Espy would go back to being bubbly. "The wagon master called a halt, inspected what was left of the wheel, and said there would be at least a two hour delay. The Countess took this as a chance to stretch her legs and went for a walk, promising her handmaiden that she wouldn't go far."

"Didn't you follow her?" Esendore asked, on the edge of his seat. Espy's lower lip shot out.

"I meant to!" she cried. "But...but...there was this starbin that seemed very interested in my bubble, and it kept chasing me..."

"You lost Dariel because you got scared by a STARBIN?" Esendore exclaimed.

"You told me to watch her, and I couldn't very well watch her if the starbin pricked me, could I?" Espy challenged. Esendore didn't say anything. Espy took a lengthy breath and continued. "I managed to lose the bird, but when I did I also lost Dariel. I searched the entire forest within a two-mile radius of the caravan, but I couldn't find her anywhere. I knew something had happened to her, but I couldn't communicate with anyone there so I decided to send a message to you."

"But your messenger did not arrive until late last night," Esendore interrupted. "The caravan's dispatch rider arrived before yours did." Espy's brow furrowed.

"He left before mine was able to, and he only knew that the caravan was delayed, not that Dariel was missing. They realized it an hour after he left and did not have another rider to spare," she explained. "As for my messengers, things seemed to...to...happen to them." She stopped and shook her head in bewilderment.

"For example?" Esendore inquired.

"The first one I sent from the village came back three hours later, dragging his zeorse behind him. The beast had thrown a shoe. The second's zeorse threw him four miles out from the village. The third would not set out until yesterday morning because he refused to ride in the dark. His zeorse, the last in the village, lay down and wouldn't get back up. The rider returned and I paid him to walk. He was the one that made it to you late last night."

"Okay, so we know where Dariel was, but where is she *now*?" Esendore asked, impatiently. "And who has her? How can I get her back? When—"

"Patience, little brother, patience," Espy chided. She put a hand to her forehead, hiding her eyes. After taking several deep breaths, she continued. "You are aware of the country Ivral, to our south, are you not?" she inquired, her voice heavy with distress.

"Of course," Esendore said, "They are always pushing the border and trying to pick a fight with our southern people. We have ignored them for the past fifty years."

"Who?" Ferdy said, speaking for the first time. Esendore opened his mouth to answer, but Ferdy suddenly remembered. "Oh, that country full of lunatics ran by lunatics? *That* Ivral?" Allee was about to laugh, but after seeing both Espy and Esendore's quelling looks at Ferdy, she stopped herself and coughed instead. Esendore turned back to Espy.

"Yes, I know where it is. So?" He was getting snappish, so Espy hurried on.

"I don't know if you remember, but there was a bit of conflict over the heir to the throne after the old sultan died. Apparently, his first-born child was a girl, but her father's advisors gave the crown to her younger brother. It did not sit well with her. She attempted to murder the advisors, but failed. She was forced to flee to a remote part of an Ivral forest. That is where she is believed to be today."

"What did they have against her being their Sultaness, her nasty temper?" Ferdy asked, trying to stay in the conversation. Espy lowered her voice to a whisper and they all had to lean in to hear her. Allee glanced at Ferdy and hid a giggle behind her hand when he rolled his eyes. Espy was too caught up in herself to notice.

"There were rumors at the time that the princess was a powerful sorceress, capable of controlling animals for her own purposes. This, added to the fact that her father had trained her in sword fighting with his warriors, scared the advisors enough to choose her brother instead of her."

"I still don't see—" Esendore interrupted, but Espy talked over him.

"Nichelle is desperate for power. Royal power. And she will do anything to get it. I believe it is she who has taken Dariel, and she plans to hold her at her forest hideaway until you do what she wants for Dariel's safe return."

"And what would that be?" Esendore whispered hoarsely, his face inches away from Espy's. She lifted her eyes to meet his.

"Taween, Esendore," Espy said, her voice harsh and loud in the little room. "Your kingdom in exchange for your bride." There was dead silence as they stared at Espy in disbelief. Esendore recovered first.

"She's mad," he spit out. "How can she think to exchange one life for an entire country? And stand up to the wrath I will bring upon her?" Espy looked like she wanted to laugh.

"Really, Esendore? Who will fight for Dariel? She is hardly known or loved by anyone except her own family. And how long will it take to muster them? Four weeks, maybe five? In case you have forgotten, His Majesty has not spared the funds for pastle guards, let alone an army. A month is more than enough time for Nichelle to tire of Dariel and pursue another goal. She is in no hurry and she has many options, for there are still those loyal to her in Ivral, those who are plotting her revenge as we speak. She could very well do away with your betrothed before you even set out to rescue her. You need to act quickly." The siblings stared at each other. Esendore finally looked away.

"I cannot act if I don't know where she is," he said, his face red. Espy sighed.

"I'm still working on that." Esendore looked alarmed.

"Would you like us to leave?" he asked, scooting back his chair.

"No, I'll be fine," Espy replied, breathing deeply. She seemed to be going into a trance, but her eyes were turning a deeper color of blue and becoming more focused. Allee's stomach gave a lurch of fear, though she didn't know why. Then Espy leaned back in her chair, her hands raised in loosely closed fists.

"Come," she said, her voice resonating like the tolling of a bell. She opened her hands and there was a noise from behind her like the lid on the clay pot had slipped. A light seemed to shine from the Effervescent, and it was immediately reflected by at least two hundred bubbles of all shapes and sizes that suddenly filled the room. The hairs on the back of Allee's neck stood on end as she watched the bubbles, each flickering with some unseen image. Beside her, Ferdy was wearing a similar look of awe. Esendore just looked scared.

The bubbles closed around Espy caressingly. She giggled and reached out to stroke one. It gave a little under her touch, but didn't pop. Another, smaller one was bumping against her eyebrow, like a child wanting attention. She picked it up with her finger and peered at it intently.

"Oh," she said, giggling at whatever she saw and flushing slightly. "You will have to wait until later." She placed it at the back of her neck, underneath her hair. It seemed to snuggle there, contentedly waiting its turn. "Now," Espy said, suddenly brisk. "Which one of you has information concerning the Witch Nichelle? I call thee forth." She held out her hand, palm up. A purple-hued bubble landed gently. Espy brought it close to her eyes, which were pulsing again. She gazed closely at it and then turned it slightly. She froze and began speaking in her bell-voice,

"You will travel due south from here one-hundred and twenty miles until you reach the southern chain of the Amalgam Mountains. There is a village there. Here you can rest and prepare yourself for crossing the mountains. Since it is high summer here and will be more so in the south, it should only take you two days and one night to cross them, but expect it to take longer. From the top of the pass, it is fifteen miles through the most rugged land in all of Taween to the witch's lair, and ten more miles will be in Ivral. You must be careful. The woman has spies everywhere. Even your zeorses could turn against you. You will be in danger the moment you leave here, yet your danger will double once you cross the borders to her own country, for she is a monarch, and thus tied to it. As for the extent of her powers, that remains to be seen." Espy stopped, still transfixed with the glowing orb in her hands.

There was a silence so deep that Allee felt it pressing on her, and she wondered how in the world she had gotten herself into this. A journey across dangerous wilderness, a witch who could control animals, *living* with Ferdy for weeks on end; it all seemed overwhelming. But even as she considered the dangers, Allee had absolutely no doubts about going. It was the kind of adventure that appealed to her no matter what the danger. And she didn't care about danger, anyway, she told herself. She would just try not think about it. Esendore's voice broke through her thoughts.

"Is that all you have to tell us?" he asked. Allee could see that he wanted to leave right away, and she almost groaned. She was sore enough after sword fighting, tripping over Ferdy and then riding for six hours. She had been hoping to at least stay at Espy's for the night. Luckily, the bubbles weren't finished. A red-tinted sphere was bumping against Espy's elbow.

"What is it?" she asked, picking it up. She looked at it closely, her brow furrowed. Something must have been of interest, for she gave it a little push and then twirled it on the tips of her fingers. She looked into it again and her eyes widened.

"Ooh, look!" she cried excitedly. "This one has found her hideaway!" Esendore scooted his chair forward, hanging on Espy's every word. Allee and Ferdy looked at each other again and leaned in closer.

Espy's eyes were moving rapidly, as if she was scanning the page of a book. "She lives in a cave," she said, "though it's not nearly as nice as mine. Ha." She smirked in pleasure and continued on in a lofty tone, "It's not very neat either. There's clothes and food everywhere.

I bet she hasn't dusted in weeks. And would you just look at the—" Esendore interrupted her by clearing his throat. She blushed and stopped gloating.

"I don't see anybody, just some dirty dishes. Maybe she isn't home, or—wait." Esendore made a groaning noise, and Allee hoped he hadn't forgot to breathe. Espy drew the bubble so close to her eyes that it touched her nose. Her voice lowered to a whisper. "There is someone. It must be her, for it certainly isn't Dariel. She's coming closer." There was a long silence as Espy strained to see who was approaching. Suddenly, she shrieked, her face aghast.

"What are you doing?" she yelled at the person in the bubble. "Just what do you think you're—" Espy let out a high, piercing scream, and Ferdy and Esendore covered their ears to shut it out. Allee's arms were rooted at her sides; she was too horrified at the anguish on Espy's face to move. The scream pitched and suddenly every single bubble in the room exploded. There was an echo of cold laughter, and then all was silent. Espy slumped to the table, unconscious. Allee overcame her inertia and ran to Espy's side, the Princes right behind her.

"Espy, Espy," Ferdy cried, picking up her arm and shaking it. Esendore cuffed him lightly across the head.

"Knock, it off, Ferdinand," he said, his voice strained. Ferdy stopped shaking his sister, but still held onto her hand. Esendore checked for a pulse and breathed a sigh of relief. "I think she'll be okay," he said, his brow smoothing. "But she should rest." Allee felt her heart slow down to its normal pace, but her head was still whirling. Ferdy looked as bewildered as she felt, but Esendore was surprisingly calm. He gently lifted Espy into his arms. Her head lolled against his shoulder.

"Evil...evil...witch," she murmured, her face contorted in pain.

"Shhh," Esendore soothed, "We'll get her." Allee hurried to part the silk curtains, and Esendore laid Espy onto her bed. She thrashed once and then lay peacefully.

Esendore and Allee rejoined Ferdy by the table, all thinking their own thoughts. Allee wished she could leave to think things over, but she didn't want to seem rude. Then she remembered the dirty dishes Espy had left in the sink.

"I'm going to clean up lunch," Allee said, breaking the silence. Ferdy and Esendore snapped up their heads, their relief at having an excuse to leave the room evident on their faces.

"I'll go see how Gnarrish is doing," Ferdy said, starting for the door. Esendore looked at a loss for what to do, but quickly decided to go with Ferdy. Allee followed them, hoping that visiting Gnarrish took them a very long time.

It took Allee forever to do the dishes. She wasn't used to not having a dishwasher and the pump for the sink only spit out a cupful of water at a time. When she finally got it full, the rest of the dishwashing went fairly well. That is, until she dropped the very last bowl and the remaining stew in it went flying. When she had finished wiping it off the ceiling, Allee was in a very bad mood and very thirsty. She had just found a cup when Ferdy blew in, soaking wet.

"It's pouring out there, you're lucky I made it," he said.

"Very lucky, I'm sure," Allee replied, filling her cup with some water.

"Of course," he agreed. "Oh, are you making supper?" he asked brightly, shaking himself and splattering the recently dried dishes with water.

"Watch it!" Allee cried, but it was too late. "I just dried those," she moaned.

"Funny, they still look wet," Ferdy said, inspecting them carefully. Allee threw the dishtowel at him. He caught it and started cleaning up his mess.

"Where's Esendore?" she asked, stacking the bowls to put them back in the cupboard. Ferdy shrugged.

"I don't know. Probably moping over Dariel or something. He disappeared in the starn somewhere," he said. "Why?"

"If you don't know where he is, then I can't set out stuff because it might get cold before he got here," Allee replied. Ferdy looked startled.

"I could go find him," he volunteered. Then he looked doubtful. "Actually," he said, "I would rather have him moping with the zeorses than moping with us." Allee agreed with him.

"Sounds good to me. Would you settle for something to drink?" He nodded and she took a pitcher of yellow liquid out of the cooler set into the counter and poured it into two cups. Ferdy looked at the food in the cooler wistfully, but didn't say anything. They sat down at the table, pointedly not looking at each other.

"So," they said at the same time. Allee blushed and looked down at the table. Ferdy stared into his cup.

"You go first," Allee said, wanting to see what he would say. He took a deep breath.

"Let me get this right. Espy has just told us that we are to travel through the wilderness for who knows how long to the country full of…full of…" he stopped, and from the way he looked at her, Allee knew that he wasn't at a loss for words, he just wanted to see what she would say. She took the bait.

"Psychopaths?" she suggested. He opened his mouth to repeat it, but stopped, looking absolutely bewildered.

"Where do you get this stuff?" Allee rolled her eyes.

"Exactly how old are you? I bet my little sister knows that word."

"I turned fifteen in March," he said stiffly.

"Interesting," Allee said, and went on with her explanation. "It means beyond being crazy. Evilly crazy."

"Okay," Ferdy said slowly, still looking puzzled, but he continued, "So we are going to the country full of psychopads that is run by psychopads—"

"*Paths,*" Allee corrected him, but he ignored her.

"So that I will have one more woman to nag at me. Hmpht." He dropped his head into his hands. "I almost wish I had risked Cardolyn." Allee smiled at him sympathetically. She was still looking forward to this journey, but her apprehension had been growing since she had seen what the witch had done to Espy.

"I know what you mean," Allee said. She took a drink of her juice and choked in surprise. The flavor was a mixture of pineapple and lemon and made her eyes water. Ferdy was looking at her strangely, so she decided to change the subject.

"So how long you think it will take to get there?" she asked. Ferdy opened his mouth to tell her, but Esendore swept into the room and answered for him.

"A week if all goes well, ten days if it does not," he answered cheerfully, sitting down on empty stool. "Are we ready to eat?" He had managed to keep much drier than Ferdy had, and for that reason plus his cheerfulness at the thought of spending ten days in the wilderness, his brother glared at him disdainfully.

Allee almost laughed at his look, but was too miffed at both the Princes' attitude that she was their servant. Then she remembered that she was and jumped up to set the table. All she could manage to find to eat was the leftover cold cuts and bread from lunch and a jar of peach-apricot stuff. She thought it was plenty, but she doubted it was fit for a Prince. Shrugging, she set it on the table anyway and sat down.

"Sorry it's the same as lunch," she apologized to Esendore; she didn't really care what Ferdy ate. "I don't know where anything else is."

"Quite all right, Alethea," Esendore assured her, spearing a piece of bread. "Anything is better than doing it myself." Allee highly doubted that he had ever made his own dinner, but she didn't say anything.

The meal was silent except for the noise of the storm. Even though the stone walls were very thick, they couldn't stop the sounds of the lashing rain and rumbles of thunder. Allee felt like the outside was an echo of her head; it had so much swirling around in it she could barely think. From the way they were staring moodily at their plates, she guessed the Princes' thoughts were the same.

When Allee rose to wash the dishes the other two remained seated. She ended up doing them all by herself, though she kept sending reproachful looks at Ferdy since she knew he could help if he wanted to. Now that she knew the way the sink worked, this batch did not take nearly as long as the last, but she was still yawning as she neared the bottom of the pile. It was only six, but she was exhausted after being awakened at four, trampled by Ferdy, bounced around on a zeorse for six hours, and led on the tour of the enormous cave system. Even Esendore noticed her weariness.

"Are you tired?" he asked, standing up. Allee nodded sheepishly. "It has been a rough day for all of us," he agreed, "I do believe it would be best if we all retired early." Allee looked at him gratefully. He smiled at her. "Come, I'll show you a room."

"Can I wash somewhere?" Allee asked, feeling way too grimy to sleep in one of Espy's immaculate rooms.

"Just step outside," Ferdy muttered, "Unless you're waterproof like Esendore." His brother didn't seem to hear him.

"Yes, of course," he replied, leading them out of the room. "This way."

As soon as they entered the hallway, they could tell that the storm has escalated in ferocity. The shriek of the wind was plainly audible. Allee shuddered at the thought of being out in the elements.

"If I went outside, I just might get my skin blown off with the dirt," she muttered to Ferdy.

"True," he said, looking mournfully at his damp clothes. "I doubt even Esendore could survive it right now."

"*You* would drown for sure," Allee told him. He looked at her reproachfully, but didn't have a retort.

Ferdy left them with a good night when they met a hallway branching off to the left. Allee recognized it to be the one leading to Espy's room. Esendore gestured to a set of doors on the main corridor right next to the smaller hallway.

"This is the bathroom," he said, pointing to the first one. "There should be everything you need in there. The other door leads to your bedroom," he continued, pointing to it. "Sleep well, Alethea." He turned and followed Ferdy down the small hallway. Feeling very alone, Allee went into the bathroom.

Predictably, it was made of stone, but it was a little less monotonous than the kitchen because of the brightly colored towels and rugs. The most welcoming thing was a real shower. Allee's loneliness evaporated and she hurried to try it out. Soap and washcloths were in the cupboard next to the sink, and Allee even found another mint-flavored toothbrush. Much to her delight, she also discovered a flannel nightshirt and pants. She quickly showered, put on the pajamas, grabbed her clothes, and left.

The hallway was very dark and very cold, so Allee was extremely relieved to find a fire burning in the hearth as she opened the door to her room. *It's almost like she knew I was coming*, Allee reflected, thinking of the pajama pants. Then she groaned. Espy *had* known she was coming. She had seen it in the bubbles. But to know about the pajama pants, she would have had to have been watching Allee as she prepared for bed. *Does that mean Espy watches me in other places?* Allee thought, panicky. *Like places I don't want ANYONE to watch me? Does she know I'm from a different world? And, most importantly, will she betray me?*

Allee quickly scolded herself for thinking such thoughts and looked around her room. It was quite bare; Allee guessed it was probably designed for Effervescent apprentices to use. The only décor was a flowered water pitcher on the nightstand next to an engraved silver brush. At first, Allee couldn't see a bed, just a stone tub full of cloth. With a jolt, Allee realized that the tub *was* the bed. She sank down on it, marveling at its softness. Her eyelids drooping, she quickly drew back the covers, which were made of furs, and snuggled deep into the mattress. Before she could even think the word "homesick", Allee was asleep.

Chapter 5

Nosing

Allee awoke shivering. Her fire was dead and the storm had caused the air in the room to grow very cold. She couldn't find any wood to start it again, so she had to be content with pulling the blanket up to her chin. She tried to go back to sleep, but after ten minutes she gave it up; even the furs were cold.

She sat up in her bed, shivering and wondering what to do. Longingly, she thought of the dancing flames in Espy's room. They would not be cold and lifeless. On impulse, Allee jumped up and ran to the door. She would go to Espy's room, warm herself, and then come back. Pleased with her plan, she opened the door.

Blackness pressed on her eyeballs. Hesitantly, Allee began groping her way to the little hallway that led to Espy's room. When her hand felt air, she turned and stuck out her left hand, feeling for the Effervescent's doorway. Even though she had been expecting them, Allee started when her fingertips met the icy glass beads. She passed through them as quickly as possible, feeling as if she had just taken a cold shower.

Just as she had expected, Espy's fire was still burning brightly. Allee knelt on the hearth, holding out her hands to warm them. As soon as they weren't freezing, she sat and wrapped her arms around her knees, letting the warmth surround her. She sighed blissfully. Suddenly, a voice came out of the darkness.

"What is your world like?" Allee jumped and turned to see Espy peering out from behind the curtain. Her heart thumping wildly in her chest, Allee realized Espy had seen her come into Betwix and she knew her secret. She tried to push down the panic that was overwhelming her.

"What...what do you mean?" Allee asked, her tongue thick and dry in her mouth. Espy tilted her head.

"One of the bubbles told me they had seen the most bizarre thing, a miracle that defied all laws of nature," she started. "A girl had appeared out of thin air! It must be a trick, I told myself, a figment of someone's imagination that the bubble had picked up by mistake." Espy spoke very calmly, but Allee could hear an undercurrent of great excitement. When the Effervescent spoke again, her voice had taken on a feverish pitch. "But now, I know better. For that mistake sits before me this very second." Espy leaned forward off her bed and a strange light came into her eyes. Allee swallowed hard.

"I can see the Past as well as the Present, Alethea," Espy continued, her voice low and deep. "I saw a ball come out of thin air. I saw you appear from nowhere. And I saw the messages that appeared on the rock. Where did you come from?" Her last words sounded dangerous. Allee started to shake. People tried to destroy what they did not know or understand; she knew that thousands of people had been murdered by their fellow human beings simply because they had been different. And here, every single thing about her was freakishly different from the rest of the world. Afraid for her life, Allee desperately began to explain herself.

"My world is called Earth," she said. As soon as the words were out of her mouth, Allee felt as if a burden had been taken from her shoulders, and a new strength entered her. "I know as much about how I got here as you do," she went on, her voice clear and firm. "I do not know why or for what purpose I came here, but I mean to find out. No matter what this world throws at me." Defiantly, she raised her head to meet Espy's eyes. She felt no fear and heard no voices; her newfound strength left no room for invaders. Espy returned her gaze.

"I do not doubt it, Alethea," she said, her tone soft. "I did not mean to frighten you. I believe you completely." Relief coursed through Allee, making her shoulder's sag.

"I haven't lied about anything," she assured Espy.

"I believe you," the Effervescent said, smiling. Allee looked down at the floor, feeling awkward, and fell silent. She heard a rustling noise, and, suddenly, Espy's long white fingers were holding up her chin. Allee did not feel certain and defiant as before and carefully avoided her eyes.

"May I ask you one question, Alethea?" Espy asked, the firelight playing upon her cheeks bones and making her eyes glow. Allee nodded, her fear vanishing when she felt the warmth in her gaze. "Why don't you tell the Princes your secret? They will believe you, and you will not have to suffer so much fear and doubt. Why are you afraid to tell them?"

"I...I...so want them to trust me, and to believe in me," Allee said, her eyes focused on a little orange flower embroidered onto her nightgown. "But how can they believe in me if they know that I am from somewhere they have never seen and never will see? A place that, for them, doesn't even exist? It would be like I don't exist. And I am...I am afraid that this...knowledge would consume them. Wouldn't it gnaw at you, if you were like them? The constant thought that there is an entire *world* that until a couple of days ago, you had no idea even existed? I...I can handle it, because I can see both worlds. And you can handle it because you see tons of stuff anyway, stuff that you don't understand. But the Princes...they will never see my world. I think...that knowledge would trouble them. Being between two worlds troubles *me*." Allee finally looked up at Espy and was surprised to see that the Effervescent had tears in her eyes.

"I am so sorry," she whispered, one tear spilling over. "Sorry that you are here, that you have to go through all of this, that you have been forced into this world so different from yours. Because now...now, Alethea...both worlds will want you...having known you. You got a taste of that this afternoon, didn't you?" Allee's eyes widened in surprise. She hadn't thought Espy had realized what her gaze had done.

"I heard...voices in my head, if that's what you mean," she replied. Espy choked back a sob, but more tears spilled over.

"That was only the beginning," she said. "Both of the worlds will be constantly fighting for you. You will not notice it at first, but as time goes on, the fight will get worse, for they know their time is running out. One day, Alethea, you will have to make a decision. *You will have to choose a world to belong to.* But for now, having seen both, you will belong to both. But the worlds do not like to share. And they don't do anything they don't like."

Allee was having trouble breathing; she felt like she was in deep, deep water and it was closing over her head. She, Alethea, was to be pitted against two entire worlds? Worlds that she could already feel fighting against each other inside of her, ripping her apart?

"I won't let them," Allee said defiantly, her voice resounding against the walls. "They will NOT control me." Espy smiled through her tears, and Allee felt her sense of impending doom lighten a bit.

"I am happy to hear that," Espy said. "I will try to help you, Alethea. I know…that…that sometimes, I do not act very responsibly, but I *will* help you. As much as I can." Espy shook her tears away and squared her shoulders. Allee smiled gratefully at her, but in her heart, she knew that she would have to rely on her own strength.

Espy rose and slid into one of the chairs at the table, laying a hand lightly on the top of Allee's head. They sat in silence for a while, each thinking her own thoughts. Then Allee thought of something.

"Is that why everyone's eyes go unfocused when I look into them? Because Earth wants them, too?" she asked. Espy did not answer right away; she seemed to be looking somewhere far in the distance.

"I think so," she finally replied. "But no one can explain all that a world does. They certainly don't react like that because they can tell who you really are just by looking in your eyes. You look the same, sound the same, and mostly act the same, even though there are subtle differences between us and you."

"So that's why the dresses don't fit!" Allee cried. Espy gave a tinkling laugh, like the sound of the glass beads in the doorway.

"That may very well be," she said. "I did have to adjust the pants for you. Do they work?"

"Yeah, they work great," Allee replied, looking down at her pajamas. "Do you have any more? I don't think they packed me any clothes." Espy looked startled.

"They didn't, did they?" she asked, her eyes narrowing. "I should have known. I will find you some. And I'll make sure Esendore realizes his negligence." Allee turned her head to hide her smile at the thought of Espy telling Esendore off. Her eyes came to rest on the blue clay pot, which reminded her of something.

"Espy, can I ask *you* something now?" she asked. Espy looked slightly surprised, but also pleased.

"I will do my best to answer anything you ask me," she replied.

"How do you see things in the bubbles? Do you use magic?" Espy looked bewildered.

"Mag-ik?" She clearly had never heard of the word.

"It's kind of...I don't know...a power you can use to do stuff," Allee said, trying to help. Espy shook her head forcefully.

"No," she said, her tone firm. "In this world, there is the power of good and the power of evil, and those who serve each of them. Nothing else." Allee tried to digest this new information.

"Everyone serves evil sometime," Allee said, voicing her thoughts aloud. "What about the power of forgiveness? Forgiveness can balance good and evil." Espy looked thoughtful.

"Yes, I suppose you are right," she replied. They both were silent again as they thought this over. A little of Allee's curiosity was satisfied, but not all of it.

"So, what else can you do with the bubbles? Other than seeing stuff?" she queried. Espy looked taken back.

"That's not enough for you?" she said. Allee blushed.

"I didn't mean that...I just...I was just wondering." Espy smiled.

"Yes, I understand. But I'm afraid I can't do much else with them. I have only been a true Effervescent for five years since my predecessor died. I still have much to learn, and I must teach myself. Even sending one to greet you sapped most of my strength. I should not have looked again, but Esendore was rather pathetic. But even if I was rested, I doubt I could have countered that...that...*witch woman*." She spit out the last words as if they were venom. Allee couldn't blame Espy. Her scream of pain was still fresh in her ears. Espy's reply had only made Allee think of more questions.

"The bubble was only sent to...to meet us?" she asked. "I thought it was a message of some kind, except I couldn't read it. I saw...flickers of light." Espy fell off her chair. Allee was too startled to offer assistance.

"What did you say?" Espy breathed, leaning in closer to Allee.

"I thought I saw...things...half-pictures, almost," she replied, absolutely bewildered. Espy sat back, a look of pure astonishment on her face.

"But this cannot be," she declared, "Only albinos, trained in the art, can see *anything*. There is no way—but maybe—yes, it could be possible..." she paused in her ramblings, and her eyes turned a feverish, bright blue. "Yes, yes it could happen, that could be why, oh, yes, yes, YES!" In an abrupt motion, she raised her hands above her head. Bubbles poured out of the jar behind Allee, who jumped and scrambled to her knees, thinking Espy had gone mad. Just as suddenly as they had appeared, all but one bubble evaporated. It was an electric blue, the same color as Espy's eyes. On impulse, Allee reached out and grabbed it. She heard Espy gasp in surprise, but Allee was too absorbed with the orb in her hands to care. The bubble tickled and Allee laughed with pleasure.

She peered into its depths, curious to what she would find. To her great surprise and delight, Allee was watching a silent movie. She could see herself and Ferdy throwing breadsticks at each other, then talking to Archibald, and then playing Deceit, but there was no sound during any of it. The picture show ended when the bubble started deflating, and Allee resurfaced from her vision, inhaling deeply when she realized she had forgotten to breathe.

"How long was I gone?" she asked Espy, trying to get her breath back. Espy was looking at her as if Allee had just given her the best gift of her life.

"You never left. It took all of ten seconds," she replied, her voice a pitch Allee had never heard before.

"Really?" she asked. "It felt much longer." Allee looked down at her hands and remembered how the bubble had felt resting there. She looked back up and grinned at Espy. "Can I do it again?" Espy's eyes bugged out of her head.

"Alethea, do you know what this means?" she asked, her whole body rigid with excitement. "If you can see into the bubbles, with absolutely no training, you just simply *must* become an Effervescent!

You are the one the craft has been waiting for; the one to restore our line!" Allee felt like laughing, but didn't.

"Yeah, right," she said. "Espy, if that was true I would have been born in *this* world, not mine. There is no use for such a talent on Earth."

"But that's why you *came*, Alethea, that's why you're here now! You have talent that belongs in this world. You need to be *here*. All we need to do is dye your hair and find you some suitable clothes, and you will be just as the other Effervescents before you."

"No, Espy," Allee said, putting as much force into her voice as possible. "You cannot make me something I am not. I am not meant for this world. You cannot change that. *I* will not change that." Espy looked at her long and hard and finally gave a deep sigh.

"You are right, Alethea," she confessed, her happiness evaporating and leaving the room cold. "You can't conform to be an Effervescent. You just have some of the qualities. You are still too different. I shouldn't have pressed you so hard. It's just so…so difficult…being the only one, doing everything alone. So…hard," her eyes filled with tears again. Allee moved her hand to pat her back, but the bubble was still clinging to it.

"Go put that in the pot," Espy said wearily. "It will be reborn that way." Allee did so and turned back to Espy, but the Effervescent was glaring moodily at the rug, absorbed in her own thoughts. Allee decided to leave before Espy came up with some other crazy idea.

"Goodnight, Espy," she said, edging toward the door.

"Night," Espy replied sulkily, still looking at the floor. Quietly, Allee slipped out into the dark passage.

Ferdy didn't mention moody when he described Espy, Allee thought as she walked back down the hall and entered her room. Now that she was warm again, her bed was, too. She lay down, thinking of what life would be like if she lived with Espy all the time. She shuddered at the very thought. *I have never been so glad not to be an albino* she thought. Then she laughed. *You idiot,* she scolded herself. *You've never been glad not to be an albino.* And with that thought, she fell asleep.

As Allee regained consciousness, she was aware of a funny noise. *It sounds like Arian when she stubs her toe,* she thought groggily. Suddenly, she sat bolt upright in bed, listening intently. The noise was a loud, persistent wailing, and it seemed to be coming from the hall. She jumped out of bed and grabbed for her t-shirt and jeans. Beside them lay a maroon button-up shirt and a pair of cream-colored pants. Allee silently thanked Espy, transferred the ruby, and donned the new clothes. Tying up her hair, she cautiously left the room.

The corridor was deserted, but the wailing noise was much louder. Allee was looking vainly for the source when Ferdy groped his way around the corner, obviously half asleep. Allee ran up to him.

"What's that noise?" she yelled, having difficulty in making herself heard over the racket. He stared at her blearily.

"Huh?" he asked.

"The noise!" she shouted. Ferdy shook his head to clear it and seemed to wake up a little more. They both listened intently for a moment, Allee fighting the urge to put her hands over her ears. Ferdy snorted and rolled his eyes.

"Oh, that's just Esendore," he said, disgustedly. "He's singing in the shower." Allee tried not to let her jaw drop. She had never heard *anyone* sing that badly. Before she could say anything else, Ferdy went up to the bathroom door.

"Oy!" he shouted. "Esendore! Could you bring it down a little?" Allee waited for a pause, but the wailing kept going.

"Don't think he can hear you," Allee said. Ferdy rolled his eyes again.

"Obviously." The singing upped a notch in volume, making Ferdy and Allee put their hands over their ears.

"Tell him to shut it!" she yelled.

"What?" Ferdy shouted.

"SHUT IT!" Allee bellowed, pounding on the door for emphasis. Abruptly, the noise stopped. Allee turned to Ferdy, aghast. He was laughing too hard to comfort her.

"You should see the look on your face!" he gasped, clutching his stomach. "Didn't know you had it in you, to tell the future King to shut it, did you?" Seeing her look, he calmed himself. "Don't worry. He'll think I said it. Thanks!" he shouted at the door. They heard a muffled reply from within, and Ferdy's face contorted as he tried to control his laughter. He turned back to Allee. "Come on, let's go get some breakfast." Allee followed him, forcing herself not to laugh.

Espy smiled cheerfully at them when they entered the kitchen.

"Good morning, sunshines," she sung out, scrambling to her feet. "What would you like to eat?"

"Whatever you got," Ferdy said, grumpy again. Allee suspected that he didn't like to be called "sunshine". Espy smiled at him again and started bringing out food, humming to herself.

Allee sat down and picked up the pitcher of juice, but dropped it with a clatter when she realized Gnarrish was behind it. His head and shoulders barely cleared the table. Allee gave him a weak smile.

"Good morning," she said courteously. He grunted in return. Allee noticed that he was only a quarter of the way through some dark liquid that was in his mug and guessed that he would be more awake when he finished. She was saved from making more conversation when Espy set a bowl in front of her.

"Boatel," she whispered, so that Allee would know what she was eating. Allee smiled her thanks.

"Would you like any, Gnarrish?" Espy asked the gnarf. Gnarrish jumped up from his chair in surprise.

"Gotta see to...zeorses," he mumbled, and left. Espy gazed after him fondly.

"He's very shy," she told Allee.

"Really?" Allee said, trying to act surprised. She thought she had a pretty good idea of Gnarrish's character. "That's strange," she continued, inspecting her bowl of oatmeal stuff. "When I first met him, he didn't even wait to introduce himself before he started talking to me." Ferdy smothered a laugh in his hand, but Espy didn't catch what she meant.

"He's different with different people," she said, absentmindedly. Then she noticed Allee was wearing the new outfit. "You look nice in those clothes."

"They fit fine, too," Allee replied. "Thank-you for remembering."

"And I'll make sure you're not forgotten in the future," Espy promised. "Mark my words." Right on cue, Esendore strode in, his hair still damp.

"Morning all," he said, pecking Espy on the cheek. She glared at him, but he didn't notice. Oblivious, he sat down and pulled over a bowl of fruit. Ferdy kept sending Allee funny looks and chuckling into his juice, but Allee ignored him. She was too busy watching Espy trying to make Esendore notice she was mad at him. But Esendore was too absorbed in his breakfast.

"Has Gnarrish gone to ready the zeorses?" he asked between bites.

"Yeah, I think that's what he said," Ferdy replied. He, too, had picked up on Espy's mood and was watching her intently.

"Wonderful," Esendore continued, "We can leave right after breakfast then." Espy's aloofness vanished.

"So soon?" she asked, her surprise evident in her voice. "I thought...I was hoping...that you would stay longer than one night." Her voice had taken on a wheedling tone and her lower lip was half-sticking out. Esendore sighed, knowing he was in for a struggle. Ferdy perked up, eager for a fight. Allee tried to ignore them and eat her breakfast.

"Espy," Esendore began, his voice just as wheedling, "I will try as hard as I can to back as soon as possible. And when I do return, I will spend a week here. I promise." Espy's pout broke into a dazzling smile.

"I will eagerly await the fulfillment of that promise," she said. Esendore drained the rest of his drink and stood up.

"Well, we should be ready to leave then. No one needs to repack; we didn't unpack anything."

"Poor Allee didn't even get a chance to pack in the first place," Espy said, her voice cold. Esendore turned to her, bewildered.

"What do you mean? We brought ample cooking supplies for her and a tentopy." Espy seemed to expand.

"What, and did you think for her to go naked?" she half-shouted. Esendore looked even more puzzled.

"But she has clothes, didn't you notice? A purple shirt, and—" He turned to Allee for confirmation, and jumped. "Where did you get those?" he asked, gesturing at her new garments. Espy looked about to burst. Ferdy was furiously nodding his head towards the door, and Allee quickly followed him out, Espy's shouts echoing behind them.

They walked until Ferdy was sure that they were safe from flying objects.

"You really know how to start a row," he complimented Allee. She rolled her eyes.

"A compliment from the master. Nice." He grinned at her.

"Yeah, I get yelled at a lot, but that makes it even sweeter when it's not me." Allee laughed, but didn't reply.

Gnarrish was leading the zeorses into the yard when they left the caves. Ferdy grabbed Lunar's reins, and Allee reached apprehensively for Dazzle's. The zeorse tossed her head, and Allee's heart rose in panic. She clung tighter to the headstall.

"Please don't do that," she whispered to her mount. Dazzle calmed down, and Allee stroked her neck. She was more nervous about staying on her zeorse than the actual journey ahead.

Majesty nickered, and Esendore appeared in the mouth of the cave, looking sheepish and laden with saddlebags. Espy followed, beaming with triumph. In one quick movement, Esendore strode to Allee's side.

"My sincerest apologies, Alethea," he started, looking just as nervous as she felt. "In my hurry to start our journey, I overlooked some things." Espy cleared her throat. "Many things," Esendore hurried on. "Please forgive me." Allee knew that he had had no part in the packing and had a strong suspicion that Ferdy or Gnarrish had left her stuff out on purpose.

"I forgive you, Your Highness," Allee said, her mind racing to find a suitable reply. "Sometimes our concern for...our...loved ones overshadows everything else." Esendore smiled gratefully at her, and Allee felt herself smiling back at him, but behind the smile she was still trying to decide if she liked him or not. He looked about to say something else, but just nodded and turned to say farewell to Espy. Allee felt someone staring at her and looked up to see Ferdy, his eyes almost bugging out of his head.

"How do you think of stuff like that so fast?" he asked, his voice half-scornful, half awed. Allee pulled herself into the saddle, thinking of a reply.

"Maybe because I don't spend all of my time thinking up horrid schemes to harass people," she said.

"I don't think about schemes all the time," Ferdy protested. "I think about food, too." Allee covered her face with her hands.

"You're hopeless," she told him. He just grinned at her.

Esendore finally left Espy and mounted Majesty. Allee could tell Espy was trying very hard not to cry.

"Oh, come on," Allee heard Ferdy say under his breath, then louder, "We'll be back, Espy."

"With Dariel," Esendore added.

"Yes, I know," Espy admitted, blowing her nose in a handkerchief. "But it gets so lonely here by myself."

"Bubbles not good enough company?" Ferdy muttered. Allee felt sorry for Espy.

"Can it, Ferdy," she warned. His eyebrows rose in surprise.

"How many different ways can you say 'be quiet'?" Allee ignored him and nudged Dazzle up to give Espy a one armed hug.

"Good-luck," Espy said. Allee let go, but Espy grabbed her arm again and whispered something else. "It would not be a wise idea to get yourself killed, Alethea. The effects on both our worlds would be disastrous."

Allee sat up very straight in the saddle, half in shock and half in disbelief. Espy smiled winningly at her, as if she had just told her to enjoy the scenery. Allee stared at the Effervescent, lost for words. No one had ever told her something so disturbing in her entire life. Allee shook her head in bewilderment and pushed Espy's words out of her mind. Numbly, she pulled back so Ferdy could ride up. Not to be outdone by Allee, he gripped Lunar with his knees and gave his sister a two-armed embrace.

"Take care," she said, tears glittering in her eyes again. Allee wished that they would just hurry up and leave. Espy was being much too dramatic. Allee hoped that the "warning" was also part of Espy's theatrics. But deep down, she had a feeling that Espy was serious. As if Esendore had heard Allee's thoughts, he called out for them to leave.

"Good-bye, Espy! We'll be back!" he shouted, kicking Majesty into a canter. Ferdy went next and Allee clung on as Dazzle followed the others. Gnarrish brought up the rear.

"Good-bye, Lady!" he called over his shoulder, his words clearer than Allee had ever heard before. She had no time to say another good-bye to Espy herself, for the trees closed around them and the Effervescent disappeared from view.

Although they were riding fast and hard, and Allee was very busy hanging on, she could sense that Esendore was disturbed about something. Her suspicion was confirmed when he pulled up Majesty and turned around.

"Why does she have to do that every single time?" he asked, exasperated. Ferdy looked about to say something, but Allee glared at him, and he didn't. Esendore ran his fingers through his hair. "We need something to occupy her," he said, almost to himself. "Something big...that would take a long time."

"I noticed that Espy's horse needs shoeing, Sire," Gnarrish suggested. Esendore nodded, still distracted.

"Yes," he agreed, "I'll send a messenger for Roeland to do that, I don't trust the village blacksmith. But shoeing is not a big enough project." He looked to the sky as if for an answer, and scowled. "Too bright out here," he grumbled, shading his eyes. "I'm still used to the caves." Suddenly, Allee had an idea.

"Skylights," she blurted. Esendore turned to stare at her quizzically.

"What do you mean, Alethea?" he questioned. Allee hurried to explain herself.

"The caves were very dark, like you said, Your Highness. Couldn't you send a group of masons from the pastle to carve skylights for Espy?" Esendore looked at her thoughtfully.

"Why, yes," he said, "That would be perfect." He warmed to the idea as he talked. "Lots of people, new messes for her to clean up, and we can space it out...the first couple could take at least two weeks..." he paused for a moment, calculating the possibilities. He looked up from his fingers to beam at Allee. "Very good, Alethea. I'll ride to the village to send a messenger right away. Thank-you very much." Allee blushed.

"Your welcome, Your Highness." Esendore frowned.

"Now, now, if I can call you Alethea you can certainly call me Esendore." Allee was extremely taken back with this offer, but she replied nonetheless.

"Of course, Esendore." He smiled at her again.

"That's better," he said, wheeling Majesty around. "I'll catch up with you later," he called over his shoulder, and he and Majesty galloped off in the direction of the village.

"Of course, Esendore," Ferdy mimicked, pulling up beside Allee. "Oh, puh-lease." Allee felt her temper flare.

"Well, at least I make an effort to be respectful," she said hotly.

"Being disrespectful is still better than acting like a—"

"Shouldn't we be continuing?" Gnarrish interrupted. Ferdy and Allee both looked at him slightly abashed.

"Of course," Ferdy said. "After you," he told Allee. Allee wanted Ferdy where she could see him.

"Age before beauty," she said sweetly, giving him a half bow in the saddle. He gave her a forced smile.

"Ladies first," he said, just as sweetly. Allee opened her mouth to retort, but Gnarrish interceded again.

"I will lead," he volunteered, "And Ferdinand will follow to show me the way." Allee smiled gratefully at him and pretended to be very interested in some pinkish yellow flowers to the left of the road as Ferdy, muttering, fell into line.

Esendore rejoined them an hour later looking hot and frustrated.

"Peasants," he spat out, before they could ask. "They seem to think that everybody is out to get them, *especially* those in authority. I had to *pay* them to send a messenger to Goldham; they wouldn't even listen to a royal order! Disgraceful." He shook his head in disgust.

"Good for them," Ferdy said under his breath. Allee felt the same way, but didn't show it. She still wasn't sure if she liked the Crown Prince.

Soon after Esendore returned, they stopped for lunch beside a little stream. Much to Allee's relief, she wasn't expected to cook at lunchtimes.

"I figure," Esendore said, lounging by the stream and gnawing on his dried meat and travel biscuit, "that if we have a short, simple lunch, then we can have a longer supper, with a fire and hot food. Will that work for you, Alethea?" Allee had no idea, but she nodded agreeably.

"Sounds great," she said, hoping that her voice didn't sound as weak as her confidence in herself to produce edible food over a campfire. From the way Ferdy was looking at her, Allee knew he had his doubts, too. Squaring her shoulders, she decided that even if her food wasn't edible, she would still make him eat it.

After another two hours in the saddle, Allee was bored out of her skull. She did not have to worry about falling off of Dazzle since they were only going at a walking pace because of the thick trees and untended road, and she was ready for something new to occupy her. To make matters worse, the scenery hadn't changed for the last ten miles. Even the birds were boring, and Allee had just seen most of them for the first time. She tried to braid Dazzle's mane, but the constant bouncing and jostling undid her efforts as fast as she could accomplish them. She noticed Gnarrish almost riding abreast of her and decided to talk to him.

"What's your zeorse's name?" she asked politely, admiring the small animal's white and roan stripes. Gnarrish jumped at her voice and avoided eye contact. Allee was surprised; she had expected him to be pleased to talk about his mount. Instead, he blushed a deep red.

"Ruby," he mumbled, and rode up to Esendore's side. Allee stared after him, open-mouthed.

"That's just too weird," Ferdy said, riding up beside her. "The first time you try to be friendly it has to be about a touchy subject."

"It's not my fault," Allee protested. "How was I supposed to know his zeorse's name is Ruby?" Ferdy laughed.

"That's what makes it funny."

"It's not fair," Allee pouted. "He adores you, and you're always harassing him. He won't even give me a chance." Ferdy snorted.

"He didn't let me decide either. He just forced himself on me." Allee raised her eyebrows.

"What is that supposed to mean?" Ferdy shrugged.

"I've know Gnarrish for what seems like forever," he said slowly, obviously getting ready to tell a story. Allee gave an inward sigh. She was beginning to notice that Ferdy had a touch for theatrics, too. "The King was throwing this huge dinner for my fourth birthday, he still liked me then, and right when we were about to cut the cake, Gnarrish charged in demanding approval to bind himself to me so that he could serve me for the rest of his life."

"No way," Allee breathed, not believing Ferdy's story one bit. "Gnarrish wouldn't do that." Ferdy nodded.

"He did. He's very bold when he wants to be. He claimed that he had had a dream where he had been told that to find his destiny, he would have to lay it in the hand of another's. So, he wakes up, and thinks, "What better person than the Prince?" And he treks off from his village in the middle of the night, travels for weeks to get to

Goldham, sneaks in on a food cart, and demands to be sworn into the Prince's service. And he was only sixteen."

"Wow," Allee said, amazed. "That's pretty impressive." Ferdy shrugged.

"I suppose," he agreed. "But gnarfs are funny people. They work *with* humans, if they ever get close to them, not *for* humans. They're too proud. But, they are also unbelievably loyal. So it's a big honor if one of them wants to serve you. But Gnarrish was still taking a risk. You don't tell the King to do anything, especially regarding his family. I bet if Gnarrish had wanted Esendore the King would have thrown him out, or worse. He was lucky he chose me. Anyway, the King slapped Gnarrish with the royal enigma, told him to do whatever he pleased with me, and he's been the only one to put up with me since." Ferdy gazed fondly at the back of Gnarrish's head.

Allee turned her eyes to the gnarf, too, barely believing Ferdy's story. It seemed so unlikely, yet she knew that Gnarrish was fearsome when fired up about something. She wanted to pump Ferdy for more information, but Esendore called for him to bring the map, and Ferdy rode ahead. With a sigh, Allee went back to braiding Dazzle's mane.

She was thrilled when the landscape finally changed to show a broad valley with a river running though it. Her pleasure soon ended when she realized that there weren't any bridges.

"How are we going to cross?" she asked Esendore, dismayed. She hadn't planned on getting wet. Esendore was also looking troubled.

"It's a little high after last night's rain," he replied, studying the rushing water. "But it's only four or five feet deep here, so I guess we'll be able to ford it without any problem." Ferdy looked at the water distastefully.

"How wet am I going to get?" he asked, wrinkling his nose. Esendore suddenly became surer of himself.

"Probably only a little, Ferdinand, and I told you when we started out that this journey wouldn't be easy. You'll soon dry again." He nudged Majesty into the water, which only came up to the zeorse's chest. Majesty snorted, but then started swimming calmly. Esendore looked back and gave a cheerful wave. Ferdy watched him with narrowed eyes.

"Ouch," Allee teased, enjoying herself immensely. In answer, Ferdy kicked Lunar into the water, splashing both Gnarrish and Allee with the spray. Allee spluttered angrily.

"Don't worry," Gnarrish assured, urging Ruby to follow. "The water will cool him off." Allee was so pleased that he had spoken to her that she instantly forgot her irritation with Ferdy. She smiled and followed him into the water.

But she was soon faced with another problem. The saddlebags that Espy had given her were made of light canvas and were definitely not waterproof.

"What will I do with my bags?" she shouted across the river, where the rest had already gathered. Esendore's face fell. He had received a lot of trouble from those bags and was reluctant to see them come to harm.

"Can you carry them above your head?" he yelled. Allee was worried that she would fall off, but she did as he said, wrapping a strap around each hand.

"What about the third one?" she shouted.

"Put it in your teeth!" Ferdy joked. Allee had had enough of Ferdy's jokes for one day. Defiantly, she unbuckled the last saddlebag and put the strap firmly in her teeth. Kicking Dazzle forward, she raised her head high so that the water wouldn't touch any part of her bag. The shock as the cold water touched her legs almost made her drop it, but she strengthened her resolve and urged Dazzle to go faster. As soon as she was on the other side, she started buckling the bags back onto her saddle. And even though it tasted horrible and her jaw ached, she fastened the one in her mouth last. When she was finished, she lifted her head to smile at her companions, but she stopped short at the looks they were giving her.

"I was joking," Ferdy said faintly.

Allee's mouth hurt too badly to reply, so she just gave him a forced smile. Esendore looked from Allee to his brother and cleared his throat.

"We'll...we'll be carrying on then," he said. Allee hid a real smile and fell into place at the back of the line.

The sky was beginning to grow dark when they came to the next spring some three hours later. Esendore stopped and looked around, appraising it.

"We will camp here tonight," he announced. He paused, as if waiting for someone to start telling him what to do. When nobody did, he cleared his throat.

"We'll need a fire," he said, almost hesitantly, but warmed to the idea as he thought about it. "Gnarrish, you can do that. Allee will help you. Ferdinand, you and I will care for the zeorses, and then set up the tentopies." He hesitated again, waiting for confirmation. Allee wondered if either of the Princes had slept outdoors in their lives.

"Sounds good to me, Your Highness," Gnarrish said, sliding off Ruby. Ferdy looked startled.

"I'm supposed to help, too?" he asked. Esendore dropped to the ground and began pulling off Majesty's saddle.

"That is the general idea," he said, his voice clipped. Ferdy dismounted and turned around to argue. Before he could open his mouth, Esendore shoved the saddle at him.

"Put that over there," he commanded, pointing to where Gnarrish had deposited his. Grumbling, Ferdy complied.

Allee slipped off Dazzle, trying not to groan. She had barely ridden a horse for a half an hour at a time, and now she had put in two days of hard riding. Her head pounded whenever she took a step. *I'll get used to it*, she assured herself. Stiffly, she began to look at what she had to cook with.

She found three skillets, a mixing bowl, two pots, a box of every utensil she had ever used in the kitchen, plus some she hadn't, and a box of plates and cups in just one saddlebag. She looked at the strange utensils in dismay. Exactly what kind of food were they expecting her to make? Gourmet? The other two bags didn't at all reassure her. One held two loaves of *real* bread, not hardtack, along with three wheels of cheese, a sack of potato-like things, a wooden box with eggs packed in saw dust, and a hind of dried meat. The other bag was devoted entirely to seasonings and baking goods.

"Baking powder?" Allee asked herself, pulling the small jar out of the bag. "What do they want from me, a cake?" Shaking her head, she put the container back and drew out a bottle of yellow liquid. It was cooking oil. Allee could have kissed it. It would make her job much easier. Her exploring was interrupted by a cough from Gnarrish. He was holding something in his hand.

"Here," he said. Allee was too surprised to look at what he was offering her and instinctively held out her hands. The bloody carcass of a squirrel-rabbit, cleaned and gutted, dropped into them. Allee swallowed hard; she had never cooked wild game before. Gnarrish frowned at the look on her face.

"It's a squirbit," he said. Allee was too confused to reply. Where in the world had he found this? He didn't appear to carry any weapons and he certainly hadn't had any time to set traps. They had only been here twenty minutes.

"Thanks," Allee said weakly, deciding not to pursue the matter. "It looks…delicious." He nodded at her solemnly and turned away. From behind them came several loud oaths as Esendore tried to get a tentopy to stay upright. Allee suddenly realized how grateful she was that Gnarrish was traveling with them.

"I'm glad you came," she blurted out. Gnarrish turned to look at her in surprise. "I don't know how I could survive otherwise," she explained, watching the two Princes. "We need to have *someone* who knows what he's doing."

"You don't know what you're doing?" he asked, seeming genuinely surprised. Allee grinned at him.

"You are looking at the biggest faker of all time," she boasted. They stared at each other for a moment and then burst out laughing.

"Keep up the good work," he told her, and still chuckling, he went to help the Princes.

Allee squeezed her eyes shut and willed the squirbit to cook itself. When it didn't, she swallowed hard and began cutting it into smaller pieces, trying very hard not to throw up.

An hour later the squirbit actually looked edible, and Allee was extremely pleased with her hash browns, made from the potatams, as she found the knobby brown roots to be called. She was also very tired, not only from the work she had had to put into the meal, but Ferdy had spent the past half-hour begging her to hurry up. She wished Esendore would turn the other way so she could hit him, but the chance never arose.

Holding her breath, she dished the food onto the plates and apprehensively waited for their reaction. Ferdy sniffed at his disdainfully.

"Here it goes," he said, and forked a piece of squirbit into his mouth. Suddenly, his body went rigid and his eyes rolled back in his head. As the other three watched in horror, he fell off his log and collapsed on the ground. Allee shrieked and felt her legs give out. She knelt beside Ferdy, her hands over her mouth.

"Allee, you killed him!" Esendore said hoarsely. Allee turned to look at him, stunned, and saw his face twitch to hide a smile. She turned back to Ferdy to see he was shaking with withheld laughter. Behind her, she could hear Gnarrish choking.

"You guys!" she yelled as Ferdy rolled on the ground clutching his side. Esendore had tears running down his face.

"You should have seen your face!" Ferdy gasped, trying to rise to a kneeling position. Allee didn't know whether to laugh or cry.

"You scared me!" she accused, poking Ferdy. He just laughed harder.

"I couldn't resist!" he said, sitting up and brushing himself off.

"Did it really taste bad?" Allee asked. Esendore wiped the tears off his face.

"No, no," he laughed. "It's great. Get off the ground and eat it before it gets cold," he finished, nudging Ferdy with his toe. Gnarrish was alternately wiping his eyes and chewing on his hash browns. Ferdy pulled himself onto his log, still shaking with laughter. Esendore handed him his plate, and Ferdy looked at it with a gleam in his eye.

"Don't you dare pull anything else," Allee warned. Ferdy flashed her an evil grin, but meekly began to eat his supper.

By the time they had finished, the light had completely faded, and the first stars were beginning to come out. Allee was not looking forward to cleaning up in the dark, but she resignedly picked up the cloth and soap and knelt beside the stream. To her great surprise, Gnarrish knelt beside her.

"If you wash, I'll dry and put away," he offered. Allee looked at him with relief.

"You would really do that?" He chuckled.

"The only other thing I have to do is tuck Ferdy in. And that only takes a couple of minutes. Besides, you need all the help you can get." He inclined his head at Esendore and Ferdy, who were squabbling over who had to sleep in the most crooked tentopy.

"I won't argue with you there," Allee said, shaking her head. Gnarrish laughed and reached out to take the dish she was holding. When they had finished, the debate had almost scaled into a two-man riot. To make them shut up, Allee quickly grabbed her bags and crawled into the offending tentopy. It took them a minute to notice.

"Alethea, come out of there!" Esendore called. "Ferdy can sleep in there, he won't mind!"

"Speak for yourself!" Ferdy protested. "Good-night, Allee, sweet dreams!" Allee saw his silhouette start walking away, but Esendore grabbed his arm.

"We can't let her sleep in there, what happens if it falls on her?" he hissed.

"If it's going to fall on me then I am *definitely* not sleeping in there! It's your fault it's crooked anyway!"

"You sat on the pole!"

"Are you—" Allee began feigning loud snores. Esendore cuffed Ferdy, who shut his mouth with a snap.

"Shhh! She's trying to sleep!" Esendore scolded.

"You're hopeless!" Ferdy snapped, and walked away. A few moments later Allee heard the sound of a tent closing, and then all was silent. Esendore remained standing by Allee's tentopy for a minute longer, his head hanging dejectedly.

"Why can't I do anything right?" Allee heard him murmur. She thought about saying something to comfort him, but he shook his head and walked away.

Allee sighed and rolled over, clutching the ruby tightly. She wished that she understood Ferdy's moods more, and Esendore's personality. Both seemed to be beyond her comprehension. *At least Gnarrish is nice*, she thought with a yawn. The ruby didn't sing to her, but it's warmth and reassurance in her hand was enough to put her to sleep.

Allee was flying over a forest of silver trees. She usually hated flying dreams because she always ended up falling, but the strong breeze that was carrying her gave her reassurance. By the time she began to descend, she was even enjoying herself.

    Gently, the breeze put her down on the floor of a clearing flooded with a strange silver light. Allee looked around in amazement, marveling at the hugeness of a tree trunk at her side. She inhaled deeply, reveling in the sweet scent of a bright pink flower. The whole place was so beautiful that she laughed pleasure. Her laugh grew and grew, until the entire clearing seemed to be made of purely of laughter and light. Then Allee realized that it was full of people laughing along with her.

    She took a step back in surprise. The strange beings were extremely tall and each held themselves with an eerily fluid grace, their misty gowns shimmering in every color imaginable and outlining every curve of their perfectly shaped bodies. Allee tried in vain to see their faces, but they, too, were veiled in mist.

    "Who are you?" she cried. Suddenly, the tallest of the beings stepped forward, throwing off her veil to reveal the face of the most breathtakingly beautiful woman Allee had ever seen. Deep green eyes gazed at Allee from a face so perfectly shaped it seemed to be cut out of marble. Golden strawberry blonde hair rimmed the perfect face and rippled down the back of the dark green mist the woman wore as a dress. It stopped just inches from the ground carpeted in silver petals. Allee was too much in awe to speak.

    "Welcome, Alethea," the woman whispered, but the voice was so powerful that it resonated in Allee's bones. Allee finally found her tongue.

    "Are you an angel?" she breathed, unable to take her eyes off the woman's face. The woman laughed, and Allee felt that there would never be cloud or shadow in the world again. She found herself smiling in return.

    "Of sorts," the woman said, her amusement plain in her voice. "I am a guardian, if that's what you mean. I am called Aeyr." Allee was overwhelmed with a feeling so powerful that it seemed to her that the entire world was singing in joy. The feeling could not diminish her curiosity, but it sent her into such a deep state of amazement that she was too shy to voice her many questions. Aeyr gave her a deep, piercing look.

"You are wondering why you are here," she said. Without the laughter, her voice throbbed painfully in Allee's ears. Allee was suddenly very afraid. She wanted her thoughts to be her own and was still angry at the voice that had mocked her so.

"Stay out of my head!" she demanded, backing up until her back rested against a tree. She glared at Aeyr fiercely. "I won't do it! I won't listen to that voice!" Aeyr took a step forward, her eyebrows furrowed in worry.

"And that is exactly what I want you to do," she assured, kneeling and taking Allee's hand. Her eyes were now level with Allee's own. Against her will, Allee felt the anger ebb out of her, and she realized that this woman would never hurt her like the voice had.

"I'm sorry," she whispered, dropping her head. Aeyr lifted it back up again.

"There is no need for you to apologize," she said. "You have been through too much not to be wary. Do not be afraid of what you heard, Alethea. The worlds can do nothing to hurt you if you refuse to let them." Her eyes, clear and intensely focused, guaranteed Allee that her words were true, and for the first time since Allee had come to Betwix, she was free of doubt. Aeyr smiled and Allee felt the clearing brighten.

"I am not afraid," she said, boldly. Aeyr's smile grew larger.

"But you were," she reminded Allee, her tone kind. "I should have explained myself sooner. I wish to help you, Alethea, not frighten you," she continued, her eyes serious. "The Effervescent's "warning" has already confused you enough." She shook her head, making Allee shiver. Aeyr noticed and was quick to smile again. "She was acting in the best way she saw fit, but her warming was not worded how I would have liked. Though I hardly did better." She paused again, her face darkening, making the whole world dark and gloomy. "I daresay my messages just frustrated you, and I must admit they did not help you the way I thought they would." Allee realized what Aeyr meant.

"You were the rock!" she accused, feeling betrayed. But then she was overjoyed. "Then you can take me home!" she cried, her heart leaping within her. But instead of sharing her joy, Aeyr grimaced. Allee's happiness went cold.

"Do you really want to go home, Alethea?" Aeyr asked, her voice full of pain. Allee opened her mouth to reply, but then stopped. She had felt a variety of emotions in the past four days, but regret had never been one of them. *Did* she want to go home? Did she really want to leave and never find out what had happened to Dariel? Did she want to go home and never get to know Esendore better? She would never have to put up with Ferdy again, but he really wasn't so bad. Did she truly want to return to all that was familiar and always wonder what she had missed? Did she want to *give up*?

"No," she said, the firmness in her voice even surprising herself. "I am going to finish this out, to whatever end." Ayer's smile covered her entire face, and Allee's heart sang with joy. Then she remembered something.

"You haven't told me why I am in this dream place," she reminded the fairy-angel.

"But I did," Aeyr replied, humor in her voice. "You are here so that I can offer my help. Will you take it?" Her voice grew in intensity until Allee's hands were halfway to her ears before she could stop herself.

"I will not have some one else do this task for me," she said, stubbornly.

"I doubt it not!" Aeyr exclaimed. "For you will have it no other way. I do not offer to do this for you; I offer to help you. Will you take it?" she asked again. Allee raised her head to meet Aeyr's eyes.

"Gratefully, I will," she said, feeling a little foolish. Aeyr laughed.

"Finally we are getting somewhere!" she cried. "It was your stubbornness that got you here, and who knows where it will take you in the end! I know nothing of your future, Alethea," Aeyr continued, her tone softer, "But I do know one thing. Stubborn people do not fall out of the sky for no reason." Allee was so startled by this response that she could not speak. Aeyr laughed at the look on her face.

"Come," she said, laying an arm around Allee's shoulders, which felt like a sunbeam on a cold day. "I have some people I would like you to meet." She led Allee over the velvet-soft grass until they were directly in front of the crowd of shimmering fire people.

"These are my students," Aeyr explained, gesturing to them. "Someday, they shall also be guardians, but they are in need of experience. I was hoping you would help me give it to them, for it will also benefit you."

"Anything," Allee said, eager to please the angel. Aeyr smiled and lifted up one of her lily-white hands. As one, the company stood up from the stone bench they had been sitting on, and Aeyr began calling names.

"Corucoa! Albaus! Scintilla, Ricolas, and Stellansas!" Five women stepped down from the platform, removing their veils as they did so.

Before Allee could get a closer look at their faces, they vanished. She spun around wildly, looking for them. With a start, she realized they were flitting around her head, shrunk to barely a centimeter in height. Instinctively, she held out her forefinger. Elegantly, the fairy people landed on it. Their beautiful faces beamed at Allee, each highlighted by a different color of shimmer.

"Hello, Alethea!" they chorused, smiling broadly. Allee found herself smiling back.

"Hello," she replied, somewhat hesitantly.

"We get to live in you nose!" one shouted. Allee looked at them in disbelief.

"My nose?" she repeated, and looked up at Aeyr for clarification. Aeyr nodded, and Allee looked back down, bewildered. "Won't that be um...uncomfortable?"

"We will make a place for ourselves," one assured her.

"It will be an adventure!" another said, giggling. Allee shivered with what she thought was excitement, but then she realized that she was freezing cold and looked down at her body. Instead of her pajamas, she was looking at blue shimmers.

"Wow," she said softly. The fairy-people giggled noisily. Allee looked to Aeyr for reassurance.

"They will stay with you," she said, a smile playing on her lips as she watched Allee come to terms with the idea of a bunch of little people living in her nose, "and watch and listen for things that they can help you with." With her words, the little people vanished again.

"What things?" Allee asked, vaguely aware that she was moving backwards.

"Your fight is also ours, Alethea," Aeyr called after her, "For you see, we are guardians of the good and of the light."

"But what does that *mean*?" Allee asked, struggling to make herself stop. In reply, Aeyr lifted her hand in farewell. Try as she might to stay awake, Allee felt herself sinking back into sleep.

Chapter 6

Getting Wet Behind the Ears

"Allee! Allee, Allee, All-ee!" The voice sounded like it was calling her from far away. Allee cracked open an eye to see Ferdy leering at her from the open tent flap.

"Good morning, darling," he said sweetly. "Did you sleep well?"

"GET OUT!" Allee demanded, looking for something to throw at him. She sat up, her tangled hair falling over her face.

"AAAHHH!" Ferdy screeched, giving a mock scream. "It's the man-eating hairball! Everybody RUN!" He pulled his head out of the tent to avoid the shoe Allee threw at him, and continued screaming.

"Go jump off a cliff!" she shouted, angrier than she had ever been in her life.

"Temper, temper," he replied. Still laughing, he walked away. Fuming, Allee hurriedly got dressed, stowing the ruby safely in her pocket, and pulled her hair into the strictest bun she could manage. Quickly, she threw her possessions back in her saddlebags. After retrieving her shoe, she left the tent.

Luckily for him, Ferdy wasn't in sight. Allee began to feel better as she watched the sun peek over the trees, searing the low-lying clouds with orange and pink. She turned her face gladly to it and the warmth burned away all traces of her anger. She gazed in wonder at the appearance of the forest. Each leaf was outlined in light, and Allee almost felt like she heard them singing.

She stopped dead in her tracks. She *did* hear singing. It was like she had a song stuck in her head, but not quite. She just was trying to figure out what tune the song was when she heard a tiny sigh.

"Warm," said a little voice inside her head. Allee started, caught her foot on a tree branch, and fell over, the events of her dream flooding over her. The fairies gave several cries of dismay. Allee sat up and looked cross-eyed at her nose.

"Don't *do* that," she groaned. "You scared me."

"Sorry," said another voice. "We won't do it again."

"We just wanted to share the day with you," said a third voice. Allee was touched with their concern and started to smile.

"Good morning?" said the first voice, hesitantly. Allee laughed.

"Good morning," she replied, and then realized what a fool she must look, talking to her nose. The apologetic voice also seemed to realize the absurdity of the situation.

"Don't worry," she said, "We won't bother you. Have a nice day."

"We can't even talk to her?" the first voice protested. Allee smiled.

"You can tell me good morning, if you want to," she offered.

"I will," the voice promised, and Allee heard them all giggle. Laughing along with them, she got to her feet.

Gnarrish, who had already started the fire, was now supervising the dismantling of the tentopies. Allee hurried to get breakfast started.

The preparation was much quicker this time; she had the bacon (or what she thought was bacon) and eggs ready by the time the tentopies had all been packed away. The meal itself was eaten in total silence. Esendore kept glowering at Ferdy, who had caused an entire tentopy to collapse on him. Ferdy pretended to be nonplussed, but he ate quickly and left, claiming that he had to make sure he hadn't forgotten anything. Esendore soon followed him.

Gnarrish helped Allee with the dishes again, and Esendore forgave Ferdy when he figured out how to roll the tentopies up so that they would fit in the saddlebags. Allee carefully packed all the foodstuffs back in her bags, and Gnarrish put out the fire. Soon all that was left to do was to saddle the zeorses, who were pawing the ground in readiness to go. Allee was more than a little apprehensive about putting on Dazzle's saddle, and her arms were so sore she could barely move, but everything went fine until she tried to fasten the cinch. She struggled with it for ten minutes and was about ready to give up when suddenly big hands closed over her own.

"Here," Esendore's voice said in her ear. "Do it like this." He guided her fingers and the cinch buckled easily.

"Th-thank you," she stammered, shying away from him. For some reason, his closeness unnerved her. He patted Dazzle's flank, smiling at Allee.

"Your welcome," he replied, his face kind. He turned away, but then turned back. "One more thing," he said, as an afterthought. "The way you mount. You're being much too hard on yourself. Don't just fall into the saddle—sit down in the saddle. Like so." He sprang nimbly into Majesty's saddle to demonstrate. Allee copied his movements and was able to mount much more easily. She surveyed the ground happily.

"Thank you again," she said, beaming at Esendore. He grinned back.

"This way it's a lot easier for both of us," he said. "Easier for you because you don't hurt yourself, and easier for me, because then I don't have to worry about you falling off." He smiled again and urged Majesty over to where Ferdy was looking at the map.

Allee stared after him, puzzled. She hadn't realized that he watched her and even worried about her. A warm, fuzzy feeling spread through her at the very thought. She felt protected, even wanted. *It's just because he doesn't want to cook his own food*, she told herself. But another part of her wasn't so sure. Before she could consider the matter more, Esendore called for them to begin, and she nudged Dazzle into her place behind Ruby.

Within an hour on the trail, Allee was soaked in sweat. She guessed it only to be about nine o' clock, but the sun beat down between the trees with a painful intensity. The heat hadn't been so bad yesterday because of the lingering cool after the storm. Allee lifted her face from the saddle, hoping for a cool breeze. All she got was a bug in her nose and shrieks from the fairies. She calmed them down and made another swipe at an insect that kept buzzing around her face. All kinds of insects were swarming around her, but she didn't have the slightest wish to know what kind they were.

The group stopped every time they reached a stream, for the horses suffered as much from the heat, if not more, than their riders. Gnarrish seemed to be taking the heat particularly hard. Allee watched half in amusement, half in longing as he dunked his head under the icy cold water. She shivered in spite of herself. She wasn't that hot yet. At their third stop, they ate lunch. Nobody talked much; they were too busy trying to keep breathing.

As the others were remounting, Allee stooped and picked up a couple of handfuls of the white rocks at the bottom of the streambed, hoping to find some way to amuse herself. At the end of an hour back on the trail, she had it. Extremely pleased with herself, she edged Dazzle over to Ferdy. He looked at her bleary-eyed.

"Have you come to add to my misery?" he panted. Allee ignored him, desperate for entertainment.

"I have a game," she announced. He tried to look nonchalant, but Allee could see that he perked up a little.

"Joy. And what would that be?" Allee was too hot to be annoyed. She took the rock out of her pocket.

"I'll say a target and then try to hit it. If I do, you have to hit it. If I miss, then it's your turn to pick. And, just to make it interesting, every time you miss a target your opponent has chosen, you have to give them another one of your rocks. The first person that is out of rocks at the end of the game loses. Okay?" Ferdy looked at her with glazed eyes, and Allee could see his hot and tired mind trying to work out what she had just said. She sighed and opened her mouth to repeat the instructions.

"Yeah, yeah, I get it," he interrupted. "Give me some rocks." Allee split the pile evenly and picked her target.

"That tree," she said, pointing to a cedar-like one about thirty yards away. Ferdy snorted.

"I'll give you two rocks if you hit that," he said. Allee tossed her head.

"You're on." She hit it, Ferdy handed her the rocks, and the game continued. Nobody really got ahead. Much to Allee's disgust, Ferdy actually could hit most of the targets. When Esendore called a halt, they were so absorbed in their sport that it took them a while to notice. Allee looked up at the sun, confused. It was a lot earlier than they had stopped last night. Ferdy voiced her question.

"Why are we stopping?" he asked. "I still have to beat you," he added to Allee under his breath.

"Majesty seems to have picked up a stone," Esendore replied. He dismounted and examined the offending hoof. He frowned at it, took a knife from his belt and pried out the rock. He eyebrows knitted together. "I can't imagine where it came from," he said, stowing it in his pocket. "There aren't any rocks like this around here, and he just started limping a little while ago." Allee and Ferdy exchanged looks, trying not to laugh. Esendore didn't notice them. "Anyway," he decided, putting his knife away, "It'll do us all good to stop for the night. It's too hot to do too much in this heat. There's a clearing up ahead." Still on the ground, he led Majesty down the trail.

To the right of the clearing was a small pond, its water sparkling in the evening light. Allee looked at it wistfully. She hadn't had a bath for two days. She noticed Esendore was also looking at the water and hoped he wouldn't sing out here. The sound would echo horribly off the steep banks. Hiding a smile at the thought, she slid off Dazzle and began finding stones for a fire pit.

Tonight the tentopy pitching went under way without too much noise, even without Gnarrish's assistance (he was fishing for their supper), but there was still one tentopy more crooked than the others. Esendore inspected it closely and declared that it must be the poles. Ferdy retorted that it was Esendore, because there was nothing wrong with it in the first place. Then Esendore tried to make Ferdy look closer and accidentally shoved him into the tentopy, which promptly fell over, taking its neighbor down with it. Allee just shook her head and continued slicing the potatams into thin strips. Gnarrish came back with four good-sized fish just as she was throwing the potatams in the skillet. He grimaced when he saw Esendore and Ferdy, who were still arguing.

"It'd be easier for us if I threw them in the pond," he muttered, dipping the fish in the batter Allee had prepared and laying them in a skillet of their own.

"If you hold their feet, I'll hold their arms," Allee promised, waiting for his reaction. He looked at her sideways.

"I want the arms," he protested, and laughing, he went to settle the dispute.

With Gnarrish's peacemaking skills, the tentopies were soon set in order. The two brothers were even joking easily with each other as Allee dished up the fish.

Only half-listening to a rather vulgar joke about a farmer and three llonkeys, Allee wolfed her meal down and hurried to wash the pans, eyeing the water in the pond with anticipation. Gnarrish noticed her rush and promised that he would finish the dishes.

Allee grabbed some soap and a towel from her saddlebag and hurried to the water's edge. Too self-conscious to undress completely, she stripped down to her thin sleeveless undershirt and rolled her pants up to her knees. Lining her possessions on the bank, she surveyed her bathtub. The pond was similar to a swimming pool, with the bank dropping straight down to the bottom, not tapering in. Taking a deep breath, Allee jumped in—and almost jumped right back out.

"That's COLD!" she gasped, getting water in her mouth and up her nose. Shrill screams ricocheted around her skull.

"DON'T DO THAT!" five high-pitched voices shrieked. Allee froze.

"Sorry, sorry!" she said, alarmed. Gently, she blew out through her nose. The screaming stopped.

"That's better," a tiny voice said. Allee smiled at how ridiculous this was and made a mental note to warn the fairies before she blew her nose. Very carefully, she began floating around on her back, reveling in the feeling of being clean again. Once the initial shock was over, the water was actually quite pleasant.

After a few rounds of swimming in circles, she swam back to the bank and began washing her hair. The soap smelled like rose petals. She could tell the fairies approved from the way her nose suddenly got very warm. She dunked her head to rinse and surfaced to find Ferdy staring at her disdainfully.

"What are you doing?" he questioned, leaning on a tree.

"Taking a bath," Allee replied calmly, lathering up her arms.

"With you clothes on?" Ferdy asked, scornfully.

"Like I'm going to take them off with you around!" she retorted. He grinned at her.

"I haven't taken a bath in two weeks," he announced.

"That's nice," Allee replied, coolly. *Gross,* she thought, but then an idea struck her, and she hid an evil grin behind her hand. She wrung her hair out and looked back up at Ferdy.

"Here, help me out," she ordered, holding out her hand for him to grab. Surprised, he leaned over. With a jerk, Allee pulled him head first into the water with a mighty splash. He disappeared for a moment and came up sputtering in indignation.

"What's all this about?" he demanded, spouting water from his mouth. Allee was laughing too hard to reply.

"Atta girl, Allee!" Gnarrish shouted, running up to laugh at Ferdy, too. "He was starting to smell." He grinned at them from the shore. Ferdy sent him a scathing look that plainly said, "Traitor!" and started climbing out.

"Oh no, you don't!" Allee said, grabbing the bar of soap and wrapping her fingers around his wrist. His eyes widened in shock.

"Nuh-uh. No way. You are not—" Allee dived for his head, but missed.

"Hold still," she said, trying again, but he dodged, still struggling to get out. Suddenly, a war cry split the air.

"Aiee!" Gnarrish, shirtless, cried, jumping into the fray. With lightning fast speed, Gnarrish removed Ferdy's shirt and threw it on to bank. Then he started soaping Ferdy's lower body while Allee attacked his torso. At first, she felt uncomfortable touching his naked skin, but after a moment she was fighting too hard to lather up his hair to be embarrassed.

"No—you can't do this to me!" he protested, squirming. "Stop! Stop, ah, that tickles! Leave me alone!" Allee and Gnarrish finished at the same time and let go. Ferdy fell back into the water and was gone so long Allee began to worry that he couldn't swim. A second later he resurfaced, howling at the top of his lungs.

"You guys have no respect for personal space, I—" he stopped, horror spreading over his face. He sniffed the air carefully. Allee sniffed, too, and realized what he had noticed. She grinned wickedly.

"NOOO!" he shouted. "I SMELL LIKE FLOWERS!" He dunked his head under again, trying to escape the smell. He stopped after five tries and leaned against the bank with Allee and Gnarrish, who were weak with laughter.

"I don't know, Ferdinand," Gnarrish said dryly, "You sure smell pretty." Ferdy grumbled incoherently, splashing some water in the gnarf's direction. Allee ignored them and surveyed the shoreline, which was surrounded by trees and various sized rocks. A big one, to Allee's right, caught her attention.

"Dare you to jump off that rock," she challenged Ferdy. He eyed it carefully, his previous trauma forgotten.

"Easy!" he replied, climbing out of the water. He walked over to the boulder, surveyed it, and scrambled to the top.

"And now," he said dramatically, looking out over the water, "the amazing Ferdinand will perform his death-defying, heart stopping, gut wrenching—"

"Just do it all ready!" Gnarrish yelled. Ferdy glared at him and leaped. His splash sprayed Allee and Gnarrish a little, but Allee thought it was rather lame. Ferdy, however, was elated.

"Did you see that?" he cried, swimming over to them. "Gnarrish, you try." Gnarrish agreed and climbed onto the rock. He took a running start and jumped. His splash was considerable for a man his size. Ferdy and Allee both cheered.

"My turn," Allee announced as soon as Gnarrish rejoined them. She hauled herself up onto the rock and then launched herself into the air, drawing her legs up to her chest in a cannonball. The water was deeper than she expected, and she was gasping for breath when she resurfaced. The looks on Ferdy and Gnarrish's faces made her laugh. Both their jaws were slack.

"That," Ferdy said fervently, "was the biggest splash I have ever seen." Allee grinned at them both.

"Why, thank-you," she replied. "Want me to teach you?" Both nodded mutely, and she moved in closer to share her technique.

A half an hour later it was too dark to continue, so they all piled out to go dry off. Allee changed into her pajamas, brushed her hair, and went out to join the others. Allee settled down on a log to watch the fire.

She gently tried to work the soreness out of her shoulders and legs while watching the flames dance before her. Soon it became harder and harder to concentrate because of some whining noise. Allee realized that Esendore had started to hum, which was just as bad as his singing. Ferdy finally got sick of it.

"We already know you can't sing, Esendore, so lay off, would you?" he asked, exasperated. Esendore looked hurt, but remained silent. Although the song had been off-key, the melody was still haunting Allee. She decided to just ask him.

"What song is it?" she queried. Ferdy groaned, but Esendore looked pleased.

"You've probably heard it before—it's an old prophecy," he explained. Allee, intrigued, quickly replied that she hadn't heard of it, and he continued. "We don't know where it came from or even who first sang it, but it goes something like this,"

"Nuh-uh," Ferdy interrupted. "You'll butcher it. I'll sing." He opened his mouth, and to Allee's great surprise, his voice was sweet and clear,

> "There they stand in the starlight,
> Their loathing stains the air,
> How can the gap be breached
> If neither of them cares?
>
> Day and Night, Dark and Light,
> Each too blind to see the other's might.
> Day and Night, Dark and Light,
> Hope grows dim, and time grows tight.
>
> There she stands in the Darkness,
> Moonlight in her hair. But she's not in the dark
> Because she chose to be there.
> How small and pale she is, underneath the moon!
> She's there on her lover's dare, this child of the noon.
>
> Day and Night, Dark and Light,
> Both ready to love, but then not quite.
> Day and Night, Dark and Light,
> Can love be wrong when it feels so right?
>
> There he stands in the Daylight,
> Fire in his hair. But he's not in the light
> Because he chose to be there.

How weak and bare he is, underneath the noon!
He's there on his lover's dare, this child of the moon.

Day and Night, Dark and Light,
Betrayed by greed, and split by fright.
Day and Night, Dark and Light,
Torn apart, too weak to fight.

There they stand in the willows,
Lightning in the air.
But how can the hurt be fixed,
If neither of them dares?
Day and Night, Dark and Light,
Speak one word, and love burns bright.
Day and Night, Dark and Light,
Bound together in twilight."

Ferdy's voice warbled, and the song ended. Everyone was held in a sort of spell, breathless with the mystery and enchantment of the song. Allee finally broke the silence.

"What does it mean?" she asked, her voice trembling. She felt very strange, almost light-headed. Esendore stared into the fire a moment before looking at her.

"Like I said, it's an old prophecy," he said, his face sad. "It appeared not long after the days when the country Ivral, always our friend and ally, started becoming…becoming…" He struggled to find a word.

"Evil," Ferdy helped. Esendore nodded.

"Evil," he agreed. "There was a long and brutal war between our countries and things started to look bleak for reconcile and peace between us again. But, out of those times this prophecy arose, a prophecy that told of love between the two countries once more, love gained by the love of two people." His face looked eerie in the firelight, almost unreal, and Allee felt as if she was looking at the prophet from the days of old, but then Esendore shrugged and the look passed.

"That's silly," Ferdy said, his voice full of skepticism. "If diplomats, tons of treaties, a war, and a whole bunch of money can't bring peace, than two people who just *love* each other," he spit the word "love" out with disgust, "certainly won't. Love can't do stuff like that." Esendore's eyes took on a dreamy expression.

"Oh, you'd be surprised," he said, his voice soft.

"Ha," Ferdy barked, standing up. "I'm going to bed." He strode off into the darkness. Gnarrish arose, too, and after bowing to Esendore, he went in the direction of the tentopies. Allee watched Esendore's long face in the firelight. He looked old, each line in his face etched with pain and worry. *It must be hard for him*, she mused, *knowing that his beloved's life depends on him*. Her thoughts were broken by a jaw-cracking yawn. She stood, trying not to wince at her sore muscles.

"Good night," she told Esendore. His eyes flickered quickly to her face.

"Oh, yes, good-night, Alethea." He seemed to forget her then, and continued staring at the fire, as if searching for the answer to something, even though he knew he wouldn't find it. Softly, Allee padded into the darkness.

After she crawled into her sleeping bag, Allee dug for the ruby. She didn't feel very homesick, just a little lonely. The jewel started singing as soon as she touched it, as if it was lonely, too. Allee relaxed as she listened. The song was the same one the ruby always sang, but every time she listened to it she noticed different things about the melody.

"What would I do without you?" she whispered to the ruby. The jewel didn't reply, but if it had, Allee would not have heard.

Chapter 7

Royal Snobs

Allee opened her eyes to darkness, wondering why she was awake. Straining her ears, she listened for what had awoken her. Light footsteps pattered past her tentopy and faded off into the distance. *Why would anyone be awake at this awful hour,* Allee wondered, guessing the time to be right before dawn. She was content to let them be awake, but after ten minutes of sleeplessness she let her curiosity get the better of her and she slipped out of the tentopy.

The campsite was softly lit with moonlight and starlight, casting everything familiar into the grotesquely unfamiliar. Allee stopped right outside her doorway, staring at the sky in wonder. The stars glittered at her, so close, yet so far away. Their beauty tugged at her heartstrings, and she stood for a moment hardly daring to breathe. The vastness almost seemed to swallow her, and she welcomed it, yearning to be as high and bright as those stars.

Before she could imagine the feeling of star traveling, she heard a noise beside her and her revelry was broken. Ferdy was standing a little ways away from her, his arms at his sides, and his head tilted upwards. Allee knew he didn't know she was there. She watched him for a moment, his back straight and proud, and his bearing haughty. Yet, for all his arrogance, Allee saw him shiver in the pre-dawn air.

On impulse, she drew closer to him, almost touching his shoulder. The faint smell of roses lingered about him, and Allee suddenly remembered the touch of his bare skin under her fingertips. She pushed the thought away and waited for him to acknowledge her. He gave no indication that he had realized that she was there, yet she knew he could see her. They each stood silently, transfixed with the heavens, lost in their own thoughts. Finally, Allee couldn't stand it anymore.

"What are you doing?" she whispered, hoping that he wouldn't resent her prying.

"I am contemplating the meaning of the universe," he replied, still gazing skyward.

"Oh," Allee replied, feeling awkward, but she couldn't think how to answer. Ferdy moved his head back and forth slowly, surveying the pattern of the stars.

"It's so dark," he breathed, shivering again. His eyes were no longer fixed on the sky, but staring straight ahead of him even though there was noting to see. Allee realized that he was not speaking of the sky.

"It's always darkest before the dawn," she said, trying to comfort him. He finally turned to look at her.

"But how do you know there will be a dawn?" he asked, his voice low and hoarse, his eyes wild with fear. Allee was taken back, but still tried to reassure him. She did not realize that she was also reassuring herself.

"Do you believe the sun will rise again?" she asked, waving her arm to the east, which gave no hint to the impending dawn. Her voice was much calmer than the emotions churning within her. He stared at her, not answering. "Do you?" she pressed. He looked at her a moment longer.

"I believe in the dawn," his eyes locked on her face. Slowly, the fear drained out of them and Allee felt another jolt of energy pass from his eyes to her own.

"Then it will happen," she assured, her voice echoing slightly in the stillness of the air. Ferdy tilted his head at her and narrowed his eyes.

"You know too much for a peasant," he said, his tone haughty again. Allee felt her temper rise, but she quickly controlled it.

"It's not too hard to know more than a royal," she replied, glaring defiantly at him. And with that, she turned on her heel and went back to her tentopy. As strange as the situation had been, she fell asleep smiling.

Allee was drifting pleasantly in that place between waking and sleeping. She sighed blissfully, feeling the morning light filter in through the canvas above her. She was just about to open her eyes when—

"GOOD MORNING, ALETHEA!" a chorus of five tiny voices shouted in her head. Allee sat bolt upright, trying to find where the noise was coming from.

"What the—" she started, then remembered that she had a host of fairies living in her nose. "Oh, um, yeah, uh, good morning to you, too!" she stammered, clutching her ears, which were still ringing with giggles. She took a deep breath, and when she exhaled, the fairies were completely silent. "Between Ferdy and the fairies I am never going to be able to wake up normally again," she muttered. With a sigh, she crawled out of her sleeping bag and started getting dressed.

Extremely pleased with herself for having the last word at their early morning conversation and waking up before him, she gave Ferdy's tentopy pole a quick kick as she went by. After hearing a sleepy grunt from the inside, she went to start the fire.

She had the flames going nicely by the time Ferdy stumbled out of his tentopy, rubbing his eyes. Allee wondered how long he had been awake last night, but immediately decided not to mention their conversation. She felt that it was better left beneath the stars

"Good morning," she said, smiling brightly at him as he sat down on a log. He watched her through bleary eyes as she sliced pieces of bacon into the skillet alongside the eggs.

"We had that yesterday," he muttered, squinting at them. "And I like my eggs scrambled." Allee sighed in exasperation.

"You know what I like?" she demanded, pulling a collapsible bucket out of a saddlebag, "I like people who do something more worthwhile than complaining." She must have looked threatening with the bucket raised over her head and her eyes flashing, for he quickly started apologizing.

"Sheesh, I'm sorry, I like fried eggs just fine, I'll go get some water, just don't hit me!" He snatched the bucket from her hands and hurried off in the direction of the spring that fed the pond. Allee watched him go with a mixture of satisfaction and embarrassment. She really hadn't wanted him to get water. *Allee one, Ferdy zero*, she thought smugly and turned to smile at Gnarrish, who had joined her by the fire.

"Wow," he said, watching Ferdy almost lose his balance on the slippery rocks. "How did you get him to do that?"

"Cheerful negotiation while threatening him with a bucket," Allee responded, dishing his breakfast onto his plate.

"Ah," Gnarrish said, and looked like he was going to say more, but Esendore and Ferdy arrived and cut their conversation short.

Esendore seemed to be in a hurry that morning. Allee guessed he was eager to make up for the lost time yesterday before the day got too hot. They did manage to get on the trail by eight o'clock and had covered several miles by their lunch break. After another hour on the trail, a scorching wind blew up and prevented Allee and Ferdy from playing the rock game. Allee was too miserable to do anything but keep her head down; the dirt seemed to cover every inch of her. Ferdy kept digging in his ear. Allee roused herself enough to become curious.

"What's the matter?" she asked.

"Water in it," Ferdy said shortly. "And now that bath didn't do any good, but I *still* smell like flowers!" Allee tried to smile, but her face was too stiff with dirt. Ferdy stopped digging in his ear and looked thoughtful.

"Today is the day for Lullaby's monthly bath," he mused.

"Sounds like you bathe your dokat more than you bathe yourself," Allee said. Ferdy gave her his you-are-crazy look, but Gnarrish, who had been listening, rewarded her with a short laugh. It kept Allee from becoming too depressed, but she was more than ready for them to stop for the evening.

By the time they did stop, it was half-twilight and everyone was exhausted. Silently, they began setting up camp. Allee started the fire all by herself since Gnarrish was busy making sure the tentopies went up without mishap. It cheered her up considerably to see the dry kindling alight and crackle merrily. She was even whistling quietly when the rest joined her ten minutes later. Gnarrish and Esendore just seemed tired, but Ferdy looked very depressed. Allee tried to lighten his mood.

"What," she teased, her voice meant only for Ferdy's ears, "are you pining for Brit?" Instead of some nasty reply, Ferdy looked at her fearfully and cast a glance at Esendore, who had snapped his head up.

"Brit?" Esendore asked, his voice sharp. Allee felt her heart sink to her knees. "The dairy maid?" Ferdy stared back at him, his eyes wide with alarm. Esendore took that as a yes.

"Ferdinand," he started, and Allee winced at the anger in his voice, her heart sinking even lower. "I *explicitly* told you to stop seeing her. She is beneath you." Even though Allee was feeling worse than she ever had in her life, a flame of anger sprang up in her on Brit's behalf. *Rank shouldn't matter*, she thought fiercely, but she was too afraid to say it.

"She's nice if you get to know her," Ferdy said.

"NICE?" Esendore exploded. "Commoners are not nice—they are simply there for our benefit. You cannot lower yourself to her level, Ferdinand! What will people say?" Allee couldn't take it anymore.

"Well, you know what this commoner says?" she shouted, standing up. "This commoner says that the whole lot of us are hundreds of times better than you and your arrogant attitude ever have a hope to be, *Your Highness*!" Fighting the urge to throw something, she turned on her heel and ran in the direction of her tentopy. Behind her, she heard Ferdy stand up.

"Esendore, you've certainly stuck your foot in your mouth this time," he said. If Esendore replied, Allee missed it by entering her tentopy. She let the flap fall and sank to the floor. She hugged herself and rocked back and forth, trying not to choke on the lump in her throat. She had never been so hurt and humiliated in her entire life. She couldn't help that she wasn't of noble blood! She tried to comfort herself by reminding her wounded pride that she was equal to anyone else in her home world, but her tactic didn't work. Hot tears pricked at her eyelids.

"I will not let him make me cry!" she croaked, and fell over to land on her sleeping bag. She didn't know how long she lay there, lost and dejected. She kept turning over and over in her mind how Esendore had seemed to like her, and how he had helped her, and then how he had just treated her. *It was like he didn't even realize I had feelings*, she thought, racking her brain to find an answer for Esendore's behavior. *Nobody has an excuse to say such things* she decided, but she still did not feel any better.

Suddenly, she heard a rustling noise. She lifted up her head, which felt very large and heavy, and realized it was dark out. She heard the noise again, and Ferdy's face appeared in the tent flap. His face was very white in the darkness.

"Can I come in?" he whispered, his voice strained. Allee crawled over to the flap, very glad to see him, and grateful for his last remark to Esendore.

"Of course," she replied, pulling the flap aside. He edged through the doorway and seated himself in the corner. Allee was extremely aware of the fact that she would never, never have let him in her tentopy normally, and now that the initial pleasure of seeing him was over, she felt extremely uncomfortable with him so close in the only private place she had on this journey. There was an awkward silence while Allee racked her brain to find something to say. She heard his stomach growl and sighed in relief.

"Oh, here," she said, groping for her saddlebag where she kept her trail rations. "You can eat this." She pushed a handful of jerky and a wedge of cheese at him, saving a little for herself. She wasn't really hungry, but she knew she should eat something.

"Fanks," Ferdy said, his mouth full of the cheese.

"Sorry it's not much," Allee said. "I just don't really feel like cooking tonight." She looked at her lap, the lump in her throat returning. It was a good thing, too, or Ferdy would have sprayed her with cheese crumbs as he choked in indignation.

"Fou don't haf to do anyfing fou don't wan to!" he cried, his words slurred by his food. He swallowed as Allee stared at him, almost wanting to laugh. "You just go ahead and be mad!" he exploded, and Allee was so surprised at the anger in his voice that she looked into his eyes. She wished she hadn't. The fury there scared her. "He has no right to treat you like that," he continued, waving his jerky in the air. "No one, except maybe him, should ever be treated like they are lower than someone else, because everybody is the same, and he treated you like you had no feelings whatsoever, no better than a dokat—no, wait, dokats have feelings, HE TREATED YOU LIKE POND SCUM—"

"Shhh," Allee said, alarmed. "He'll hear you!"

"WHICH HAS MORE BRAINS THAN HE DOES!" Ferdy bellowed, his face scarlet. He stopped yelling, but continued breathing hard. "It's all true, Allee," he said. "And he should know it. He can't hide from the fact that he is too wrapped up in himself to care about others." With the word "care," Allee's mind flashed back to the night before, when she had seen Esendore hunched in front of the fire, care etched in every line in his face.

"He's under a lot of pressure," she said, aloud. "He cares about Dariel, and he's worried that—,"

"He still has no excuse to be nasty," Ferdy snapped. Allee felt unbelievably better knowing that Ferdy was on her side, but his anger disturbed her.

"He's stressed out," Allee said, wondering why she was defending Esendore. Ferdy finally seemed to get his anger under control.

"I guess you're right," he said slowly, his face thoughtful. "And usually when he's stressed he goes and gets—" Ferdy cut himself off, looking startled.

"Gets what?" Allee asked.

"Uh...advice," Ferdy said, hurriedly. "Advice. He goes and asks Cardolyn or one of the King's council for help. Even though *I'm* on the King's council," Ferdy snorted at the thought of Esendore asking him for help. "He isn't used to not having people to give him advice," Ferdy continued, smiling nervously at Allee. "But he can't do that here," he added, almost to himself. Allee thought Ferdy was acting extremely weird, but dismissed the feeling quickly. She smiled back at him.

"Thanks," she said. Swallowing her pride, she went on, "You've made me feel a lot better." Ferdy looked at her as if she had just sprouted two heads.

"Your welcome," he said, suspiciously, his eyes narrowed. They stared at each other for a moment. "Commoner," he added.

"Royal snob," Allee retorted, all her good feelings toward him vanishing. He laughed and disappeared out the tent flap. Allee decided then that both Princes were obnoxious jerks.

Allee changed into her pajamas, but wasn't sleepy yet. Her mind was still spinning with all that had happened to her, and sleep refused to come. She decided to go for a walk to clear her head and ducked out of the tentopy.

The night was warm and bright, the wind that had plagued them all day a tiny breeze. Allee turned her face upward to catch it, letting it sweep away all of her inner turmoil.

Relaxed, she tried to find a familiar constellation. She had just found one that looked a little like the big dipper when a voice spoke at her shoulder.

"They are very beautiful tonight, aren't they?" it asked. Allee jumped, her heart beating wildly when she realized who it was. It took all of her self-control not to turn on her heel and go back to her tentopy.

"Yes, Your Highness," she replied, her voice stiff. Abruptly, Esendore was standing in front of her.

"Alethea, don't be angry," he implored, his face strained with worry. "I...I never meant to hurt you. Those things I said...I would give anything to take them back. I feel so terrible—" his voice broke, and his face crumpled. Allee felt her anger ebb a little. She took a deep breath.

"It's okay," she said, a weight lifting off her shoulders as she forgave him. His body sagged with relief. "I understand," Allee said quickly, to let him know she really meant it. "I know how worried you must be about the Countess, I—"

"Oh, Dariel!" he cried, his face a mask of pain. He looked so much like one of Allee's little sisters after tripping and falling that, from habit, Allee reached up to pat his shoulder. To her horror, he collapsed in her arms.

"I miss her so, so much, it's like this...this huge hole, inside me," he wailed. Allee braced her legs so as not to collapse under him. She decided that this was the most ridiculous thing that had ever happened to her. The Crown Prince was bawling on her shoulder. Gingerly, she patted his back.

"Shhh, it'll be okay," she soothed, the awkwardness of the situation preventing her from saying anything else. "It will be alright, Esendore. You'll find her."

"I'm trying," he wept. "But it's so hard, Alethea! And no one understands, no one knows how horrible it is to love her and not know where she is, or what's happening to her, or even if there's a hope that she's alive!" Allee felt the same emotion she had felt earlier that morning when Ferdy had despaired.

"Espy would know if she's dead, Esendore," she said, her voice sounding funny to her ears. "And there is always hope. You just have to look for it sometimes. Just like you're looking for Dariel. You're doing a great job," she assured, wincing a little at the half-lie. She wracked her brain to find something to comfort him with and then faked a laugh as a thought struck her. "They might even make it into a song," she mused aloud, hoping she didn't sound too corny. "The valiant Prince, never yielding in search of his betrothed." Esendore stood up.

"You really think I'm doing a good job?" he asked, his tears shining in the moonlight.

"No one could do it better," Allee said, believing it so he would. He have her a wobbly smile.

"Thank-you, Alethea. You don't know how much this means to me, I—"

"You're welcome," Allee said, cutting him off. She already felt weird enough without him starting to gush like Espy. His smile grew stronger, and he straightened his shoulders. Allee knew it was safe for her to leave.

"Good night, Esendore," she said, edging back toward her tentopy.

"Good night, Alethea," he replied, just as softly. And Allee knew that he would not despair so deeply again. More bewildered than when she had left, Allee entered her tentopy. She didn't need the ruby to sing herself to sleep that night. She did it herself, trying to find something that rhymed with "valiant Prince".

Chapter 8

Monsters and Maids

When Allee stuck her head out of the tentopy the next morning, she was quite a bit more cheerful than the downcast sky above her. She had been fully awake and dressed by the time the fairies had "greeted the day" as they called it, and she had finally done something important on this crazy journey that did not include cleaning up after people.

Sadly, her cheerful mood didn't last long; a gray drizzle started and Ferdy kept cursing his wet socks, reminding her how little fun riding with him was going to be. She hoped the drizzle would quit before too long or she might be in just as bad of a temper as he sounded.

Gnarrish already had the fire going for her, along with a funny-looking pot stuck above it. A moment of awkward silence hung in the air after Allee said good morning, but to her great relief, he didn't say anything about the night before.

"There's hot teoffe in the pot," he explained, seeing her curious gaze. "I always like a little on damp days like this." A particularly loud oath from Ferdy's tentopy made Allee wince.

"I think some people are going to need more than a little," she replied, unpacking the skillets. Gnarrish sent a look at his master's tentopy.

"I have plenty," he assured, and went off to find some water. Allee began slicing a loaf of bread for toast to go with a jar of purple jelly Gnarrish had found inside the teoffe pot that Espy must have put there. Almost as an afterthought, she threw some cheese into the eggs and scrambled them. *At least Ferdy will have one less thing to complain about this morning,* she guessed.

"Hey, plape," Esendore said as he joined them a minute later. "That's my favorite." Allee noticed that he looked paler than usual, but otherwise he seemed just fine.

"Zesty, huh?" she asked, using the first word that popped into her head. He looked at her for a moment and then burst out laughing.

"Zesty?" he repeated. The amusement in his voice made Allee laugh, too.

"Haven't you ever used that word?" she questioned, teasing him. He looked surprised.

"If I have, it wasn't to describe *toast*," he replied.

"It tastes better when it's zesty," Allee told him, taking a bite out of a piece.

"If you say so," he replied, popping an entire piece into his mouth. Allee smiled at him and finished hers off. She looked up as a shadow fell over her.

"Good morning, Allee," Ferdy said, extremely courteously. Allee was pleasantly surprised at his attitude. He was much more cheerful than she had expected him to be.

"Good morning," she replied, her heart feeling lighter.

"Good morning," Esendore said to Ferdy, but his younger brother completely ignored him and grabbed a piece of the toast. Esendore's face fell, as did Allee's heart. *Here we go,* she thought grimly and dished out the eggs.

Ferdy glared at Esendore throughout the entire meal, making Esendore so uncomfortable that he excused himself before eating another bite. *He didn't even get to eat more of his favorite jelly,* Allee thought sadly. She saved a piece to give to him later. Gnarrish drained the last of his teoffe and went to go help the Prince take down the tentopies. Ferdy moved to follow, but Allee grabbed his arm.

"Look, Ferdy," she started, but paused, trying to collect her thoughts. She did not want to alienate Ferdy right after he had started acting decent towards her. She took a deep breath.

"Don't treat Esendore like that," she said, hoping she didn't sound hypocritical. "He apologized last night. And he really meant it, so I forgave him. Everything's—"

"You WHAT?" Ferdy interrupted, his eyes growing wide. "You FORGAVE the stupid—"

"If I can forgive him, then you certainly can," Allee said, hiding her red face by stuffing the food back in the saddlebags.

"But, Allee—" Ferdy protested. "Those things he said to you—"

"He's sorry," Allee said firmly, looking Ferdy in the eye. "And I believe he's sorry. That's all that matters." He opened his mouth to say something else, but then Gnarrish called for him. Ferdy sent her one last look as he walked away, and she breathed out in relief. It didn't say "traitor", as she had feared, but instead was the look he reserved especially for her. It was the "you are crazy beyond all possible craziness" one. Allee sighed and turned back to the dishes, marveling at her stupidity for getting herself into this mess.

Ferdy seemed to forget his earlier annoyance with her after they had been on the trail awhile. The drizzle had stopped, but the clouds were still hanging low in the sky, which made the day extremely humid. Allee was eager for something to take her mind off the weather and was very pleased when Ferdy rode up beside her.

"Do you want to play the rock game?" he asked. "I still have to beat you." Allee rolled her eyes and grinned.

"In you dreams, Ferdinand," she retorted. "Bet you three rocks you can't hit that rock." She pointed to an upcoming boulder.

"Ha," he scoffed, measuring it up. "You underestimate me." He missed.

When they stopped for lunch, Ferdy was out of rocks, and Allee had one. She was quite boastful about her win, but he protested that she had said the first person out of rocks at the end of the game lost, and the end of the game was when they stopped at the end of the day. Allee wasn't surprised that he had found a loophole, but she still argued with him all through lunch. Finally, she gave in just to shut him up. They refilled their pockets and continued, a little more competitive than before.

"Three rocks that I hit that bush," Allee challenged.

"I don't think so," Ferdy replied, his words dripping with disbelief. At the last second, a bird burst out of it and she overthrew in surprise. Ferdy chuckled as Allee handed over the rocks.

"Pathetic," he said, gloating. Allee didn't say anything. She knew she could get him back. He began scanning for his target. His eyes focused on something in front of them and his face lit up. "Two says I hit Esendore's head," he declared, his tongue sticking out the edge of his mouth as he concentrated on his aim.

"Ferdy," Allee warned, but he threw before she could stop him. Thankfully, the shot went wide, hitting Gnarrish instead. He turned around to look at them. They looked at the ground innocently. Gnarrish rolled his eyes and reined in Ruby.

"I think I had better start playing this game of yours before I get my head knocked off," he said, and announced his target. Ferdy and Allee grinned at each other, and the game went on.

Ferdy kept trying on and off all day to hit Esendore, but he never hit him. Allee suspected that he wasn't trying very hard, in fear of what his older brother would do to him. She couldn't imagine Esendore wrestling with Ferdy like she had seen other older brothers do to their younger siblings, but, then again, where had Ferdy learned to be so ornery?

"This time I'll do it," Ferdy announced as the afternoon was waning. "And I'll give you five rocks if I don't." Allee and Ferdy were both tied at six rocks each. Gnarrish had three, so he was out.

"I'll win after all," Allee said. "Go ahead and try." Esendore stopped to look at something right when Ferdy threw his rock. It hit him squarely in the middle of his head, but nobody noticed. They were too busy gaping at the change in scenery.

As Allee pushed her mount to the front of the line to see what everyone was staring at, the sun came out and she was suddenly blinded. When her vision cleared, she realized what the light had reflected so brightly off of.

"Mountains," she whispered, her breath taken away by their hugeness. The sun glittered off their snowy peaks, dazzling the group's eyes while it stood open-mouthed in wonder. Rock was piled up thousand feet by thousand feet to end in jagged, purple peaks. Allee had never seen mountains before, but she guessed that these were the size of the Rocky Mountains. At their base stretched a wide, grassy plain, its many grasses rippling in the light wind. The plain was cut in two by the brown waters of a medium-sized river. Three miles away, by Allee's reckoning, the forest began again at the base of the mountains. At its edge was a small village. Allee quickly took in the mountains' surroundings and then involuntarily began staring at their snowy heights again.

"Please don't tell me we have to cross those," Ferdy said in a tiny voice, breaking the spell. Allee could barely tear her eyes away from the splendor before her, but she did. Going over those monsters had not even crossed her mind. Esendore looked almost as terrified as she felt. He cleared his throat.

"Well, yes," he started, his voice very small as his eyes swept over the scene before them. He squared his shoulders and turned to look at them. "There is a pass," he assured, pointing to their left. Much to her relief, Allee could distinguish the pass easily. Still, the journey did seem daunting.

"Esendore!" Ferdy practically shouted, his eyes bulging. "Are you CRAZY? It'll take a WEEK to cross them!"

"No," Esendore said, firmly. Allee was very relieved to see that he acting more sure of himself. "It will only take two full days of hard riding. I will get you to the other side, Ferdinand. Do not doubt me." He nudged Majesty forward. Ferdy looked defeated for a moment, but then thought of something else.

"But, but, Esendore," he started. Esendore stopped to look at him. Ferdy seemed to take heart. "But, Esendore, do you know what mountains these are?" Esendore rolled his eyes and was about to snap back at his younger brother, but Ferdy pressed on. "Esendore, these are the GARGONS!" Allee took another quick look at the mountains and agreed wholeheartedly with their name. Esendore tapped his fingers on the saddle impatiently, and Ferdy rushed on.

"Do you know what lives in the Gargons, Esendore?" Esendore was looking angrier by the moment and opened his mouth to reply, but again Ferdy wouldn't let him.

"Alzius," he said, his voice lowering to a whisper. The air, which had been pleasantly warm a moment before, suddenly went cold, and the wind swirled around them. Allee shivered. Esendore sat unmoving, his jaw clenched. Ferdy seemed to be getting desperate.

"Esendore, you know what I'm talking about. You've heard the tales about bloodthirsty monsters that prey upon wanderers in the mountains. *Those* mountains." He stopped to gesture to the peaks in front of them. Suddenly, Allee didn't think they looked so spectacular anymore. They looked cruel and cold. Esendore didn't say anything.

"Esendore, please," Ferdy begged, a waver entering his voice. "The rumors...they say that the monsters can FREEZE their victims with one stare so that they are easy targets. That—"

"I *know* what the stories say," Esendore snapped, pushing his windblown hair out of his face. "I know more about those mountains than I care to. But there is *no other way*." His face drew on a look of pure determination, and he spurred Majesty down the ridge. Ferdy bowed his head in defeat. Allee let her eyes fall upon the mountains one more time, searching the peaks intently, but she did not know what for. The only noise to break the frosty silence was the sound of Majesty's hooves as he picked his way down the slope. Allee urged Dazzle to follow, sneaking a glance at Ferdy as she did so. She saw him look one last time upon the Gargons and swallow very hard.

Esendore was waiting for them at the bottom. He sighed when he saw their long faces.

"Oh, cheer up," he said, trying to lighten the mood. "Just think, tonight we will be able to eat real food on a real table, and sleep in a real bed. Though, I do doubt the food tastes as good as Allee's." He smiled at her, somewhat hesitantly.

Allee knew he was still trying to make up for last night, so she smiled in return, even though the gesture was a little forced. She was not looking forward to being among lots of people again. She always seemed to make a fool of herself. Esendore seemed to take heart from her smile. "The inn is quite good here, or so I've heard," he went on, smiling encouragingly at all of them. "The Roaring Avalanche," he added. "I'm sure we'll all feel right at home."

"Any roof sounds good for me, Sire," Gnarrish said, clucking his tongue at Ruby.

"Good to know," Esendore said, looking very optimistic. He kicked Majesty into a canter. Allee sighed and looked at Ferdy. He shrugged his shoulders at her unspoken question.

"I'm still glad I didn't risk Cardolyn," he said. Before Allee could reply, Lunar started to trot ahead. Silently agreeing with him, she hurried to catch up.

The zeorses must have sensed the stalls awaiting them, for they traveled faster than they had all week. But when the group neared the hustle and bustle of the village, which was actually a good-sized town, the animals began to shy and sidestep. After four days in the wilderness, they had grown unaccustomed to a lot of noise. Rather than risk being thrown, their riders dismounted.

Allee was very relieved. She doubted her would have been able to stay on a nervous zeorse and now she could watch the townspeople without them noticing her. She gave herself a crick in her neck looking at all the people and buildings. Most of the villagers eyed the newcomers with suspicion and distrust. Allee could hardly blame them. Their fine livery and the Prince's "traveling clothes" made everything surrounding them drab and dull. Allee tried to hide her blush in Dazzle's shoulder. She hated not being trusted by her own kind of people.

Suddenly, a frantic shout tore through the air.

"Seek shelter! Seek shelter!" it cried, "Mad bull coffalo on the loose! Out of the street! Take cover!" Screams of surprise and fear erupted from shoppers and pedestrians, who quickly ran into shops. Esendore and Gnarrish stepped into the shadows of an alleyway, pulling Allee and Ferdy with them and using the zeorses as shields.

Allee peered over Dazzle's shoulder, curious. She felt quite safe with Esendore's arm around her shoulders and Dazzle's bulk solidly in front of her. She stood on tiptoe to watch the action. She didn't have to wait long. Around the corner of a store across the street appeared a huge, black bull. Twelve feet tall and bellowing with rage, he looked like something out of a nightmare. If Esendore hadn't been behind her, Allee would have taken a step back in surprise.

The animal's mean little red eyes surveyed the empty street, and he snorted and pawed the ground, looking for something to take his anger out on. *You aren't going to find anything*, Allee thought smugly, but her then her breath caught in her throat. Something *was* in the street—a very small something. It was coming out of a vacant lot between two shops, its back to the bull and oblivious to the danger.

"It's a little kid!" Allee cried, her voice echoing off the sides of the buildings. The bull saw the child in the same instant. He shook his massive horned head and charged. Without thinking, Allee tore loose from Esendore's grasp and ran out into the street.

"Allee!" Esendore screamed, but Majesty spooked at the oncoming bull, and he couldn't stop her.

Allee hadn't heard him anyway, her entire being was concentrated on the child, who had now realized its peril and was frozen with fear. The bull let out a bellow of triumph, and Allee put on one last burst of speed—

"Gotch ya!" she yelled, snatching the kid inches from the bull's horns. Caught up in her momentum, she lost her balance and both of them tumbled into the hollow under the boardwalk. Dust billowed around them, and a cheer went up from the onlookers.

Allee started coughing uncontrollably and pressed her head against the cool dirt to steady her nerves. Her hands were cut and bleeding, and she knew her right side was going to be one big bruise tomorrow, but otherwise she was unhurt. *Esendore's going to kill me* she thought, trying to catch her breath. When she had gotten herself back under control, she lifted her head. Soft brown eyes stared back into her own. Allee tore her gaze away before she could freak the poor kid out even more. Then she heard a shout from above,

"You can come out now, we got him under control!" Allee breathed a sigh of relief and turned back to the child.

"You all right, k—" she started, but then stopped, and turned the "kid" into another cough. It was not a child gazing back at her with wide eyes, but a female gnarf. Allee guessed she was just a little older than herself.

"Are you alright?" she asked again, and sat up, wincing at the pain in her right side. The gnarf still didn't say anything. Allee turned to study her face. *Maybe she's in shock*, she thought, but the look on the face opposite from her was not one of trauma, but of deep awe. Allee had seen that look right before Cardolyn had started making a big deal about the dead taranion. Allee realized what the gnarf was thinking.

"Oh, no—" she sputtered.

"You saved my life," the gnarf said, her voice surprisingly rich and syrupy for how small she was. Allee raised her hands in front of her in exasperation.

"What is *with* you people and your "you saved my life" stuff?" Allee practically shouted, backing out of the hole. The gnarf crawled after her, her face glowing.

"You have saved the lives of others, Lady?" she asked, her eyes dripping with admiration. "I do not doubt it. Your Ladyship just radiates greatness, no one could deny it."

Someone was helping Allee to her feet now, and twenty hands were slapping her back while their owners voiced their appreciation. Then she was hit so hard she had the wind knocked back out of her, and Esendore had her in a vice-like embrace.

"You are…you are…" he whispered hoarsely, trying to find words to describe his feelings. Allee could feel him trembling underneath her. She tried to pull away, uncomfortable, but he kept an arm around her shoulders.

"Pretty stupid," Ferdy said in her ear, but he was grinning. Allee gave him a shaky smile in return.

"I owe you my life, Ladyship," the gnarf reminded her.

"Shhh," Allee said, embarrassed by all the attention. The gnarf didn't listen.

"I call for you as witnesses," she shouted to the huge crowd. Abruptly, they became silent. Allee froze.

"What's going on?" she muttered, looking at Esendore from the corner of her eye.

"Hush," he admonished, squeezing her tighter. Allee began to panic.

"We answer you with the use of our eyes and ears," the crowd chanted. Allee realized vaguely that this was some type of ceremony.

"Without this Lady," the gnarf shouted, her voice gaining volume as it echoed off the store fronts, "I would not have my life." Allee was too numb with shock to protest as the gnarf sent her a loving glance. She took a deep breath. "So in gratitude, I give it to her, to do what she will." Allee felt her jaw drop open.

"We hear it and see it and witness it," the crowd replied.

"So may it be!" the gnarf yelled.

"So may it be," the crowd answered. Allee was feeling extremely dizzy and knew if Esendore hadn't been holding her up that she would have fallen over. The gnarf dropped to one knee and bowed her head as the crowd cheered and clapped.

"My name is Gnilli Diggr," she said, her gaze directed at the dirt. "Please accept my humble thanks, Ladyship. I am yours to command."

"Call me Allee," Allee said, automatically. She looked from Esendore to Ferdy to Gnarrish, completely dazed. *Help me*, she mouthed at Ferdy, but he shook his head and gestured subtly at Gnarrish. Allee remembered what he had said about it being a great honor to have a gnarf in your service, but right then she didn't care. She reached down and pulled Gnilli to her feet. The crowd clapped respectfully and then began to disperse. Allee didn't notice.

"Are you sure?" she pleaded, still holding onto Gnilli's warm brown hands.

"Allee," Ferdy warned, and Allee swallowed hard. She decided that she would have to accept Gnilli's offer with as much courtesy as she could muster.

"I look forward to your companionship," Allee said, her tongue dry and thick in her mouth. Gnilli smiled widely at her, and the knot in Allee's stomach loosened. She found herself smiling back. Gnilli peered around Allee to give a shy glance at her companions.

"Oh," Allee said, remembering that she had to introduce them. "This is Esendore, Ferdinand, and Gnarrish." She pointed to each as she said his name. Gnilli eyes bugged out of her head, and she put her hand over her mouth with a frightened squeak. Allee couldn't figure out for the life of her why, but then she remembered that royalty didn't exactly drop into mountain villages. *I need to go to bed*, she moaned to herself. *How could I forget that?*

"Oh, *yeah*," she said aloud. Ferdy rolled his eyes.

"You are so dumb," he hissed. Allee's temper flared, and she felt more like herself. He bowed to Gnilli.

"Prince Ferdinand Nikolas Denerite, at your service," he said, his voice solemn. Gnilli looked terrified. Esendore flicked Ferdy on the forehead.

"Stop that," he scolded as Ferdy frowned at him. "You're scaring her." He smiled kindly at Gnilli, but she didn't seem any less frightened. Suddenly, Allee realized something and quickly pulled Esendore aside. He sent her a look, but didn't resist. "Esendore, I don't think it's a good idea to flaunt your station here," she said.

"What did you just say?" Esendore asked icily, trying to shake her off. Allee held back a sigh. This was going to be more difficult than she had thought.

"That woman is bound to have spies, looking for us," she explained, hoping he wouldn't be too thick headed. "Spies that would only know our names and not our appearances."

"The witch uses animals to do her bidding, remember?" Esendore protested. Allee clenched her teeth to keep from loosing her temper.

"I know," she said, enunciating every syllable, "but she could have planned an ambush or something. An ambush operated by humans. Just in case, maybe we should play it safe." Esendore thought for a moment, and Allee held her breath.

"You are right," he decided, his face very thoughtful. "I'm very glad you thought of this. I'll try to be more careful in the future." Allee exhaled in relief. *We will have a much easier time fitting in now*, she thought happily. They turned back to the others, who were waiting in bewilderment. Ferdy threw a suspicious look at Allee, who ignored him and went to Gnilli's side.

"Gnilli," she said, trying to think of a simple way to say what they were doing without giving their entire mission away. She decided to be frank. "Gnilli, our journey is one of some secrecy. We can't let people know who we are. So, as you're first task, I'm asking you to keep quiet and not to tell anyone our real names, okay?" Gnilli nodded, her eyes confused. Allee's heart twisted within her. She didn't want to hurt her new charge.

"Yes, we must remain anonymous," Esendore said, smiling encouragingly. He turned to Ferdy and Gnarrish. "That goes for you two, also. We need to keep a low profile." Ferdy nodded. Esendore seemed to take this plan to heart. He pointed a finger at Ferdy. "If anybody asks, you are Frederic," he said.

"That's my least favorite name in the world," Ferdy muttered, but Esendore ignored him.

"And I am Dainian," he continued, frowning in concentration. "We are traveling with our um…sister to visit some friends over the mountains." He blushed slightly, and Allee wished he had let her come up with the story. They neither looked nor acted like siblings. But he seemed to think he was doing a fine job, for he continued on surer of himself. "Allee, you can use your shortened name. Gnarrish, you come up with something suitable for yourself."

Gnarrish nodded gravely, but Allee could tell he was trying not to laugh at Ferdy, who was rolling his eyes behind his brother's back. Gnilli turned to look at the other gnarf as if seeing him for the first time. Her puzzled face broke into a grin.

"I know you!" she cried, overjoyed. "Your Aunt Gnolly lives on the same street as my uncle and I! She will be very pleased to see you!" Gnarrish blushed as Ferdy rounded on him.

"You never told me you had family here!" he exclaimed. Gnarrish blinked at him.

"I didn't think family reunions were a priority on this trip," he said dryly. Ferdy frowned at him and drew himself to his full heights so he looked more commanding.

"Gnarrish," he said, his voice serious, "I command you to visit your aunt." He paused and went back to his normal voice and posture. "There, now, you go visit her. People need to talk to their aunts, it's good for them." He realized what he had just said, and slapped his forehead. "Did I really just say that?" Gnarrish chuckled.

"Of course you didn't," he replied, grinning. Ferdy made a face at him. Gnarrish just laughed. "See you in the morning!" he said, shouldering the pack that had been sitting by his feet and starting off for his aunt's house.

"Bright and early!" Ferdy called after him. Gnarrish waved lazily to show he had heard and disappeared around the corner.

Ferdy rolled his eyes while Esendore shook his head fondly. Then he turned back to business.

"Now," he said, his voice brisk. "We need to find the inn. I told that starn boy to bring our bags there after he saw to the zeorses. Would you know of it, Gnilli?" Gnilli hesitated, still unsure of him. Ferdy realized her discomfort before Esendore did.

"It's not that we don't trust you, Gnilli," he assured her. "It's that we don't have time to explain it to you now."

"I'll tell you everything you want to know as soon as we find the inn," Allee said, trying to make her understand.

"And some food," Ferdy added. Gnilli looked from one face to the other and, looking much more at ease, grinned.

"That will not be difficult, Masters and Lady," she said, her smile growing larger. "My uncle owns it! I could find the Frosty Mug with my eyes closed."

"The Frosty Mug?" Esendore interrupted, puzzled. "I thought it was 'The Roaring Avalanche'." Gnilli giggled.

"It was," she laughed, "Until my uncle bought it some five years back. He changed it because he said he likes aleer much better than an avalanche. You can meet him for yourself, it's just right over here!" She trotted off, waving for them to follow. Allee and Ferdy looked at each other and snickered.

"I think I like this uncle all ready," Esendore said, smiling, and they followed the small figure down the street.

The Frosty Mug was a clean, well-run establishment, with its whitewashed front rising two and a half stories above the ground and its brightly painted sign swinging in the evening breeze. A smaller, plainer sign was nailed directly above the door, which was open, spilling light into the dusky street. Allee craned her neck to read it.

> *All ye who sup and do not pay*
> *Shall be merrily beaten a night and a day.*

"Steal something, Ferdy," Allee whispered in his ear. "I want to see you merrily beaten."

"You first," he hissed back. Allee couldn't retort; she was too busy trying to get her eyes to adjust to the bright interior of the inn. Her eyes could finally focus when she thought she had gone deaf. An ear-splitting roar shook the inn as the entire house cheered her successful rescue of their favorite aleer maid. Beet red, she hid behind Esendore, but Ferdy dragged her back out again to be embraced by a very excited gnarf, his white hair and mustache bristling with gratitude.

"My thanks cannot be put into words," he said, one arm wrapped about his flushing niece. Allee tried to say something in return, but all that came out was a squeak.

"She says 'your welcome'!" Ferdy shouted over the town people's babble, enjoying Allee's discomfort immensely. Gnilli's uncle smiled broadly at her, and Allee finally got her voice back.

"It wasn't that big of a deal," she muttered, trying to stop blushing.

"Nothing could have been bigger!" he cried, waving his free arm wildly. "I am Gnilli's guardian, but I am glad that she has another one! Naught can make me happier than seeing her safe and in the service of such a noble and gracious Lady such as yourself, and you, Lords," he bobbed his head respectively in the Princes' direction.

For a second, Allee was afraid that Gnilli had told the secret of their identity, but realized that anyone could tell Esendore and Ferdy were noblemen just by looking at their clothes. *At least no one knows which noblemen they are*, Allee thought. Suddenly, Gnilli's uncle clapped his hands and two human boys appeared behind him.

"Whatever you want, I will do everything in my power to make sure you get it," he said, a pad and pencil seeming to come out of thin air. "Command me." Extremely embarrassed at his enthusiasm, Allee started speaking before Esendore could have a chance to do something, in Ferdy's words, "Esendoreish".

"We need four beds," she started, thinking fast as he scribbled. "Counting Gnilli, for tonight, in two separate rooms, if you have them, and food and drink for all of us, if you can spare it." She was trying to be polite as she could, but he seemed to take offense.

"'If I have them', 'if you can spare it'," he mimicked, his moustache bristling. "Child, you just saved the life of my niece! You can have the whole house if you want it!" he shouted. His customers looked up in surprise.

"Let them eat their food!" Allee cried, laughing, and they turned back to their conversations. "In that case, I want two rooms with two beds in each of them, and as much hot food as we can eat, and three baths, two in one room and one in mine. Two, if Gnilli wants one. Will that work?"

"And if it doesn't?" he countered, teasing her.

"That's too bad!" she declared. He roared with laughter and slapped her on the back.

"That's more like it!" he shouted, and snapped his fingers at the boys. "Draw the baths for the gentlemen," he commanded, and they ran to do his bidding. "Gnilli, you can take care of the Lady's." Gnilli, her eyes twinkling, followed the boys. "And now," the old gnarf said, turning back to Allee with a flourish of his pencil, "I beg your name of you, Fair Lady."

"Well, it's certainly not Fair Lady," she replied. He roared again, and this time tears leaked out the corner of his eyes.

"I beg your pardon," he gasped, wiping at them with his apron. Allee could feel Esendore shaking with suppressed laughter behind her and couldn't help grinning. The man's laugh was contagious.

"My name is Allee and this is Dainian and Frederic," Ferdy winced at the sound of his new name. "My brothers," Allee continued, cringing at the lie, but she knew there was no getting around it. "We are traveling to see our friends over the mountains." Allee did not feel so bad about that part of the story. After all, Dariel was a *very* good friend of Esendore's.

"Splendid, splendid," the gnarf said, bowing at Esendore and Ferdy. "You couldn't have picked a better time. The pass over the Gargons could not be safer. You should make good time." Allee noticed Esendore sent a gloating look at Ferdy, who shrugged.

"And your name, Master Gnarf?" Allee asked. He looked startled.

"Ah, forgive me! I am forgetting myself! I am Gnathan, your humble servant, whether I like it or not, right?" Allee knew he was teasing her again.

"You better believe it," she replied. He chuckled.

"Ah, if more women acted like you I might consider finding myself one." Allee blushed, not sure if this was a compliment or not. She felt Esendore stiffen beside her and wondered why he had suddenly become so protective. She didn't like this new attitude at all. One of the boys appeared back at Gnathan's elbow and whispered in his ear.

"Your rooms are ready," the gnarf explained, waving the boy away. "Follow me, please." He led them through the crowded bar room, up a short flight of wooden stairs, and opened the first door on the left, beckoning Ferdy and Esendore inside.

"This can be your room, my Lords," he said, bowing them in. Allee moved to stop Esendore to tell him something, but he already knew what she was going to say.

"I'll scrub him to an inch of his life, don't worry," he promised, smiling wryly. Ferdy glared at both of them as Allee smiled back.

"You're going to get wet, Esendore," he warned, and the door closed behind them. Gnathan chuckled and opened the door to the adjacent room.

"If it pleases you, Lady, this room is yours," he said. Allee let the "lady" go, knowing that it made him uncomfortable to call her anything else, and stepped inside. The room was simple, but clean, from its whitewashed walls and crisp white and blue curtains to the wooden bed and dresser.

"You have certainly found your calling as an innkeeper," she told Gnathan, making him flush under his tan. Gnilli appeared in the doorway of an adjoining room.

"You bath is ready," she said, drying her hands on a towel hanging on the edge of the bed.

"Then I will leave to prepare your meal," Gnathan said. "Any requests?" he asked, his hand on the door.

"Just no internal organs," Allee said quickly, to make sure her first real meal in five days would be a decent one. "Or anything closely related to them."

"I can do that," he laughed, and bowed his way out. Allee shook her head in amusement and turned to Gnilli, who was waiting to help her with her bath.

"I can bathe myself," Allee said, gently, and Gnilli bit her lip, unsure of what to do. "But could you do something else for me?" Allee continued.

"Anything, Lady," Gnilli replied, her eyes shining.

"I want to be your friend, not your master," Allee said, grasping one of the gnarf's hands. "So please, please, call me Allee." Gnilli nodded solemnly.

"I will go find your things," she said, walking over to the door and opening it. "Allee," she added, smiling shyly. Allee smiled encouragingly and went to take her bath.

The warm water was heavenly, but Allee didn't linger for long. She was more hungry than dirty and quickly returned to the other room to find Gnilli pouting on the bed.

"You own not a single dress!" she cried, horror in her voice. Allee grinned in spite of herself.

"Nope. And even if I did, I wouldn't wear it." Gnilli made a disgruntled noise.

"That's what the Young Prince said," she said. Trying not to laugh, Allee threw on the blue shirt and cream-colored pants Gnilli had found and began brushing her hair.

"Don't let me forget," she said, thoughtfully. "We'll need to get you some shirts and pants, too."

"What?" Gnilli yelped. "I couldn't...I can't...it won't work. I—"

"It won't work for you to ride behind me in a dress, either," Allee reminded her. She knew that Gnilli would not like dressing like a man, but the only way she could see the gnarf coming with them was to ride behind her. She didn't know what would happen when Dariel joined them. She couldn't picture the Countess riding astride even if they did find a zeorse for her. "Tomorrow we will have to see if your uncle has anything you can use." Gnilli sighed.

"I suppose you're right," she sighed. Allee tied up her hair and jumped off the bed.

"Come on," she called, heading for the door. "I'm starving. Hope you don't like internal organs because they're not on the menu."

"Yuck," Gnilli agreed, and followed her out.

Ferdy and Esendore were already seated at a table in the corner by the stairs.

"You took a *long* time," Ferdy complained as they sat down. "What did you do, decide to take a nap?"

"Oh, hush," Esendore said, poking him. "You just got here two minutes ago." Ferdy immediately looked sheepish, and Allee rolled her eyes. Gnathan appeared moments later bearing platters of food.

"No internal organs or anything even closely related," he said, setting down the plates of potatams, ducken, and bread.

"You are absolutely marvelous," Allee said, filling her plate.

"Agreed," Ferdy said, tearing off a piece of bread.

"Thank-you, thank-you, you're too kind," Gnathan mumbled. His pen and paper appeared again. "And what to drink tonight? Lord?" He turned to Esendore, pencil poised.

"The house special," he said, smiling at the gnarf. Gnathan nodded.

"The same for you, Lord Frederic?" Ferdy looked at Gnathan like he had offered him something poisonous.

"No!" he said so forcefully that several people looked up in alarm. Allee was taken back. She assumed that the "house special" were the tankards she had seen earlier. All ages of people were drinking out of them, including some that looked younger than Ferdy. She had thought he would want to prove he could do anything Esendore could. Gnathan's bushy eyebrows knitted together in surprise, and before Ferdy could make a scene Allee interrupted.

"We'll just have water," she said, smiling. Gnathan nodded again, and left. Allee raised her eyebrows at Ferdy over her plate, but he ignored her and began cutting up his ducken. Allee shook her head. *I'll never understand him* she decided and began enjoying her meal.

Gnathan soon returned with the drinks.

"Anything else?" he queried, setting the cups down. They all shook their heads (their mouths were too full of food), and he left to join a game of Deceit.

None of them said anything other than "pass the butter" during the entire meal, but when they had finished, Allee was eager for human conversation, or, rather, conversation that wasn't with Esendore, Ferdy, or Gnarrish. Besides, Esendore was preoccupied with the talk at a table near them, and Ferdy was involved in a dart game against Gnathan. Allee kept noticing him sending worried glances back at Esendore, but she couldn't figure out why and decided she must be imagining things.

"Your uncle is very nice," Allee commented, watching him compliment Ferdy on a well-thrown dart.

"Yes," Gnilli said, her eyes misting slightly. "I am very fortunate to have him." Without any urging from Allee, she explained. "My parents died in the epidemic of Blossom Fever."

"The same one that killed the Queen?" Allee asked softly. Gnilli thought a moment before nodding.

"Yes, I guess so. I've really never made the connection before. We are very cut off from the pastle out here." They sat in silence a minute and watched Gnathan stick his tongue out in concentration as he aimed for his next throw.

"He will miss you," Allee said suddenly, feeling guilty that she was taking his pride and joy away from him.

"Yes," Gnilli said, but she did not sound sad. Allee realized that Gnilli was looking forward to seeing new things, and felt better. "He does not like to iron the linens." Allee laughed.

"I see wrinkled sheets in the Frosty Mug's future," she predicted. Gnilli laughed in agreement. "But that cannot be all you do around here," Allee pressed, eager to hear about her new friend's life. She was not disappointed. Gnilli enthusiastically described her usual day at the inn. As she listened, Allee decided that she had no desire ever to start a hotel chain.

"Allee," Gnilli inquired a little later, looking puzzled. "Would now be a good time to ask you *my* questions?" Allee took a quick look around. There was nobody except Esendore within listening distance.

"Go for it," Allee replied.

"Exactly why are you here?"

"I have no idea," Allee said without thinking. Seeing Gnilli's face, she changed her answer.

"Just kidding," she said, trying to think of a good reply. "Have you ever heard of the Prince's betrothed, Dariel?" Gnilli shook her head. Allee took a deep breath. "Oh, boy, here we go..."

The story took much longer than Allee had anticipated. When she had finished, her voice was very hoarse and she was more then ready to go to bed. Thankfully, she had told it so well that Gnilli didn't have any questions, so Allee was free to let her attention wander. She rolled her neck on her shoulders to try to get the kinks out and looked around.

She noticed that Ferdy was no longer absorbed in his dart game, but was staring at something else. Allee let her gaze follow the direction he was staring in and saw that he was looking at Esendore, who was acting extremely odd. His head was wobbling slightly on his neck, and his eyes didn't seem to be able to focus on the shaking hands spread out in front of him. Suddenly, he slumped forward on the table. Allee stood up in horror. Ferdy was at his side in a second, almost like he had been expecting it.

"What's the matter with him?" Allee gasped, running around the table to his side, Gnilli right behind her. Ferdy, looking grim, was throwing Esendore's arm over his shoulder.

"Distract her," he hissed, nodding his head at Gnilli. Allee threw a quick look over her shoulder at the gnarf, who was looking somewhat suspicious. Allee didn't understand, but she complied.

"Gnilli," she said, getting under Esendore's other arm, "go turn down my bed and then find my night clothes, please." Gnilli gave Allee one more bewildered look and fled to do her bidding.

Allee and Ferdy gave a mighty heave and got Esendore suspended between them. Beads of sweat had broken out on Ferdy's forehead, but Allee didn't think Esendore was all that heavy. Luckily, their table was at the back of the room so nobody noticed the odd threesome. Allee gave a breath of relief; she knew Ferdy wanted to avoid all the questions that he could.

Just to make sure nobody was looking their way, she glanced back over her shoulder. For some reason, she thought that something looked wrong with their table, but before she could recognize what it was, she had to concentrate on climbing the stairs and getting the Princes' door open. Ferdy did it for her, forcing it open with a kick. Allee winced and readjusted Esendore's weight.

"Ferdy, what's wrong with him?" she asked again as soon as they were inside. "The food couldn't have been—" With a flash, Allee realized what had been wrong with the table. There had been five empty aleer tankards sitting on it.

"Oh," she breathed, "He's drunk."

"Quiet," Ferdy growled, slamming the door behind them. Her mind reeling, Allee let Esendore sink onto his bed while Ferdy bolted the door. The Crown Prince sighed blissfully and started humming. And for once, he was on key. That made Allee even more worried.

"Do you think he'll be okay?" she asked, her voice calmer than the emotional turmoil inside her. She had never, ever dreamed Esendore would do something like this.

"Of course," Ferdy snapped, walking over to the window and peering out. "It's no different from the other times." He drew the curtains closed, even though they were on the second story and it was after eleven. Allee didn't know how more shocked she could get.

"This has happened before?" she demanded, astounded. She had thought that Esendore had simply underestimated the potency of the ale. Then realization hit her like a brick.

"That's what you were going to say yesterday," she accused, thinking back to the episode in her tent. The expression on Ferdy's face didn't change, but Allee saw his eyes flicker in recognition. She pressed on. "You said that Esendore went and got advice when he was stressed out, but you were really going to say that he goes out and gets drunk!"

"So?" Ferdy said defensively. "He's got a lot to deal with! You said so yourself! So who cares if he tries to relax once it a while? I certainly don't." He moved over to his brother's side, and ignoring the humming, jerked the bedclothes over him. Allee gave a silent prayer in thanks that at least he was a happy drunk.

"Is it really every once in a while?" she asked, her voice shrill and her heart pounding. She did not want Ferdy to hate his brother, but she didn't want him to fight his battles for him either. And that was exactly what it sounded like he was doing. "Or does it happen a lot?" From his the look on his face, Allee knew the answer.

"He gets stressed out a lot," Ferdy protested. "So, naturally, he tries to relax a lot. It doesn't mean anything."

"It means EVERYTHING," Allee said pointedly.

"IT DOES NOT!" Ferdy yelled, shocking Allee into silence. She glared at him, wondering why he was being so defensive. Ferdy closed his eyes, trying to get himself under control. "It's not a problem," he said. Allee raised an eyebrow and snorted in disbelief. He glared back at her, but then wavered a little. "And even if there is a problem, it's only a little one." Allee's sympathy instantly vanished at his stubbornness.

"Then he still needs help," she insisted. "I'm sure there are other alternatives when he's stressed out. If the Duchess knew—"

"NO!" Ferdy shouted. "I'm the only one who knows, I'm the only one he's trusted to tell, and you and me are the only ones who are going to know!"

"He just told you so he wouldn't have to worry how he was getting to bed," Allee objected. "He's using you—"

"STOP!" Ferdy bellowed. Allee glared harder at him, furious at the way he was treating her, like she was wrong and he was right. Ferdy's breath was coming in gasps, but he was no longer excited. Instead, it seemed that all the energy had drained out of him and his shoulders slumped.

"Just try," he said, his voice so low that Allee could barely hear him. She leaned it closer and found herself looking into his eyes. The pain there disturbed her, but she held his gaze, trying to help him with what he had to say. He took a deep breath.

"Just try to understand," he continued, looking at his outstretched palms. "I am doing this, putting up with this because if the people would find out that the Prince, the *Crown* Prince, got drunk—even just on occasion—the story would grow and be distorted until there wasn't a scrap of truth in it anymore, and pretty soon, His Highness is a stupid drunken fool who is never sober and it would just be…just be," he stopped, and his hands clenched into fists as he struggled to find the words.

A whirl of pictures flew through Allee's mind, pictures of people distrusting the royal family even more, of Esendore as a laughingstock, and even a horrible one of a peasant revolt. *I do understand*, she realized. Ferdy's back was to her as he stared at his sleeping brother, and though Allee felt extremely awkward doing it, she touched his elbow.

"I understand," she said softly, trying to think of how to comfort him. "And I will help you as much as I can." He didn't say anything. "You really are very brave for doing this," she added softly. Ferdy still didn't reply, but Allee could tell that he was thinking about what she had just said. Esendore suddenly let out a moan.

"Ferdinand," he croaked. Ferdy went over and wet a cloth in the nightstand pitcher, then placed it over his brother's forehead. Esendore stirred once and then lay silent.

"You can go if you want to," Ferdy said, his voice weary. Allee's heart ached for Ferdy as he gazed mutely at the burden that had been forced upon him, this burden that he carried without a complaint. She yearned to help him, but she knew that she couldn't do anything more than encourage both of them.

"Okay," she said, her voice soft. She edged towards the door and stopped, her hand on the knob. "But, Ferdy," she added, unsure of what to say. "I'm…I'm just next-door if…if," she stopped, lost for words.

"Yeah," Ferdy replied, turning around the look at her. Allee felt herself flush. "Yeah, I know." Before her blush could get any deeper, Allee fled to her room.

The brightness of her chamber made Allee pause in the doorway to let her eyes adjust. Gnilli had lit every candle in there.

"Allee?" came the gnarf's concerned voice. "Allee, what happened?" Allee came completely into the room and saw the small figure sitting stiffly in the chair by the bed.

"Just too much food and drink after hardly any on the trail," Allee explained, closing the door to hide her face, fearful that it would give her half-truth away. She was also surprised Gnilli hadn't guessed. Surely she had seen other drunks pass out before. Or maybe the mountain people could hold their liquor with more dignity. She turned back around to find Gnilli much more relaxed.

"You don't have a night gown," she said in an accusing tone. Allee smiled at her, too tired and depressed to laugh.

"Yeah, I know," she said. "Throw me my pajamas." Gnilli looked at her disapprovingly, but handed over the clothes. Still smiling, Allee went into the bathroom to change. When she came out, only one candle was burning and Gnilli was in her bed, asleep. Allee gazed fondly at her as she climbed into her own. *She is too nice for me*, she thought, trying to get comfortable.

The bed was very soft and much better than a sleeping cloth on the ground, but Allee's just couldn't stop tossing and turning. She was even too disturbed to go find the ruby. But, for once, it wasn't her thoughts that kept her awake. It was the retching noises coming from the next room.

Chapter 9

The Gift of the Alzius

Allee awoke to total darkness the next morning. She didn't know exactly what time it was, just that it was early enough that nobody in her right mind should be awake, but, unfortunately, as she had proved when she chose to go on this crazy trip, she was not in her right mind and therefore she should get ready to go or they wouldn't be able to cross the mountains in two days. The room was quite warm, but Allee shivered at the thought of crossing those monsters. She was spared from dwelling on her new worries when a crash reminded her of her problems next door.

"Esendore!" Ferdy's muffled voice cried. "You can't have forgotten how to WALK!" In her relief that they had both survived the night, Allee didn't catch Esendore's reply, if he had replied at all. Quietly, so as not to wake Gnilli, she got out of bed and began to get dressed.

"Morning?" asked an extremely sleepy voice inside her nose. Allee almost smiled.

"Sort of," she whispered back. There was a small squeak, followed by a flurry of light as the rest of the fairies awoke.

"Good morning!" they called, their enthusiasm not dampened in the least by the early hour. Allee shook her head in exasperation and stuck the ruby in her pocket as always. She wasn't quite sure why she carried it with her at all times, but it seemed to offer some sense of security. She knew she needed all she could get and started looking for the saddlebag with her socks in it. She had accidentally put them in the one with the pots and pans during yesterday morning's rush.

Much to her disgust, she found that she had one of Ferdy's bags instead. Along with a slingshot, a pad of paper, a squashed loaf of bread, and a jar with something slimy in it, the bag held three pairs of socks. Revolted with the slimy thing and the total waste of a saddlebag, Allee decided to borrow some. She picked the cleanest pair and noticed that they were extremely heavy. Surprised, she pried the socks apart and a little leather bag fell into her hand.

"Ah," she said softly. "So here's how we pay our bill." Quickly making up her mind to go find Gnathan to pay and buy some more food for the rest of their journey, Allee donned her stolen socks, stuffed her feet into her shoes, and slipped out the door.

She groped her way down the stairs in pitch black, and much to her relief, she saw a chink of light at the bottom of the kitchen door. Pushing it open, she was startled to find that she had either grown or the room had shrunk. All the counters only came to a little below her waist and the cupboards were no higher than her head. She realized that the room had been modified to fit Gnathan and Gnilli's shorter stature. *Funny*, she thought, *I haven't even noticed their small size that much*. Even though both gnarfs only came up to her shoulder, their personalities made them seem much bigger. Suddenly, she heard a noise to her left and she turned to find Gnathan kneading bread in his nightgown. He did not seem surprised to see her.

"Good morning!" he said, brushing off his hands on his apron and pouring her a glass of aplrange juice from a pitcher by his elbow. "Hoping to get an early start at crossing the Gargons?"

"Early?" Allee repeated, looking at the darkness outside the window. "It's so early it's late." He laughed and patted her arm with a floury hand.

"Don't worry, it won't catch up with you until later," he assured. "You're young still. Now, it's us old people that know what early is." He yawned and stretched. Allee yawned in reply. He chuckled, and covered his ball of dough with a towel. "What supplies do you need?" he asked, knowing why she was there. Allee eyed the towel.

"Bread for sure," she replied, going over all their supplies in her head and realizing that she had no idea what she was doing. She decided to guess. "The kind that travels well. And some dried fruit. Oh, and milk since we can keep it cold. We have plenty of dried meat, but fresh would be good if we can get it. I wouldn't want to take anything you need." He waved her apology away and began packing a leather bag full of anything he could lay his hands on. The supplies were all neatly tucked away in less than five minutes.

"This should be enough to last you for a while," he said when he was finished, setting the bag in front of her. She smiled gratefully at him and brought out the little leather bag.

"Including this, supper and the rooms, how much do we owe you?" she asked, taking out some gold pieces and breathing a sigh of relief when she saw that they had the number of their amount engraved in them. Gnathan seemed alarmed.

"Nothing, nothing," he insisted, taking a step back. "I couldn't take anything after what you did for Gnilli, I just couldn't." Allee was too grateful for his kindness to let him go without a reward.

"And I," she said firmly, shoving six pieces into his hand, "couldn't *not* pay you, for your service to us, and for the outstanding way you have raised my new friend." Gnathan gave her a long look, and silently took the coins.

"You are most noble, Lady," he whispered.

"I'm more stubborn than anything," Allee replied. Suddenly, the door opened behind her and Ferdy walked in. Allee tried not to look at him just in case her face would reveal something to Gnathan, but she couldn't help noticing the deep rings under Ferdy's eyes.

"You've gotten the supplies?" he asked, but before she could answer he spied the bag. "Great. Do we need anything other than food?" Allee quickly thought of Gnilli.

"Oh, that reminds me. Gnilli needs clothes suitable for riding astride. I was hoping you would have something she could wear."

"Ride astride?" Gnathan repeated. "Oh, I bet she likes that idea." Allee smiled in return. She was too sleepy to make much of an effort for conversation. He knew the answer anyway, and chuckled. "Of course," he assured, winking. "I'll find her something appropriate."

"Take as long as you want to say good-bye to her," Allee told him. He nodded, handed Ferdy his own cup of aplrange juice, and disappeared behind another door. Allee watched him go, a smile playing on her lips. She missed him already, and she had just met him last night. The smile soon faded as she turned back to Ferdy and remembered the mess they had upstairs.

"So," she said, trying to find out what the plan was without seeming to pry. Ferdy passed a hand over his eyes.

"I think he's pretty much recovered since I poured the sober-up drink down his throat, but we're going to have to tie him to the saddle," he said wearily. "So while I go find Gnarrish and get the horses, I want you to pack our stuff and find some rope. Try to hurry. We wanted to get at least half way today." Allee nodded mutely and resisted the urge to try to comfort him. She knew she couldn't say anything to make their job easier. He seemed to know what she was feeling and nodded at her as he left the kitchen. Allee took a deep breath, squared her shoulders, and followed him out.

Back in her bedroom, Allee woke up Gnilli and sent her down to her uncle. As soon as the gnarf was out the door, she began packing her stuff into her saddlebag. It was the best she had repacked all week, but she was still surprised to see all the room left over. She left it open for Gnilli and decided to go next door and pack up the rest.

She didn't bother to knock and stole softly into the room, startled to find Esendore dressed and lying on top of his bed. She breathed a sigh of relief when she realized he was asleep and hurriedly began picking up clothes.

During her last sweep of the room, she spied a pair of socks under the bed and dove for them. As she used a hand to push herself back out, someone grabbed a hold of her wrist. Biting back a scream of surprise, Allee found herself looking into Esendore's eyes. She didn't need to worry about bothering him; she doubted they could go more unfocused, but she ducked her head nonetheless.

"Allee," he said hoarsely, trying to bring her head back up. She kept looking at the floor. She didn't want her eyes to betray how disgusted she was with him. His hand let go of her wrist and dropped to his side.

"Allee, please don't do this," he begged, a waver entering his voice. "I...I know I'm being selfish again, and that all I do is be selfish, but I don't want to be. I'm trying really hard." Allee tried to keep from making a noise of disbelief, but she couldn't help it. She felt Esendore slump even lower.

"Allee, please," he implored again. "You are the last person in the world I want to have mad at me." Allee looked up in surprise. He had to be joking. But his face was more serious than she had ever seen it.

"Truly, Allee," he said, his voice stronger. "I see it in your face that you don't believe me, but I swear I'm not lying to you. I've never had anyone like you to have a true, unbiased opinion about me. You have never lied to me about what I'm like just to make me happy, and you never will." Against her better judgment, Allee felt herself believing him. He noticed and hurried on. "Please, Allee, please understand...you...and Ferdinand...you make up the parts of me that are missing. Like we're all a family...a real family. I have always wanted one. Please, Allee. Please forgive me." His voice ended in a whisper.

Allee looked at him with a mixture of pity and bewilderment, trying to find something to cling to in the whirlwind of emotion that was roaring inside of her.

"He's such a jerk," she thought, but then she remembered the waver in his voice and her heart softened.

"He's just confused," she decided, but then she remembered the way he had frightened her.

"He's irresponsible," she told herself fiercely.

"No," the other part of her said, *"he just needs someone to take care of him. He can take care of himself,* she argued. *He's a jerk...he's so pathetic...he's selfish and he's—"*

"He's sorry and I can't help that I have a forgiving nature," she told her analyzing, practical self, and all of a sudden the whirlwind stopped.

"I forgive you," she said aloud, smiling her brightest smile at him. He gave her a weak grin in return. Allee knew she was being stupid, but she had to ask anyway. "Am I the big sister or the little sister?" she inquired. He gave her a real smile and fell back onto his pillows.

"Both," he whispered, closing his eyes again.

"If you say so," Allee said, rising slowly to her feet and gathering up the saddlebags. She only had to carry three; the rest had been left with the zeorses.

"Tell Ferdinand I'm sorry," Esendore croaked. Allee thought Esendore should tell Ferdy himself, but she humored him.

"I will," she promised, and edged out the door. She turned around and almost ran into Gnilli.

"How do I look?" the gnarf asked, throwing out her arms. Allee appraised her carefully, glad for a distraction. Her charge was now garbed in what Allee considered "normal" clothes. The crisp cream shirt and tightly woven brown pants looked ready for anything. Allee nodded in approval, but a voice other than hers was the first to praise Gnilli.

"You look absolutely stunning," Gnarrish said, standing at the head of the stairs with his head tilted to one side. Allee had never heard him compliment anyone before, but by the way he was looking at Gnilli, Allee knew he meant every word. Gnilli knew it, too, and blushed prettily. Gnarrish tore his eyes away from her to address Allee.

"Ferdinand sent me to see if you were ready," he said. Allee wondered briefly if Ferdy had told Gnarrish about Esendore's condition and decided that he had probably made something up. However, she also knew Gnarrish wasn't stupid and he probably had guessed what was really going on.

"Yep," she said, holding up the saddlebags. "I just have to find some rope." Gnilli looked puzzled.

"I know where some is, but I don't understand why you need it," she said, wrinkling her eyebrows. Allee thought fast, but Gnarrish beat her to it.

"Lord Esendore still isn't feeling well," he explained smoothly. "He is going to need to be secured to his zeorse." Gnilli's mouth formed a round O, and she nodded.

"I'll be right back," she promised, and raced down the stairs, blushing as she passed Gnarrish. He watched her go with a funny look on his face.

"Can you get him going by yourself?" Allee interrupted him. He snapped his attention back to her.

"I think so," he said, looking thoughtfully at the closed door. "You can take the saddlebags down to Ferdy. He's loading up the zeorses."

"Great," Allee replied, starting down the stairs. "Good luck." He nodded and opened the door.

Allee groped her way though the common room and threw open the front door. The rush of cool air blew away most of her misgivings. She took a deep breath and looked around. The morning was even foggier than the day they had left Goldham. Allee bumped into Ferdy before she saw him. They both yelped in surprise and stood looking at each other.

"Esendore says sorry," Allee blurted, not knowing why she had to tell him this very second. Ferdy snorted.

"Fat lot of good that's going to do us," he snapped, grabbing the saddlebags from her. Allee felt her temper flare.

"At least he's in a good mood," she snapped back, feeling her good feelings toward the younger Prince vanish. Ferdy lashed on the bags, his back to her.

"I don't need him in a good mood," he said tersely, "I need him to be able to ride!" Allee was ready to snap at him again, but thankfully, Gnilli appeared with the rope and their squabble ended.

Esendore was able to walk out under his own power, but as soon as he was on top of Majesty he slumped in the saddle, clearly exhausted. Ferdy and Gnarrish tied him on while Allee taught Gnilli how to mount. The gnarf had never ridden anything larger than a llonkey before and was very nervous. Allee had never really ridden *anything* prior to four days ago and felt like she was the blind leading the blind, but she did manage to get Gnilli seated comfortably behind her without too much mishap. She was feeling quite optimistic about the journey until she realized Ferdy was going to lead them, and then she began to fervently hope that he knew where they were going.

They rode for almost a half an hour through the mist before a sign loomed at them. GARGON PASS it proclaimed boldly, and Allee gazed apprehensively at the sheer cliff sides that formed the walls of the pass. *Maybe it won't be so bad*, Allee thought as she craned her neck upward. The jagged, gigantic peaks were mostly invisible in the dark, but Allee could still hear the shriek of the wind as it whistled around them. She looked quickly back down at her saddle. *Nope*, she decided, looking from the mountains to Ferdy's white face, *we're doomed*. Taking a deep breath and trying to cheer herself with the fact that at least she wouldn't be hot anymore, she nudged Dazzle into line behind Gnarrish.

Midmorning they stopped to gnaw on the travel biscuits and unpack the heavy cloaks and gloves they had brought for this part of the trip. Allee shivered as more flurries of snow came off the peaks around them and tried to find something good about their situation. *At least Esendore has woken up enough so that we could untie him*, she mused, watching as the Prince choked down his biscuit. *And Gnilli hasn't fallen off yet*, she added, thinking of the gnarf's solid presence behind her. Now that she had gotten the hang of riding astride, Allee hoped Gnilli wouldn't hold onto her waist so tightly. She was finding it difficult to breath. A little more cheerful and a great deal warmer, Allee remounted Dazzle and the party continued on its way.

Soon after their stop, the sun finally decided to make an appearance, breaking through the thick mass of gray clouds to illuminate the mountainside with a dazzle of light. For the second time in her life, Allee felt like she was in a different world. In front of her was a sparkling vista of white and sunlight and behind her was the entire country of Taween. She had to keep looking over her shoulder to gape at it. She had never been so high in her entire life. Most of the terrain was forest, but every so often was a glisten of water or smoke from a village.

The brightness of the snow made her see spots, but she couldn't help looking at it. The zeorses were very interested in the white stuff, too. They kept stopping to sniff it gingerly and would sometimes even stick their noses in. As soon as they felt how cold the snow was, they would snort and prance excitedly.

Everyone was having a hard time keeping their mounts under control, so as soon as they reached a semi-clear spot Esendore, who was quite coherent now, said it was time for lunch. Allee dismounted gratefully, and after assisting Gnilli to the ground, began unpacking the new supplies. She had a tough time doing so; Dazzle kept dancing around to look at the sparkling world around her. Allee was thoroughly exasperated by the time she was done.

"You'd think they've never seen snow before," she commented. Ferdy looked at her in surprise.

"They haven't," he said, pouring some grain into Lunar's nosebag. Now it was Allee's turn to be surprised, but before she could ask, Ferdy explained. "I haven't seen much in my life either. It hardly ever snows in Goldham." He lifted his boot free of a drift and shook the snow off of it. "Good thing, too. Nasty cold stuff it is." He was about to say something else, but Esendore called for him, and he went off to help. Allee didn't agree with Ferdy. She liked snow and was eager to play in it.

She wolfed down her lunch and started strolling around the campsite, both to keep warm and to hear the snow crunch under her feet. With pleasure, she noted that today was the first day she could move without the hindrance of sore muscles. As she walked next to Lunar she noticed a peculiar device hanging to his saddle. Upon closer inspection, she realized it was a shield. She was certain it hadn't been there before, so she guessed Ferdy had bought it in town.

"Hey, Ferdinand!" she yelled. He looked up from his jerky and squinted at her. "What's this for?" He didn't answer right away, and Allee was instantly suspicious.

"Umm...I bought for umm...avalanche," he replied, and quickly looked back down at his lap. His excuse sounded incredibly lame to Allee. Plus, Ferdy's ears were red, which was usually a good sign he wasn't telling the whole truth. Allee had a hunch that he was worried about the Alzius again. She doubted that this mythical creature would bother them, but for some reason, she shivered as she thought about the animal. Pushing her worries out of her mind, Allee looked at the shield thoughtfully.

"Can I look at it?" she asked, intrigued by its shape. Ferdy looked back up at her, his puzzlement plain on his face.

"I don't care," he replied, and, shaking his head, went back to his meal. Allee unbuckled the device and carried it over to where the others were eating and resting. Esendore was staring off into space, Ferdy was finishing his jerky, and the gnarfs were deep in conversation, so no one noticed as she slipped into the middle of the shield, giddy with her plan. She surveyed the edge of the dell they were camped beside, looking for the smoothest way down.

"What are you doing now?" Ferdy asked, coming up behind her. Allee felt her eyes light up, and her plan changed to a scheme.

"Come closer, and I'll show you," she said, trying not to grin. She couldn't believe he was falling for the same trick she had pulled on him at the lake, but innocently, he took another step. Allee grabbed his arm, pulling him onto her sled. With a kick of her foot, they went flying down the hill.

"Aaarrgghh!" Ferdy yelled. Allee shrieked with laughter, loving the joy of a successful trick and the feel of the wind against her face. Suddenly, the sled hit a rock and they both went sprawling. Allee quickly bounced back up and began brushing herself off, her cheeks stiff from the combined effects of smiling and the cold. Once she was done, she looked around for Ferdy and found him lying spread eagle on his back four feet away. Half-worried, she walked over to make sure he was all right. He looked back up at her with a beady eye.

"You are a total MANIAC," he stated calmly, and for a second Allee was afraid he was mad at her. Her fears soon vanished as an evil grin spread across his face. "But let's do it AGAIN!" he shouted. Allee laughed at his eagerness and, after digging out the shield, followed him back up the slope. The others hadn't even noticed Ferdy and Allee had been gone.

Ferdy was about ready to clamber back on the sled when he noticed Esendore staring moodily into space. A wicked look came over his face.

"I have the most awesome idea," he whispered to Allee. Thinking she knew what he had in mind, Allee nodded, trying with difficulty to hide her own grin.

"Do it," she whispered back. Ferdy chuckled evilly and then wiped the smile off his face.

"Esendore!" he called, his voice full of concern. Allee wondered what story he had this time. Esendore snapped his head up.

"Yes?" he answered, giving his brother a little smile.

"I don't think my shield is balanced," Ferdy explained, pointing to the shield sitting on the ground. *Oh, this is going to be good*, Allee thought, folding her arms across her chest and trying to look innocent. Esendore got up and came over to inspect the offending device.

"Seems alright to me," he said, nudging it with his toe. Ferdy rolled his eyes at Allee, and she stuffed her mitten in her mouth to keep from laughing.

"You have to sit in it," Ferdy said. His eyes were gleaming, but his face was a mask of innocence. All of Allee's faith in Ferdy's storytelling ability vanished. *Esendore's not stupid*, she thought, but Ferdy went on smoothly. "You sit in it, and if it balances your weight it's good, and if it doesn't, the shield is bad. Could you try it for me?"

Allee thought Esendore had to have a terrific hangover to fall for that, but he did.

"Like this?" he asked, settling himself in the middle.

"Perfect," Ferdy replied. Allee took that to be the cue. With a mighty push, they sent Esendore rocketing down the valley. He gave a high-pitched yell, ramped over a flat boulder, and landed in a huge snow bank with a flurry of snow. He appeared moments later, spluttering and covered with it.

"I am going to BEAT you two!" he yelled, laughing so hard he could barely get the words out. Ferdy and Allee were both doubled over, clutching their sides.

"Ooh, we're so scared!" Ferdy challenged. Allee was laughing too hard to say anything. Leaving the sled, Esendore raced back up the slope and grabbed Ferdy by the waist, pulling him down into the snow. His other hand snaked around Allee's ankle and tripped her. Laughing, Allee tried to smother Esendore's face with snow. Ferdy managed to get free and then leaped back on top of his brother. His momentum was great enough to send all three of them rolling down the hill. Allee had never spun so fast in her life, especially on top of somebody else. In a heap, they landed in a snow bank and lay there, panting.

"You are simply horrible at wrestling, Ferdinand," Esendore said, breathing heavily.

"Oh, yeah," Ferdy shot back, sitting up. "Well, you scream like a girl."

"Do not," Esendore protested. Allee ignored them and starting waving her arms to make a snow angel. They were too busy squabbling to notice. As soon as she felt she had made a big enough one, she carefully stood up and surveyed the result. It was a little lopsided, but still unmistakably an angel. Ferdy and Esendore stopped bickering to stare at her creation.

"What is that?" Ferdy asked.

"A snow angel," Allee said proudly. She knew that angels existed in Betwix because Aeyr had said she was one.

"I can do that," Esendore declared, lying back and throwing out his arms. Not to be undone, Ferdy followed suit. Allee started laughing again. They looked so ridiculous. When they had finished, she helped pull them up and they all inspected the finished product: three almost-perfect snow angels.

"Great job," Esendore said, putting an arm around each of them. To Allee's surprise, Ferdy didn't resist. She smiled in relief, pleased that Ferdy had forgiven his brother.

Esendore took one last look at the angels. "We will have to see if they're still here on the way back," he added. Allee looked up at him, startled. This was the first time he had mentioned the return trip. They must be closer to their destination than she had thought. She sneaked another peek at Esendore, and gulped. His face told her that they were very, very close.

"Hey, snow people!" a shout interrupted them, and they all turned to look. Gnarrish was peering at them from the top of the hill. "Do you want to get to the other side by nightfall or not?"

"Coming," Esendore called, squeezing Allee's shoulders in a comforting way. She smiled at him again and realized that she trusted him once more. She just prayed that he wouldn't do something to make her wish she hadn't put her faith in him again. Ferdy grabbed his shield and, with Esendore's arms still around them, they walked up the slope.

When they mounted back up, Gnilli decided to ride with Gnarrish, saying she didn't want to strain Dazzle. Gnilli weighed so little Allee doubted it mattered, but she was glad there was no one to bother when the snow in her hair melted and trickled down her back, making her squirm.

Four hours after their lunch break, Allee was cold, damp, and bored. To distract herself, she reached down and plucked up some snow, which was now almost up to her stirrups. She played with it for a little bit, modeling it into a duck, and then a chicken. The feet wouldn't stay on, so Allee looked for a place to get rid of it.

On impulse, she threw the ball at the back of Ferdy's head. He jumped and looked up, thinking it had fallen from the peaks above them. Allee snickered and bent down to grab another handful. When she straightened, she was met with a face full of the white stuff. Spluttering, she tried to wipe it off with her mitten.

"How stupid do you think I am?" Ferdy asked, grinning wickedly with another snowball in his hand.

"Very," said Esendore, who was in front. Ferdy turned to insult him back and received a snowball in the face. Esendore roared while Ferdy laughed good-naturedly.

"I walked into that one," he admitted, brushing it off. Still chuckling, Esendore turned back to the path in front of him. Allee wondered who was being stupid now. *Honestly*, she thought, *turning your back on Ferdy with a snowball in his hand*? And sure enough, with a flick of his wrist, Ferdy sent his weapon sailing into the back of Esendore's head.

"Gotcha!" he yelled triumphantly. Esendore replied with another quick barrage of snow, and in his enthusiasm, got Allee, too. She retaliated, and Esendore answered with two snowballs, hitting both Allee and Ferdy.

"Is that all you got?" Ferdy challenged, spitting out snow. Esendore laughed, and turned around to grab another handful. But instead of turning back, he paused, looking at something between Majesty's ears. Allee and Ferdy's snowballs exploded at the back of his head, but he didn't move.

"Hold you fire," he said, absently. "And come look at this." Obediently, Allee and Ferdy nudged their zeorses next to Majesty. Gnilli and Gnarrish had dropped back during the heat of the battle, but now joined the others. Allee craned her neck around Esendore's shoulder, and her breath suddenly caught in her throat.

"Whoa," she said weakly. Ferdy whistled. Hundreds of feet bellow them spread the other side of the Gargons. To the east and west, smaller mountain chains to seemed to stretch forever. Directly in front of them spread the total wilderness of the Gargon foothills. Some of the hills could very easily be considered mountains. Black trees spread for miles and miles without interruption, giving the land an air of secrecy and gloom that seemed sinister in the fading daylight. Unlike the forest of Taween, no cheerful glimmers of water or homey wisps of smoke broke the trees, just darkness as far as the eye could see. Allee strained her eyes for just one hint of civilization, or of any life, even of a bird, and she thought she saw a shimmer like a heat wave on the far horizon.

"What is that?" she asked, pointing, not able to bear the silence any longer. Esendore and Ferdy squinted at where her finger lay.

"Probably the fumes of their evil cult sacrifice fires," Ferdy said moodily. Esendore rolled his eyes.

"You don't know that unless you see it happen," he chided.

"I don't see Allee take showers, but I know she does," Ferdy retorted. Allee and Esendore both hit him. Ferdy rubbed his arm and glared at them reproachfully. Esendore massaged his temple. Allee was trying to get over the idea that Ferdy thought about her taking showers.

"So I don't KILL," he said, sending Ferdy a scathing look, "my younger brother, I think we'll camp right inside the timber line." Ferdy was still miffed and remained silent, but everyone else expressed approval. "Besides," Esendore added, looking at Majesty in concern. "I don't think the zeorses should go much further."

Allee looked around at the mounts. Even though the air was quite cool, all the zeorses were breathing hard and sweating. She felt bad, but she was still glad they were going to stop soon. She did a quick tally and decided that out of the twenty-four hours in this day, she was going to be awake almost twenty of them. Slumping in the saddle with fatigue, Allee pressed Dazzle to follow Majesty.

After a half and hour of picking their way down the mountainside and getting almost nowhere, Esendore decided that they would lead the zeorses. Allee pushed her weariness out of her mind by concentrating where every footstep fell on the rocks. She didn't even notice that the timberline had begun again until she saw grass poking out from the snow under her feet. Surprised, she looked up to see everyone else already unpacking. Suddenly, Allee felt her strength return, and she vigorously began taking off her saddlebags.

Esendore, Ferdy, and Gnarrish unsaddled and hobbled the zeorses, who immediately collapsed to the ground and rolled away their tiredness. Allee began gathering wood for a fire. Just as she was ready to light the timber, Esendore stopped her.

"I don't think it would be wise to flaunt our position this close to the enemy," he said in a low voice. Allee was startled at this reminder of the closeness to their destination, but she tried not to show it.

Instead of cooking, Gnilli helped her lay out cold ducken along with a loaf of bread and some slices of cheese. The others flopped down beside them as soon as the tentopies were pitched. They didn't use any plates and drank out of their hip flasks, so, to Allee's great relief, she didn't have a single dish to wash. Still, she was bored and a little lonely without anything to do. She didn't even have anybody to talk to. Esendore was almost asleep by the fire, Gnilli and Gnarrish were talking again, and Ferdy was brushing Lunar. Eager for something to occupy her, Allee decided to explore.

"Can I go for a walk?" she asked Esendore's motionless form. He cracked an eye.

"Don't go too far – it'll be dark soon," he replied, closing it again.

"I won't," Allee assured. "Bye!" she called back, speeding down the first path she found. She assumed the track was made by some kind of animal. Esendore flipped his hand in recognition and went back to sleep.

Allee just walked in a wide circle around the camp, but she still felt like she was cut off from everybody else. After living with them for five days, she was more than ready to have a little breather. What she loved most was the absolute silence. She paused just to listen to it. Suddenly, she heard a strange cry. Allee took a step back and half-crouched behind a bush, her heart racing.

"Hello?" she called, her mouth dry, thinking of all the horrible things that lived in the wilderness. "Is anyone there?" She began to think it had just been her imagination when the noise came again. She felt herself break out in a cold sweat, but then she thought of something. "Ferdinand," she shouted angrily, "If you're trying to scare me, it isn't working!" Much braver with the thought of what she would do to him if she found him, Allee looked around the bush. What she saw almost made her hide again. Sitting in the middle of the snow-patched path was a baby wolf cub. It seemed as startled to see her as she was to see it and let out a small mew of surprise. Allee felt her shoulders sag in relief.

"Oh, hello," she said, softly, her heart melting at its helplessness. "Are you lost?" It whined piteously. Allee shifted her weight to make herself seem smaller and less threatening. "Poor thing," she soothed, hoping it wouldn't run away. She sat down so as not to scare it. Holding out her hand, she whispered, "Can I touch you?" In one fluid movement, the cub crawled into her lap. Allee froze, but soon relaxed as it snuggled into her lap.

"Oh," she breathed in awe, digging her fingers into its fur to scratch behind its ears. It sighed blissfully while Allee marveled at the deep, dark gray shade of its coat. For some reason, the color made Allee guess that the cub was a boy. "You are so beautiful," she crooned, rocking him slightly. Suddenly, she heard a crashing sound in the trees in front of them. Allee stood up, holding the baby closer to her chest, her heart pounding again. She didn't even have time to speculate before a group of men with loaded crossbows in their hands stumbled into the clearing. They saw her and froze, their eyes bugging out of their heads. Allee's breath was coming in ragged gasps, but she stared boldly back at them. The men recovered their composure first.

"Put the Alzius down, girl," the tallest said quietly, slowly raising his bow. "We need to kill it before it kills you." Allee's brain was having trouble processing this information.

"Alzius?" she repeated, looking down at the innocent animal in her arms. He gazed trustfully back at her, and, with a feeling not unlike an electric shock, Allee realized he had purple eyes set in a near-human face. Seeing his faith in her, Allee drew her arms tighter around him.

"No," she said, defiantly, her voice echoing in the stillness. She heard several of the men gasp. "He isn't hurting anybody." The men goggled at her, dumbstruck.

"It's bewitched her," one muttered, recovering his voice. Allee felt her temper rising and resisted the temptation to stamp her foot. The leader seemed to be getting desperate.

"Just put him *down*, girlie, please," he implored, taking a step toward her. Allee took a step back.

"He isn't hurting anybody," she said again.

"No," the man replied, sighing in exasperation, "But he will when he grows up and turns into a blood thirsty monster, so we need to put an end to him *now*." Allee was really angry now.

"Oh," she said, her voice shaking in withheld fury. "Well, in that case, if you kill him, you'll have to kill all *your* children, too, because they might hurt somebody when they grow up." The men all stared at her blankly. Allee glared at them. The leader glared back and turned to confer in harsh whispers with his comrades. Allee's hold on the Alzius relaxed slightly, but she still held herself tense, straining to hear their conversation.

"Fine," she heard the leader snap. "We won't kill it!" Allee exhaled in relief and, before they could change their minds, turned and raced into the forest. There were surprised yells from behind her and then the sound of their heavy boots crashing through the underbrush as they took pursuit.

Allee madly pushed on, her fury and relief making her blind to everything around her. All she cared about was the baby Alzius and getting him as far from those men as possible. Finally, she could run no more and she collapsed on the ground, her back against the bare side of the mountain she had run to. Frantically, she checked the cub for any scratches and breathed a sigh of relief when she could find none.

"Thank goodness you're safe," she whispered, rubbing his fur against her cheek.

"Thanks to you," another voice answered. All the hairs on the back of Allee's neck stood up, and she winced in pain as the voice ricocheted around the inside of her head. One hand on her temple, she scrambled to her feet and whipped around to see whom the voice belonged to. Trotting towards her was a larger and much more powerful version of the creature she held in her arms. Allee was too much in awe to be frightened.

"No problem," she muttered, unable to think straight. The Alzius stopped to stare at her thoughtfully.

"That was a very brave thing you did," it said, its voice making Allee think of frozen rocks and icy peaks. But this time it didn't echo so badly.

"I'm more stubborn than anything," Allee said, weakly. Suddenly, Allee heard a small whisper like snow falling, and she realized the Alzius was laughing. She gave a small smile in return as the great animal sat down and wrapped its long gray tail around itself like a cloak. As soon as it had gotten situated, it held out its arms. To Allee's great surprise, they were not a dog's forelegs, but remarkably human-like. The paws even had thumbs. Carefully, she deposited the baby into them and hugged herself, trying to keep in his warmth. Without him, she felt very small. The Alzius looked at her charge with such devotion and affection Allee instantly knew she was a female. Allee felt better knowing that these strange creatures had such deep feelings.

"Is he yours?" she asked, curious to find more about the cub. The Alzius looked up from crooning at the baby, her face wrinkled in surprise.

"I did not give birth to him, if that is what you mean," she replied, searching Allee's face to see if that was the answer she wanted. "But I care for him as if were my own. All of us do, for he is all of ours." With her last words, her voice echoed again, and Allee forced herself to resist the desire to put her hands over her ears.

"So...is he like your king?" she inquired, bracing herself for the voice. But this time it was soft with bewilderment.

"King?" the Alzius repeated, clearly unfamiliar with the word. "Does a king belong to his people by knowing every thought that they ever conceive? Is a king someone who loves his people so that *they* can love? Cares so *they* can care? Fights so *they* can fight?" Allee struggled to find words for a reply, perplexed with the Alzius's answer.

"Not exactly," she said, trying to think of a way to explain a king. The Alzius explained for her.

"Then Skyreae is not king," she said firmly. "More of...more of..." Her brow furrowed as she tried to find a suitable word. Then she relaxed and smiled. "More of a keeper," she decided.

"Ah," Allee said, and even though her mind couldn't work it out, her heart understood. Suddenly, the Alzius flowed gracefully to her feet. Even on all fours, she was on eyelevel with Allee. After tucking the cub into a net made from spun frost that hung from her neck, she turned back to Allee, who was again dumbstruck in wonder.

"We have been watching you, Alethea," she said, her voice lower and softer than Allee had heard it before. "For you have done many things worthy of our attention." Allee desperately tried to interrupt, knowing that she wasn't going to like what was going to happen next, but the Alzius kept talking. "And thus, there is something that I can do to aid you in your struggle." Allee stopped trying to fight whatever was going to happen and watched, enchanted, as the creature before her exhaled gently, and a soft snow began falling. As the flakes touched Allee's bare skin, they glowed with a bright blue light. With each snowflake, Allee felt a sensation like a electric shock. Then she realized that she was glowing. The creature smiled at the look of wonder on Allee's face and began to chant:

Three dangers you have braved,
Three lives you have saved,
Cardolyn, Gnilli, and Skyreae,
So the gift of life I give to thee.
When you cry it will be your say,
To give life or to take it away.

The Alzius lifted a hand in farewell, and suddenly, dense fog closed all around Allee, pressing on her eyeballs. She stood rooted to the spot, the Alzius's words reverberating over and over inside her head. *What in the world does that mean*, she asked silently, screaming and laughing at the same time. Allee felt like she was falling far, far away, never to return. Her nerves were on fire. Briefly, Allee wondered if this is what it felt like to be struck by lightning. The pain pitched, and, with a noise like thunder, disappeared. Allee stood motionless, her mind trying to come to grips with what had just happened. But before she could recover her wits, she was enveloped in a crushing embrace. Allee blinked and realized that the fog was gone now, and the sky was dark. She wondered how long she had been standing there.

"You have got to stop doing this to me," Esendore said, squashing her to his breast. Allee shook her head, trying to get rid of the mist that clouded it. She felt like she was waking up from a very, very long sleep and she had to concentrate with all her might to figure out what Esendore was saying. "...didn't come back and then the villagers came and said that they had seen you and talked to you, but you had taken off with one of those horrible *monsters*—" Allee snapped out of her daze like someone had slapped her.

"They are NOT monsters!" she said fiercely, pushing Esendore away from her so she could glare at him. The effect was kind of ruined; she couldn't get her eyes to focus. "I don't know what kills stuff, but, Esendore, I swear it isn't them." He looked at her dubiously, and she feverishly went on. "Esendore, I *talked* to one. She was extremely nurturing, doting even! They wouldn't hurt anybody, Esendore!" Her voice reached a higher pitch as she remembered more details of what had just happened. "They...they even gave me a g—" she cut herself off, suddenly wary of telling anyone about her gift. First of all, she wasn't even sure if it wasn't a curse. And second, she had to believe it happened before she tried to convince anyone else that it did. "She gave me a good feeling," she finished, very lamely. Esendore looked at her with blank confusion, which instantly switched to worry.

"Let's get you back," he said, steering her in the direction of the forest. Allee meekly let him lead her, her head spinning. They had only been walking for five minutes before she spied the tentopies through the trees.

"See," she said, her mind trying to focus on something other than snow and an echoing voice. "I didn't go very far."

"Oh, Allee," Esendore said, trying to sound exasperated, but too relieved to be convincing. Gnilli ran over to them as soon as they entered the clearing.

"Lady, Lady, are you all right?" she cried, grabbing Allee's hand.

"Yes," she replied, wishing she could think straight so she could tell Gnilli not to call her "Lady".

"Did you actually see one?" Ferdy asked excitedly, joining them. "Did it hurt you? What did it look like?"

"Fluffy," Allee replied stupidly, wanting to scream in frustration at the haze that blocked her mind.

"Fluffy?" Ferdy repeated scornfully. "You're even more crazy than you were before."

"That's enough," Esendore said firmly, guiding her to the tentopy she now shared with Gnilli. "Allee is going to bed now." He opened the flap and watched her crawl numbly inside. "Good night, Allee," he said, softly, and he gently closed the flap.

Allee mechanically got into her pajamas and crept into her sleeping bag. She wanted to think about what had just happened, she wanted to recall the baby Alzius's warmth to take away the chills that racked her body, and she desperately wanted to explain to Gnilli why she just could *not* call her "Lady", but her exhausted brain wanted sleep, and it won.

Chapter 10

Presents

Allee sat bolt upright and stared into the darkness, trying to think of what had awakened her. Beside her, Gnilli was still snoring softly, so it couldn't have been the gnarf, and she didn't hear anything outside the tentopy. She thought harder, knowing it was important. She had been dreaming…she had been dreaming about a party, a party for her…she had received a box of ferret treats for a present…she didn't even have a ferret. *That isn't important* she rebuked herself sternly. She put a hand to her forehead, forcing herself to remember. A party…for her…With a jolt of surprise, Allee realized the party had been her birthday party. Allee felt all of her strength leave her and she laid back down.

"Today is my birthday," she whispered into the darkness, which consumed this revelation without an echo. "I am fifteen today." Still, she heard was no reply, not that she had been expecting one. No "Happy birthday, sweetheart!" from her mother, no threats of birthday spankings from her father, no sticky hand-made cards or pencil holders from her little sisters, nothing but darkness and emptiness. Fiercely, Allee pushed the emptiness away. *At least I'm as old as Ferdy now,* she thought, trying to encourage herself. Loneliness threatened to overwhelm her, but luckily she was still exhausted from her ordeal, so she rolled over and went back to sleep.

Allee had one more dream that night. No ferrets in this one, though. It was a nice dream, filled with silvery green light. Suddenly, Allee became aware that she was not truly dreaming. She opened her dream eyes to see Aeyr's smiling face right above her head. They were sitting on a tussock of the silver petal strewn grass in Aeyr's forest. Before Allee could shout with joy, Aeyr bent down and kissed Allee on her forehead, pressing something into her hand.

"Happy birthday, Alethea," she said. Allee smiled in return, and as suddenly as it had come, the light vanished. Allee opened her real eyes to find the tentopy filled with a soft, early morning glow. Allee looked down at the thing cradled in her hand. It was a circlet woven of small threads of silver with blue flower-shaped gems studded at equal intervals around the circle. From the gems branched other silver chains at least a foot long, each ending in another blue flower. With a gasp of awe, Allee realized it was a headdress, to be worn in her hair.

"Oh, pretty," a voice sighed, and Allee whipped around. But Gnilli had already left. Then she remembered the fairies.

"Thanks," she replied, smiling at the gorgeous piece of jewelry in her hands. She doubted she would ever have an occasion to wear it, but it was so beautiful she didn't care. Gingerly, she wrapped it in one of her undershirts and stowed it in a deep pocket of her saddlebag. As soon as she was sure it was safe, she got dressed and crammed the ruby into her pocket, feeling much better about spending her birthday in Betwix.

When she stepped outside, her attention was immediately drawn to the campfire. At first she was confused, since Esendore had told her it was dangerous, but then she realized that it didn't matter if people saw them anymore. She had already revealed them to that group of men last night. Comforting herself with the possibility that the men would not tell anyone, she walked over to join the others. They all stopped talking to stare at her, and she was just wondering what was wrong with her now when—

"Happy Birthday!" Ferdy cried, holding out a huge, slightly misshapen, birthday cake. They laughed as Allee stood gawking.

"Who...what," she stammered, looking from one to the other. "How?" Her mind simply could not get over the fact that she was staring at her very own birthday cake with a fifteen carved in the top.

"I heard you talking in your sleep," Ferdy said proudly. Briefly, Allee wondered why he had been awake at that hour, but she was too happy to think about it long. "And so then," Ferdy went on excitedly. "We baked—," There was an ah-hem noise from behind him, and he rolled his eyes. "Okay, Gnilli," he looked at the gnarf with a "Happy now?" She nodded, and he continued. "Okay, so Gnilli baked it, but I tested the batter, and wha-la!" He seemed enormously pleased with himself. Allee finally found her voice.

"That's so sweet," she said, smiling broadly at all of them.

"Nah," Ferdy replied, the evil gleam coming back into his eyes. "We were just sick of your cooking." For once, Allee didn't even think of hitting him. Instead, Esendore flicked him with his fingers.

"You are hopeless," he scolded. Ferdy stuck his tongue out at him. "Sorry it doesn't have any frosting," he told Allee.

"It's perfect," she declared, beaming at him. "We are having it for breakfast, aren't we?"

"I love birthdays," Gnarrish sighed. Allee laughed and began cutting up her birthday cake.

In Allee's opinion, it was the best cake she had ever eaten. And to top it all off, Gnilli did the dishes for her so Allee had more than enough time to pack her things just the way she wanted them. As she tied on the last saddlebag, she heard footsteps behind her. She turned to smile at Esendore, who was holding one hand behind his back and looking extremely sheepish.

"I felt bad that I didn't have anything to give you," he started, and Allee began to protest that she didn't need anything else, but he kept going. "Since Gnilli and Ferdy baked the cake and all, so—" He took a deep breath, and brought his hand out, palm up. "Happy Birthday." Allee gasped in surprise and delight. Resting in his cupped hand was a silver necklace with a heart-shaped crystal heart bound with more silver.

"Oh, it's beautiful," Allee breathed, her hand at her mouth. She had never even dreamed of getting two gorgeous presents in one day.

"I took it from the trade goods," he explained, dropping it into her other hand. "Let me see you wear it." Happy to comply, Allee quickly fastened it around her neck. The heart settled warmly in the middle of her chest. She touched it with her finger and beamed at Esendore.

"I'll wear it always," she promised, taking one last look and then slipping it inside her shirt so it wouldn't get scratched.

"That's a long time," he replied, teasing her.

"Not for things like this," she said, truthfully. He laughed and went to go saddle Majesty. With a light heart, Allee went to go see if Gnilli needed help finishing up.

Allee tried to carry that feeling of happiness with her the rest of the day, but the difficulty of the trail worked hard to make her miserable. This side of the mountain was much, much steeper than the north side. In addition, it had about a thousand more trees. The trees hid everything; ground, sky, even the very air seemed full of leaves and branches. As a result of the stifling closeness of the vegetation, everyone sank further and further into an unshakable gloom.

They almost didn't even stop for lunch; the group was reluctant to break its concentration on the harrowing business of getting off the mountain. After lunch, Allee couldn't decide if things got better or worse. The ground did finally level out, so they didn't have to lead the horses in fear of going over their mounts' ears anymore, but with the flatter ground came, if possible, even more trees. In some places what meager path they had suddenly ended at the base of a huge conifer.

"Crazy squirbits," Ferdy would mutter. Then Esendore would get out the axe meant for chopping firewood, and he, Ferdy, and sometimes Allee would carve a path in the wilderness while Gnarrish and Gnilli cleared away the brush. It would not have been so bad if the forest hadn't been so horribly stuffy. Allee began to feel claustrophobic and longed for the open plains she was used to.

When the time to stop for the evening finally came, they could not find a single place for them to set up camp. Everyone looked around in despair as the trees seemed to press in even closer.

"Let's just keep going," Esendore said. With a sigh, the zeorses plodded onward.

The sun had set an hour ago and they had been forced to light torches before they found a clearing. They were even too tired to rejoice at the little bubbling spring that ran right next to it. Slowly, they went to perform their assigned tasks. Weariness was evident in every move they made. The zeorses didn't even have the strength to roll in the leaves, but collapsed on them instead.

Lethargically, Allee began building the fire and cooking supper while the tentopies were put up. Watching how hard it was for them to lift the heavy poles, she almost suggested to Esendore not to pitch them if he didn't feel like it. She knew that they could fall asleep anywhere tonight. They ate the fried ham and toast in silence, too tired to talk. As soon as they had finished, Allee moved to do the dishes, but Esendore, stretched out on the ground, put a hand on her arm.

"Just leave them," he croaked. Usually zealous about cleanliness, Allee just nodded, and sat back down. She was too tired to get ready for bed just yet, as were the others. But, as usual, Ferdy quickly got his strength back and began pestering his older brother.

"Hey, Esendore, I have a question," he said, poking him to make sure he was still awake.

"Ask," Esendore grunted in reply. Ferdy grinned wickedly, and Allee perked up to see what he had up his sleeve this time. "Do you remember the most interesting part of today?" Esendore grunted again, and Allee almost laughed out loud in spite of her weariness. Trust Ferdy to find something interesting in a bunch of horrid trees. "It was without doubt," he paused for effect, "The dead wolverear we saw." His companions groaned, Esendore the loudest.

"No, I don't remember that," he snapped, "That was so disgusting my mind just blocked it out."

"I wish I could block disgusting things out," Allee said glumly. "Then I could forget Ferdy even existed." Everyone stared at her for a second and then burst into laughter, including Ferdy. Esendore roared. As soon as they had laughed themselves out, Gnarrish and Ferdy began discussing the habits and traits of wolverears. Allee tuned them out, letting her weary body relax. It stiffened again when she felt a touch on her hand.

"Thanks, Allee," Esendore whispered, smiling at her. She risked a quick look in his eyes to see that he was entirely serious. "I really don't think we would have made it this far if you hadn't come with us."

"I-I'm glad you think so," Allee stammered, not sure what to think.

"I know so," he replied, and went back to listening to Ferdy and Gnarrish's discussion. Allee watched the embers of the fire glow, several emotions churning inside of her. They weren't overwhelming, just a little disturbing. She had never felt so *confused* before. Esendore was absolutely bewildering. She didn't know if she liked him being so nice to her. For some strange reason, she liked Ferdy's abuse better. With him, she was herself. Esendore made her feel like she was responsible for him. But she was really still a child of fifteen, and the sensation of being the adult made her feel very awkward. Ferdy's voice faded back into her daydreaming.

"I've heard they mostly eat squirbits — Allee, why is your nose glowing?" Allee jumped and everyone turned to gawk at her. She looked down, cross-eyed, and the brightness of her nose made spots before her eyes. She pinched the bridge, hard. There were several squeaks of surprise.

"Oh, sorry," a voice said, and the light disappeared. "Very busy, you know." Allee shook her head, wondering how she was going to explain this one. She decided to play dumb.

"Glowing?" she asked, innocently. "I don't see it." Ferdy squinted at her. Esendore made a noise of disbelief.

"Come on, Ferdinand," he said, exasperated. "Her *nose* was glowing? I think you need to go to bed." Ferdy frowned.

"It must have just been the light," he decided. His frown got deeper, and Allee hoped the darkness would hide her blush. "But I could have sworn..."

"It was just the light," Esendore chided. "Drop it." Ferdy shrugged and continued talking to Gnarrish and Gnilli.

Allee waited long enough so as not to seem suspicious and announced that she was going to bed. Gnilli was listening, enthralled, to a story Gnarrish was telling, so Allee entered their tentopy alone.

She undressed quickly and slipped into her sleeping bag, sighing as it pillowed her achy muscles. Her vow to herself not to dwell on her family's absence on her birthday was holding strong, and would have held strong, but she was so tired her defenses came shattering down and homesickness assailed her. The feeling was the worst it had ever been, and she hated her weakness in letting it bother her. *People love me here, too,* she told herself fiercely, thinking of the way Esendore and Gnarrish treated her like a little sister, and Gnilli was becoming a close friend. And Ferdy...well, she was pretty sure Ferdy liked her, too. But, try as she might to reassure herself, she knew her new friends couldn't replace her real family.

Seeking comfort, she dug out the ruby and lay down with it next to her cheek. Its warmth and familiarity comforted her, but her mother's face inadvertently swam before her eyes. This had been the first birthday she had ever missed. Allee knew she would still be sad if she was in Goldham, but sore, exhausted, and lost in the wilderness was a horrible way to spend a birthday. *Curse the witch who got me into this* Allee cried silently, and try as she might to prevent it, a single tear rolled down her cheek and landed on the ruby. As soon as it touched the gem, the ruby burned white-hot in Allee's hands. She bit back a scream, her mind trying to comprehend what was happening to her, but the pain was too much, and she was knocked unconscious. And when she awoke in the morning, she remembered nothing past the tear.

Chapter 11

The Ruby and the Duel

As Allee opened her eyes the next morning, the first thing that she noticed was the large amount of light that was seeping into the tentopy, and secondly, she couldn't hear any voices from the campfire. She looked around in alarm to see Gnilli sleeping peacefully beside her, and the bottom dropped out of her stomach. They had overslept! Fumbling in her hurry, she got dressed and fished the ruby from her sleeping bag. Leaving Gnilli sleeping in case she was mistaken, Allee slipped quietly out the tent flap. Like she had guessed, it was already mid-morning.

She hurriedly built a fire, cursing herself for being so lazy. She had just gotten the kindling burning nicely when she heard footsteps behind her. She turned to see Esendore, still in his pajamas, stretching and yawning. She almost forgot her panic at the sight of the bright purple polka dots covering his sleepwear. She shook her head, angry with herself for getting distracted

"Esendore!" she cried, and he looked at her in alarm. "We overslept!" The alarm quickly left his face and he shrugged.

"Nah," he replied, fighting another yawn. "We could sleep until noon if we wanted to." Allee stared at him, wondering if the polka dots had gotten to him, too. They were in somewhat of a hurry, or at least they had been the rest of the week.

"Huh?" He smiled at her.

"Allee," he said, gently. "The witch's lair is only a good two hours ride away." With the force of a brick, Allee realized that today was the seventh day. Today was the day that they had planned to reach their destination. She felt her legs go jelly-like as she struggled with her new revelation.

"Oh," she said in a tiny voice. "I wasn't keeping track of how far we've gone." She wished she had paid better attention; maybe she would have been more prepared. Esendore smiled again.

"I'm glad to know that at least one of us isn't thinking about it all the time," he said, half to himself. His smile had vanished. Allee's heart went out to him. She knew he thought obsessively about Dariel. "I guess it to be about eleven now," he continued, much louder. "So if you want to you can make a brunch, and we'll eat just once."

"Sounds great," Allee agreed, trying to cheer him up. His smile returned.

"Everything's great for you," he said, shaking his head. Allee didn't know how to reply, so she didn't. "I'll go get dressed," he added, and walked away. Allee watched him go, pondering his words. She wondered if the reason for Ferdy's wakefulness the other night had been due to the closeness of their goal, and suddenly, she felt just as worried as Esendore sounded. *None of us have any idea of what we're doing*, she realized, *or we wouldn't be so worried*. Allee pushed her anxiety out of her mind and focused on their meal.

Gnilli and Gnarrish rolled out of their beds twenty minutes later, both extremely apologetic for sleeping late. Allee assured them that they were fine, but Gnarrish went hunting to make up for it, and Gnilli insisted on going to search for edible berries. Allee stared after them, shaking her head in frustration.

"Ah, the stubbornness of gnarfs," Esendore mused, lounging beside the fire and listening to Allee mutter at their unquenchable persistence. She barely had time to agree with him when Gnarrish came striding out of the forest, swinging a cleaned bird Allee guessed was a quailant. Whistling cheerfully, he dropped in into the skillet and then went to help Gnilli find the berries. Allee watched him go, speechless.

"How does he do that?" she sputtered. Esendore chuckled.

"Amazing, isn't it?"" he acknowledged. "But he won't tell anyone. Some ancient gnarf haunting tactic, I guess." He shrugged to show how much he knew about the topic. "But it sure works. You really should spit that," he added, taking the quailant out of the pan. "I'll show you." As Allee squeamishly watched, he deftly cut a few branches and made a crude spit. "Ta-da!" he declared, sticking the quailant over the fire. Allee laughed at his childishness and built the blaze up higher.

Ferdy stumbled out of his tentopy when everyone else was sitting down to eat.

"You guys are loud," he complained, dishing himself a bowl of rasueberries.

"I thought your snoring would cover us up," Esendore teased. Allee was surprised that he was able to keep his sense of humor with the pressure now so heavy, but was pleased all the same. In fact, they talked and joked more at that meal than they had all week. They weren't obviously nervous or apprehensive; they had had grown close enough together that they just liked to talk. Allee chattered with Gnilli happily as they did the dishes while the others joked and laughed while they took down the tentopies and saddled the zeorses.

Their cheerfulness came to an abrupt end as they watched Ferdy and Esendore strap their swords onto their belts, the first time they had done so. For some reason, Allee felt no fear, only sadness because she could not help them. She sighed in a mixture of frustration and apprehension.

"Please, Lady," Gnilli's voice pleaded, interrupting Allee's thoughts. "Don't look like that." Allee looked up to where the gnarf was mounted on Ruby.

"Look like what?" she asked absently. Gnilli winced.

"Don't look like things are all that bad," she explained, slowly. "For it makes me sad, too." Allee was so taken back she could not speak. When she finally did get her tongue back, Gnarrish had returned from helping Ferdy and led Ruby to stand by Majesty. Silently, Allee mounted Dazzle, her heart heavy with the seriousness of the situation. Her brow furrowed with worry, she fell into line behind the others.

The path through the forest was now clear enough that Allee did not have even the smallest distraction from worrying about the ordeal ahead. After an hour of almost making herself sick, she decided to find out what the plan of action was.

She looked for Esendore, but his face showed he was deep in concentration so she didn't bother him. The gnarfs were pointing at plant life and talking quietly, lost in their own little world, but they probably didn't know anything anyway, so Allee sidled up to Ferdy, who was picking leaves off the trees and shredding them in his lap. They rode in silence for a little while, neither knowing what to say. Finally, Ferdy gave a little cough.

"So," they said at the same time, just like they had at Espy's. That day seemed a long, long time ago to Allee, but she still remembered that she had blushed just like she was doing now.

"You go first this time," Ferdy said. Allee was surprised that he remembered.

"What are we going to do?" she asked bluntly, knowing that he didn't want her to be nice about it. Ferdy ran his fingers through his hair, making it stand on end.

"I don't know for sure," he confessed, "But I think Esendore is planning to confront the witch alone—"

"ALONE?" Allee exploded, shocked. "We can't let him do—"

"Just wait!" Ferdy interrupted, holding up his hand. "I wasn't done yet. He's going to make her *think* he's alone, confront her, ask her nicely to give Dariel back, negotiate—"

"And if that doesn't work?" Allee asked. Ferdy held up both his hands.

"I'm getting to that!" he declared, glaring at her. Allee decided to keep her mouth shut for a while or she would never find out what was going to happen. After a breath, he went on. "And if negotiation doesn't work, he'll challenge her to a duel, winner gets Dariel." Allee didn't want to know, but she asked anyway.

"A duel to the death?" she whispered. He nodded slowly. Allee inhaled sharply.

"That's how it's supposed to be," he said. She stared at him in disbelief. "But it's usually to whoever begs for mercy," he assured her quickly. Allee was only a little bit relieved. "But he doesn't expect to duel," Ferdy added. Allee's relief grew as he explained. "Esendore is pretty sure the witch will strike a bargain with him. This whole scheme was so she could get land. He gives her enough money to buy some, she gives him Dariel, and they're married the week after next. Easy as that." He smiled at her reassuringly, but she could tell he was reassuring himself as much as comforting her.

"But what about us?" she inquired. "We can only watch?" Ferdy rolled his eyes.

"Pretty much," he said, disgustedly. "He said I could only help if she cheats." He stopped and swallowed hard as another thought struck him. "Or if he—," Allee realized what it was a millisecond before he said it.

"Don't say it," she commanded. They sat in silence for a moment, but Ferdy quickly recovered.

"You know," he said, his voice low as he looked around to see if anyone was listening. Allee leaned in closer. "There is a way you could help." As if knowing she wasn't going to like what he had in mind, he hurried on. "We really need someone to take the gnarfs on some errand while we deal with the witch." Allee pulled back from him, shocked. She felt as if the world was crashing down around her. She wanted more than anything to be there with Esendore and Ferdy, not discarded since she had no value in a fight. Seeing her face, Ferdy quickly explained while Allee numbly listened.

"It isn't like that!" he said, as if had read her mind. "You can fight! I've seen you—you've beaten *me*! If we could have it any other way we would, but we just can't have Gnarrish there. You've seen him. If he gets some dumb idea that he can help, he will. He won't care if I've ordered him to stay back, he'll jump right in. And as for Gnilli, we can't let her get hurt; she has nothing to do with this. We can't risk them interrupting. Please understand, Allee. It's the only way." His eyes implored her to see reason, and Allee's mind did understand, but her heart protested with all its might. She wanted so badly to be able to see the enemy, after so long of hating her, but she also knew that if Esendore's negotiations went wrong because of Gnarrish, it would be disastrous for all of them. She swallowed hard and took a deep breath.

"I'll find something for them to do," she said, trying not to let her disappointment show. Ferdy's face folded into a relieved grin.

"Great," he said. "I'll go tell Esendore." And with that, he left her. Ignoring her aching heart, Allee began racking her brain for a good wild goose chase.

When Esendore halted them an hour later Allee had decided to make Gnarrish and Gnilli help her do laundry. The scheme wasn't very creative, but her heart just wasn't into it. Thinking of what she was going to say, she unsaddled Dazzle slowly and carried her saddle to the pile. Dusting her hands off, she looked around for her charges. Allee's neck swiveled on her head an entire minute before she realized that they were absolutely nowhere to be seen. She couldn't believe her eyes. The gnarfs had been next to Ruby just a moment ago.

"Ferdy," she started as he came over to dump his saddle, thinking he could have sent them somewhere, "where did Gnarrish and Gnilli go?" Ferdy gave her a funny look.

"Think real hard, Allee," he said, straitening his stirrups. Allee stared at him uncomprehendingly, totally confused. Just an hour ago he had been begging her to find something to keep the gnarfs busy and now it sounded like he done the task for her instead.

After a moment of staring at each other, Ferdy sighed in exasperation. "Don't tell me you haven't seen how they have been looking at each other." A tiny ray of enlightenment pierced Allee's fog as she remembered all the times in the past three days that Gnilli and Gnarrish had been talking together, walking together, or riding together.

"Wow," she whispered. "They're in love." Ferdy smirked as she struggled to come to grips with this newfound knowledge.

"Brilliant, Allee!" he said. Allee was still puzzled.

"But why would they leave when they knew we were so close to our destination?"

"Did *you* tell them?" Ferdy asked. Allee thought a moment. They would have had to be pretty dense to miss the signs, but she had never told Gnarrish or Gnilli how close they were to the witch's lair.

"No," she said slowly.

"Then they don't know because Esendore and I certainly never told them. And Gnarrish wasn't there when Espy described our journey, remember?" Everything was clearer to Allee now, and she could feel her heart rising back up into its rightful place as she realized that she could go with the Princes after all. There was just one last thing.

"What kind of a date is this?" she asked, waving her hand at the forest. Ferdy shrugged.

"By gnarf standards, a great one." He snorted. "They'll probably look at fungus or something."

"They have my blessing," Esendore said, joining them, his job of hobbling the zeorses finished.

"Mine, too," Allee and Ferdy said together. Allee wrinkled her nose while Ferdy made a face. Esendore gave a strained smile.

"Come on, you two," he said, and began leading the way down a crude path to their right. They traveled along it silently, but Allee was so happy the silence didn't bother her at all. She knew she should be more serious, after all they were about to fight a witch and somebody was probably going to get hurt, but she couldn't help herself. Her revelry was abruptly broken when she ran into Ferdy. He didn't even notice; he was too intent on whatever lay in front of them. Allee peered around him to see why and gasped in surprise.

Out of the forest in front of them rose a two-foot high shelf of black rock ending in a wide-mouthed cave. The shelf strongly reminded Allee of pictures of lava rock in the Hawaiian Islands that she had seen, but she knew there were no volcanoes for hundreds of miles. Before she could take a closer look at it, Esendore had pulled her onto the ground behind a boulder.

"Now," he started, but then stopped to glance back at the cave. Allee and Ferdy both nodded encouragingly at him. He took a deep breath and continued. "I am going to talk to her first. Then, if she won't make a deal, I'll fight her. Ferdinand, you WILL NOT show yourself unless she cheats or I lose. DO YOU UNDERSTAND?" Allee had never heard Esendore so stern, but then again, they had never been in this kind of a situation before. Ferdy gulped at the iron in his brother's voice and nodded.

"I understand," he said in a small voice. Esendore tried to smile at him, but the gesture came out as a grimace.

"Good," he replied. He turned to Allee. "You make sure he does just that," he told her.

"I will," she promised, swallowing the lump in her throat.

"I know," he said. He stopped again, struggling to find words.

"You guys—" he started, but his voice broke, and he couldn't go on. Ferdy and Allee each grabbed a hand, which were cold and sweaty, and squeezed. He finally gave them a real smile. "See you in a little bit," he whispered. And with that, he turned his back on them and strode across the shelf until he was six feet from the mouth of the cave. Ferdy and Allee knelt on the ground and nervously peered over the boulder, their shoulders touching.

"Nichelle!" Esendore called. His voice was strong, but his shaking hands betrayed his true feelings. Allee jumped. She had forgotten that the witch had a name. There was total, eerie silence and Allee was just wondering what would happen if the witch wasn't home, but then—

"What do you want, Esendore?" a high, cold voice came from the cave. "And cut the chitchat. I think I know already." With her last words, the witch slinked out of the cave.

"Oh," Ferdy groaned softly, "She would have to be a looker." Allee wanted to hit him, but she was too busy staring. She had never even dreamed that a witch could be as beautiful as the creature standing before them. Golden cheekbones were set off by deep red lips and snapping black eyes. Long, wavy, black hair framed her proud nose and chin while perfectly tanned arms hugged her dress, the exact color of red as her lips, to her flawlessly molded body. Luckily, Esendore's mind was set on Dariel, and he could not be distracted.

"I ask for you to yield up the Countess Dariel Eloquente Farholt, whom you have taken captive. The Countess is the betrothed of I, Crown Prince Esendore Sanumuel Denerite of Taween," he boomed, strength and pride in every inch of his bearing. "The Crown of Taween is willing to negotiate a price for her safe return." Allee was quite impressed by Esendore's speech and knew that he had probably been practicing the entire journey to make it sound so convincing.

Hardly daring to breath, Allee waited for the witch to name her price. She certainly was taking her time to think it over. She was obviously toying with Esendore.

"How about," she started, and Allee felt Ferdy tense beside her, "no?" Ferdy's breath went out in a whoosh, and Allee felt like crying, but Esendore's face didn't change, though his eyelids flickered for a second. Nichelle noticed and smiled maliciously.

"You see, Esendore," she began, her long, blood red fingernails tapping her chin while she reveled in his discomfort. "I don't want your money, and I certainly don't want your betrothed. I only want what I feel I deserve." Esendore let his puzzlement show for a second, but quickly masked it again. Nichelle's smile grew larger as she let her bombshell drop.

"I want your kingdom," she whispered. Esendore's face showed open horror. Nichelle flipped her hair behind her shoulder, still grinning. "And you know as well as I, that this means I have to get rid of *you*. And your pathetic younger brother. I suppose he is around here somewhere." She let Esendore take in her words and then laughed at his open fear. Allee decided that the sound was the most awful noise she had ever heard.

"Oh, no," Allee whispered, fear squeezing her heart. Ferdy closed his eyes for a second, but quickly reopened them.

"Not good," he agreed, his eyes round. The witch stopped laughing to smile maliciously at Esendore. He stared back at her, unmoved, his face set in grim determination.

"So what'll it be?" Nichelle continued. "Staff?" She waved her hand and a long black rod appeared there. Ferdy sucked in his breath as Allee watched with her mouth open. The witch had just defied all the laws of physics.

"She's sold herself," Ferdy breathed. Allee didn't know exactly what that meant, but she still cringed. Esendore didn't move a muscle.

"No?" the witch asked, shrugging. The staff disappeared. "Bow and arrow?" Another weapon materialized. Esendore remained silent. Nichelle sighed. "Very well then. Have it your way. Sword." The steel appeared in her right hand, its hilt glittering with rubies. Esendore drew his own diamond-studded sword. Nichelle crouched in a battle position, and Allee felt her heart wrench inside her. She yearned to look away, but couldn't. Nichelle gave another evil smile.

"Go," she whispered. In the blink of an eye, the clearing was resounding was the crash of metal on metal. The duel had begun. And in that instant Allee knew that this would be not be a fight until one of the duelers begged for mercy, but a battle fought to the death.

"Tell me now," Allee whispered. "How good of a swordsman is Esendore?" Ferdy didn't answer. Allee put her face against the stone and tried not to weep.

The combat seemed like it lasted for days, the times when Esendore was on top seconds and when he wasn't-hours. Neither Nichelle nor Esendore managed to hold the upper hand for very long; although Nichelle was obviously the better swordsman, Esendore was motivated with an unreal strength. Finally, Esendore managed to drive Nichelle into a corner of the rock. He almost had her in a fatal position when out of nowhere came a huge black bird of prey, its claws driving for Esendore's face. He ducked to avoid having his eyes scratched out and Nichelle jumped out of her corner. Allee watched in horror, wishing she could scream out at this injustice.

"That would be cheating," she whispered to Ferdy, and with a cry, he drew his sword and raced over to help his brother. Nichelle saw him coming and licked her lips in anticipation.

"Lovely," she said, raising her sword to meet him. Allee realized how stupid they were being to allow both Princes to be fighting a death fight with their kingdom at stake, but she could see no other way. Her heart left her throat and moved into her mouth. And still the battle raged on.

At first Esendore and Ferdy seemed to be overpowering the witch, but then she switched hands and attacked with renewed vigor. Allee realized that this woman was a much, much better swordsman than Esendore was, and she had just been playing with him before to tire him out and see if she could draw Ferdy into the fray. Ferdy was better with a sword than his brother was, but his limited experience was an obvious downfall.

Allee could hardly watch as Nichelle held both Esendore and Ferdy against the rock wall. For a second, despair overwhelmed her, and then in the next, she had made up her mind. Coolly, she went over her plan. She would sneak up on the witch, grab her from behind, and then let Ferdy and Esendore deal the final blow. The deed would not be cheating, because Allee had just noticed the shadow of a second sword in Nichelle's right hand. She was using her powers to beat them.

Allee stood up and leapt for the shelf, but in her eagerness she caught her foot on a tree root and was sent sprawling, catching her hip on the edge. Allee rolled onto her stomach as pain shot through her. She realized that she had landed on the ruby. Biting her lip and closing her eyes against the pain, she dug it out of her pocket, almost crying out when she saw that it had broken into three pieces.

In frustration at her clumsiness, she threw the pieces across the shelf and turned onto her other side. Her mouth dropped open in a silent shriek. Standing beside her was a very confused-looking young woman, her thin white shift clinging to her frail body. The woman kept rubbing her eyes like she had just woken up. Allee stared at her and from somewhere in her deep confusion, she realized that this woman was Dariel.

But WHERE did SHE come from, Allee cried silently. Her gaze caught on one of the ruby pieces, and the truth suddenly dawned on her. *Stupid, stupid* she berated herself, hitting her head against the rock. *All those nights it sang to you and you never questioned why. Dariel had been imprisoned in the ruby*! Allee looked back up at the Countess, all plans of helping Esendore and Ferdy pushed aside for a moment as she contemplated this new phenomenon. But Dariel didn't notice Allee lying on the ground at her feet. She was too busy staring at her Prince.

"Esendore?" she called, her voice trembling, her confusion so great that she didn't notice that he was kind of busy. Esendore peered around the witch to see who had called his name. He almost dropped his sword.

"DARIEL!" he cried. With the sight of his beloved, the fatigue of fighting for almost an hour seemed to vanish. His sword arm was renewed, and with several quick slices, the witch collapsed at his feet, unmoving. "Dariel?" he said again. He stared at her suspiciously, realizing that she could be a trick.

"Oh, Esendore!" she cried, running to him. Esendore dropped his sword as soon as they touched and wrapped his arms around her, kissing her passionately. Allee watched them in fascination, still unable to understand what had just happened, and then looked at Ferdy. He was resting against the cave with his eyes closed, but Allee could see a smile playing on his lips. She stood up, laughter in her own throat, when she saw movement at Esendore's feet. Suddenly, her laughter died cold as she realized that the witch was not dead.

More swiftly than Allee could shout, Nichelle was on her feet with a bow and arrow in her hands, grinning crazily at the two lovers. While Allee drew breath to scream, Ferdy opened his eyes and leapt to stop the witch, but an invisible force knocked him back against the rock, and he slumped to the ground, unconscious. And as Allee's tormented scream burst from her throat, Nichelle loosed her arrow. As if in slow motion, Allee watched it spin through the air, enter Esendore and continue through Dariel. The back of her white shift blossomed with red. With a short cry, they crumpled to the ground.

Allee felt her world go black.

"NO!" she screamed, rage and horror occupying every part of her mind. Blindly, she scrambled onto the shelf and picked up Esendore's fallen sword. It was heavier than she normally would have been able to lift with one hand, but Allee's adrenaline was pumping at an obscenely high rate.

As soon as she touched the sword, Allee's mind was suddenly clear, and her fury became cold and calculating. Nichelle looked up from her inspection of the fallen lovers.

"You," she hissed, her eyes glittering with hate. Allee was surprised that Nichelle knew her, but she was consumed with her anger and could not show any other emotion.

"What about me?" she asked, her voice taking on a cold, metallic quality that she had never heard before.

"You," Nichelle repeated, the sword reappearing in her hand. Allee looked at it and almost smiled. She welcomed a fight, even one to the death. Maybe it would take away the pain that was ripping her heart apart. "You were supposed to go with the gnarfs on an errand," Nichelle spat. "Your zeorses assured me that you would not be here to mess things up again."

"Oh, I'm sorry," Allee said sweetly, taunting her enemy. "But love got in your way again. Not that you would know anything about love." Nichelle smiled in return.

"It has put a cramp in my operation," she admitted. "But unlike what you are thinking, sweetheart, I have loved before and am very capable of doing it again. I just don't let my emotions control me, and, unless I am mistaken, you are letting your feelings overrule your reason this very moment. Do you really think you can fight me, girl?" Hearing this, Allee wanted to hurt the witch even more.

"You said that I have messed things up before?" she asked, her heart beating against her rib cage as Nichelle began to circle her. The witch gave a strangled laugh.

"Yes, but you were too stupid to know you did." Allee frowned at her.

"I resent that," she said, watching Nichelle's chest muscles for signs of an attack. Her answer seemed to make the witch furious.

"Well, do you know what, girl?" she shrieked, her face a livid red, "I resent you killing the taranion before it could kill Cardolyn, I resent you not listening to my second assassination attempt through the ruby, I resent you distracting the coffalo so he couldn't trample the Princes, and I—" she paused, her face no longer beautiful but contorted in rage, "I RESENT YOU BEING HERE TO GET IN THE WAY!" She lunged, and Allee was ready for her, but she could never have prepared her body for the shock of the initial onslaught. This was nothing like to what she had experienced with Ferdy in the practice ring. Her muscles screamed and her legs wobbled while the tip of Nichelle's sword cut a thin line down her left arm. Allee pushed with all her strength and the witch sprang back, licking her lips.

"First blood is mine," she whispered, and attacked again. Allee fought with her entire mind and body focused on simply staying alive, something she had never had to do before, not even in her nightmares. She managed to draw blood next, cutting the witch's thigh with a low blow, but Nichelle soon made up for it by grazing Allee's knee enough to make her limp. The nightmare became ten times worse when she nicked Nichelle's eyebrow and the witch retaliated by slicing along Allee's hairline. Allee screamed, her head exploding in white-hot pain as blood mixed in with the sweat and trickled down her neck. Nichelle leered at her, laughing crazily.

Gasping in pain, Allee's mind went back to the day when she had been in the middle of a brightly lit arena, and a face had been leering at her just like that. Oh, what she would give to see his face again! With Ferdy's face swimming before her, she lodged Esendore's sword tip underneath Nichelle's hilt and pulled with every ounce of strength she possessed. Nichelle gasped in horror and her sword went flying out of her hands to land somewhere behind Allee.

Allee marveled for a second at her success, a big mistake. Taking advantage of Allee's hesitation, Nichelle jumped on top of her, knocking them both to the ground. The sword went spinning away from the impact, but Allee never noticed. They rolled over and over, Allee trying to find just a little more strength in her exhausted body.

Somehow, she managed to come out on top. Struggling to stay that way, she bit and pinched in a way she had never would have believed herself capable of.

As she fought, she spied a shard of the ruby within reaching distance. Desperate for a weapon, she held Nichelle down with her knees and grabbed it. She raised it high over her enemy's head to drive it down with all her might, but then paused. In fascination, Allee watched as a droplet of water started to roll off of the glittering gem.

For the second time that day, everything slowed down. Allee could look from the tear to the witch's fear filled face without the witch having time to renew her efforts to dislodge her. Even Allee's realization *it's my tear* came to her painstakingly slow as the droplet fell down, down, down, to land onto the witch's forehead with a splash that echoed around the clearing. Nichelle gave a high, rage-filled scream and Allee answered it, all of her frustration, fury, and hope pouring out of her and into that tear, sealing the Alzius's gift. The clearing seemed to explode with a tremendous flash of light, and Allee fell over onto her back. The witch had vanished.

Allee lay still, firstly to make sure she was still alive, but mostly because she couldn't do anything else. Her head was still bleeding, her arm and knee felt like they were on fire, and her hip was one big dull throb, but she was breathing. Hearing a noise, she lifted her head up to see Ferdy crawling toward her. There was a purple lump on his forehead, a gash above his eye, and he was having trouble breathing, but he was in one piece.

"You okay?" he croaked.

"I'm okay," she responded. They were about ready to smile at each other when they heard a groan. They met each other's eyes to see the exact same fear in the other's face. In desperation, Allee reached for Ferdy's hand. He met her half way, and hanging on to each other with all the strength they had left, Allee and Ferdy crawled as fast as they could go to the fallen lovers.

If Allee had not been half dead herself, she would have screamed in horror. Esendore's face was deathly white except for the blood on his lips, and Dariel's was blue tinged. Ferdy collapsed by his brother's side while Allee sat by Dariel.

"Esendore," Ferdy choked, grabbing his hand. "Oh, Esendore, I—" Allee saw the pale fingers squeeze Ferdy's hand, and she caught up Dariel's in her own. To her surprise, they grasped back.

"Thank-you for singing," she mumbled to Dariel, not knowing why she needed to say that right now. The Countess's green eyes fluttered slightly.

"You helped me as much as I helped you," she whispered, and opened her mouth to say more, but the pain was too great, and she gasped instead. Ferdy and Esendore were oblivious to Allee and Dariel's exchange. Ferdy was too absorbed in the feeble rise and fall of his brother's chest. He finally couldn't take it anymore.

"Esendore, don't die!" he cried, his breath coming in ragged gasps as he fought to keep himself under control. Esendore's eyes opened in surprise, and Allee wanted to hide her face to the calmness she saw there.

"Death is not such a bad thing, Ferdinand," he murmured, his breathing fast and shallow. Ferdy's face contorted in pain.

"How can you say that?" he demanded, "You don't know that! You can't know that! Esendore, you aren't GOING TO KNOW THAT!" Esendore coughed, getting angry himself, and fresh blood spotted his lips.

"Look at me, Ferdinand," he commanded, grabbing Ferdy's shirt collar. "Look at me."

"I'm looking, Esendore," Ferdy half-sobbed, his shoulders shaking. "I'm looking." Esendore took a shaking breath.

"Trust me, Ferdinand," he whispered, his voice almost normal. "From here there is no place to go but *up*. A beginning, not an ending. And do you know why?" Ferdy was too overcome with emotion to reply, but he shook his head. "Because," Esendore said softly, letting go of Ferdy's shirt. "I believe that the good will not let me go down any further. Can you try to understand that for me, Ferdinand?"

"I'm trying," Ferdy half-sobbed. Esendore nodded and lay back down.

"You will understand," he assured, his voice a whisper again. "Ferdinand, someday, you will understand what death is. And I hope that day is not for a very long time. The fact that you are even trying is remarkable. But that is who you are. Always trying." He smiled at his brother and reached up with his remaining strength to ruffle his hair. "You shall make a great King. *Because you are always trying.* Just keep doing that for me." Ferdy kissed his brother's hand.

"I will," he promised, his eyes bright with his oath. "I will do it for you."

"No," Esendore reprimanded. "You will do it for your people."

"Our people," Ferdy corrected. Esendore smiled and squeezed his hand.

"Our people," he agreed. He turned to Allee, and she trembled as she looked into his eyes, but they did not go unfocused. Mist was already gathering in their depths.

"Good-bye, Allee," he whispered. All he said was her name, but, for Allee, he could not have said a more perfect goodbye.

"Good-bye, Esendore," she whispered back. Esendore looked back up at Ferdy and smiled at something he saw in his brother's face.

"You shall make a great King, Ferdinand," he said again, his serenity and happiness making his face seem less deathlike.

"Esendore," Ferdy begged, his eyes shining with withheld tears. "Don't leave me here alone." Esendore made a small noise of disbelief.

"Alone?" he repeated, getting some of his old spirit back. "Certainly not. You will have Allee." He turned to smile at her, and Allee softly smiled back. "And I—" he turned to his beloved. Dariel let go of Allee's hand to grab his. "I will have Dariel." Esendore and Dariel kissed once more, and together, they died.

A queer silence penetrated the clearing. It was not eerie, or even deathly, or indeed one that had touched that clearing for a very long time. The silence was one of peace.

Allee put her fist in her mouth to keep herself from crying out and ruining it. She tried in vain to make her exhausted and beaten body to stop shuddering, but she could no longer control it. Slowly, she lifted her eyes up to look at Ferdy, who returned her gaze. They each took a choking breath, and suddenly they threw themselves into each other's arms, sobbing.

Allee cried for the voice that would no longer sing her to sleep, for the loss of the woman behind it, and for the horrible waste of a life. She cried for Esendore, for everything she didn't know about him, for everything she did, and because he wouldn't be able to see if their snow angels were still there, wouldn't get to laugh at her and Ferdy's antics, and would never need her to comfort him again. And she cried for both Dariel and Esendore, who hadn't had the chance to begin their life together, to get married, to have children, or to grow old together. Instead of sharing a life, they were sharing a death.

Slowly, Ferdy and Allee's sobs slowed to the occasional hiccup and they sat in silence, sharing in each other's strength. Ferdy took a shaky breath.

"Allee," he said softly. Allee stirred herself from her cocoon of grief and lifted her head off his shoulder to look into his eyes. There was such sorrow there that she wanted to cry again.

"Yes?" she replied. Tenderly, she pushed a lock of his hair behind his ear. He took another breath.

"Allee, what happens if I mess up?"

"Then you fix it," Allee said, her voice as firm as she could make it. She was so tired and hurt that she could barely keep herself going, but she knew that Ferdy needed her. He looked down into his lap and wrung his hands.

"But what if I can't fix it?" he pressed. "What if the people get mad? Allee, I'm so afraid, what if—" He stopped, horror filling his eyes until Allee felt it entering her, too. His voice came out as a whisper. "What if they don't like me?" He was so alone, so helpless, and so *scared* that Allee reassured him in the only way she could. She kissed him.

After a moment, they broke apart and pointedly avoided looking at each other. Ferdy gave a little cough and blushed deep red.

"Well," he said, looking at Allee from the corners of his eyes. Allee was about to smile at him when his attention became fixed on something behind her. He frowned.

"What's that noise?" Wondering what could possibly happen to her now, Allee listened.

"It sounds like hoof beats," she said, slowly. They both looked at each other, panic-stricken, and tried to stand up. Even using each other for support, they couldn't make it to a kneeling position. They finally gave up and turned to face whatever was coming with their arms intertwined.

Out of the trees burst the heavily muscled torso of a man in his late fifties. His face was cold and proud, but it immediately showed relief when he saw the two small figures on the ground.

"They're here," he called back to somebody behind him, his voice deep and resonating. He moved so that they could see the rest of him, and Allee realized that the man was a centaur. But he wasn't just any centaur. Upon his steel gray flank was burned a tree with a crown on its canopy.

As if remembering another lifetime, Allee recalled the book about centaurs she had read, and the page that had described the Wealder, the King of the centaurs. Unless she was grossly mistaken, the centaur before them was none other than the Wealder himself. And unless she was again mistaken, if the Wealder was here then there was a great possibility that his son was with him. She knew her guess was correct when Ferdy gave a surprised croak.

"Neiy?" he called out. The centaur's shaggy brown head appeared over his father's shoulder, and his face broke into a relieved smile.

"Thank-goodness, you're—," Then his eyes grew large as he realized who lay behind them. All the color drained out of his face, and his mouth formed a round O. The Wealder also showed surprise, but he had no color to leave his face in the first place.

"Oh, Ferdinand—" Neiy started, but his voice broke, and he shook his head. Ferdy and Allee just stared at him, too exhausted to wonder what he was trying to say.

"Just tell him," the Wealder rumbled. Neiy looked back up and took a deep breath.

"I'm so sorry, Ferdinand," he began, his eyes and voice showing how much he felt for them in a very un-centaur like way. "But we have to take you back to the pastle, right away. Your father, he's-he's—" he stopped again, bit his lip, and then whispered, "He's dying, Ferdinand."

Allee felt Ferdy slump beside her and tightened her grip on his arm to reassure him; even though her own breath was coming in gasps again as she realized that they had to make another long journey. Allee did not think the clearing could get any more silent, but it did. She could actually *hear* the torrent of emotion swirling around inside Ferdy and combined with her own internal battle, it sounded like a windstorm. She wanted to scream, "Just leave us alone!" but she knew the act would be pointless. The Wealder cleared his throat.

"He commands an audience with you. The girl may come, too," he explained, his voice and face showing absolutely no emotion. "We have volunteered to take you to him, if you are up to our way of traveling." Allee knew that she and Ferdy weren't up to anything except breathing right now, and she had a feeling that the centaur's way of traveling couldn't be very relaxing. She also knew that the offer was an effort by the centaurs to mend broken ties between their race and the human's, and that if they did not go with Neiy and his father, they would never make it to the King in time.

Allee knew all of this, but she what she wanted more than anything else in the world to sleep, and to stay asleep until all of her grief and pain had gone away. Instead, she offered her good arm to Ferdy, and he wearily stood up. The centaurs did not move to help, knowing that Ferdy and Allee would ask for their aid if they needed it.

As soon as Ferdy was semi-steady on his feet, he reached down and pulled Allee up to stand beside him. She swayed slightly, feeling like she was going to throw up, but Ferdy steadied her with his hand and the feeling passed.

"We will go," he said to the Wealder, looking straight into the centaur's cold gray eyes. "Just show us the way."

"It would be my pleasure," a high, clear voice rang out. Wearily wondering what was happening now, Allee turned to see a huge, white-winged horse land lightly on the edge of the rock shelf. It folded its enormous silver wings and took a couple of steps forward as Ferdy and Allee stared open-mouthed. The creature ignored them, her attention focused on the centaurs, who were both showing signs of complete shock.

"They are not up to a twelve hour journey," she said in her bell like voice. Allee felt it resonating in her bones and felt a little of her strength return as the woman-horse talked.

"Especially one that requires extreme concentration. They shall come with me."

Allee realized that she had heard this voice before, but her tired mind refused to remember when or where. The Wealder seemed to come out of his state of shock.

"We wish you well," he said, bowing to the ground. Neiy, still gawking, was a little slower, but he quickly followed his father's example. Allee was still trying to figure out where she had heard the woman's voice when Ferdy solved her problem.

"Who are you?" he breathed, his voice full of awe. Allee realized whom the woman was a second before Aeyr answered.

"An angel," she replied, smiling her soft smile. Her eyes flickered to Allee. "Of sorts. Please hurry." The smile left her face and they were reminded of their urgency. While Allee was squeezing every bit of warmth and strength out of the smile that she could manage, Aeyr knelt and extended a wing to give them a handhold. Ferdy moved towards her and without him for support, Allee collapsed.

Before she had really realized what had happened, she felt herself being swept up into Neiy's strong brown arms. Relieved, she laid her head on his shoulder to see the Wealder bending over Dariel and Esendore, his fingers ready to snap the arrow shaft so that he could move them.

"Wait!" Allee's strangled cry echoed around the clearing. She threw out her good arm, struggling to free herself so that she could stop him. "Don't take them apart!" The echo of her cry died, and the peaceful silence returned.

Breathing heavily, she watched in relief as the centaur nodded solemnly and began gathering fallen branches to make a sling. Her last fit of passion made Allee's limbs turn to jelly. Neiy arranged her like a rag doll on top of Aeyr, and Ferdy put an arm around her protectively. Neiy stepped away, his hand raised in a silent farewell. Allee tried to do the same, but her arm wouldn't move. Somehow knowing what she wanted, Ferdy raised it for her, and Neiy moved to help his father.

"Don't let her fall," Aeyr instructed, and began pumping her wings.

"I won't let her fall," Ferdy promised, and Allee leaned back against him, confident that he would keep her safe.

They burst above the treetops into a glorious red sunset that made the dark and gloomy forest seem almost friendly. But then again, Allee wasn't sure if the light was red or it was just the blood encrusted on her eyelashes. At that thought she felt sick again and closed her eyes, falling into an exhausted stupor.

"Is Alethea asleep?" Aeyr asked a half an hour later. Allee heard her, but couldn't get herself to make any movement to show that she had. She didn't need to. Ferdy knew she was awake.

"I think so," he said.

"She needs to sleep," Aeyr replied. The only other sound in the gathering twilight was the soft whoosh of her wings.

"She going to need more than sleep," Ferdy said, his arm tightening around Allee. "She's pretty beat up. I don't know what would have happened if she hadn't done what she did."

"You are wondering how she killed the witch," Aeyr said, voicing his unasked question.

"Yeah," Ferdy said, squirming as he realized Aeyr could partially read his mind. "I am."

"How much do you know?" Aeyr asked. Allee felt him tense in concentration.

"I was knocked out for the first part," he said, slowly, "and then when I came to, Allee was on top of the witch and it was like...like," he paused, and Allee could tell he was having a hard time remembering what had happened and wondered just how hard he had hit his head. "A star," he said finally. He hurried on, more sure of himself. "It was like a star fell from her hand, and when it hit the witch, there was this most awful noise, and then...silence." He shivered as he remembered the last part. "I just don't understand how it happened." Aeyr's great wings beat again before she responded.

"You are aware that Alethea had a meeting with one of the Alzius, are you not?" she questioned.

"Yeah," Ferdy said, his voice surprised at this change of topic. "But what does that have to do with anything?" Aeyr turned her head back to stare at him for a second before continuing.

"Everything in this world, Ferdinand," she said, her voice grave. "They are not the monsters you think they are. Entirely the opposite."

"But, there is *proof* that they are vicious," Ferdy protested.

"And are there not also documents recording the horrendous acts centaurs have committed?" Aeyr fired back, the steel in her voice making Ferdy and Allee both cringe. "Along with the atrocious acts committed by dragons, mermaids, and especially your own race? Have you not just *witnessed* one, Ferdinand? Is the behavior of a few enough to condemn an entire race?" Ferdy was mute, his mind processing this information. "Is it?" Aeyr pressed. There was silence as Ferdy tried to come up with an answer.

"Of course not. That would be ridiculous," he finally said. Allee felt Aeyr relax underneath them.

"Then you are already well on your way to becoming a King," she said, her voice back to normal. Ferdy sagged with relief, and Allee wished she could congratulate him for passing his first test. They lapsed into silence again until Ferdy got his tongue back.

"I still don't understand how Allee killed the witch," he reminded Aeyr. She sighed, but withheld laughter laced her voice.

"Patience," she chided. "I am trying to help you understand the best I can. Are you also aware that Alethea saved the Alzius sovereign?" Allee felt Ferdy's jaw drop on top of her head.

"N-n-no," he stammered. "She neglected to mention that."

"Sounds like her," Aeyr said, her voice half amused, have exasperated. "But she did. And in gratitude for saving the life of their child-Keeper, in addition to Cardolyn's and Gnilli's, they gave Alethea the gift of life."

"What does that mean?" Ferdy asked. Allee listened harder, eager to have her power explained.

"It means," Aeyr said, her words slow and deliberate, "that when Alethea cries, she can decide if the person that receives her tears lives or dies. But, the way I understand it, she can only do this three times." Ferdy gave a squeak of surprise.

"Say that again," he said, his voice faint. Aeyr sighed.

"Alethea has the power to kill or resurrect just by thinking it. If the emotion is so powerful that it brings her to weep, whomever that tear touches will receive whatever she was thinking of at that time. That was the way it worked just an hour ago. According to my sources, Alethea was very frustrated last night, and she cried onto the ruby. Since Dariel was held by the witch's spell, it could not harm her, so it just stayed there. But since Alethea had been thinking of the witch's death when that tear fell from her eye, Nichelle received its full potency, and thus Alethea killed her." Allee felt Ferdy start to shake in suppressed excitement.

"She still has two left, doesn't she?" he asked, his voice trembling wildly. "That means that...that she can save Esendore and Dariel!" Allee's heart leaped inside of her as she realized what he meant. But then her elation faded just as quickly. She doubted she could squeeze any moisture out of her eyes right at the moment. She wished she wasn't so tired!

"No, Ferdinand," Aeyr said gently, and Ferdy deflated like a balloon. "The time for the gift to be effective has passed. This gift must be administered right away or its power will not work. And even if Alethea had tried before I doubt she could have accomplished such a feat. She was much too near death herself to be thinking of life." Allee felt Ferdy trembling and she squeezed his hand to comfort him. She would have tried with all her might, had she known. Aeyr felt him shake.

"Do not let yourself be burdened with their death, Young Prince," she said, her voice kind. "For you fought bravely, and there was nothing that anyone could have done. Your brother and his betrothed were ready for death, and they went peacefully, surrounded by the two people who loved them the most." Allee heard Ferdy give a huge, shuddering sigh and she felt some of her own pain leave with it.

"Thanks," he whispered.

"One of my duties is to inspire hope," Aeyr replied. Allee guessed Aeyr's response was her way of saying, "You're welcome."

"Then just one more question," Ferdy said, his voice back to normal. Aeyr gave a nod of assent. "Why didn't Allee kill me when she cried? I do have burn marks all over my shirt." Allee experienced a small jolt of surprise. She had never thought of that.

"I told you," Aeyr said patiently. "Alethea was much too exhausted to use her gift. Those tears were only of sorrow, nothing else. But now, even normal tears will have side effects for Alethea. She will have to be more careful from now on. She has already done a splendid job of adapting. She was more courageous than I had ever hoped she would be." Allee finally found the strength to object. She cracked open an eye to glare at both of them.

"I am more stubborn than anything," she muttered. Ferdy shook his head in exasperation while Aeyr gave a tinkling laugh.

"You and your stubbornness," she said, shaking her luminous white mane. "I hope it sees you through the night. We're here." Allee sat up, startled, to see the pastle rising up before them out of the darkness. Aeyr must have used some sort of power for them to have arrived so quickly.

Aeyr swooped to one of the pastle's towers and hovered before a tiny, lighted window, its glass-frosted panes blurring the room on the other side. Ferdy reached over and pushed it open, throwing a leg over the sill as he did so. Aeyr held him steady so there was no danger of falling, but he still hesitated, nervous to leave the only source of comfort he knew. Allee smiled at him.

"I'm right behind you," she promised, holding out her arm for him to pull her in. He reached over and when their hands clasped, Allee felt much of her strength return. She squared her shoulders, ready for whatever lay ahead.

"Believe in the good," Aeyr whispered, and she disappeared into the night. Ferdy and Allee looked at each other one last time and then slipped over the windowsill.

Allee was surprised to find that the room was actually quite gloomy; the yellow glow seen from the outside had given the impression of a well-lit interior. Instead, the grand chandelier hanging from the ceiling was dark; the entire room was lit by two candles flickering in a sconce by the door, which was opposite of the window. The rest of the tower was lavishly decorated in the royal colors of bright blue, black, and silver. Heavy tapestries depicting various scenes from the history of the Denerite family adorned the walls, and the floor was covered in thick blue carpet. However, the furniture in the room was strikingly plain and consisted of two wooden chairs, a nightstand, and a sagging bed. The lumpy, sweat-reeking bed was the least attractive thing in the tower, but Ferdy's entire attention was fixed on it, his body rigid with dislike. It was then that Allee realized that there was a *person* under the black satin covers.

"So you're finally here, are you?" the old man asked, his voice surprisingly clear for someone who was dying. "And you do not have good news for me." Allee saw Ferdy's lip tremble.

"No, Your Majesty," he said, his normally cocky voice a defeated whisper. "I am sorry to have to tell you this, but Prince Esendore is dead at the hand of Nichelle the exiled Sultaness of Ivral." The old man looked startled.

"Goodness, boy, you don't have to tell me all about it. That strange woman already has. I don't want to know the details anyway. I want to talk to *you*. Come here." Allee felt herself stiffen at the man's tone. He didn't even sound sympathetic for Ferdy or sad that his eldest son was dead. *Doesn't he care* she wondered silently, the pain in her own chest making her wince.

Ferdy took a hesitant step forward, Allee on his heels. The old man looked his son over with a shrewd eye. He ignored Allee.

"Sit," he commanded, and they sat. He continued to stare, and Ferdy looked back at him coolly. Allee was too interested in what she was seeing to be completely indifferent. The King's appearance was not at all like she had expected. She had envisioned an arrogant, proud face with snapping blue eyes, rather like an older version of Esendore.

Instead, the face before her was worn and tired, aged before its time with lines of pain and worry etched as deep as they would go. But what was most shocking were his eyes. Allee quickly looked away from them, afraid she would be lost in the endless black pools of sorrow. This was a man who had lost the thing he had most loved in his life.

"So, you are to be the next King of Taween, then, Ferdinand?" the old man finally asked. "And I suppose then that I must give you my blessing." Ferdy gulped, and nodded.

"Yes, Your Majesty," he said quietly. The King's beady eyes squinted, attempting to get a better look at the sad figure sitting before him.

"You are correct if you are thinking that I am not pleased with this turn of events," he said, closing his eyes and settling back on his pillows.

"Yes, Your Majesty," Ferdy said again, even more quietly. The old man seemed to gather his remaining strength and leaned forward.

"I must admit, you have always been a tremendous rascal," he started, and Ferdy's shoulders slumped as he prepared for a barrage from his father. "Never had any sense of honor or dignity, never cared for your responsibilities, or even tried to act your station. You broadcasted your emotions to the entire pastle. I have hardly ever received news about you that I liked, Ferdinand."

"I'm sorry, Your Majesty," Ferdy whispered, tears shining in his eyes as he tried to keep himself in control. He had been through too much to not let his father's words bite him. Allee felt her temper rising, but quickly stomped it down, knowing that this was not a time to interfere.

"You will have to change that, Ferdinand, before you become King," his father admonished, shaking his finger. "There will be no time for such foolishness."

"I understand," Ferdy said, his voice shaky. Allee thought the old man smiled then, but he if he had, it was the scariest-looking smile she had ever seen.

"Good. You cannot make the same mistakes I have, Ferdinand. Kings must not show emotion, must not feel emotion." Pain flickered in his haunted eyes. "I have learned this the hard way," he said softly. "And have regretted feeling deeply every moment of this so-called life I have been living. You must not make mistakes, Ferdinand, for they will never stop coming back to trouble you." Ferdy was shaking now, trying to hold all of his emotions inside his exhausted body. Allee couldn't stand it any more.

"You're wrong," she said, her voice echoing in the stillness of the room. Instantly, she regretted her outburst. Why couldn't she keep her big mouth shut? The King finally noticed her.

"What did you say?" he whispered, his eyes boring into her.

"You are wrong," Allee said again, every word deliberate. With every passing second those haunted eyes rested on her, her desire to look away grew larger. Taking a deep breath, she plowed on. "Your Majesty, I believe your thinking is corrupt. You *have* to make mistakes or you won't ever learn anything. It is not our acts that condemn us, Your Majesty," she paused to give him a cold stare, but then she saw the astonishment in his eyes, and she let her face relax. "What condemns us are beliefs like that one," she ended. Ferdy stirred beside her.

"Believe that you can be forgiven, and you will," he said softly. He looked as surprised as Allee felt at his addition. The old man stared at them for a moment more, but Allee had a feeling that he wasn't looking at them, but at something far away. Suddenly, he gave a great, heaving sigh, and when he turned back his eyes had lost some of their hopelessness.

Ferdy looked from Allee to his father with a mixture of disbelief and bewilderment.

"What did you just do?" he whispered. Allee couldn't answer because the King had sunken back on his pillows again, his strength obviously failing.

"Ferdinand," he said, his voice less clear than before. Ferdy leaned in so he could hear him better. "I would like to apologize to you, but I'm afraid there's just too much I don't know how to say. There are so many things that I could have done for you that I didn't. So many things..." his voice trailed off as he a dry, hacking cough wracked his body.

"It's all right," Ferdy said quickly. His father shook his head feebly, trying to get himself under control. Gasping, he spoke again.

"It is not all right, but I thank you for saying it just the same." He winced. "I am going about this all wrong, aren't I, girl?"

"No, Your Majesty, you're doing fine," Allee said, relieved that he had gotten her message. He gave a weak smile.

"Pity I don't get the chance to talk to you longer," he said, and paused. His eyebrows knit together. "No," he said quietly, turning to his son. "Do you know what the real pity is?" Ferdy shook his head. His father reached out and grasped his hand. "That I never took the chance to talk to *you*, my son." Ferdy swallowed hard and a different set of tears glistened in his eyes.

"I still love you, Father," he said, choking back a sob.

"Thank-you for calling me that," the King whispered. "It is good to hear that word one last time. I love you, Ferdinand." He closed his eyes. "Was I truly a father?" he asked, his voice faint.

"You will always be my father," Ferdy replied, a single tear trickling down his cheek.

"Then I am happy," his father said, and he was gone. Ferdy kissed his father's hand and laid it next to the other. Allee grabbed Ferdy's other one and squeezed. He smiled at her through his tears.

"Thanks," he said.

"Any time," she replied, concentrating on trying to hide her ragged breathing. She felt like her head was going to break in two, if her heart didn't first. Ferdy took one more look at his father and then stood up.

"Let's go," he said, wiping his eyes and walking to pull open the door. Allee got up and silently followed him out of the room.

Cardolyn was sitting on a little wooden chair right beside the door and jumped up when she saw them. The questions on her lips died as soon as she saw their faces. The news of the King's death was plainly written there. Unable to control herself, she fell on them, sobbing.

They patted her back, each of them dry-eyed. Both of them were out of tears. As soon as Cardolyn had recovered herself, she held them at arm's length.

"You two are a sight," she admonished, blowing her nose loudly. "You need a bath and some hot food, not to mention new clothes. I can't believe how—"

"We need to sleep," Ferdy interrupted. Even in her stupor, Allee realized that she had never heard him speak with such authority. "Anywhere. Just find us somewhere. Now. Please." Allee could feel her forehead bleeding again, and her arm and knee were throbbing so much that she swayed as he spoke. Cardolyn put a hand over her mouth, aghast, and nodded.

"Alethea's room is closest," she said, picking up a candle from a holder in the wall. "Follow me." Ferdy grabbed Allee's arm and led her after Cardolyn. They stumbled down a spiral staircase and two long hallways before they stood before Allee's door. Cardolyn unlocked it and they entered the room. Ferdy threw himself on a couch while Allee crawled into her bed. She was asleep before Cardolyn could shut the door.

Chapter 12

Saying Goodbye

Allee slept harder than she had ever slept in her entire life, only briefly disturbed when it felt like someone was slathering fire on her forehead and sticking needles in her arm. The second time this happened she dozed instead of slept. Finally, she found that she was awake enough that she could talk, but only with huge effort.

"Hey," she groaned to no one in particular. "How sick am I?"

"Pretty sick," replied a cocky voice. "But, trust me, you look much worse."

"Ferdinand!" Allee cried, struggling to open her eyes, but finding that there was something wrapped around her head. Blindly, she then attempted to sit up but found out she couldn't do that either. She gave a cry of frustration. "If I could move I'd—"

"OUT!" bellowed another voice. Allee was shocked into silence. She hadn't thought Meli could get that angry. "Your Majesty, you asked if you could see if she's all right, and as you plainly just demonstrated, Alethea is FINE! OUT!"

"Bye, Allee!" Ferdy's voice called out, but Allee couldn't reply. Her outburst had used up what little strength she had recovered and she was already being sucked back into blissful oblivion.

Allee opened her eyes slowly due to the fact that she had some foreign stiff object plastered to her forehead. She reached up to touch it and realized that it was a bandage. As soon as her fingers brushed the cloth, her skull started throbbing. She groaned, cursing herself for not paying attention to how long the witch's sword had been. Then she heard a rustling noise beside her.

"Lady?" a quivering voice asked. Painstakingly, Allee turned her head and strained to see into the semi-darkness. Her face broke into a grin when she realized the voice belonged to Gnilli. Allee was very glad to see that the gnarf had gotten home safely.

"Hello," she replied, trying to sound cheerful. "How are you?" Gnilli stared at Allee for a second, and then, to her mistress's great surprise, burst into tears.

"Lady, lady, I'm so sorry," she sobbed; burying her face in the bed cover while Allee stared at her in shock. "I left you, Lady," she bawled, her words muffled by the cloth. "I left you to make myself happy. I pursued my own wants before your needs. I am so ashamed. I-I—" She was overcome with misery and couldn't go on. Allee braced herself for the pain she knew would follow movement and reached out to pat Gnilli's shoulder.

"Hey," she said softly as the room spun around her. "Gnilli, don't worry about it. I can't even begin to tell you how happy I am that you did not have to see what I saw, go through what I went through. Just think, Gnilli, if you had been there, you wouldn't be able to take care of me now because you might have been hurt, too. This is better isn't it?"

"But I left you!" Allee sighed and tried a different approach.

"Gnilli, there is nothing I want you to do more than to be happy," she said, putting as much sincerity and warmth in her voice as she could muster. "And I know you were happy then because you were spending time with the man you love." Gnilli's sobs slowed, but she didn't reply. "Weren't you?" Allee pressed. She saw the fabric move and knew that Gnilli had nodded. Allee breathed a small sigh of relief, but Gnilli quickly began berating herself again.

"I bound myself to you!" she protested. "I promised to be with you, and serve you, and protect you! And I failed!" She began to weep again. Allee had had quite enough of tears.

"Then you can't swear yourself to Gnarrish, can you?" she pointed out. Gnilli finally looked up at her with wet, wide eyes. "For that is what you are planning, isn't it?" Allee continued, saying each word carefully. "You want to get married, right?"

Gnilli nodded, her eyes getting even wider as she realized that if she married Gnarrish she could no longer devote all of her time to her mistress. Allee decided to take a risk, knowing that if she did not convince Gnilli to lead her own life now, she never would.

"And, I do believe, His Majesty," she didn't know why she called Ferdy that, but she did, "has already released Gnarrish from his servitude." Gnilli nodded again, more slowly this time. Before the gnarf could do anything else, Allee sat up. Trying not to black out, she laid a hand on her gnarf's head.

"Gnilli Diggr," she said formally, trying to think of the right way to do this. Gnilli stared up at her in bewilderment, then astonishment when she realized what her mistress was about to do. Allee ignored her and continued. "I release you from your oath to be my everlasting servant for another promise." She paused to look in to Gnilli's overflowing eyes, but this time the tears were ones of joy.

"Anything, Lady," Gnilli whispered, grabbing Allee's other hand. Allee smiled.

"A promise to be my everlasting friend." A smile appeared on Gnilli's own face.

"I accept all terms," she said promptly.

"So may it be," Allee said, sealing the pact. They looked at each other a moment longer, and then Allee enveloped Gnilli in a hug. When they had parted, Allee lay back down on her pillows, exhausted.

"So," she started, eager for news. "When's the wedding?" The gnarf looked back down at her lap, and Allee knew she wasn't going to like what Gnilli had to tell her.

"Tomorrow morning," she mumbled.

"Tomorrow morning?" Allee repeated, thunderstruck. "Already? I don't know if I'll be up to moving around so soon." Gnilli didn't say anything, and Allee realized what the problem was. "Oh," she said softly. "I can't come." She looked down at her hand and bit her lip to keep her emotions in check. Gnilli grabbed her hand again.

"Oh, Lady, don't be sad!" she cried, on the brink of tears yet again. "It's not your fault, truly it isn't. It's just our people's custom, to marry in secret, without onlookers. I wish more than anything that you and His Majesty could be there, but our law says that a couple have to begin their life together *alone*. I'm so sorry." Allee didn't mind in the least now that she knew she couldn't do a thing about it.

"Gnilli, it's fine," she assured, smiling. "I understand. You and Gnarrish should respect your customs. I don't mind at all." Gnilli looked startled.

"Really?" she asked. Allee's smile grew wider even though it made her cheeks hurt.

"Just hurry back," she replied. Gnilli gave a small hiccup in reply. So that the gnarf couldn't fret even more, Allee continued with her questions.

"How long have I been asleep?" Gnilli paused for a moment, thinking, and Allee realized she had been asleep a lot longer than she had thought.

"A night and two days," she said finally. "Since it's now about nine o'clock in the evening. We've been quite worried about you, Meli and me, that is. But Caysa promised that you'd be all right," she gave Allee a dazzling smile. "And you are."

"What kind of stuff did she put on me?" Allee demanded, aware of a funny smell that seemed to cling to her. "It burned like mad." Gnilli frowned.

"We're not quite sure," she admitted, her eyes flickering form Allee's bandaged arm to her forehead. "It came from a little blue jar that...that," she paused as she struggled to find words to describe what had happened, "appeared...on your bed side table early yesterday morning when Caysa was trying to figure out what to do with you. You were bleeding pretty badly, so she just grabbed the first thing she could, which was this salve, and slathered it on. The bleeding stopped right away. Meli said it smelled like rose petals, but I thought, I thought," she paused, her eyes getting a far away look. "It smelled like moonlight." Allee decided that she had better change the subject.

"How did you and Gnarrish get here?" she inquired, unnerved by Gnilli's behavior. Gnilli blinked, broken out of her revelry.

"Huh? Oh, that was also very strange," she said, her eyebrows knitting together as she tried to understand it so she could put it into words. She sighed in frustration. "You know how the centaur's are the guardians of earth?" Allee nodded; she had read it in the centaur book. Gnilli looked relieved. "Well," she continued, more sure of how to describe their journey. "It had something to do with that, but I'm not exactly sure how." Allee shrugged, pretty sure she wasn't coherent enough to try to understand something extremely complicated.

"That's okay," she said, but Gnilli was already trying her hardest to describe their journey.

"They took us to these two gigantic trees," she was saying, concentrating hard, "And said some strange words...and then the trunks turned into these...I dunno...windows. They felt like ice, and squeezed me awfully, but we made it back a few hours after the sun had risen yesterday. We left just a little after dark." She stopped to shiver. "The trees were the worst way I'd ever traveled, but I was ready to get back in them again as soon as we had entered the city. It was just tomblike because of His Majesty's death. And cold," she shuddered again, remembering. "Cold like everything else had died, too. I was afraid for you, Lady."

She looked at Allee with wide eyes, and Allee felt herself start to shiver, but forced herself not to. "I'm fine," she reassured Gnilli, black grief rising to the surface as she said so. She gulped and smiled feebly "Just a little weak, that's all." Gnilli smiled back at her, and Allee remembered something else she wanted to ask.

"Do you know what His Majesty died from? He wasn't that old." Gnilli looked thoughtful.

"They said he had a lump on his stomach, that seemed to be...to be...eating him up," she said, slowly, not explaining who "they" were. *Cancer*, Allee realized, but she knew that the disease had not been the only cause of death.

"And a broken heart," she said to herself, but Gnilli heard her.

"Yes," she agreed, nodding. "He did love his Queen very much. But now he can be with her always. He was buried beside her this afternoon."

"WHAT?" Allee half-shouted, sitting up again. "They've already had the funeral? And I missed it? But-but—"

"LADY!" Gnilli cried, pushing her back down again. "Calm down. Only the family can attend. It is the law. You missed nothing." Allee obediently lay back, panting. She had wanted to see the old King laid to rest, sort of as closure. But she knew there had been no way she could have attended and decided she would try to forget about it. The she thought of something.

"Does that mean that Espy is here?" she asked. Gnilli frowned, and for a second, Allee wondered if Gnilli knew who Espy was, but the gnarf's reply assured her that she did.

"She is, but no one is very happy about it," she said. Allee was surprised, but was pretty sure of the reason.

"Didn't want to leave the bubbles, did she?" she guessed. Gnilli nodded solemnly.

"She said...she said," she looked around fearfully, and then leaned towards Allee, her voice low. "She said that since her father had never bothered to see her when he was alive, that she couldn't be bothered to see him buried." Allee gave a low whistle.

"What did His Majesty do?" she asked, unable to keep herself from using Ferdy's new title.

"He said some things about his sister that were not nice at all and then stormed out of the pastle. He sent armed guards on the fastest zeorses in the starns and they brought her back tied to a saddle. So now she's here."

"Ooh, I'm glad I was asleep," Allee said. "I bet she made a scene." Gnilli nodded again.

"She is pouting in her old chambers. His Majesty won't let her leave until sometime next week." That reminded Allee of Ferdy's new role.

"When's his coronation?" she queried.

"When the period of mourning is over," Gnilli replied quickly. Allee was surprised at the large amount of news the gnarf had picked up in such a short time, but she was glad nonetheless. "And His Majesty has set the mourning period to be one month for the Countess, two for the Prince, and three for the King. He said that it is so short because we have been in mourning for the Queen long enough to make up for it." Allee quickly did the math in her head.

"Six months," she said aloud. Briefly, she wondered if she might possibly be home before then, but before she could think about it too much, she turned her attention to the thing that had been bothering her since the mention of the law against non-family attending the King's funeral.

"If only family can attend the King's funeral," she started, struggling to find the right words to state her question. "Does that mean that I...that I..." her voice lowered to a whisper as a lump rose in her throat at the thought, "That I can't see Esendore and Dariel laid to rest?" She waited, wondering if she could bear the answer.

"Oh, Lady, do not worry," Gnilli assured, patting her hand. "It was only a law the old King had set regarding his own funeral. It does not apply in the least to the Prince and his betrothed. Anyone who wants to can attend." Allee sighed in relief, but her grief just squeezed her heart harder.

"Great," she said, not knowing what else to say. She was beginning to get sleepy again, and she couldn't think straight. Gnilli smiled at her and reached over to draw the blanket up to her chin.

"Go to sleep, Lady," she instructed. "You will need to be rested for the burial tomorrow."

"Happy wedding," Allee murmured, struggling to think of something better to say than that. Gnilli's smile grew wider.

"Meli will be here if you need something," she said. Allee smiled sleepily back.

"Don't call me...," she mumbled, but she was asleep before she could finish.

The next time Allee opened her eyes she was greeted with cheerful late morning sunlight.

"Lady, you're awake!" Meli cried, standing up from her chair by the window. Allee groaned.

"Not you, too!" Meli clapped a hand over her mouth, her eyes dancing.

"Oops, I forgot," she said, trying not to giggle. "Gnilli said that you were being touchy about that again." Allee rolled her eyes.

"You called me that on purpose," she accused. Meli gave a tinkling laugh.

"I had to check if you were okay," she answered calmly. "If you didn't get mad, I'd know you weren't." Allee laughed for the first time in three days.

"It's good to see you," she said, smiling at Meli. Meli beamed back.

"Not half as good as it is to see you," she replied, walking over to smooth the bedclothes. "You couldn't imagine the fright you gave me when I came in to wake you up ten days ago, and you weren't there." *Ten days,* Allee asked herself silently. *It's only been ten days? It feels like a lifetime.* She pushed that thought to the back of her head and smiled again.

"I bet Her Grace blew her top," she said, picturing Cardolyn's reaction in her mind.

"Her top?" Meli repeated, her eyes wide. "She blew the roof! She was already upset with Their Highnesses for leaving without her consent, but when she found out they'd taken you, too, she was furious!"

"That must have been a sight," Allee mused wistfully. She almost wished she could have seen it. *Almost.* Meli nodded fervently.

"The kitchen boys were placing bets on when she'd collapse from shock." Meli giggled, and then shrugged. "She never did though, so Caysa got all the money."

"*Caysa* placed wagers on Her Grace?" Allee asked, astounded. Meli laughed at Allee's expression.

"That's exactly what the kitchen boys looked like. She put it under a false name so they wouldn't know it was her. But don't worry, they'll get her back." Suddenly, the clock out in the courtyard bonged and Meli jumped. She looked out the window, surprised. "And I wager that if I don't get you fed in the next half-hour, we're both going to be in trouble." She left the bedside and hurried over to the little breakfast table.

"Come eat," she called over her shoulder. Allee suddenly noticed how hungry she was. After all, the last time she had eaten had been almost three days ago. She slid slowly off the bed, pausing to let her head stop spinning and adjust the loose lilac shift she was wearing. She limped over to the table, but stopped dead when she realized what they were eating. Roast quailant. A picture of Esendore merrily showing her how to build a spit flashed before her eyes, and she winced.

"Is something wrong?" Meli asked quickly, noticing Allee's discomfort. Allee swallowed hard, willing the image to go away. The picture disappeared, but the pain remained.

"I'm...I'm not sure I'm ready for that yet," she said slowly, trying to dislodge the lump in her throat. Meli looked horrified.

"Oh, Allee, I'm so sorry," she apologized, hastily covering the tray back up. "I never thought how weak you must be after not eating for three days. Of course you couldn't choke down a quailant. Here," she finished, stuffing an aplrange in Allee's hand and pushing her into a chair. "You start on that while I ring for some soup. It won't take long." Allee obediently bit into her fruit, wondering why Meli didn't even want to leave her to go get a bowl of soup. She didn't mind in the least, though. Meli launched into a story about Caysa and one of the kitchen boys, and Allee was able to push her grief out of her mind.

By the time she and Meli, whom Allee had persuaded to eat with her, had finished, Allee was weak with laughter. It was much better than being weak with fatigue, so she welcomed it. But her pain returned when Meli mentioned getting ready for the funeral. Allee took a deep breath, her grief back on the surface.

"I'm ready," she said, her voice as strong as she could make it. Meli touched her arm sympathetically and handed Allee the under dress with the petticoats. Mechanically, Allee went to the bathroom to put it on. When she returned, two dresses were laying on the bed. One was an unornamented black satin, its sleeves made of light gauze so it wouldn't be so hot in the summer afternoon. The other garment was navy blue with similar sleeves, but with a few ruffles and flounces. Allee stared at them in disbelief.

"I have to wear TWO?" she demanded. Meli giggled.

"Don't sound so pleased," she joked, but when she saw Allee's face she quickly sobered. "The black one is for the service and the blue for the banquet afterwards," she explained. Another picture of the first time Allee had ever seen Esendore sitting proud and stern at the high table swam before her eyes. She stamped it out.

"Is the banquet mandatory?" she asked.

"You are the guest of honor," Meli said quietly. Allee sighed, and tried to make light of the conversation. She would try anything to make the ache in her chest go away.

"I'm the guest of honor at a *funeral* banquet?" she repeated. Meli realized what she meant and stifled another laugh.

"I'm so glad you're better," she said.

"Not quite," Allee replied, but her voice was so low that Meli didn't hear her. Instead, she picked up the black dress and held it out, almost gingerly. Allee sighed again and raised her arms over her head so that she could put it on. As usual, it didn't seem to fit or look quite right. To make matters worse, Allee's white bandages stood out even more when contrasted with the black, making her look like a battered china doll. Meli did a good job hiding the one on her forehead by arranging Allee's hair over it, but she still felt ridiculous.

"You like fine," Meli assured, fastening a heavy gold and garnet medallion on her neck. With a flash, Allee remembered Esendore's present, and her hand flew to her throat.

"Where's my necklace?" she demanded, her heart thumping wildly. "The one he gave me for my birthday? I promised—"

"It's right here," Meli interrupted, alarmed, taking it off the nightstand. The light caught the crystal and flashed in Allee's eyes, forcing her to blink and calm down. "We were afraid you would break it, tossing around as you were," Meli continued. "Would you like to wear it instead?" Allee nodded.

"Yes, please," she said, her voice weak with relief. She didn't know what she would have done if she had lost it.

As soon as the Meli's fingers had secured the clasp, the sun warmed crystal settled into the hollow of Allee's throat. She closed her eyes and let its warmth reassure her. *Everything's going to be all right* she thought she heard a voice whisper, but when she opened her eyes to see who it was, the only thing she saw was Meli holding out a pair of black shoes and gloves. Allee put them on without protest. Wordlessly, Meli led her to the door and opened it. Cardolyn, dressed from head to toe in black dress and veil, was waiting for them.

"Ready to go, dear?" she asked, trying to smile. Allee nodded mutely, waved good-bye to Meli, who had never met Esendore or Dariel and would therefore not attend the services, and followed Her Grace down the wooden staircase, along the library corridor, and out into a small flower garden only about half full with somber people. Most of them were nobles but Allee guessed a couple of them were merchants or peasants by their dress. Allee did not know anyone except two boys from Ferdy's classes and the Count and Countess Farholt. The Countess was sobbing openly while her husband, pale with grief himself, tried in vain to comfort her.

Allee turned her head, her eyes beginning to burn. But Allee knew that from now on she would have to deny herself the pleasure of releasing her emotions in the form of tears. Crying was just too dangerous. The next time, she might do more than just burn some holes in a shirt. She shivered, just thinking of what could happen if she let go of her control. She realized then that Cardolyn had come to a halt.

Ferdy was waiting for them in his own funeral best, complete with silver circlet, at the head of a path that led down a hill. Espy was standing beside him, almost unrecognizable for the heavy black veil, but before Allee could greet her she moved off into the crowd.

"Do I look any better?" Allee asked to get rid of the depressing look on Ferdy's face. He looked startled, but his eyes lit up faintly as he remembered their exchange.

"Much better," he replied, rewarding her with a tiny smile. He nodded at his aunt, who bobbed her head in return, and turned to lead the procession. Allee took a deep breath and followed.

The garden, even if it was neglected and overgrown, was in all of its summer glory. Under any other circumstances, Allee would have loved to look at all the different kinds of flowers growing there, but she was too wrapped up in her grief to even notice.

She focused all of her attention on her shoes and fought to keep it there. After walking for five minutes down the same brick path, Ferdy made a right turn and passed through a low stonewall into the royal cemetery. Huge, elaborate crypts stretched for acres, the glistening marble contrasting sharply with the emerald green grass. Ferdy led them to a vault near the edge of the grounds, its newly cut black marble seeming to absorb the bright rays of the sun and reflect them back in cruel darts of light. On top of it perched an angel, her serene face gazing down into the heart she held in her hands. On a raised platform in front of the tomb lay a single large coffin. Allee stopped to stare at it, slowly processing what it meant.

"You didn't take them apart," she heard herself say aloud. Ferdy turned to look at her, his eyes sad.

"How could we?" he replied, but before Allee could say anything else, a man in billowing black robes appeared and the service began.

Allee watched the entire ceremony numbly, neither listening nor watching what the man was doing. Instead, she kept her eyes fixed upon the white marble casket, never blinking even as six heavily muscled men lifted it into the tomb. The only time she even flinched when the door closed, and the realization that Esendore and Dariel were gone forever truly hit her.

    The ominous clang ringing in her ears, Allee grabbed her crystal pendant and held it so tightly she felt a cut on her finger begin to bleed. The pain managed to keep her emotions under control, and she thought she heard a snippet of song, but it was very faint and far away. She strained her ears to see if she could catch it, and to her surprise, the more she concentrated the louder it got, until she recognized it as the song that Dariel had used to sing her to sleep at night. Except that now, Allee could understand the words that floated over to her across the warm summer air:

> *Do not worry; do not sorrow,*
> *For you know not the tomorrow.*
> *There is a greater force,*
> *Who will guide you on your course.*
> *Hold in faith and offer trust.*
> *It will help you do what you must.*
>
> *Do not worry; do not fret,*
> *For the journey is not over yet.*
> *Yes, there will be grief and pain,*
> *But joy will be yours again.*
> *How do you know what is glad,*
> *If you do not know is sad?*

    Allee was so absorbed in the song that she jumped when she felt Ferdy slip his hand into hers. She smiled at him, happy that he could hear it too, and let the words wash over her.

> *There will always be a bitter end,*
> *An empty hole that none can mend.*
> *It will leave you lost and hollow,*
> *But do not fear, beginnings follow.*
> *Do not be leery of a fresh start,*
> *For the strength lies in your heart.*

Do not worry; do not sorrow,
For you know not the tomorrow.
There is a greater force,
Who will guide you on your course.
Hold in faith and offer trust.
It will help do what you must.

The song slowly began to fade away, until only one bar could be heard, very close to Allee's ear:

Do not worry; do not sorrow,
For you know not the tomorrow.

She looked up, startled, to see Ferdy peering intently down at her and realized that he had sung those last two lines.

"That was really beautiful," he said. "I didn't know you knew that song." Allee looked back at him in bewilderment.

"What are you talking about?" she asked. "It wasn't me who—" Suddenly, it occurred to her that she *had* been singing, but it had been someone else who had given her the words. She looked up at Ferdy, her heart lightening with newfound joy.

"I'm glad you liked it," she replied, her smile growing wider. She felt Cardolyn's arm on her shoulder and was aware that the service was over. After giving her a smile of his own, Ferdy disappeared, mingling in with the crowd. Dazed, Allee let herself be swept up in the funeral procession. Gently, Cardolyn led her back to her room.

Meli was waiting for her and helped her change while Allee floated in a detached aloofness, her heart and mind going over and over the words of the song and finding comfort in them.

Her revelry came to a crashing halt when Allee tripped on the stairs leading to the high table. Although she felt more like herself, she had another bruise to add to her already impressive collection. She even managed to smile at Ferdy as he gave one of his wicked grins. Nobody else seated there noticed her.

"Still haven't figured out those steps?" he asked, pulling out her chair. His seat, she noticed, was a gilded throne.

"No, I haven't," Allee replied acidly. "Because no one around here believes in pants." Ferdy looked startled.

"Than what am I wearing? A kilt?" He looked down at his lap to make sure. Allee was surprised to find out that they had kilts in Betwix, but didn't let her surprise faze her.

"Wouldn't put it past you," she retorted.

"Oh, really?" Ferdy started, but then the trumpet blew to announce the arrival of dinner. They did not proclaim guests in respect for the deceased.

Even though Allee had eaten only a short while ago, she found that she was hungry again and dished up the linguini stuff that was set before her. Ferdy was talking to Dariel's father, who was seated on his left, and Cardolyn, on Allee's right, was occupied with the guest on her right, so Allee didn't have anything to occupy her other than her food. She didn't feel much like talking anyway, so she watched the crowd. With a jolt of surprise, she realized that in addition to the merchants and nobles, all sorts of commoners were also seated down below. So many tables had been added to make room for them that the people sitting on the edge were pressed up against the wall. The higher classes surveyed the lower with looks of contempt while the peasants looked suspiciously at the food and drink that was offered to them and jumped at small noises. For some reason, Allee knew Ferdy was behind the intermingling of the classes.

She scanned the crowd again, looking for any traces of mourning other than their clothes, which were even gloomier than what they had been wearing before the King's death. Not a single one of the people looked even remotely sad; instead, they kept sneaking apprehensive glances at the high table. When they saw Allee watching them, they would blush and quickly look away. She always smiled back to be friendly, but she didn't think they ever saw her.

The looks increased and conversation died down as the food was cleared away until total silence reigned. Ferdy heaved a sigh.

"Here I go," he muttered, and got to his feet. Allee watched him intently, hoping and praying that he would say the right things.

"People of Taween," he called, throwing out his hands. His subjects stared back at him balefully. He swallowed hard, but never faltered.

"I thank you for coping with these difficult times," he continued, his eyes scanning the crowd for even one sign of interest. "I will make sure that they do not last much longer." At this statement, there were some murmurs, but they were quickly silenced so as not to miss Ferdy's next words.

"I know most of you did not agree with my father's way of ruling things," he went on, his voice getting stronger. There were murmurs of surprise at this statement. Cardolyn gasped in horror, and Allee wondered how she could have been so blind to how feared and unloved the King had been, but she quickly turned back to what Ferdy was saying. "And I respect that," Ferdy added.

Finally, he got some reaction. The people were now looking at him with interest, even admiration. He became surer of himself.

"But I am not here to talk about the past," he said, "but the future. I hope, with your help, to make this country one to be remembered by visitors and loved by all who belong to it." A general buzz of puzzlement arose as the people digested this. Ferdy knew what they were wondering.

"Yes," he assured them. "I have refused the offers of a co-ruler from my father's advisors, and will rule this country myself. That is, if you are willing. If you are willing," he paused to let his eyes sweep over his people. "I will start an entirely new beginning. If you are willing." He stopped and bowed his head, waiting for their judgment. Allee looked at him in astonishment; she didn't know he was capable of such stirring words. Silence stretched and then—

"Aye!" one man cried out, jumping to his feet. "Ye have my consent, Majesty."

"Mine, too!" another shouted.

"And mine!" came another. As if a dam had been broken, the Hall erupted with cheers and shouts of "You have my consent!" until it became a huge, steady roar. Ferdy finally looked up, grinning at his ecstatic people.

"So may it be!" he shouted.

"SO MAY IT BE!" they roared back, and with a cheer, they fell back to their drinks and conversation. Ferdy sat back down and wiped the perspiration off his forehead. Allee stared at him, wide-eyed.

"Wow," she said simply. He grinned at her and took a long swig from his goblet.

"You only say that when you're really upset about something, so was it really that bad?"

"I didn't say that!" she protested. "I think it was an excellent speech."

"I—" he started, but stopped. Now it was his turn to be surprised. "You did?"

"Brilliant!" Allee said generously. And she meant it, too. She was still tingling. Ferdy turned a deep, violent shade of red, and, instead of replying, began conversing with the Count again. Allee shook her head in exasperation, and immediately wished she hadn't. Something ripped, and wetness spread underneath her bandage. She realized that her head had torn open again. Muttering to herself, she stood up to leave.

"Why, what's wrong, dear?" Cardolyn asked. Allee gave her a reassuring smile, but she doubted it looked convincing since the room was spinning.

"My head tore open a little," she said, touching her bandage lightly. Cardolyn looked sick, and Allee quickly got off the dais before Her Grace was ill.

Meli was waiting for her at the door that led to the hallway with the wooden staircase, and she helped Allee up to her room. She assembled the necessary bandages and salves as Allee changed into her pajamas.

"Lie down on the bed," she instructed. Allee was only too happy to comply. She was starting to feel woozy again. Meli's concerned face blurred before her eyes, and Allee fought to keep her in focus, but she knew she was loosing the battle. "It's okay, Allee," Meli assured kindly. "Go to sleep if you want." But Allee already had.

When Allee awoke the next morning to find late morning sunshine streaming in again, she was thoroughly sick of sleeping. To her relief, her friends had finally trusted her to be by herself, and she was alone. She was able to dress herself in the plainest maroon dress she could find, do what she liked to her hair, and simply grab a banagrant instead of eating a big breakfast.

Leisurely eating and licking the juice off her fingers, Allee felt happier than she had in days. However, she was so used to company that she began to feel lonely. As soon as she was finished with her breakfast, she set out to find somebody to talk to.

Her hallway was completely empty, so she decided to go downstairs, but the ground floor was equally unoccupied. Feeling deserted, Allee turned down the corridor that led to the library, entertaining the idea of finding a book to read. Then her ears picked up the faint sound of people laughing.

Allee followed the sound to a staircase, climbed it, and found herself to be on the same level as her room, but in an entirely different wing. It seemed to be an art gallery of sorts. While working her way towards the voices she examined the paintings and statues lining the walls and gazed with interest at the ornate columns holding up the roof. The laughter was very loud now.

Peering into a doorway at the end of the gallery, Allee saw an open balcony overlooking the sewing houses. Ferdy, Lou, and Raf seemed to be very interested in what was happening below. Suddenly, Raf dropped something over the edge, and all three boys snickered in appreciation. Then Lou saw her.

"Hey!" he greeted her, sounding surprised. Ferdy and Raf whirled around, their eyes wide, but when they saw who it was, they relaxed. Allee began to suspect that they were doing something they shouldn't be.

"You can come watch if you want to," Raf offered. Pleased to be included, Allee walked over to join them. All three looked startled.

"Get down or they'll see you!" Ferdy hissed, pushing on her shoulder. Allee knelt, wondering what was going on.

"Okay," Raf said, scooping something out of a bucket in front of them. "Watch this." He half-stood while his companions peered over the edge to the courtyard below. A woman was walking across the stones with a basket of snowy white laundry.

"Fire," Ferdy whispered, and Raf launched what was in his hand. Allee watched it sail across the courtyard, realizing that is was a ball of mud. With a plop, it dropped at the woman's feet, splattering her dress. She shrieked, and the basket of laundry went flying. She looked around for her assailant in bewilderment, saw the soiled laundry, and burst into tears. The boys collapsed in a fit of laughter. Allee was horrified.

"Ferdinand, how could you?" she cried, scrambling to her feet.

"Shhh!" he said, pulling on her skirt to make her kneel back down. "She'll see us!" Allee tore the cloth out of his hands.

"GOOD!" she shouted. "I hope the people do see you doing such a wonderful job of looking out for their best interests. For, as you said in that PACK OF LIES last night," she paused for effect, and he stared at her in shock, "they are your people and *you* are their King." She glared at him while he stared open-mouthed back at her. She lowered her voice to an almost-whisper. "They *believe* in you, Ferdinand, and this is how you thank them? What will they think of you now?" she asked, imploring him to understand how stupid and irresponsible he was being. Ferdy glared back at her angrily.

"I meant every word I said last night," he said, also on his feet. Allee gave a short laugh.

"Great job you've done proving it," she retorted. Ferdy, his breath hard and ragged, continued.

"And, as for what they think of me," he said, "They, unlike some people, will understand that I'm just trying to have a little FUN!" Raf and Lou were too startled to speak, for which Allee was grateful.

"Fun is NOT hurting people!" she shouted. "You, of all people should know that. Ferdinand, YOU ARE THE KING!"

"I don't know how to be King!" Ferdy yelled.

"Then LEARN!" Allee bellowed. And before she could really loose her temper and throw something, Allee turned on her heel and raced down the gallery. Blind with fury, she ran until she was out of breath. Which, considering her present state of health, was not very far. Suddenly very weak, she sank down in the shadow of a pillar and buried her face in her hands.

"Idiot! Idiot!" she told them, feeling better for saying it aloud. But the rest of her thoughts she kept in her head. *I don't know how to be King*, she mimicked, silently. *He's so stupid! I can't believe I kissed him!*

A few minutes later she heard familiar footsteps.

"Go away!" she ordered, not looking up. She thought he had listened, but when she peeked through her fingers he was sitting beside her, his head also in his hands.

"Mimeorry," he mumbled. Allee knew what he had said, but she was too angry to care.

"What?" she asked. He brought his head up to look at her.

"I'm sorry, okay?" he said. "You're right, I'm wrong. That was a very irresponsible—

"And idiotic," Allee reminded him. He grimaced at her.

"And idiotic thing I did. It's just that—" he stopped and dropped his head, struggling to find the right words. When he looked back up, there was the same fear in his eyes that Allee had seen three days ago. He took a deep breath.

"Have you ever had something really important just thrown on you?" he started, his tone urgent. "Something that you knew you had to do, even though you'd never even considered doing it before and the thought of actually performing this task almost paralyzes you with fear?" Allee couldn't help but give him a small smile.

"That's the kind of feeling that made me fight the witch," she replied. He tilted his head to look at her better, his surprise plain on his face.

"Oh," he said simply. He looked down at his feet, and Allee waited patiently. "Do you know what I need?" he asked, looking back up. Allee opened her mouth to reply, but he interrupted her. "Don't answer that." Allee ignored him.

"I think you need a place where you can remember...and not have to worry about running a country or being a king...to just...I don't know...heal." she said, slowly. She knew that no matter how much she hated him at times, she really needed him to help her get over her grief. He nodded.

"But I can't just *leave*." Allee thought hard.

"Couldn't you just...stay here...but...take a break?" she asked.

"I'm not hiding from my responsibilities any longer," he replied.

"That is the last thing I want you to do," Allee said quickly. "It was just a suggestion." They were silent a moment, each thinking their own thoughts.

"Do you remember that he promised to visit Espy...right before we left?" Ferdy asked, his voice almost a whisper. This was the first time Ferdy had mentioned Esendore directly, so Allee knew whatever he was going to say was important to him.

"Her chambers here are plenty big for three people," he continued, his voice stronger as he warmed to his idea, "And we could rest for a couple of days. No one has to know we're there. And that way we could...we could still keep his promise." Allee thought that this idea of hiding right under everyone's noses what a bit far-fetched, but she knew that this was the only way Ferdy could come to terms with his grief.

"All right then," she said, briskly, standing up and brushing herself off. "Let's go." Ferdy scrambled to his feet, giving her his you-are-crazy look.

"Cardolyn will not like this one bit," he objected. Allee sighed.

"This is YOUR idea," she reminded him.

"I was joking!" he protested. Allee glared at him. He knew he hadn't been joking just as much as she did.

"Number one," she started, "You are the King."

"Oh," Ferdy replied, "so NOW I'm the King. I thought—"

"Number two," Allee said loudly, her voice drowning his out. "Cardolyn is easily distracted. And number three, your cousin Archibald adores you and likes her. It won't be that hard for him to explain the situation to her."

"Oh, no," Ferdy protested. "I am not going make him help me with anther scheme; it's too soon after the first one." He gave a short laugh. "He won't want to do it anyway."

"I won't want to do what?" Archibald asked brightly, coming around the corner. Ferdy gave a little yelp of surprise

"That's scary," he said. Archibald gave him a look, and Ferdy flushed. "Nothing," he said quickly. Archibald rolled his eyes.

"Ha," he barked. "Then you tell me, Alethea." Ferdy sighed and opened his mouth to explain, but Allee beat him to the punch.

"We want you to tell Her Grace that Ferdy and I are going somewhere to recuperate. We'll be close by in case of an emergency, but unless it is, we are…um…indisposed," she said, making her point clear and concise. Archibald frowned and Allee's heart sank.

"I'm sure the Duchess would understand if you wanted time alone," he said. Ferdy, who had been sputtering the whole time, finally found his voice.

"But she'll make it way too complicated," he complained. "And she'll want to come with us. I just want to keep this as simple as possible." Archibald nodded understandingly and stroked his chin.

"What do you want me to tell her when she notices you're gone?" he asked. Allee grinned as she realized he was agreeing to their plan.

"The truth," she replied. "We've gone somewhere for a day or two, and if she or anyone else desperately needs us, we'll be there."

"We're going to be with Espy, just so you know," Ferdy added. Archibald chuckled.

"Hmmm," he said, looking from one to the other, his eyes dancing. "It sounds easy enough. I accept." They smiled at him gratefully. He smiled back and then clapped his hands, making them both jump. "Well, get going!" Hardly believing their luck, Ferdy and Allee trotted down the corridor.

"I still feel bad," Ferdy muttered. Allee shrugged.

"So reward him by appointing him to your council or something," she replied. He looked at her as if she had just sprouted two heads, but before she could ask why he was already shouting back at his godfather.

"Archibald!" he yelled.

"Yes, Your Majesty?" he answered.

"For you services to the Crown," Ferdy said, trying his best to sound formal, but failing miserably, "you are now an official member of the King's Council! See you in a few days!"

"Have fun!" Archibald replied. Allee caught one last glimpse of him laughing before they rounded the corner.

"Services to the Crown," she repeated, shaking her head. Ferdy grinned at her.

"I was going to do that anyway, I just hadn't gotten around to it," he retorted. Before she could fire back, he raised his hand. "Here's what we'll do. You go get your stuff, I'll go get mine, and I'll meet you at the base of the wooden staircase."

"Done," Allee replied. He grinned at her and disappeared around the corner.

Allee was at the meeting place long before Ferdy; she hadn't needed anything but the pot of salve and some pajamas from her room. He motioned for her to be quiet and then pressed on a knob in the staircase. Another secret passage way opened.

"I KNEW IT!" Allee shouted triumphantly. She had been hoping they would travel through the tunnels again. Ferdy just shook his head exasperatedly and pushed her into the passage.

This tunnel was very different from the first one they had traveled through. Instead of going down, it climbed up and was made almost entirely of stairs. Allee was dizzy and out of breath by the time they stopped. As soon as Ferdy opened the door at the top of the stairs, Espy crushed them into an ecstatic embrace.

"I missed you!" she cried, squeezing them so hard they couldn't breath. "The bubbles told me you were coming, but I thought they were off since they are in a new place..." Allee tuned out the Effervescent's chatter and looked around. They were in a perfectly round room furnished like a sitting room. And, sure enough, the little blue pot was setting by the fireplace.

"Be right back," Ferdy suddenly said, turning back to the passage. Allee stared at him.

"Where are you going?" she asked while Espy still babbled in her ear. He grinned wickedly.

"I asked Roeland to bring Lullaby to the staircase. I have to go pick her up." Allee rolled her eyes.

"You're crazy," she replied. He shrugged.

"If I'm going to be holed up with you and Espy, I am going to need something to keep my sanity," he said, and disappeared back down the tunnel. "Oh, and I'll be in one of the bedrooms if you need me. There's other tunnels connecting all the rooms in this tower," he called back, and was gone. Allee shook her head and let Espy drag her into the kitchenette.

"I am *so* glad you came," Espy chattered, pouring Allee a glass of pinon juice. Allee smiled ruefully, wondering if Espy had drawn a breath since they had arrived. As she looked at the pinon juice, memories of Espy's house and all the times after it overwhelmed her. Allee gulped and sat down. Espy saw her face and instantly shut up, as if Allee had flipped a switch.

"Do you want to talk about it?" she asked, her voice both kind and sad. Allee took a deep breath. After hearing the strange song at the funeral, she had come to terms with what had happened, and the grief was no long overpowering. But, with the closure of Esendore's death, a new idea had occurred to her. Allee thought a moment, trying to pin the feeling down.

"There's something I've realized, that has nothing to do with...with Esendore...but yet has everything to do with him...but I'm not sure why I just suddenly realized it," she said, slowly.

"Maybe if you would say it aloud, it would help," Espy suggested. Allee took a big gulp of pinon juice (she was finally getting used to the flavor) and swallowed.

"Before I came here," she started, letting what she wanted to say form completely in her mind before she actually said it. "I assumed that every action I did spoke louder than the words I said and the things I thought. Even the unimportant actions, the ones I didn't think anyone but me noticed. But now," she paused, staring deep into her cup as if it would cup up with words she wanted to say. Espy didn't push her, and eventually Allee went on.

"But now, I have realized that actions are important, and so are words and thoughts, and I should plan them carefully, but what is important," she took another deep breath. "Really, really important, is my beliefs. For it is," she paused again to look up at Espy. "It is faith that makes up the world."

"Then I think it is time for you to go home," said a voice that shook Allee's bones. She whirled around to see Aeyr standing in the doorway, her brightness chasing even the deepest shadows away.

"Home?" she echoed, drowned by a rush of memories.

"Yes," Aeyr replied, smiling at Allee's eagerness. "You have done what you needed to do. And learned what you need to learn. You are ready. I will take you to the portal now." Allee's feeling of joy disappeared.

"Now?" she repeated, suddenly unwilling. "I can't go now! I haven't said good-bye to Ferdy!" Aeyr looked as startled as Allee felt. Her green eyes grew deeper as she considered Allee's request.

"You may say good-bye to His Majesty if you hurry," she said finally. Allee went limp in relief.

"Where are the bedrooms?" she demanded, turning back to Espy. Much to Allee's distress, Espy didn't answer her right away; she was in too deep of a state of shock. Allee wanted to shake her.

"Through that door," the Effervescent said finally, pointing to it, her voice faint. "He's in the second one on the left." Allee leapt up from her chair, almost knocking it over in her haste.

"You cannot tell him where you are going," Aeyr reminded her, her voice gentle. "He will not understand."

"I won't," Allee promised. Aeyr sighed, making the candles flicker.

"Very well," she said, and Allee whisked by her to get to the door.

"Wait," Aeyr called, her voice making the very marrow of Allee's bones reverberate and forcing her to stop and turn. Aeyr laid a long white finger on her forehead.

"I need to fix this," she explained, and before Allee could say another word, the room was filled with a blinding flash of light, and she was gasping in shock as the pain from the cuts on her arm and knee, as well as the gash of on her forehead, suddenly disappeared. She reached under her bandage and found her hairline. Her fingertip met smooth skin.

"How did you do that?" she demanded. Aeyr smiled and shrugged.

"The salve, for one," she replied. Then her eyes grew serious. "The power of good does many things, Alethea, and healing is its specialty. I just helped it along." Allee gave her a long look, not exactly comprehending what the angel has just said. Shaking her head, she gave up and dashed out of the room.

She had no trouble finding the door and knocked softly, praying that he was back from getting Lullaby. Her knock was answered by a muffled,

"Come in." Taking a deep breath, she opened the door. The room was small, just big enough for a bed, a washstand, and a fireplace. Ferdy was kneeling on a rug in front of the hearth, his dokat on his knees.

"Hey," she greeted him.

"Hey," he returned, stroking Lullaby's ears. Suddenly, all that Allee had planned to say deserted her. How was she supposed to say good-bye without really saying good-bye?

"Enjoying your vacation?" she asked, not caring how lame that sounded. He raised his eyebrows. They had only been here twenty minutes.

"Sure," he said, shrugging. "You?"

"Yeah," she replied, dragging her foot against the floor. "It's more of an escape for me, though. I have to leave whenever I think Cardolyn might want to teach me how to curtsy." He gave her a small smile, and she could tell that he was preoccupied with something.

"Are you ready to be King?" she asked. He shrugged again.

"I think so," he said.

"Esendore had faith in you," she reminded him. "And I do, too." He finally gave her a real smile.

"Thanks," he said. Allee felt that she had said as much as she could.

"I need to get back," she said, turning to leave, her heart thumping wildly as she realized that this could be the last time she ever saw him.

"Hey, wait, Allee," Ferdy called after her, and she stuck her head back in the doorway. "What did you come in here for anyway?" Allee swallowed hard.

"To wish you good luck," she said simply, holding her head high. He rolled his eyes. Allee's heart leapt at that familiar motion.

"Are *all* commoners as strange as you are?" he asked. Allee wrinkled her nose.

"Only if all nobles are as snobbish as you," she retorted. He just laughed. Allee smiled sadly, wishing she could tell him, but knowing that she could not.

"Good-bye, Ferdy," she said, softly, and with one last long look at him, she went back down the hall. She felt a strange feeling churning up her insides, but before she could name it she was back in the kitchen, where Aeyr was waiting for her. Espy was gone.

"Did you say good-bye?" Aeyr queried. Allee gave a weak nod.

"As much of one as I could give," she replied.

"You have done enough," Aeyr assured. "I have instructed the Effervescent to tell His Majesty your story when I deem he is ready."

"Where is Espy?" Allee asked, surprised that she hadn't waited to say good-bye. Allee knew Aeyr's perfect features couldn't look disgusted, but they came really close.

"Weeping," she said shortly. "But I believe she will recover. She told me say good-bye in her stead." Allee looked at her shoes, a lump rising in her throat. Aeyr lifted her head back up with her warm fingers.

"Do not be sad, Alethea," she said, her voice washing Allee with reassurance. "For you have touched their lives for the better. They will never forget you." Allee felt her heart lighten, and in the blink of an eye, Aeyr had transformed into the winged white horse. Her wingtips brushed the walls, and she had to crouch to avoid hitting her magnificent head against the ceiling. Wondering how they were going to get outside, Allee climbed on her back, comforting herself with her last image of Ferdy, his body tall and proud against the glow of the fire. The room was filled with another flash of light, and they were flying over the city of Taween.

What seemed like three wing beats later, they were on the cliff face and Allee was sliding off again. She stared at the rock while Aeyr turned back to her human form.

"It is open for you," she said gently, placing a hand on Allee's shoulder. "I wish you the best, with all my heart." Suddenly, Allee remembered something.

"What happened to my fairies?" she demanded, touching her nose. "They disappeared the day of the fight." Aeyr looked surprised.

"They came to get me. That was their task. How else do you think I knew I needed to bring you back?" Aeyr smiled as Allee digested this new information. "Thank-you for helping me teach my wards," she added.

"You're thanking *me*?" Allee repeated, astounded. Aeyr laughed at the expression on her face. Allee was still shocked. "YOU are thanking—" Aeyr interrupted her by enveloping her in an embrace. Allee felt a warm, fuzzy feeling spread all over her. "Now go," Aeyr said, giving her a little push. Allee stepped forward, but instead of meeting solid rock, Allee fell into thin air. A prickling sensation began behind her eyeballs. *Don't sneeze and mess it up* she told herself sternly, and closed her eyes. When she opened them, she had to grab a hold of a branch to keep from falling out of the tree.

"Didjya find it?" a voice called. Allee looked down to see Arian peering up at her. Allee realized she was back in her old clothes and automatically dug in her pocket. The fetch ball was still there. She stared at it in shock.

"Yeah," she said, faintly. "Yeah, I did." Then she heard another voice,

"Girls! Dinner!" Allee's mom yelled. Allee's heart leapt at that familiar sound, her mind struggling to comprehend what was going on. Everything was happening too fast.

"Hurry, Allee, I'm hungry!" Arian pleaded. Allee clambered down from the tree and stood staring at her little sister. How long had it been since she had seen her? On impulse, Allee folded Arian to her in a crushing hug.

"HEY!" she protested, squirming. "You crazy sister, get off me!" She wiggled out, and with a scathing look in Allee's direction, started off towards the house. Silently, Allee followed her, soaking in the formerly familiar sights and sounds that were now strange to her.

She jumped back in surprise when the rush of cold air met her at the door. She had almost forgotten about air conditioning. Tenderly, she placed the fetch ball in the hall closet and breathed in the familiar smells of cheeseburgers and baked beans.

Still walking as if she were in a dream, Allee washed her hands and sat down at the table. Her mother smiled at her, and Allee stared unblinkingly back, unable to help herself. Part of her wanted to jump up and collapse in her mother's arms, bawling, but another part held herself aloof, wondering how she could readjust to her family after being away so long.

Seeing her strange expression, her mother gave her a worried frown and gave Allee the biggest cheeseburger. Allee ate it slowly, her mind slowly processing everything that was happening to her.

After dinner, Allee helped with the dishes, just as she had promised herself she would, so many days ago. But the process didn't go as smoothly as she remembered. She kept bumping into her mother and always seemed to be in the way. Finally, Allee couldn't stand it any more. As soon as her hands were free, she wrapped her arms around her mother.

"I love you, Mom," she whispered.

"I love you, too, Allee," her mother replied, her voice plainly showing her surprise. She tried to put her chin on Allee's head like she always did, but then she jerked back. Allee was now too tall. "You just keep sneaking up on me," her mother complained. Suddenly, Allee didn't feel so glad to be home anymore.

"I'm going outside," she said, pulling away.

"Okay," her mother answered, giving her daughter another worried look. Allee tried to reassure her with a smile, but her mouth just wouldn't work.

Allee went for a short walk around their farm, going to all of her favorite places and visiting her animals. She was very glad to see all of them, but they just couldn't make the hollow feeling in her chest to go away. Allee continued to walk around until dusk. The darkness caused the feeling to grow worse. In desperation, she returned to her hammock tree and stared up at the branches. *Did it really happen* she asked herself. She felt a lump rise in her throat as she wondered if she had just imagined it all. Then, something glittering in the shadows caught her eye.

Allee reached down and picked up the headdress Aeyr had given her as a birthday present. Her hand immediately went to her throat, where Esendore's gift was still snuggled against her chest. *Yes, it happened*, she thought. But instead of being comforted, Allee was even lonelier. *What if I never see them again* she wailed silently.

Defeated and miserable, Allee went into the house, took a shower, and crawled into bed. Now that she was back in her own bed she had thought she would drop off right away, but she waited a long time for sleep to claim her. Too many thoughts crowded her mind. *What if they forget me? What if I forget them? Can I ever go back?*

"I don't want to be done with Betwix!" she cried silently, and silently, sleep finally came.

She had a very strange dream. She was back at Espy's apartment, sitting at her kitchen table. However, neither Ferdy nor Espy seemed to be able to see her.

"She went HOME?" Ferdy said, his tone outraged. "Without even saying good-bye?" Allee had never seen that look on his face before. Espy, her beautiful blue eyes red and puffy, gave him a sad smile.

"Did she really not say good-bye, Ferdinand?" she asked gently. Ferdy thought a moment, and then pouted.

"That was the worst good bye I've ever heard," he said grumpily. Espy patted his arm while he struggled to accept Allee's departure. He shook his head in frustration. "So she's gone, just like that?" he continued. "Without an escort or anything?" Espy gave him a real smile this time.

"Allee believes in the power of good," she said, simply. "And, therefore, the power of good will watch after her." She said something else, but the vision faded away before Allee could catch it. She smiled and rolled over in her sleep, the hollow feeling evaporating. Espy was right. Allee believed in the good, and the good would see her through.